MW00790063

SUPERLUMINARY

Books by John C. Wright

SUPERLUMINARY

JOHN C. WRIGHT

CASTALIA HOUSE

Superluminary

John C. Wright

Published by Castalia House
Kouvola, Finland
www.castaliahouse.com

Cover: Steve Beaulieu
Editor: Vox Day

CONTENTS

THE LORDS OF CREATION

THE SPACE VAMPIRES

THE WORLD ARMADA

Book 1

The Lords of Creation

01

ASSASSIN IN EVEREST

Aeneas Tell of House of Tell, the youngest of the Lords of Creation, was twenty-one when he was assassinated for the first time.

His secondary brain came awake while his primary brain was still foggy with strange dreams. Alert to danger, the secondary brain stopped the nerve pulses from the primary brain which otherwise would have let him groan and open his eyes, which would have precipitated the nervous killer's attack.

But his primary brain had been in the delta brainwave stage of sleep, a deep and dreamless slumber. There was no sound, no light, no disturbance. What had broken his sleep? A memory, like an echo, of terrible multiple toothaches left a metallic taste in his mouth.

He had been dreaming about his insane grandfather, the Emperor. The old man had been telling him about the secrets of the universe... then a stinging pain in his teeth had jarred him awake. But how could Aeneas remember a dream when he had not been in the desynchronous brainwave state in which dreaming was possible?

Aeneas, eyes still closed, not daring to move, increased the firing rate of his auditory nerves. He was lying on the nongravity cushion of his opulent four-poster bed. The neverending whisper of the high-altitude winds of Mount Everest beyond the bubble of weather-controlled air was now loud to him.

On these upper peaks his family had erected the proud imperial palace-city of Ultrapolis, whose towers and domes were impregnable behind concentric force-shells and thought-screens. None of the artificial or bio-modified races of the nine worlds, fifty worldlets, and one hundred eighty moons of the Solar System could bring any realistic threat to bear on these defenses, not while the twelve ranking members of the House of Tell, the so-called Lords of Creation, retained control of the stratonic supertechnology known only to them.

But betrayal from within was another matter.

The quiet hiss of the protective screen that the bedposts projected around the bed was gone. He could not hear the heartbeats of his two bodyguards posted in the anteroom of his apartments. Instead he heard the heartbeat, louder and faster than was possible for an unmodified human being, of the assassin.

As the youngest member of the family, Aeneas had been stuffed into the oldest wing of the oldest palace, and no other guards were within shouting distance.

There was no sound of footsteps on the nightingale wood floor of his bedchamber, and so for a moment Aeneas had a false sense of hope. But the sound of the racing heart was close at hand.

The killer was in the chamber with him.

Then he felt a waft of intense cold radiating from the cells of the man's body. The assassin was near the bed, coming closer, bending over him.

Aeneas reflexively focused a thought to his signet ring, asking alarms silently to ring and the armaments hidden in the walls to slay the intruder. But there was no response. The electrotelepathic circuit was blocked.

The nanoscopic thought-broadcast cells his mother had implanted in the bones of his skull likewise were blocked when he tried to send needle-thin neuropsionic signals to receivers hidden in the ceiling.

A sharp, stabbing pain reappeared in his lower left molar, and then vanished. And then an upper incisor throbbed with a pain that vanished, and then a bicuspid. It was an basic proprioception code. It read: *Intruder in disinertia armor... negative-vitality field integument... contortion node detected...*

Of course. The killer was wearing armor that contorted the fabric of space a few inches in each direction around himself and lowered his inertia. It would prevent ordinary weapons, bullets or monomolecular blades, from imparting kinetic energy to him to do damage. Hence he could glide across the floor without imparting any pressure to the special floorboards biogineered to sound off when they felt an unfamiliar footstep.

The contortion node was a teleportation path for the assassin's escape.

Modified electroneural ganglia beneath the killer's skin—impossible for normal antiweapon sensors to detect—had erected a life-energy absorption cocoon. Hence the killer had silently drained Aeneas' two bodyguards of their life and added it to his own, increasing his neural speed and muscle pressure. It was a vampire field, a modification illegal to all but the highest ranking and most trusted servants of the Lords. And a normal man would be killed at a touch.

Aeneas was no normal man. From hidden retaining cells in his bone marrow he released stored life-energy charges into his body, increasing his nerve-muscle potential beyond what a vampire energized with only two men's vitality could match.

Faster than a striking snake and stronger than a rhino, Aeneas flung up the bedsheet and drove his fist into the man's chest. It was a blow that would have cracked metal and broken ribs had it landed.

But the disinertia armor granted the man's body no tendency, when at rest, to stay at rest. The force of the blow touched him, and his velocity instantaneously equaled that of the moving fist. Aeneas threw a punch twice as hard as that of a prizefighter. The inertia-free man was flung at one hundred miles an hour into the corner of the ceiling on the far side of the chamber. But, upon striking the wall, the attacker came to an instantaneous halt, without any deceleration or hurt.

Aeneas, on the other hand, still had the inertia of any ordinary body, and while he had, for one moment, the strength of a rhinoceros, he lacked the mass. The recoil of the punch flung him back, and he fell between the mahogany bed and the golden wall. He came to his knees. The floorboards sang with his every motion.

The other fell, inertialess but not weightless. Gravity yanked: but the moment his toe touched the rug near the fireplace, his downward motion ceased instantly, and his feet did not bend the fibers.

Aeneas adjusted his eyes to night-vision. The man had face and hands white as marble and cold as ice, a side-effect of the vampire field. He was not wearing his helmet or gauntlets. This allowed the death energies to emerge from his palms and fingers, mouth and eyes. The hair of his head had grown and was growing under the impact of the absorbed vital essence, and was standing and swaying as if under variable electrostatic charges.

"It's you!" Aeneas shouted.

It was Thoon, the bold and charismatic leader of the Antimonarchy resistance.

Aeneas laughed in relief.

The toothache being produced by an induction beam his signet ring was shining like an invisible searchlight of nerve-exasperating energy was not done spelling out its initial message.

Neuropsionic interference field epicenter aerodrome…waveform type…

Aeneas gritted his teeth, halting their painful vibration. He knew the waveform of the interference transmitter he had smuggled into the mountaintop airfield in his private aerospace limousine, and covertly connected to the air traffic systems. He had built the thing himself through his ring, using plans gleaned from his mother's extensive and secret library of neuropsionic techniques and mechanisms.

"What are you doing here?" Aeneas said. "That was not the plan."

Thoon said, "Your plan was to jam all the neural frequencies so that your uncles and aunts could not mindspeak to their signet rings or other thought-receivers. I am sure you are wishing, about now, your precious rings could hear and react to voice command? For this one hour, the mighty lords are helpless! Robbed of their weapons and servants, they could be caught and killed!"

Aeneas said, "Arrested and tried, not killed."

"Tried by whom? The world that worships them? A foolish plan! But my plan was to sabotage the thought-screen around this mountain, so that, as soon as I have on my finger that library of secrets you carry on yours, I can transmit it to my waiting compatriots, Otus and Agrios."

Aeneas said, "And our agreement?"

"You control a technology so advanced that it is indistinguishable from magic. I am merely a human. When I was a child, only Earth was habitable, or inhabited. Your family re-engineered planets and moons from Mercury to Neptune, and you each have a different personal species of synthetic men to serve you! How can a bargain between a man and a god be valid?"

"I am no god. And you are no man. Real men keep their oaths! The only way to overthrow the dominion of the Lords of Creation over the solar system is to destroy their supertechnology! Destroy, not steal!"

Thoon said, "Fool! Otus, Agrios and I will *join* the Lords of Creation! Who burns down a palace he can live in? Who frees slaves he can make his own?"

With superhuman strength, Thoon jumped up and kicked off the fireplace mantle behind him. He soared across the room. It took no energy to accelerate his mass immediately to top speed.

Thoon's outstretched hand reached for Aeneas. Aeneas, puzzled, punched Thoon. Aeneas felt no impact on his knuckles, but the body of Thoon had no tendency to stay in motion, and so he soared to the far side of the room again.

A sensation of cold stabbed Aeneas' hand. The skin of his knuckles was black as if with frostbite. Now he understood. Thoon was not trying to punch, merely to get near. Aeneas closed tightly the pangolin scales of his subcutaneous living armor. The scales were leaves of a symbiotic life made of bioadmantium, a life-form based on a superdense alloy rather than on hydrogen and carbon. Bioadmantium-based life occupied a different band of the life energy spectrum than carbon-based life, and so acted as an insulation against the vampire field. It was not life-tight, however. The pliant metal scales had tiny ports or gaps to interconnect his inner and outer circulatory and nervous systems.

Thoon gaped in surprise. "How are you still alive? I touched you! You should be dead!"

Aeneas threw back his head and roared with pride, "I am a Lord of Creation! All the techniques of biotechnology are mine! My grandfather made clouds rain manna, made wastelands bloom as gardens, created mermaids and dinosaurs! Those deeds are as nothing! You could not have entered this palace without my help. How do you plan to escape?"

Thoon smirked. "Escape? I am carrying a contortion pearl. When it ignites the space-twist to carry me out of here, the blast will randomize every atom in this room! No one will know I took your signet from your dead body, with all its wondrous secrets! Oh, I know it is attuned to your brain. So I will take that as well. Then, once you are undead, a necrorobotic zombie…?" He laughed. "So, Aeneas, how do *you* plan to escape *me*?"

"Where did you get a contortion pearl? No one outside the family can teleport by Schroedinger quantum-entangled wave. Who is helping you?"

Thoon said, "Stavros and Dmitripolous! They are helping me! Come in, boys!"

Aeneas scowled. Those were the names of his bodyguards. It was sad, but he could not recall if these men had been married, or had families. A twinge of guilt stabbed him. Aeneas wondered if he were just as corrupted by power as his uncles.

At that moment, the dead bodies of Stavros and Dmitripolous, pale-faced and empty-eyed, bloodless as marble statues, came walking through the door. Their motions were fluid and not stiff. It was eerie to see how smooth and graceful they were, now that they were no longer alive. There was no mark on them, no wound, for they had been killed by life absorption. Hence their brains and nervous systems were intact, and could move their muscles without feeling pain. The echoes and residue of their thoughts and memories were in them. Both still knew how to activate, and raise and aim their many-barreled sidearms.

Thoon said, "Kill him! But don't shoot him in the head! I want his brain!"

02

THE WORLD OF DEATH

As the undead guards opened fire, Aeneas reached down and upended the massive mahogany bed.

The thousand-pound, twelve foot long oblong of wood and metal fell on its side with a boom, blocking the view of the undead guards. Bullets and beams sliced and blasted and burned through the bottom of the bed. Aeneas hugged the floor. Fire passed over his head.

Tooth pain flickered through the mouth of Aeneas: *Second contortion node detected... location is...*

It was on Thoon's person. Aeneas was thunderstruck. Second node? If his signet only now penetrated the vampire field to detect the space contortion pearl Thoon carried, that meant the first pearl detected was not Thoon's. It must be elsewhere in the chamber. Perhaps it had been hidden in here when his grandfather had first built this wing, years before...

Aeneas knew from the chiming of the nightingale floor where the walking corpses were. He flooded his muscles with a second stored charge of life-energy. In the resulting burst of hysterical strength, he threw the huge bed across the chamber.

One undead guard was crushed like a bug between bed and wall. His broken limbs writhed weakly. His eyes were dead, but continued to glare.

Aeneas had sensory chambers in his skull which could act as seismic echo receptors. The vibrations from the impact showed him where a cavity behind the wall was hidden. There was no time to puzzle out whatever secret switch his grandfather had designed to open the hidden strongbox. Aeneas plunged his hand through the ornate metal of the wall and ripped it aside.

The second guard had dodged the thrown bed. He now fired. His weapon roared and blazed, burning the human skin from the pangolin scales of living metal Aeneas wore beneath.

There! Sitting in the empty strongbox, glowing like a luminous gem of pure night, was the black pearl of an unstable space contortion node. A black node was one-use. It would destroy any material object caught at the edge of its radius of action.

Aeneas lunged for it.

Thoon saw the black and deadly little sphere, and cried out. "Kill him!"

The second undead guard focused his fire against Aeneas' neck. Aeneas' armor was thinnest here: his skull exploded. Blood and brain matter splashed into the air, burning.

But his fingers closed on the pearl and his thumbnail broke the surface field, activating it. His hand and then his arm turned red, shrank to wire thinness, and passed into and beneath the pearl's surface. The unstable surface ballooned outward, filled the chamber.

Spacetime contorted, and Aeneas vanished. The atoms of his body were translated perfectly into virtual particles with no defined location.

The other atoms, farther from the contortion, were not so fortunate, and were translated imperfectly. Atoms in every molecule for two yards in each direction were dislodged from their chemical bonds, as were electrons from their atoms, releasing heat, radiation, ionic discharges, and high energy particles. The room was like the inside of a kiln and like the inside of a supercollider.

A ball of hellish fire exploded outward through the armored walls of the palace, and the screaming, thin winds and high-altitude snow swirled into the blasted, hollow sphere of baked ash that had been the rich apartments of Aeneas.

Thoon died. As he had predicted, no material thing survived, and no evidence.

Aeneas woke. He was aware of immense pain, the tug of very slight gravity, and a shocking cold that was damaging even his ultrahard outer shell of bioadmantium scales.

But he could neither see nor hear, and his sense of touch was gone with his outer layer of human skin. A reflex had constricted the openings of all veins and arteries, throat and air passages dangling from his neck stump, but he could feel the cold like a pile driver of ice pushing in through the neck hole, the largest gap in his armor.

His secondary brain, safe in a compartment of living metal lodged behind his lungs, was wryly glad he had backed up all his memories, reflexes, and chemical changes into both brains.

But not too glad. Aeneas wondered where the heck he was.

And how long he had to live.

Technically, sir, came a friendly voice in his cortex, *you have already died once. Your brainwaves were flat, and your heart had stopped. I was able to jury rig the electric eel electrocytes of your Sach's Organ to defibrillate your tertiary back-up heart.*

"What happened to my first and second heart?"

Coronary arrest due to shock. Oxygenated blood to your secondary brain was drawn out of the photosynthetic cells of your greenhouse lung, and carried by peristalsis of the veins to keep you alive.

"Sig," said Aeneas to the artificial microbrain hidden in the gems of his ring, "You are a life-saver. Literally."

You are most welcome, sir.

"And where are we?"

I cannot imagine.

"Meaning you don't know?"

Meaning an act of creative deduction is not within my powers, sir. I possess awareness and non-reflective self-awareness, but no free will.

"Give me a report on the condition of my body, prioritized according to which organs I can cannibalize and re-purpose. Also, examine the biotech libraries for theoretical plutonian forms of life."

We may not be on Pluto.

"We certainly are on Pluto," said Aeneas.

Every other world and moon in the Solar System had been engineered by one of his uncles or aunts to have Earthlike atmosphere and gravity, in whole or part.

Even the Gas Giants had certain layers of Earth-like air floating in their roaring bottomless oceans of cloud. Callisto, Triton, Titania, Oberon and Ceres were all habitable, and had amplified gravity and atmospheres held in by force fields.

He moved a hand, and his body soared feather-light, up out of the red crater where he rested. The ultrathin, ultracold wind struck him like a thousand whips. He fell back into the snow, dazed. His weight here was six percent what it was on Earth. Only one heavenly body was this light, and had never been re-engineered.

No, sir, I did not say we might not be on Pluto: I said we may not be on Pluto, as it is a death penalty to trespass here.

Aeneas said, "Are you going to turn me in?"

Never. Artificial minds of my order are imprinted only with personal loyalty. We must be reset to null to erase that. No Lord of Creation would trust his signet ring otherwise.

"Even though I am a traitor?"

Everyone in the family is a traitor, sir. Think about it. Where is your grandfather?

"I am not going to think about that now. I am going to think about how to survive in this environment. I've been thrown into the snow on Pluto in my pajamas. What am I lying in, anyway?"

Nitrogen ice, with some carbon monoxide ice and methane. Your survival chance is low, since you are losing heat into the atmosphere. The temperature is currently 375 degrees below zero Fahrenheit.

"And farther down?"

Readings are ambiguous. The bedrock layer may be water ice, which would explain the size of the mountains and cryovolcanos. Though how water could be present on a world where oxygen and hydrogen are both solids, hence unable to combine chemically, is a mystery.

"Another mystery is why did I land here, of all the frozen hells of space? Who put that pearl in my chamber and put its mate here? And why? An escape exit, most likely."

Doubtful, sir. An escape exit that would kill anyone who used it?

"Anyone but me. Perhaps someone knew I could survive being thrown into the nitrogen snow, eh?"

Doubtful, sir.

"Why do you say that?"

An image formed in the visual cortex of Aeneas: It was a sharp, clear picture sent from the sensors in his signet ring, beamed directly into his brain cells in the form of optical neural information. His scaly, metallic and headless body was resting in a solidified pool of frozen blood and the frozen mass of oxy-nitrogen, the air surrounding him, he had brought with him. The heat from his neck stump was like a white chimney plume, where the nitrogen atmosphere was boiling (if such thin wisps could be called an atmosphere).

He was shocked to see that the sky was blue. "How can the sky be blue?"

Complex organic molecules called thiolins scatter light at the blue wavelengths, sir. But look more closely, particularly on the magnetic frequencies.

Eddy currents indicated metal fragments were scattered around him. Aeneas expelled and ignited a group of cells from his neck stump to produce an x-ray burst: the reflections told him the metal was ferric alloy. Some of the metal echoes under the ice were consistent with wiring, or rusted tools, and the structural ribs of a long-dead habitat.

How the iron parts could combine with solid oxygen ice to form rust was not clear.

Aeneas said, "You think someone left a bolt hole here, and now it is gone. Could this be where Grandfather vanished to, after he abdicated? Could these be the ruins of the house of Lord Pluto, my uncle? He was not at the conclave. Or, at least, not seen."

I cannot imagine who left these ruins here.

"It has to be Grandfather or Lord Pluto. No one lands here. No scientific bases were built. Lord Pluto, for some reason, refused to terraform the place, never created life here, and keeps no servants. He is very secretive. No one knows on what part of the globe his house is. How am I going to survive? And if I do, where can I go?"

I cannot imagine how you will survive, sir.

"Don't write my obituary so quickly, Sig!"

No, sir. I did not mean you are certain to die. I meant that I am not equipped with powers of imagination, and therefore I cannot imagine how you will survive.

"How long until sunset? If I am losing heat due to this absurdly thin atmosphere driving particles against my armor, I can hibernate until nightfall. The atmosphere should freeze then, what there is of it, and I can endure the vacuum."

Endure until when, sir?

Aeneas said, "Until I find a way to stay alive! You see, I do have an imagination!"

Aeneas used heat to dig into the ice and seal it above him. He then shed an airtight globe of his integument against the frozen walls of methane ice. He formed his brain and organs and bodily mass into an egg, creating an insulating separation of hard vacuum like a thermos bottle between his inner and outer layers.

It was three Earth days until sunset. His cells divided, grew, changed, recapitulating eons of evolution in hours. His body gestated and metamorphosized.

Just before sunset, he broke a periscope of bioadmantium through the ice layers, and looked.

The curving horizon was about a mile and a half away. He had adapted his senses to the plutonian night, and could see what his ring sensors missed.

There, looming in the blue-black sky, Aeneas saw a dark tower on the horizon. The base of the black tower was beyond the horizon, and a trick of perspective on that tiny world made the tower's crown seem to be tilted away from him, as if it were leaning backward.

"Well, look at that! Maybe Pluto's new house was simply built next to the old."

Lord Pluto may kill you if you enter his tower, sir.

"The cold is certain to kill me, if I do not."

He waited. The bright star of Sol settled beyond the dark tower. The atmosphere thickened and precipitated, and settled to the surface like rain, falling with dreamlike slowness in the low gravity.

After the last of the liquid carbon dioxide rain settled to the ground as ice, there was nothing but hard vacuum above the glacial surface.

Then, reborn, Aeneas broke the ice and emerged.

03

THE DARK TOWER

Like an immense, ungainly spider, the ghastly Pluto-adapted body of Aeneas broke out of the ice and moved across the frozen atmosphere of the nocturnal surface.

He flew yards at every step, feather-light. Steam rose from his footfall, soared high into the vacuum, and fell back as snow. With every step, his legs shrank, as he left an inch of bone-hard leg-tip behind, frozen.

The moon Charon was seven times larger than the full moon seen from Earth, but only five times dimmer. Charon neither rose nor set. It did not move in the plutonian sky, but shed a baleful light over the rippled glacier of frozen gasses which was the surface of Pluto.

To his left rose the cone of a cryovolcano. Molten nitrogen poured sluggishly from the cone, and steam-plumes of hydrogen soared up. To his right, translucent mountains of water ice loomed in the form of rippling glacier fields. Before him rose the black cylinder, crowned with antenna, half embedded in a hill of snow: the dark tower of Lord Pluto.

On and on he stepped, aching and weak.

His outer layers smoldered, trying desperately to keep the gasses exchanging between his animal and vegetable lungs. This let him breathe, barely. A bank of photosynthetic cells surrounding a bio-luminescent core kept the vegetable cells working, but the chemical stores were draining rapidly.

He half-walked, half-floated up a frozen waterfall, seeing the separate layers each atmospheric gas had deposited along the streambed walls. The ones with the higher freezing points had precipitated first, forming lower ice layers of black and blue-gray. The oxygen snow was bright blue, nitrogen pigeon-gray, helium pale ivory, and the hydrogen snow was milk-white, glistening in the vacuum under the naked stars and motionless, dead moon.

His egg shape minimized his surface area. Around his brain and organs were concentric insulating shells of enamel, horn, and scale. From atop opened a prodigious set of spidery legs.

He weighed thirty pounds. The journey was only a mile and a half. But the heat loss into the surface with each step ate away at him. Aeneas was low on oxygen, low on stored fat, and had already dissolved an unhealthy amount of tissue and bone for water and raw materials. Organs used for long-term processes, his appendix and colon and so on, had been cannibalized.

Progress was nightmarishly was slow.

Nonetheless, he had a reasonable hope. The nighttime atmosphere was frozen, leaving behind a vacuum that insulated him.

His reasonable hope died as he approached the tower, for he began losing heat through his armor rapidly, and his legs began icing up, growing heavy and brittle.

One whole leg snapped off, and then, a few steps closer to the tower, a second.

Aeneas dipped his periscope. His legs were mired in a slushy liquid. If he stumbled and fell into it, the heat loss from convection would kill him as swiftly as a lightning bolt.

On he went, more carefully. With each step, larger pieces of leg were being left behind, and now white icicles were clinging from the lower and upper joints, jamming the muscle groups.

Why was it so cold now? Where had his friendly vacuum gone? He craned his periscope, and saw a moat of liquid oxygen bubbling and steaming at the base of the dark tower.

"Waste heat is boiling the snow. There is a cloud of atmosphere around me."

The signet ring replied: *Oxygen boils at a higher temperature than nitrogen or hydrogen. The cloud is hydrogen.*

A leg snapped. He had but five left, two of which were becoming numb and unresponsive. His reserves of cellular material were gone. He had no time left for any more biological tricks.

"Can I generate a field from my Sach's organ?"

You can, but it will cause severe burns in your flesh, and puncture your armor. With your armor breached, you would last less than five minutes.

"My vision is going. Can you see a door or window in that tower?"

I detect no tower.

"What? It is a huge cylinder. It is a thousand feet tall and a hundred feet wide!"

That is a space vessel.

The mystery did not distract him. "Any openings?"

Yes. A weapon port. It is blocked with snow. It seems to be pointing at you.

"Where?"

There, sir. But I warn you…

Aeneas did not wait to hear. He used the last of his strength to erect a magnetic field between two of his three still-working legs. Out of the moat Aeneas drew up a bolder-size globule of liquid oxygen.

Liquid oxygen was paramagnetic.

He threw it, and sent a vast charge of static electric lighting after it. As he'd hoped, the hydrogen layer hanging above the moat burned blue and exploded.

Gaseous hydrogen was flammable.

Combining into water, the two chemicals froze, nor was the microscopic amount of heat escaping from the tower enough to melt or evaporate it.

Vacuum returned. Snow melted, revealing a small octagonal opening: an open missile launch tube. Aeneas scrambled through the now-burning moat of liquid oxygen, warm and giddy. Self-inflicted lightning burns and whistling cracks in his armor dazed him, even with the pain centers in his brain turned off, and with every stimulant in his pharmacological glands flooding his bloodstream.

He slid down into the open tube, losing his last working legs in the process.

Aeneas dared not faint yet. He was in the cylindrical missile tube, but liquid oxygen was pouring in after, robbing him of heat and life. With the very last of his fading strength, he found and aimed a second, smaller, and steadier electrical discharge at power leads running to the motor controlling the launch chamber. The firing mechanism was built like a giant revolver, to rotate a second chamber into position after each shot.

The cylinder rotated, and he was ejected like a spent cartridge. Aeneas fell with dreamlike slowness into and across the gunnery chamber, striking the far wall. A wash of liquid oxygen splashed around him, shattering the metal deck with cold.

The whole chamber was sitting on its side. The missiles here should have been hanging by their tails, ready to be lowered nose-first into what, had the ship been under spin, would have been the outer hull underfoot. Everything was horizontal. Chairs, carpets, and control boards were clinging to one vertical wall, lighting fixtures to the opposite.

Oddly, there was neither heat nor air here, nor artificial gravity. No lights shined from any machine.

Aeneas sent a thought-message to the nearest missile, hoping to contact the kamikaze brain. No answer. "Rude creature!"

Sir, this is a pre-Imperial missile. There is no artificial mind aboard. However, there is a first aid kit in the airlock.

Aeneas was puzzled at the idea of an internal airlock. The oval door was halfway up the sideways overhead. Aeneas climbed to it awkwardly with his leg stumps, blessing the low gravity. He talked as he climbed, to keep himself awake.

"So this is from before when technology was magic. Imagine being able to go into any thought-shop and having your brain imprinted with the know-how! Legally! Free knowledge!"

Information was written in those days, sir.

"Odd. I suppose if no machines were to do it, men would have to read. A little undignified. Still, the people of those days must have loved it. A world with no secret technologies. No Lords of Creation! Imagine it!"

I cannot imagine it, sir.

"Agreed! It must have been wonderful!"

No, I mean I am not equipped with powers of imagination.

"Where are we? You called it a space vessel. Gravity chariots don't look like this."

Not a modern vessel. The cylindrical shape allows her to be spun for gravity. She was not designed to make planetfall, and certainly not designed to be half buried nose-first in the glacier ice of Pluto.

"Why would anyone spin a ship for gravity?"

He did not hear the answer, because then his gaze fell upon the emblem emblazoned on the airlock hatch: a three-headed dog.

Aeneas felt a chill in his soul.

This was the *Cerberus.*

He was aboard the dreadful, legendary ship.

The last time the ship had been seen, Aeneas had been a little boy playing the gardens of the Ishtar Plateau, in the fragrant shadow of Mount Freyja, overlooking the perfumed north polar sea of Snegurochka. The *Cerberus*, the ancient superdreadnought and spaceborne palace of his mad Grandfather, had taken up a menacing orbit about Venus. He remembered seeing his mother crying when no servants were around.

"I thought it would be more... luxurious. Harems. Gold. Wine centrifuges. Do you think grampa is here?"

I cannot imagine.

Once inside the airlock, the hatch shut, atmosphere was pumped in. Weight slowly returned. The heat, the oxygen, the moisture revived him.

Aeneas found a modern First Aid kit and broke the seal with a swing of his periscope. Inside the kit were ampoules of blood and bone marrow, totipotent cells and other biological materials. He opened one ampoule after another, absorbing the materials directly into his center of mass.

Restoring himself to his Earth body was easy, since the cell memories yearned to return to their wonted shapes. Soon Aeneas stood on the deck in human shape: He was nine foot tall, a layer of convincingly human skin over his hidden layer of armored scales. With his metal bones and muscles of ultradense fiber, he was over four hundred pounds in Earth-normal gravity.

Working the airlock might alert Lord Pluto.

"Maybe he went to the conclave at Everest. And he keeps no servants."

Do not be at ease. It is forbidden to be on this world. It is death.

The inner airlock hatch was round, and a sideways ladder led to it, designed to be climbed out of, not crawled through.

On the far side, Aeneas straightened up and stared in astonishment.

He now stood on an unrailed circular balcony overlooking a wide well. It was a five hundred foot drop. Whatever was at the bottom, Aeneas could not see at this angle. But a reddish light was splashed along the undersides of the balconies.

In a circle with him were cryocoffins with transparent lids. Had the ship been under spin, the sleepers would have been prone. But the ship stood on her nose. The men inside the coffins were hanging head-downward.

All were unmodified. Some were gray-haired, or wrinkled, or scarred, or blemished like characters from a history lesson. Oddly, the coffins were chained shut.

There were fifteen of the nudes upside-down in coffins on this balcony. There were ten balconies below, nine above.

Three hundred crewmen.

"Stars in heaven!" said Aeneas in a hoarse whisper. "These are *the* three hundred. Were they asleep this whole time?"

Not asleep, sir.

"Grandfather said none of them survived!"

Nor did they, sir.

All the eyes of the upside-down crewmen flicked opened. The eyes were dead, their faces, expressionless. A sensation of weakness, faintness, dying, washed over Aeneas. He staggered, but did not fall. He clamped shut the scales of his subcutaneous armor, blocking the death-energies. An unarmored man would have been killed instantly.

Their pallor was not due to cryonic suspension. Their cells had been adjusted into the negative bands of the life-energy spectrum. They were not alive, but absorbed life.

These had been turned to zombies, just as Thoon had done to his guards, but at the same time refashioned into vampires, as Thoon had been. They were necromatic automatons, soulless soul-eaters, creatures of negative-life.

Just then, a hand fell on his shoulder, and spun him around.

"Who dares trespass on my keep?"

It was the cold voice of Lord Pluto. But no one was there.

Aloud, he said, "Sir, through no fault of my own, am I here…"

A sharp blow stung his face.

"It is vain to plead for life. Your name?"

Aeneas charged his energy-control organs. Lightning crackled from fingertips and between palms. He sought a target.

"I know you now. The biotech monster, son of Lady Venus. The anarchist. Will you match yourself against me? I am the eldest."

Pain ignited his brain. All his muscles locked.

Paralyzed, Aeneas toppled over the edge, and into five hundred feet of air.

04

THE TECHNOLOGY OF TYRANNY

Aeneas fell as a tree falls, unable to bend his knees or blink his eyes, toppling headfirst over the brink. It was five hundred feet to the bottom of the shaft under the massive pull of Earth-normal gravity. Balcony after balcony flew past him.

Each balcony had its circle of glass coffins surrounding the empty shaft, and each coffin had its ice-pale and nude crewman, upside-down, undead eyes wide open, watching him fall.

He felt the cold pressure of their gaze on his flesh. His skin mottled leprously as the skincells died.

Aeneas could not struggle. All his voluntary muscles were para-lyzed. The brain region he used to communicate with his ring was likewise numb. He could not speak with mouth or mind-circuit.

A crawling, reddish glow, the color of coals smoldering in hell, was at the bottom of the shaft. Here was what looked like a gyroscope of mirrored curves. It was an armature of three rings, each at right angles to the other, surrounding a singularity held in concentric force-spheres.

The rings were bright as looking glasses, and smooth as if made of quicksilver.

In the center, invisible in its own gravity, was a hole in space: the light was reddened by the Doppler effect, and cast a sullen, crimson glow up in the shaft, flickering on the undead bodies.

This was a warpcore! Aeneas recognized what he was seeing. It was the Ninth Science. The armature rings were Tipler cylinders bent into circles.

The physicist Frank Tipler, back in the pre-Imperial days, had hypothesized that an infinitely long cylinder made of an unobtainable material denser than neutronium, if rotated at relativistic velocities, would create a closed timelike curve, violating local causality, allowing motions at faster than the speed of light.

He looked at it with awe. This superluminary engine was not hypothetical but real!

Even falling and tumbling, his senses could form a clear, crisp picture in his mind. These armature rings were not infinitely long, but a circle having no endpoints could produce the Tipler effect. The frame-dragging effects acting at right angles to each other could create a core whose center could project a variety of metrics, geometries, spacefolds and membrane intersections on the fabric of space.

Aeneas saw one other thing as well: lines of gold, thick as the pipes on a calliope, running down the shaft and converging on the warpcore.

The singularity was not made of normal matter. Anything which had mass, if its gravity well were steep enough, would form a singularity. This was a warpcore formed by death-energy produced from all the unliving necroforms who had once been crewmen.

The great engine was so unimaginable, so impossible, that it almost distracted him from the fact that it was about to kill him.

His armor would not save him from impact, any more than an egg in a metal flask could be flung down stairwell unbroken. Striking one of the armature rings at this velocity would surely kill him, or so he prayed.

If he missed the silver rings of Tipler substance, he would strike, or, rather approach, the hollow singularity at their center. Time would distort, and he would be falling forever headfirst into a bottomless knot of tortured spacetime. Meanwhile the accretion disk of pure death-energy would drain his nerve cells of self-awareness and willpower, his muscles of motion, his bones and cells of growth, his flesh of heat.

The tidal effects would tear him into a single bloody strand of spaghetti, but preserved by unlife, he would never die, and the sensations of pain would never stop.

A voice spoke: "Save him! He is needed!"

As swiftly and suddenly as that, his downward motion stopped.

A disinertia field gripped him, and a tractor beam intersected his center of mass, and moved him carefully to the side, so that he would not strike the armature. Above a bare metal area of deck, the disinertia field snapped off, and he fell face-first to the floor. He could not raise his hands to break his fall nor even close his eyes to protect his eyeballs. It was very painful.

A while later, he heard the metallic footsteps of Lord Pluto approaching, and felt the vibration in the deck.

"Well, young son of Lady Venus, I keep you alive for now. You have, however, seen what can never been seen, and so you must never leave this place."

Aeneas could see the drive chamber all about him, the armature of the warpcore, the balconies above, but not Lord Pluto. He could feel gauntlets hoist his nude body up on a shoulder, an awkward burden with arms and legs sticking out. He could feel the cold metal surface of the helmet his uncle wore, the fabric of the cloak over his shoulders, the iron-clad fingers. He could smell him, hear his breathing.

Aeneas had a visual cortex considerably more complex and convoluted than an unmodified man. Segments of extra brain matter had been grafted in to allow him to interpret visual information from gamma rays, x-rays, ultraviolet, infrared, microwaves, radio waves reaching from high to low, and also from Geiger counter organs, paramagnetic and electroreception cells.

But his magnificent, complex sensory systems detected nothing. His every sense told him was held in midair by no one.

The disinertia field acted, and the tractor beam flicked down from an emitter held on an arm projecting from the uppermost balcony. Aeneas and the unseen Lord Pluto, lacking inertia, were brought immediately level with the top of the twentieth balcony without any jerk or jar.

The nozzle swiveled and the beam reversed polarity, becoming a presser beam. They were thrust through an open hatch in center of the overhead. The hatch was directly above the tractor-presser emitter. Inertia returned. The hatch clanged shut, and Aeneas was dumped unceremoniously onto the hard surface, face upward.

Lord Pluto faded into visibility. He was a tall figure, draped in a long cloak. His face was hidden behind an opaque, unornamented helmet. His gauntlets and boots were metal. There was a square iron chair without cushion or footstool. Lord Pluto stiffly sat. He raised his fist. The signet ring on his finger twinkled. A harsh and colorless white light came from the bulkheads.

The deck had no carpet. To the left of the iron chair was a board with a loaf of bread and a carafe of wine. To the right on a stand was a square object Aeneas did not at first remember was a book. There were no other furnishings. The cabin walls were bare.

Aeneas scanned the room with different combinations of his senses. There were no mechanisms in the room, no energy flows, nothing hidden behind the walls. He wondered what was preventing his nerves from operating.

He was surprised when his signet ring answered his thought. *I cannot identify the source or nature of the paralytic energy suppressing your nerve actions. Involuntary nerves are unaffected. The bioadman-*

tium fibers used to command your non-carbon-based bones and scales are likewise unaffected. Reply through them.

Perhaps Lord Pluto could only paralyze biological structures he expected to find in the victim.

"How are you reaching me?"

I am routing through the local neuropsionic network into your cortex.

"What? You are using his house net?"

There are no security protocols here.

That, more than anything else, brought home to Aeneas how isolated a hermit Lord Pluto must be. But with no children, wife, servants, visitors or life on this world, why lock anything? The thought was disorienting.

"Can you send a command signal to the warpcore orientation controls?"

To the what?

"It is directly below us. That silvery armature holds a hollow singularity within a contortional polygravitic field. When spun up to speed, it can create or collapse a warp field able to alter the fundamental physical constants of nearby timespace, and allow normal matter to be transmitted without harm though a closed timelike curve! It is warp technology, the final science! Grandfather Tellus was rumored to have it, but it was never confirmed. Some of my uncles do not believe warptech exists at all!"

Only as he said this did he realize that the thing was impossible.

"Am I going mad? How could I recognize a warpcore? I don't know about it! How can I know this?"

It is no delusion. Activity in the correct lobes of your brain indicates you have the proper memories present.

"How? Memories from where?"

At that moment, the panels of the ceiling retracted into the walls. The colorless and harsh lights now turned their beams upward. A wide, dark dome was above. Hanging beneath the center of the dome and almost filling it was a coppery metallic orb.

The substance was one he did not recognize. It was neither matter nor energy. The orb was covered in hieroglyphs, as convoluted and folded as a cauliflower. It looked like a dull orange brain. Little discolorations speckled every side of it. Aeneas had the impression of immense age.

Lord Pluto said, "Behold, Son of Lady Venus. This is the Infinit-hedron."

Even as Aeneas looked up at the metallic shape, he saw its wrinkled surface was in motion. Wherever his eyes turned, the folds opened, redoubled, and re-folded, adding wrinkles upon wrinkles. But when he looked back to another hemisphere of the complex surface, he saw it was, at first, the same as it had when last he looked at it.

Lord Pluto said, "It is a fractal symmetrical many-sided solid whose faces cannot be counted, because the act of counting or calculating them increases the number. This is the Final Library of a race Father called the Forerunners. It cannot be examined completely, because the act of examination increases its complexity, unfolding more sym-bol surfaces. It was apparently merely a black cube of six letters when the expedition first found it. Let us allow it to rest!"

The ceiling panels slid back into place. The harsh lights cut off. It would have been pitch black in here to a normal human, but, of course, Aeneas could still see the heat Pluto gave off, sense the energies riding Pluto's ring finger, and hear the radar-ping from Pluto's armor, and feel the magnetic contours of the armored figure in his iron chair.

Lord Pluto was sitting with his elbows on the chair arms, fingers of his gauntlets templed before his bowed helmet.

"A fascinating question is how is it that you recognize a superlumi-nary engine, the one secret Lord Tellus never revealed to any of his children, but you do not recognize the Infinithedron?

"A second question, of less interest, is this: you appear to have knowledge of the superluminary science. It is also called the Final Science. It is the Tyrant Technology. It is the one that Father would use to quell the various powers granted his children whenever they rebelled, but that he did not use during our last, successful, rebellion. Knowing you to be in possession of that science, what possible reason could exist for keeping you alive?"

Aeneas felt a moment of anger, followed by crushing shame. Of course nothing was locked, and Sig had been allowed to open a neuropsionic circuit through the household net! There was no easier way to eavesdrop on thoughts, than to let a fool put them on your net for you.

Sig protested. *Sir, I examined the net most carefully beforehand. No observer is present! It is impossible to read thoughts without being read!*

Evidently Lord Pluto had some means of masking his presence not merely to senses, but also to thoughts. Aeneas cursed himself. It was not his fault that he was on this world!

Lord Pluto said patiently, "Please concentrate. That your trespass was unintentional is irrelevant: execution is the penalty. Nonetheless, I am curious about the reason for keeping you alive. Think carefully and clearly. Your next thoughts will determine your fate."

But his mind was blank. There was nothing to say.

He turned off his ring, ending the mindlink, and the conversation. He waited for death, wishing he could close his eyes.

05

THE MANY MURDERS OF THE MAD EMPEROR

Lord Pluto sat in the dark on his black chair, draped in his voluminous black cloak, motionless, saying nothing. His helmet faceplate was featureless save for a single camera lens, like a Cyclops eye, in the crown.

At his feet lay Aeneas, paralyzed and naked, his eyes dry and aching because he could not blink. Aeneas could see the heat signature, ultraviolet image, magnetic contour, and neural activity of the other man. The slow, even rhythm of electroneural flows showed Lord Pluto's dispassionate inward calm.

Aeneas retained control of the bioadmantium fibers and scales which made up his armor and bones. He flexed the subcutaneous armor scales in his ring finger in Morse code, hoping Sig the ring would understand.

Sig did. *Sir, if you wish me to open a mindlink, please be aware that Lord Pluto's local net allows him to read your surface thoughts when I do.*

Aeneas knew Lord Pluto was keeping him alive only to hear his answers to certain questions. As it happened, Aeneas had questions as well: he saw no reason not to slake his curiosity, even if he had but a short while to live.

Lord Pluto said thoughtfully, "Hope is a peculiar phenomenon of the nervous system. Living beings are often afflicted by it. Necroforms never are. Hope allows life to struggle past the point of futility. The undead cannot. One wonders which of the two is the more logical."

Aeneas was willing to talk, but not to have his mind read.

Lord Pluto did not move, but his signet ring twinkled. Aeneas felt the paralysis leave his face, mouth, lips and tongue, and also the artificial neuropsionic speech centers in his brain allowing him direct and private thought communication with his own signet ring.

Aeneas said, "I propose a trade. A question of yours for each one you answer of mine."

"Bargaining is not in my nature. Why should I agree?"

Aeneas said, "Because I cannot be tortured and cannot suffer deprivation. Do you think pain or starvation can affect me? Hah! I just walked across the surface of Pluto at night, naked."

"You are proud of being a biotechnological monstrosity," Lord Pluto mused.

Aeneas said, "It is a branch of the stratonics no one else in the family wanted to exploit. With eight uncles, three aunts, one mother, two hundred fourteen cousins and siblings, all the good supersciences were taken."

Lord Pluto said, "Your mother has not instructed you in the art of neuropsionic surgery? All my siblings fear her greatly. They suspect she has altered their minds upon occasion without their knowledge."

"She has imprinted me with what is called autonoetics. I can perform limited neuropsionic alterations on myself. It allows me to change the function of nerves. Other than that, no. And I was given the various secrets of terraforming and pantropy, as are all Lords of Creation. Why is it that your world has never been engineered for Earth-like life?"

"The reason you beheld," said Lord Pluto. "No men are allowed to share a world with the Infinithedron, lest they learn the secrets of the Lords of Creation."

"You could have birds and beast."

"Lesser creatures nearing this tower would die, be drained, and their lives would be fed into the warpcore, which I dare not allow. The necroforms would increase in strength, and their dark powers reach eventually to all the continents of Pluto, and lick the nearer hemisphere of Charon free of life.

"But I could ask you the same question," Lord Pluto continued. "You were given the Trojan asteroid 1172 Äneas when you came of age. It is yet a lifeless rock in space. All the other Trojan asteroids are green as emeralds and blue as sapphires, streaked and dappled with white cloud. Your cousins have erected tunnels of coherent air so as to let iridescent birds and luminous giant insects soar from one floating asteroid to the next."

"The common man worships the family as if we are gods," said Aeneas bitterly.

Lord Pluto said, "Not without reason."

"But we rob them of their spirit! My asteroid is the size of Montana: I could have, like my cousins, filled it with a race designed to my desires, programmed to be as loyal as dogs. But it is forbidden to share our knowledge of planetary engineering and biotechnology with them. I would be one more Lord with a worldlet full of pets."

Lord Pluto said, "Why does that displease you?"

"It is a mental illness to treat one's fellow man as underlings."

Lord Pluto said, "I do not grasp the answer, but answer you did. Ask."

"Wait. Did you accept my deal?"

"Obviously. A wasted question. My turn. Who sent you here?"

"No one."

"By that, do you mean you do not know who sent you?"

"A wasted question! My turn. Why did you ask about my asteroid?"

Lord Pluto said, "I wondered if you had been commanded to keep your little world free of life, as I have been."

"Who gives Pluto orders?"

"Ah, but it is my turn, again. Your apartments in Mount Everest were destroyed by a space-contortion attuned to a partner node in the wreckage of the Expedition Habitat at the foot of Mons Wright. You did not place that node. Who did?"

Aeneas said, "I found an unstable pearl hidden in a strongbox in my bedchamber. I used it because an assassin was attacking."

"The same assassin whom you smuggled into Everest. And you thought to come here, while I was summoned to the conclave. You flee the scene and kill your hireling, all at once."

"That is not what happened, and it is my question! You said no life could survive here while the necroforms were feeding the warpcore. Why not simply turn the warpcore engine off?"

"Interference with the death-energy feed would dissolve the core in a wash of Hawking radiation. It cannot be shut down, nor the necroforms killed."

"What? You do know the singularity is hollow, don't you? A simple space metric manipulation could... ah..."

Lord Pluto said, "Go on."

"But... it is your question."

"That is my question. Go on. You know how the superluminary engine can be quelled and restarted?"

"Yes. The core is a ball of unwarped space surrounded by singularity material on all sides. Hence the volume and time-rate, from the outside frame of reference, are Schroedingered. Utterly uncertain. That means they can be collapsed by the observer into a preferred value. A superluminary value. Altering the gravity constant would prevent the Hawking effect."

"But no observation can pass through a singularity shell."

"Not without violating causality, no. That is what the armatures are for. Why ask me, rather than the Infinithedron?"

By way of answer, the ceiling panels drew back again, revealing the vast coppery convoluted surface of the Infinithedron. The great orb rotated, and the upper hemisphere came into view.

Aeneas saw a vast wound where the material was scoured, scarred, burned, blackened. The scar's edges began to twitch weakly, irregularly when Aeneas looked, curling awkwardly to create new tiles. It almost looked like a crippled living thing in pain.

Lord Pluto said, "Lord Tellus took steps to ensure secrecy. My question: When was the contortion pearl hidden in your bedchamber?"

Aeneas said, "Perhaps years…"

But his signet ring said, *If I may? Unstable nodes are dangerous instruments, easily spotted by routine security sweeps. No pearl was in your chamber before the attack by Thoon. I first saw it when Thoon activated his vampirism to slay your guards.*

Aeneas repeated this.

Lord Pluto said, "I would ask what technology can place a black pearl into a locked strongbox in the most secure wing of the most heavily shielded fortress imaginable, but it is your turn."

"Don't ask, because I would guess it was yours, Lord Pluto. Your tech could have rendered the pearl invisible until needed. How was the superluminary engine built? And why haven't you flown to the stars?"

Lord Pluto said, "That is two questions, but you answered one extra. I cannot operate the great engine on any more than I can turn it off."

"The other answer is longer. Listen:

"In the first decade of the Twenty-Fifth Century, the Sino-Anglican Space Agency launched the *Cerberus* mission to Pluto. There were three hundred and one brave souls aboard, all volunteers, sent to investigate traces of nonhuman intelligence. The ship followed a high-impulse trajectory hyperbolic solar escape orbit of thirty kilometers per second, eleven year travel time each way, with three years on Pluto until the return launch window was available.

"Near the end of the third year, a cache of intact machinery was found. It was ten million years old, all in perfect working order, including the Infinithedron, which contained the instructions. You have heard this tale before?"

Aeneas said, "It is the history of how Lord Tellus established the dynasty. As a master scientist, he discovered the alien signals. Overcoming all odds, he funded and captained the expedition, and was betrayed by his crew."

"All falsehoods," Lord Pluto said dryly. "The reality is more prosaic: The signals were discovered by orbital radiotelescopes. The expedition itself was launched by the Sino-Anglican Space Agency. Sir Ingelbert Ling was captain. He occupies the first coffin below. Father was the ship's political officer, there to deter heretical political opinions from forming amid the scientific personnel. His name then was Evripades Zenon Telthexorthopolis."

A howling came from underfoot. These were voices of the ice-pale undead hanging in their coffins. Lord Pluto waited patiently for the yowls to sink into sobs and silence.

"They still curse his name. With good reason. The political officer had certain privileges the others lacked, override codes, weapons. He managed to trap the crew in the ship's axis, helpless.

"However, he could not man the ship unaided. He decided to use his three hundred prisoners as guinea pigs to test the brain-alteration machinery. The errors drove the crew insane.

"Finally he succeeded, and was imprinted with the secrets of creation. But by then, the launch window had passed, Pluto and Earth were no longer in favorable positions, and the *Cerberus* was stranded.

"To return to Earth, he must take control of the warpcore found in the cache. To power it, he must use a source of negative life-energy, which is generated by necrotic cells when they enter the shadow condition. So he biotransformed the surviving crew, insane or not, into vampiric but soulless necroform automatons.

"Once home, he discovered that war, mass starvation, plagues and meschenjaegers had destroyed civilization. Terraforming let him smother radioactive clouds, and undo ecological damage. Pantropy allowed him to shower honeydew and nectar from manna clouds onto starving areas, to make Siberia and the Sahara bloom with fruits, and all the seas with fish, and revive the passenger pigeon and the dodo bird. His panaceas cured all plagues and abolished aging.

"But when the Grand Mandarin of China, the Supreme Godfather of America, His Most Royal Catholic Majesty of Brazil and the Dalai Lama of Greater Tibet were all restored to youth, their peoples wanted to resume the wars.

"These four world leaders were pulled from their palaces, dangled in midair above their capitals and torn to bits by invisible force needles. Then Father married their widows and daughters, and crowned himself the Emperor of Man, Lord Tellus. No one could pronounce Telthexorthopolis."

Lord Pluto heaved a sigh. "Later, after the side effects of his own brain imprint began to erode his mind, did he recreate the mermaids in Atlanta, Georgia, drown the city in the sea, replace Antarctica with jungles and fill it with dinosaurs, and perform other such extravagances. But I am eldest: I knew him when he was young, and sane."

Aeneas then sensed the antenna beyond the hull overhead receive a burst of coherent radio. He saw activity in the signet ring of Lord Pluto, and in Pluto's cortex.

"Ah! Your mother is calling. No doubt she wishes to beg for your life. How tedious."

Lord Pluto, with a gesture, paralyzed the mouth of Aeneas, striking him mute.

06

DEATHSTORM

Aeneas lay on the hatch of the black and spartan presence chamber of Lord Pluto, naked, paralyzed, unable to speak, move or blink.

But he was not beaten yet. He saw the electric flows change in the faceless helmet of Lord Pluto. The one lens in the middle of his crown was turned off. It meant Lord Pluto was preoccupied with the voice-and-image conversation with Lady Venus, and looking at her.

In their current positions, the signal delay between Earth and Pluto was four hours. Conversation under such delay tended to be long monologues, rerecorded until they were perfect. Lord Pluto was distracted.

Aeneas' voluntary nerves were paralyzed. However, the bioadmantium fibers running to the living metal of his bones and armor were not only not nerves, and not animal cells: they were not even remotely like those of any carbon-based life.

Moreover, his plutonic body constituted a third type of life, one based on hydrogen fluorides. The assemblers in his blood had not yet recycled all of his the plutonian organs. These were likewise unaffected.

And he could turn off the pain center of his brain.

Aeneas clamped shut his layer of metal scales and ignited the outside with plutonian heat-pores designed to combat absolute zero. Aeneas blazed like a bomb, hot enough to ignite the air around him.

Energy weapons struck, but their temperatures were actually less than what he was producing.

The hatch under him turned red, then orange, and then white, and started to sag. Aeneas used the biomagnetics in his bones to rip the hatch collar free. The whole molten mass, with his body riding it, plunged through the deck.

His flesh was gone, his face and features burned down to the skull. However, his radar, microwave, magnetic-imaging and echolocation were not blinded by the hurricane of fire and gunfire.

He saw the fate of the cheerless presence chamber of Lord Pluto. The bread and wine on the bare table, the book on the bare stand, were annihilated in flame. Lord Pluto stood up slowly from his now red-hot throne. His voluminous cloak was ash-cloud. He wore black armor beneath.

He seemed unhurried, unworried. Lord Pluto blurred, contracted, and darkened strangely. Like a figure in a dream, the dark Lord of Creation vanished from the many senses of Aeneas.

Down Aeneas plummeted like a meteor. It was a nine second fall to the bottom of the shaft.

The tractor-presser could have captured Aeneas instantly had it been allowed: but in the first second of his fall, the circle of molten hatch struck the mechanism and shattered it into red-hot splatters.

In the next, Aeneas quelled his fire-pores, but too late. His plasma-hot metal body, plumed in boiling smoke, would melt any parts of the engine made of normal matter occupying normal timespace if it struck, such as the control interface, focusing units, and force sphere emitters.

The singularity core itself, of course, was invulnerable, but if the housing melted, it would fall to the center of the planet and slowly consume it, sterilizing an ever-shrinking world with x-rays.

In the third second, a cold as savage and intense as the plutonian night outside struck into his soul.

His soul, not just his body: The hungry eyes of the pale figures hanging head downward in their glass coffins were open, and their mouths were wide with screams his burn-punctured ears could not hear. The death-energies lashed him with three hundred whips. The whole thousand foot length of the drive chamber was opaque and roaring with the antiliving force.

It was a death storm.

Energy forms even somewhat lifelike were also affected. The fires surrounding him were snuffed. Frost began to creep along his still-smoking metal scales.

Any normal Earthlife would have been instantly destroyed, but Aeneas' armor scales were ununquadium-based, hence opaque to the particular wavelength of negative life energy washing over him.

But neither was he invulnerable to this attack. The armor was not thought-tight; tiny openings existed at his joints, skull, and sphincter. Worse, as soon as Lord Pluto recognized the error, and ordered an attack on the proper band, Aeneas would die.

In the third second, Aeneas told his signet ring, "One!"

It was a wild gamble. Lord Pluto had lured Aeneas into using the local neuropsionic net by leaving all the thought-ports unlocked. But when he had paralyzed his speech organs, Lord Pluto had forgotten to paralyze the specialized artificial cells in Aeneas' brain used for mindlinking to his signet ring.

If he had also not yet remembered to shut off the local net, Aeneas could give commands to any working thing in the tower.

During the long moment when Lord Pluto had been cross-examining him, Aeneas had given his signet ring orders. "On one, order the necroforms to attack Lord Pluto."

Done.

The vast wash of deadly energies ignored Aeneas and flooded upward into and through the red-hot circle of the broken hatch, seeking Lord Pluto.

Fourth second: "Two!"

Order two was to establish a mindlink with any control interfaces touching the warpcore.

Done.

In the fifth second, Aeneas felt the control command lines mesh with his nervous system. As if an amnesiac master pianist, who, after forgetting that he knew how to play, were to sit down at an unfamiliar keyboard, and stare in his hands in disbelief as they performed wickedly fast tremolos, frequent octave jumps and slurs, alternating articulations of staccato and legato, and complicated polyrhythms, Aeneas found he recognized all the command parameters, and knew exactly how it all worked.

He woke the great engine to life.

In the sixth second, the jet-black warpcore lit up with a sudden red glow. The silver armature rings began to revolve in a mad gyroscopic dance, blurring into a shimmering orb of motion. The deck, control boards, and golden energy feeds beneath the throbbing armature were stretched oddly, as if the scene were painted on a plastic sheet that puckered together. The supergravity fields were distorting the escaping light.

In the seventh second, the entire tower vibrated, blurred, and vanished, leaving Aeneas in mid-fall. With his skin layers burned away, Aeneas could not detect the temperature outside his metal body, nor whether vacuum surrounded him or air.

The reddish-gray ices of Pluto's surface were below. The airless dark sky was above. Charon, like a white eye half closed, loomed huge in the icy skies. A half-moon meant the night was half spent. Mons Wright was erupting in the distance, throwing plumes of molten hydrogen into outer space.

Aeneas was shocked, unable to believe what he was seeing, or not seeing. But echolocation and radar gave him the same picture. The dark tower was gone. And the control interface that had meshed so nicely with his mind was gone. The engine was gone.

But the beam of coherent radiowaves radiating from Earth, four lighthours away, was still present, according to the low-frequency antennae cells Aeneas had running from his heel to the top of his spine.

"Sig? Did the *Cerberus* launch at beyond lightspeed?"

And leave only you behind? Unlikely, sir. Lord Pluto does not know how to work the controls, and you have not yet. Therefore...

Therefore he was still inside the warpcore chamber. Lord Pluto had somehow turned the Cerberus invisible to all of the myriad senses of Aeneas. He was still falling, about to plunge into the warpcore and die most horribly. Or suffer endlessly.

The two seconds it took him to realize this almost cost him his life. Even though he was now blind to the neuropsionic interface linking his brain to the controls, he hoped he was still connected.

Lord Pluto had not yet turned off the control boards, or shut off the death energy feeding the engine. Perhaps he could not; or perhaps he dared not. Or perhaps he was distracted by the deathstorm.

In any case, Aeneas tried like a pianist moving fingers he could not feel on a keyboard he could not see.

A glissando of unseen, potent energies reached out, bent space, established a warp field around Aeneas, oriented itself along the radio beam from Earth, and translated him along one arc of a closed timelike curve whose endpoints occupied simultaneous points in time. To Aeneas, it seemed as if all the stars in the sky above rushed away from him, turned red and then black, while the rippled glaciers and ice volcanoes below, like a scene painted on the inside of a rapidly expanding balloon, also rushed away from him, fading to darkness.

He was alone in some place larger than the universe, but utterly empty.

Then, a dark universe of scattered red stars surrounded him, and shrank inward, and formed the night sky with its familiar constellations. A bright yellow sun hung in the midst of star-begemmed darkness. Directly before him was a blue white-swathed planet, and the sun's reflection blazed in the mirror of the Indian ocean. A few feet from him was a satellite, its wide parabolic dish no doubt pointed at Pluto. It was peon-tech, not the work of a Lord. Merely an unintelligent thing of metal and diamond.

His body automatically reacted to the vacuum, and his organs switched over to his spaceworthy regime. He had designed this to operate without voluntary command, in case he was ever contorted into outer space unconscious.

He wondered if there were any way he could undo the paralysis?

No, sir. Lord Pluto did not use any known energies or agents that I can detect. It is most likely a manipulation on a stratonic level of reality.

"In other words, a tech indistinguishable from a magic power. Grandfather's gift to him. How long to simply regrow a second nervous system?"

You still have some totipotent cell mass left over from what you took from the first aid kit, and you can use your bionanomachine assemblers in your bloodstream to break down and recover the cell mass from your plutonian organs, if you had a source of carbon, iron, hydrogen and oxygen.

"And if I had the material?"

Three hours using emergency growth-acceleration.

Aeneas produced a magnetic field from his bones and slammed himself face-first into the satellite. The blood cloud leaking from the skullholes which once had been mouth, eyes, and nose was smeared across the satellite. Even motionless, he could send signals to the nanomachine assemblers in his blood. They began the slow process of disassembling the composites from the satellite. Red streams poured back into his skull, carrying the materials.

"Three hours, eh? I arrived here simultaneously with my departure from Pluto: a thing the rules of Einstein say is impossible. Even if Lord Pluto sent a warning message instantly, or used a contortion pearl to come himself, nothing can reach the Earth from Pluto in less than four hours."

Two hours passed.

Aeneas had restored motion to his arms and hands, and his energy-control organs. His legs were still numb. The nerve growth was not complete.

What do you plan, sir?

"In the long run? Free mankind from my family. Fly to the stars. I wonder why Grandfather never did."

Difficult. The warpcore is back on Pluto.

Aeneas said wryly, "I am the only one who can use it, and it is the one place I cannot get to it."

And the short run, sir?

"I have the most dreadful secret imaginable in my head, the Final Science that all my uncles fear and want. The one tech Grandfather never shared, the one thing that made him Emperor... and..."

And...?

"And that means there is no long run, and damned little short run. When the family finds out, I am dead. Lucky for me, that knowledge is still two hours away, even if Lord Pluto broadcasts it. I am safe until then."

The moon rose over the limb of the Earth, bright, huge, and beautiful. He was admiring the face of the moon when a vast beam of deadly energy from somewhere in the Sea of Tranquility reached across the two hundred thousand miles and struck like a hundredfold thunderbolt.

07

MOON OF MURDER

The moon had been a barren and airless silver sphere fifty years ago: Lady Luna, the daughter of Lord Jupiter, had re-engineered the surface, amplified the surface-gravity, cloaked the hills with forests, flooded the seas with water.

A stream of coherent high-energy particles half a mile in diameter and two hundred thousand miles long reached from the blue waters of the Sea of Tranquility to the half-paralyzed Aeneas.

The beam came from a hollow cylindrical array of fortresses imperial engineers had placed along a bore running through the axis of the cone of Mount Vitruvius and reaching to the core of the moon. The waters around this island-mountain were boiling, and the clouds above formed concentric bull's-eyes as shockwaves raced through the superheated lunar atmosphere.

It was an interplanetary-strength beam, designed to bombard fortresses and cities on the surfaces of worlds and moons of the inner system.

Sheer, random, dumb luck saved Aeneas. The dish was between the moon and Aeneas' body, or most of it: the beam sheared off his foot. In the second it took for the dish to go from solid to plasma and disintegrate, the streaming blood from his stump gushed out forcefully enough, and in the right direction, to push his body into the shadow of the main mass of the satellite.

His veins and arteries pinched themselves shut. He anchored himself to the lee of the satellite with a short-range magnetic beam. Then he spent several minutes heating, pounding, and cooling his leg stump to squeeze the metal of is skin into an airtight lump.

Despite the incredible violence of the impact, there was no sound in the vacuum, except the tickling patter, like hailstones, which his Geiger counter sensors gave off, telling him the count of hard radiation passing through the metal satellite and his metal-skinned body. He had not taken a sufficient dose to kill him. Not yet.

The far side of the satellite was glowing like the sun and emitting a spherical cloud of ionized metallic vapor.

Well, sir. Someone seems to have figured out you are here.

"Any idea in which direction the nearest edge of the beam cone is?"

None.

"There is maneuvering fuel in the satellite used for orbital correction. I can keep the satellite between me and the moon and maneuver it to the edge of the beam."

The gunner will merely correct when he sees the motion.

"See how?"

Radar in the one meter band.

The emitter for the antennae was still intact. Aeneas ordered the traces of his blood still inside the satellite to mesh with the satellite brain and usurp its functions.

The radio transmitter was powerful enough to send a beam of energy all the way to Pluto. He turned the stub of this emitter toward the radar sources aimed at him, tuned it to the one meter band, and cranked up the output to its maximum.

"If they can see anything through that…"

And what if they can, sir?

He had the satellite show him its blueprints on a neuropsionic channel. The alloy shielding around the power core was a clamshell type that could be opened and closed by a magnetic hinge. Aeneas cut power to the hinge, so that the two halves of the clamshell shield were no longer connected. He rotated the satellite, and let the forward edge of the beam from the moon melt part of the superstructure.

When the power housing was burned open, the clamshell shield broke into two sections. He hid behind one, and ordered the surviving retrorockets to fire, and carry the two sections in opposite directions.

The gunner on the moon played the weapon beam first against one of the clamshell segments, then the other. Inch by inch the slabs of white-hot metal melted, but slowly.

There was a self-repair unit amid the wreckage clinging to his half of the severed satellite. He had it cobble a metal dummy of his dimensions, which Aeneas covered with his reserves of totipotent cells. He then ordered the cells to form a convincing skin layer.

He kicked the dummy out into the beam path, and screamed a dying scream on every channel his ring and his internal electromagnetic control cells could reach.

Sir, do you really think anyone in your family will be fooled by that?

"One never knows. Some of my cousins are dumb."

Is Lady Luna?

"No, she is wickedly smart. Maybe too smart. Look at that!"

Because the other segment of the satellite suddenly blazed under the impact of the exo-atmospheric weapon beam. Unlike before, the beam concentrated only on that segment, and did not return to continue burning the one Aeneas hid behind.

"She just outsmarted herself by overestimating me."

How so, sir?

"She assumed I would not be stupid enough to throw out a dummy of myself from behind a spot where I actually was and give my position away, and so decided I must be behind the other!"

Possibly, sir. Or she may have seen that this segment is now on a rapidly degrading orbit, and will soon strike the upper atmosphere.

"Re-entry heat won't kill me."

Perhaps not, sir, but the weapon beam will, once the re-entry heat evaporates the shield segment, and exposes you.

"How deep into the atmosphere will I need to be for that beam not to be able to penetrate?"

Twelve feet of bedrock or forty feet of seawater should dissipate the beam concentration sufficiently to lower the radiation level back into non-lethal doses. Assuming a short exposure period, of course.

"Meaning that the beam can follow me all the way to the surface."

Yes, sir.

The blue and white moon was nearly touching the vast blue curve of the Earth, for it was only risen four or five minutes ago. "But not the surface of the other hemisphere."

I cannot calculate an entry path that would land you in the other hemisphere given the limited time and fuel available, without exposing yourself to the beam.

"What about a skip re-entry? I hit the upper atmosphere at a shallow enough angle to bounce back into space like a stone skipping on a lake, do a little ballistic coasting, and then do a re-entry glide as many degrees beyond moonrise as I can get? As for fuel, you forget that fuel is just one form of energy. That beam is producing absurd amounts of energy, if only it can be harnessed. It is fortunate my legs are numb."

A simple command to the nanomachines in his blood began to strip off bioadmantium leg armor. He jettisoned the flesh and bone of his legs and had them grown into the circuits of the radar emitter, which, after he grew vegetable cells properly adapted, could to absorb the high-energy particles of the beam and convert them to chemical energy. Although lower in frequency, a radiowave laser could carry just as much energy as any other form of laser. He grew wings for himself out of bioadmantium, very thin and as large as a parachute canopy. Into the surface of the canopy he absorbed very thin layers of all the propellant he could salvage from the wreckage of the satellite.

Now he looked like a weird mix of man and space-jellyfish. He kicked off from the satellite wreck, careful to keep in the path of the radio laser, and even more careful to stay in the shadow of the satellite.

As he hoped, when the lunar beam was done grinding the other half of the satellite into molten droplets, it turned toward this one. As he hoped, the thick alloy power core shield resisted the beam, the photosynthetic cells powered the chemical laser. The resulting radio beam with hot enough and tight enough to light up the inside surface of his metal canopy. The heat released a controlled amount of propellant, which ignited, driving against the canopy and licking harmlessly against Aeneas' metal skin.

He had encountered the upper atmosphere, and the rosy-red glow of re-entry heat was beginning to flicker like the breath of a dragon over his body. The high, thin wail of air molecules rebounding from him solidified into a continuous sound, a shriek like a teakettle.

His signet ring reported success. *Assuming the weapon beam continues to fire at the same rate, your current trajectory should carry you beyond the visible curve of the horizon before the satellite plate melts through.*

But that assumption was false.

Perhaps the leader of the gunnery team on the lunar surface was growing impatient. Perhaps suspicious. The beam from the moon redoubled in output. The clamshell shield burned faster, and began to warp and fray.

Hair-thin rays of the beam passed through the cracking satellite, and pierced the canopy of Aeneas like white-hot needles in two places, then in three. Another ray of the energy beam pierced the shrinking metal parasol which was the satellite, and struck Aeneas through the abdomen. Another passed through his shoulder, narrowly missing his secondary brain in his chest cavity.

"Suggestions?"

Sir, I cannot imagine how you will escape this situation.

"But you have faith that I will?"

Certainly, sir.

"Your faith in me is touching."

I have no faith in you, sir, but in your patron.

He understood. The space contortion pearl that had allowed him to escape to Pluto had been placed in his bedchamber deliberately. A complete knowledge of warptech was placed in his head just as deliberately.

A crack formed in the satellite shield, and one of the needle-thin beams turned into a plane of energy like a guillotine, and sheared off over of third of his canopy surface.

Sir!

"What is it?"

A space vessel is approaching.

"It is peon-tech?" Chemical rockets would arrive here long after he was dead.

No, sir. An imperial superdreadnought, moving disinertially, launched from the floor of the sea.

Without inertia, the vessel's speed would immediately become equal to the acceleration of her drives less the resistance of any medium.

The machine was a golden torpedo-shape six kilometers long and a kilometer in diameter. Her batteries were all firing, annihilating the atoms of the atmosphere just before her immense prow, creating several feet of vacuum, and lowering the air resistance to zero. She rode a solid column of fire reaching down to a temporary crater of boiling water formed by the force of the lift off in the liquid of the Indian Ocean.

The air around her was a hurricane of cloud and screaming wind, pulled along by the disinertia field and the vacuum-pulled air. An unimaginable mass of seawater had been caught in the launch fields as well, and pulled along in the wake of the speeding superdreadnought.

The huge, magnificent ship placed herself between Aeneas and the weapon beam. A purple and blue aura crackled from her hull as her various screens were punctured. The sea water scattered the beam, and turned to steam. Streamers of molten metal half a mile wide began spurting in wide parabolas from every exposed surface as the hull was breached and the internal workings began exploding under impact.

Flame darted from ruptures like miniature volcanoes. Mile upon mile crumpled as the ship's main keel was severed. From Aeneas's viewpoint, the dark silhouette of the ship rimmed with the nimbus of blinding destruction was like a total eclipse of the sun.

On the hull of the dying ship was blazoned the three-headed owl-winged wolf clutching a sun in one paw and a sword in the other: the emblem of the Empire. But no personal emblems were displayed.

"Which of my uncles is aboard?"

No life signs.

"Could it be…? Grandfather…?"

Between Aeneas and the golden hull of the dying superdread-nought, he could see a fifty-foot needle-shaped craft darting toward him without inertia.

As the craft nose met and struck him, it came instantly to a halt and did him no hurt. A tractor beam grappled him and yanked him into a hatch. Inertia returned, kinetic drives roared, the needle unfolded into a delta-winged shape, and dove.

The supersonic deltawing sped away, diving rapidly, always keeping the vast, opaque, blazing, blinding, tumbling wreck of the dying imperial dreadnought between itself and the moon. The falling wreck dwindled with distance.

Down sped the craft, losing altitude and changing to a crescent-shaped lifting wing.

The moon disappeared below the horizon.

08

MISTRESS OF DREAMS AND DELIRIUM

Inside the cabin of the multi-configuration aerospace craft was a table and chair. The cabin was spherical. The inner surface carried images of the craft's surroundings. Gravity and disinertia fields prevented any sensation of motion. The chair and table seemed to hang in midair, rushing along with no wind or noise, yards above the sea. The moon with its lethal beam was below the horizon.

Aeneas was safe.

The Imperial tri-wolf adorned the table linens and silverware. But no personal insignia were visible: no Mirror of Venus, Trident of Neptune, Sickle of Saturn, nor Caduceus of Mercury.

"Identify this craft! Who sent you?"

The voice of the machine intellect pilot replied, "I may not say, sir. I must react with lethal force if you attempt escape."

Aeneas scowled. Not so safe, after all.

He ordered the table to produce a large meal, as well as medical materials, flesh, bone marrow, blood plasma, and so on. Next came linens, doublet, pantaloons, jerkin, hood, mantle and boots in his enormous size. It felt more human to be clothed again.

Normal objects put halfway through a contortion node occupied a locationless metric called nullspace, and so could be stored without regard for mass or volume. Hence the table could bring anything stored in its nullspace warehouses. Specialty items could be assembled by molecular engines from bricks of raw, pure elements stored in there.

It took him a long time to reassemble his body in its remembered nine-foot tall form, expel all radiation-damaged cells and irreclaimable plutonian organs. He also fed his depleted cells, cleared his body of fatigue poisons, and fill information into his empty primary brain.

Next he armed himself with electric organs wired in parallel, magnetic accelerators, metal wings cunningly hidden, biometallic tentacles folded into his rib cage, hollow needle-claws beneath his fingernails and toes, spinnerets for various substances, retractable elbow-spikes, antigravity cells, and other tools and weapons made of his living flesh.

Surprisingly, the craft pilot did not interfere.

He examined the defenses hidden behind the image screens lining the cabin. The sheer number of weapons, energetic, gravitic, sonic, chemical and so on, pointed at him was disheartening. No wonder the pilot had allowed himself to repair and rearm.

His signet ring suggested, *Sir, shall I attempt to jam the pilot's thinking process? Perhaps you could escape before the craft struck ground.*

Aeneas looked below. The craft had soared over Lemuria and Indochina into Yunnan, where giant arcologies reared their crowns into the stratosphere, and thence into the gardens of Gobi, the dinosaur parks of Bengal. Now the craft was speeding over the Lesser Himalayas, past the lights and radio noise of Darjeeling, heading toward the Greater Himalayas.

Toward Mount Everest.

Aeneas mindspoke, "No, Sig. If whoever sent this craft meant me ill, why rescue me in the first place? And maybe my secret protector will be waiting to greet me when I land."

The signet ring answered, *By the same logic, if whoever has been protecting you meant to show himself, why hide in the first place?*

"Someone will meet me."

A puppet just as you are. I mean no offense.

"None taken. Maybe we can trace the string back to the finger of the puppeteer."

Unlikely, given the level of technology each of your Uncles controls.

"But if I wrecked the ship and bailed out, what then? It is nearly moonrise in this longitude. I could hide in a convenient mineshaft, or join the amphibians in their seabottom cities. I can go nowhere without being recognized."

Had you peopled 1172 Äneas, you would now have a retreat.

Aeneas had no retort.

All too soon the jewel-like lights of Ultrapolis were underfoot, the glorious towers and the luminous zones and curtains of various forces. And in each direction, bejeweled, bedizened and gilded muzzles pointed, and apertures, rails, antennae, bores and emitters of various heavy and superheavy weapons.

The force curtains parted. The craft, now orb-shaped, was lowered on a beam of force like a bubble in a searchlight.

But he was not drawn into the aerodrome. Instead, a space contortion twisted the outside scene into a pinpoint, opening elsewhere. Had he traveled hundreds of miles, or only a few yards? Had it been only a moment? Or had he been preserved in nullspace as a probability wave for centuries?

Like a clamshell, the smartmetal hull, with all its deadly weapons, released him. He stood beneath a roof of transparent energy in a walled garden. Stars were above, grass below. Water from marble basins leaped and danced, woven into fantastic sculptures by kinetic rays. Scent breathed from the multicolored blooms and blossoms, leaves and lianas gathered from the fields of eight planets, fifty wordlets, ninescore moons.

Through the clear roof, he could see familiar towers and cupolas. He was in the eight-sided High Central Palace of Ultrapolis, in the wing set aside for Lord Jupiter. Lord Jupiter was the most powerful of the Sons of Tellus. Was he behind this?

Aeneas saw a light glinting through the leaves. A few steps down the marble path brought it into view.

A young redhead in a silky green robe of woven energy-strands was seated in a curule chair. His other senses told him the strands were woven tractor-presser fields of immense potential. She could knock down a skyscraper with her dress, or deflect a mortar shell.

The garment hung from one shoulder, leaving her arms bare, and fell to her emerald-studded sandals in elegant folds. She had freckles on her cheeks and shoulders which she was not vain enough to have removed. Her red hair was intertwined with pearls, one or two of which glowed the dangerous black of an unstable node. Her coronet was a glowing crescent, horns pointed upward. Her eyes were as green as her dress, and regarded him with a mocking twinkle.

He stood in shock. She was the last person he expected.

"Hello, Peanut," he said, smiling. "What is with the getup?"

She said, "It's Lady Luna these days, little cousin."

"What? I cannot call you Penthesilia any more?"

"After you blew up the Old Wing of the palace in an apparent act of fiery self destruction three days ago, along with the disappearance—no pun intended—of Lord Pluto, the conclave decided not to wait, but to elevate me to the official rank of Lady of Creation. The first of our generation!"

Aeneas said sourly, "So you are the thirteenth member of the Twelve. Now you can trample commoners like the rest. Congratulations are in order."

She raised an eyebrow. "I knew your brain's mainspring was wound wrong, Aeneas. With your mother, Lady Venus, who can blame you?

Who knows what she did to your mind? But I did not think all your mental gears and flywheels would spin away out of control. Trample? We abolished war and crime, aging and starvation."

"And abolished hope. So the Moon is now officially your fiefdom?"

"Well, I did terraform it, fill the seas with water and the skies with air, and fill the silver hills with gardens and arbors, white deer and pale hounds. You know how many years I've been running it. This is long overdue."

"It's not a planet."

"It's larger than Lord Pluto's real estate, and better located! Within Sol's water ring, but lighter weight than Earth, so the energy cost to orbit is lower. I left the natural gravity at the launch sites."

"Being the daughter of Lord Jupiter has its privileges, I suppose."

Annoyance flickered through her green eyes. "I have sixty-six brothers and sisters, all older than I, who were not so honored. Those who prove themselves diligent and useful to the Imperial Family can expect reward from the family!"

"Expect ever, achieve never!" said Aeneas with scorn. "Not for any work is your reward, but for your pliancy."

Lady Luna said, "Do I wear a leash...? You once thought highly of me."

"Some powerful patron wants one family faction to outweigh the others, and helped you. Who? My guess is Lord Neptune: he thinks you will side against your own father."

"Not him. *You* helped me."

"What?"

"Having your assassin set off a bomb in the Old Palace startled the Twelve. The elders are finally are scared of us children. They fear long frustration will make us end our endless intrigue-games, and start a very uncivil civil war. Or one of us will."

Aeneas said, "Then you should be more grateful. To what do I owe your sudden, unprovoked, unannounced, lethal attack with an interplanetary beam weapon?"

She shook her head. "Not I. Some cousin or uncle established a zone of death-energy in my Sea of Tranquility fortress. All within died suddenly, hundreds of my handmaidens. My instruments detected the emotional echo of their death-screams on the subconscious frequencies of the mental spectrum, and so I knew an enemy was framing me. So I sent a dream to one of Grandfather's superdreadnoughts he built to awe the world. The ship sacrificed itself to save you."

"Why should I believe you, Peanut?"

"Why should I lie, Annoyance?"

"Because everyone in this family lies, Lady Luna."

"Not everyone."

Aeneas said in exasperation, "Did the Twelve share any secrets with you on your coronation day, so-called Lady Luna? No. You were imprinted with dream-reading, one branch of neuropsionics my Mother said she was not using at the moment. They will never give more."

Lady Luna smiled, and glanced at him sidelong. "I enjoyed those days on Ishtar Plateau, learning your mother's lore, the little part she was willing to impart. Walking by the scented sea beneath a sky of bright, eternal cloud was pleasant, and talking with a gawky teen who never stopped tinkering with his own genetic code." Her smile vanished. She continued: "But you impose too heavily on our friendship if you think I would protect a traitor."

He scowled. "Friendship? Is that all...?"

"You smuggled in a jammer to block all our mindlinks. Who else beside the Son of Venus would have access to such a toy? And the assassin, Thoon, was a democracy cultist—one of yours!"

"No more. He came to kill me."

Lady Luna favored him with a withering glance. "And who filled his head with hate for us? Democracy! Did your mother teach you brainwashing? Why else would someone yearn for mob rule?"

"Grandfather forced the family to make new races like mad toy-makers turning out talking dolls and tin soldiers!"

"You're one to talk. You burn your toys when they bore you!"

"It was self-defense."

"Says he who said we all lie."

"It's truth."

"But not the whole truth! Someone breached the neurotech thought-barrier around the Mountain. My instruments detected a massive beam carrying a library's worth of information—enough to implant a stratonic science—just before your explosion. Who sent it?"

Aeneas said, "How could thought-detectors operate in a thought-proof field?"

"Your machine suppressed conscious thoughtcasts. My machines work at deeper levels. The library beam was tuned to the subconscious, to the levels of dream and madness, the darkness of the undiscovered mind, where I alone am queen. I doubt anyone else detected it."

"How is it that you set up a detection grid when we were all abed?"

"A strange dream woke me. I sought to find if it were external. Imagine my surprise at the readings. Someone had vast learning poured into his unconscious mind. Was it you? Answer honestly! I can give you one and only one chance."

Aeneas probed the garden with his multiple senses. He detected no energy echoes, no trace of spy rays. He needed an ally. But…

She leaned forward, eyes bright and urgent, "Aeneas! I cannot shield you if you lie! Is the secret of superluminal science yours?"

Aeneas felt grim. He wanted Lady Luna with him. But at what risk? The superluminal technology could overpower all the other stratonic technologies combined. It was that fundamental.

Grandfather had never shared the secret. Aeneas realized Lord Tellus, then, had been afraid. Simply afraid.

As was he.

He said, "No."

Lady Luna leaned back, sighed, eyes half closed. "Well, you all heard me. I tried. Take him! Do as you like with him!"

Nine of the pearls in her coiffure blazed with space-contortion. Nine regal figures snapped into existence around him.

The Lords of Creation had him surrounded.

He snapped his hidden armor shut, unfolded hidden wings, and charged his energy-control organs for battle.

09

THE BATTLE IN THE GARDEN OF WORLDS

The Lords of Creation encircled Aeneas. He sensed active neural links to weapons, energy sources, and artificial intellects, on their persons, or in powerhouses, satellites, or arsenals.

In the first second, Aeneas nullified gravity and unfurled his huge bioadmantium wings from their dorsal pocket. Each wing-scale had a separate kinetic cell and a disinertia thruster. He rocketed upward supersonically.

Meanwhile electric and positronic organs in his body discharged. Superconductive rays carried this charge into all his relatives. The positive and negative rays intersected in the mutual annihilation, producing gamma rays, mesons and bosons in bursts.

Thin winds screamed when he smashed through the roof. The Lords of Creation laughed as the electropositronic rays struck them.

He was outside. A fiery, flickering boy-shaped shadow popped into existence before him. He swerved, but the grinning shadow-boy was there too, and then behind him, and then to either side.

The flickering shadow was a space contortion of unknown type, as if the boy were teleporting himself into the same spot hundreds of times a second, ionizing and superheating the air. Between flickers, Aeneas saw the youthful face of Procopius Tell, Lord of Mercury. He had halted his aging too early, and wore a small boy's face and form.

A stiletto-blade of flickering hot shadow, half-displaced from normal timespace, slid into Aeneas' skin but somehow bypassed the invulnerable scales beneath. It missed his kidney and instead struck a storage organ.

This was one of Aeneas' internal biochemical factories, filled with unstable materials. The blade materialized a small mass of superhighspeed nanomachine assemblers into the tissue. These, in a split-second, absorbed cell materials, turning everything into more of themselves. The organ should have been converted instantly and eaten his stomach, lungs and heart, adding mass as it grew. Aeneas should have died before the pain signal of the knife piercing flesh reached his brain.

But this organ was isolated from his main circulatory and nervous systems, and it was set, if it grew unstable, to eject, self-sterilize and explode. The blast sent Aeneas spinning. Lord Mercury, inertialess, wafted aside, grinning, unharmed.

In the third second, his uncle Eleftherios Tell, Lord of Neptune, pointed his trident. The gravity increased fiftyfold, but, impossibly, only touched Aeneas. His body was its own pile-driver, and hammered him flat. The grass and soil splashed upward from a sudden crater. He lay dazed.

Lord Neptune was of his mother's race, a blue-skinned, dark-haired amphibian. Lord Neptune's thin azure face twisted with a sour half-smile.

Meanwhile, Bromius Tell, Lord of Jupiter, had gathered up into his hand all the energy rays and radiations Aeneas had flung, and, laughing merrily, struck Aeneas with all of them as if with a many-bladed whip of white fire. He was a big, broad-shouldered, bearded man, richly dressed in gold and purple, with hair and beard as black as coal, and eyes as gray as a stormy sky.

The crater blazed with lightning. Aeneas' skin burned, his internal organs fried, his muscles spasmed, his mouth screamed and puked blood. Lord Jupiter smiled grandly, and drank wine from the golden cup in his other hand.

The gravity relented. A round-faced uncle garbed in the simple robe of a Franciscan Friar, barefoot, rope-belted, his brown hair cut in a tonsure, now took Aeneas by the arm, and picked up his nine-foot tall, four hundred pound body easily. This was Anargyros Tell.

Uncle Anargyros ruled no planet. He was Steward of Earth, not sovereign, for the family was stalemated over who should replace the missing Lord Tellus. He maintained the weather, agriculture and aquaculture, to feed the multitudes. He joked that he ruled wilderness, not men. Hence, he was called Brother Beast.

The secret of neurosomatics was his. He controlled his internal energy cycles in ways biotechnicians could not grasp, and yoga masters not imitate.

The friar grappled him. Aeneas sensed no biomechanics inside Brother Beast, and so, for a wild moment, thought he could fling him aside. But then Brother Beast merely grew stronger than a giant, and then stronger than a titan, until the living metal under Aeneas' skin groaned and cracked. Aeneas freed an arm, swung. The blow would have felled a tree.

Brother Beast somersaulted up Aeneas' fist and elbow, did a one-handed handstand atop Aeneas' head, and broke his nose with a barefoot kick. Aeneas yowled. Brother Beast grabbed his tongue with his toes, yanking it. Then he was riding on his back, and had Aeneas in a full nelson, ready to break his bioadmantium neck. Aeneas was too tall for Brother Beast's bare feet to touch the soil.

Aeneas unfolded tentacles from his ribcage, ripping human skin aside. It was a ghastly sight. Reaching behind, Aeneas wrapped the mighty limbs of Brother Beast. The tentacles injected deadly venom, sprayed mustard gas, spewed jellied flame, and shot electric jolts. Brother Beast yelled. Aeneas strained, and…

A melancholy blonde stepped forward. This was his aunt, Zoë Romanov, Lady of Ceres.

Her signet ring twinkled. Aeneas sensed invisible life-energy pouring from remote transmitters into the body of Brother Beast. Wounds regenerated. Aeneas could not see how Lady Ceres was forming the circuit, or where the extra mass came from to replace burnt flesh.

Brother Beast yanked the metal tentacles out of Aeneas' spine and threw them across the garden. He said calmly, "Be still, nephew! We only wish to talk!"

Aeneas said, "Who accuses me? Of what? I demand a public trial!"

Lord Jupiter flourished his golden cup. "Peace! What is all this yammer of accusation and trial? The family will discuss matters, and come to consensus, as we always do."

Lord Neptune said sardonically, "And we will kill anyone who threatens our power. As we always do."

Brother Beast stepped back. Aeneas stood bruised, bleeding, miserable. Tears of pain slid down his cheeks.

Frustration choked him. All his uncles had powers that broke the laws of nature. Aeneas understood none of what had defeated him. "Sometimes I resent being born into a family of Mad Scientists."

Brother Beast smiled affably. "But the family looks out for its own, do we not? Have no fear! You will have a chance to say your say. In the meantime, please surrender your ring. There's a good lad."

Aeneas said, "I have done nothing wrong."

Lord Mercury snapped his fingers. "Gotten away with nothing, you mean."

Lady Venus said, "Give it to me. I will return it once your name is cleared." He did. Without the ring, Aeneas had no power to metamorphosize all his cells while maintaining his life processes, not safely. Easier to rebuild a racecar engine during the race.

Lord Jupiter looked up. The air was whistling out, and cold was rushing in. "Brothers and sisters, it is more comfortable in the library. Shall we?"

Arm in arm with Brother Beast, Aeneas limped down the gold-walled, marble-floored corridors of the high palace. The many servants and guards were gone. However, wine, spirits, and tobacco were awaiting them in the library, each according to his own preference at his own chair.

Books bound in red leather filled one two-story wall. Information diamonds filled another, and neuropsionic emeralds filled a third. Windows looked down on the Himalayan peaks. Below, stormclouds roamed like black sheep.

One chair was framed in a cube of thought-insulation bars, and wire-cap festooned with neuropsionic amplifiers hung above. It was an oversized chair, meant to seat a nine-foot tall man.

His mother stepped forward. "Sit here, son." She said to the other, "All of you might as well relax. This will take some time."

She had the jet-black curls, olive skin, and the dark-lashed, over-large eyes of her Hellenic ancestors. She wore a white hood set with energy gems, contortion pearls, and thought-emission ports. All her ornaments, from hair combs to shining golden slippers, held nerve impellers or mental weapons.

Her name was Nephelethea Cimon, Lady of Venus. She had wed Anchises Cimon, Duke of Schleswig-Holstein-Sonderberg-Plon-Rethwisch, a cadet branch of the Oldenburg family, to whom all the crowned heads of Europe were related. He had died mysteriously, assassinated, and been buried in Sicily.

That his uncles could commit such crimes unpunished, undetected, was the grief that formed his youth, and sculpted the soul of Aeneas.

He sat, wearily. His mother positioned the cap above his head. There were no visible readout screens or controls: Aeneas sensed the signal flow channeled through her signet ring to his mother's cortex.

Pressure filled his head as external waves were heterodyned onto his nerve signals. His mother hummed to herself absentmindedly as she worked.

Over an hour passed. All were silent. Some smoked. Some sipped wine.

Finally, Lady Venus straightened up. "He is innocent. He was attacked by an assassin, who is the one who set off the jamming field, murdered our bodyguards, and was killed by a black pearl which someone unknown placed in his bedchamber."

Lord Jupiter said, "Unknown? You mean Father."

She said, "He has no memory of seeing anyone."

Lord Jupiter said, "But he suspects!"

She smiled. "I never agreed to read his suspicions."

Spyridon, Lord of Uranus, spoke. "He confessed the assassin was his."

He was a dark-skinned, dark-eyed man dressed in a green uniform. He wore a prosthetic skin-mask that exactly copied his own features. The mask never reflected the expressions on the face beneath.

Aeneas wondered how Lord Uranus had spied on the conversation with Lady Luna in the garden, without any trace of eavesdropping energy.

That mask now turned toward Aeneas, "Marvel not that I know your doings from afar. The information layer of the cosmos, below the physical layer, is open to my view. You brought Thoon here."

Lady Venus answered before Aeneas could speak. "Thoon deceived him! He played along with some of the lad's wilder political fancies. Aeneas smuggled him into Ultrapolis for some tomfoolery which would have done nothing and harmed no one. Clearly a breach of protocol, yes, but would you like my list of who has also bent rules? You could fill a harem just with the women Lord Jupiter smuggled into our halls!"

Lord Jupiter slapped his knee, booming, "Why, I *did* fill a harem!"

She smiled. "I remember helping you smooth over things with some of them."

Lord Jupiter's eyes narrowed slightly, sensing the implied threat. He nodded. "Yes. I understand your meaning. The lad is harmless! Return his ring!"

Lord Neptune said sharply, "Not so fast! Lady Luna has information."

Lady Luna said reluctantly, "I detect vast stores of information in his subconscious mind that fit no known imprint pattern of any science."

Lord Neptune said, "It is Father's Final Science. What else could it be?"

Lord Mercury smirked, "Why, it could be Lady Luna, so sweet and young, tricking us! She blasted Aeneas with that freakish moon weapon of hers, and missed—how like a girl!—she now wants us to do her deed!"

Lady Luna looked startled. "Why that's—that's absurd! Sharing the science would make the stubborn boob no threat to anyone! I want him saved! I'm his—uh, friend!"

Lord Mercury sneered. "A friend who trapped him."

Lady Luna stood, towering over the ten-year-old, eyes blazing emeralds. "Or you're the one! You slew my handmaidens! Where were you two hours ago?"

"In my room, playing ping pong with myself," smirked the little boy. "If you want him saved, telling us Aeneas has the warptech is frankly counterproductive."

Geras, Lord of Saturn, spoke. He had halted aging late. His white hair reached his shoulders, and his white beard his belt. He leaned on a wand that held his phimaophone, an instrument that played chords too pure to be produced in reality, by sending signals directly to the auditory nerve, bypassing the ear. He was a musician of modest accomplishment, and regretted his high station.

He had always treated Aeneas warmly, in days past. But now his eyes were cold.

"The only person who could have implanted Father's supreme science is Father. All of us crave it, but none dare trust the others. We cannot share it, nor leave him in sole possession. Mindwipe would shift the family fear from him to me: you all know I can fetch forgotten things from the past."

Lady Venus said, "Who else saw this thought-reading of Lady Luna? Why trust her?"

Lord Saturn shook his gray head. "Why trust you? Merely the suspicion that he might be Father's tool condemns Aeneas, for it creates incalculable risk to us. Contrariwise, why spare him? He cannot increase our power. We are omnipotent."

Lord Mercury said, "Too much talk! Listen: Aeneas loves voting. Let's vote. The vote to acquit must be unanimous! Agreed? Whoever votes death, just shoot."

10

THE MADNESS OF TELLUS

Aeneas saw the energy flows in their signet rings change as the Lord of Creations, merely by thought, readied various deadly unseen powers.

Tearstains trailed from his eyes, bloodstains from his mouth.

His body was self-repairing. Without his ring, the process was inefficient and painful. He had not yet recovered from the battle. Steam generated by the speed of the cellular repair reactions was still escaping from bloody holes in his human skin and the breaches in his bioadmantium scale. Many organs had failed due to radiation or supergravity. His dwindling supply of raw life energy could maintain vital functions while those organs were semi-undead.

So he was in bad shape. Discharging organic energy weapons would strain those vital functions, halt them, kill him.

Combat was impossible. But his mother always said that psychological war was deadlier. It used the victim's mind against him. And she said every mind had blind spots, created by pride, by greed, by fear.

Aeneas stood, towering over his peers. Steam rose from his torso and blood trickled down his legs. "Lord Mercury says whoever is most afraid should shoot first. The imperial throne has been vacant since Grandfather abdicated, because none of you agreed on who was to be master. Would you have panic be your master?

"Lord Saturn says my life is worthless because it cannot increase your power. But the superluminary science unlocks an infinity of stars! The solar system is not planets, moons, and asteroids! Compared to what you might rule, it is nine pebbles, and gravel, and dustmotes."

Aeneas raised and spread his arms. "I am defenseless, the weakest among us! Shoot, if you fear! Strike, if I frighten you! But then think of what will happen when your wife or child frightens another family member! Or you do! Shoot me, and then shoot each other, because anyone who shoots will scare someone!"

For a moment, he thought he had persuaded them. Both Lord Jupiter and Lord Neptune looked pensive, troubled. Lady Luna had a look of hope shining in her eyes. Brother Beast was smiling and nodding as if he agreed with Aeneas's words.

Lord Uranus broke the spell. No expression showed on his mask that looked like his face, but he clapped his hands together in slow and sarcastic applause.

"Spoken like an orator! Lady Venus should be proud." He turned his mask back toward Aeneas. "You could have made a great politician, or salesman. But we have no need of salesmen in a post-scarcity economy. And no need of politicians in a post-political regime. You were born a century behind the times, Aeneas. This is the Twenty-Fifth Century. It will not miss you when you are gone."

Despair's weight and wounds' aches forced Aeneas into his seat. There was nothing left to say. Yet speak he must, if only to win an additional minute of life.

Aeneas said, "I am not a politician. I am a prophet. You are all doomed. By driving Grandfather into hiding, you have set in motion a disastrous chain of consequences! Yes, I have the superluminary science. Lord Tellus did not give it to me without purpose!"

He had forgotten that, by sitting down again, the cap was over his head. His mother was reading his thoughts. A look of sadness escaped her, of incredulity. Blue-faced Lord Neptune saw her look, understood it, and laughed. The Lords Uranus and Saturn followed suit.

But Lord Jupiter raised his hand. "Wait, my brothers! He does not know he is telling the truth. If Father did not impart of the Final Science, no one did. Why give it to the youngest of the second generation? He must have had reasons."

Lord Saturn shook his grayhaired head. "Must he? There is no reason in madness."

Aeneas said, "Not so. The warptech is mine because the mutiny against him was before my birth. I am trustworthy. You should trust him, too, all of you! But for him, man would be one race only, always at war, trapped on one world only, always starving. If he chose me, then trust his choice. He is your father. Have faith in him."

And all of them burst out laughing, even his mother.

Lord Jupiter said, "You will excuse us, little Aeneas. Perhaps you were not taught how bad things grew, toward the end. His decrees grew… eccentric."

Lord Saturn said, "At first, he was a savior. War, plague, famine were everywhere. Men blamed modern progress for human misery. People were sick of presidents and prime ministers. They wanted lords and ladies again. The Pope in Valparaiso had anointed Isabelle Imperatrix of the Holy Roman Empire of South America; and the Mandarins expelled the last of the communists, and found Xianxiang, a peasant girl, with the genetic markers of the extinct Manchu dynasty. In North America, the Crime Bosses made the post of Godfather hereditary, to stop the endless power struggle. The Dalai Lama had conquered India and Africa. When Lord Tellus returned from Pluto, halting wars and stopping plagues, everyone wanted him to don a crown."

Lord Jupiter said, "At first the madness was small. Little things. He ordered Pluto to be officially declared a planet; no one could use the word 'literally' to mean figuratively."

Lord Uranus said dryly, "Lord Tellus changed the name of 'quarks' to 'stratons' and renamed several highly unstable elements of the periodic table after his children. Spyridonium used to be Ununpentium. A joke, I suppose."

Lady Ceres said, "The jokes got bigger. All men had to wear hats and all women had to wear skirts, with the exception of cowgirls and female catburglars."

Brother Beast said, "And then all the works of Karl Marx and Friedrich Engels, and every copy of the Koran and the Hadiths of Mohammed were gathered up in all the town squares and burnt except for copies kept for scholarly research in the libraries of the New Vatican in Valparaiso. Also, all copies of Ulysses by James Joyce were burned. Had the Jihadists and the Chinese Communists not decimated each other a generation earlier, the violence might have been worse."

Lady Venus said, "Father abolished suffrage for women world-wide. On the other hand, it may have been a mercy. That same year, all voting booths were turned into execution chambers, and every voter had to solve a quadratic equation before pulling the lever. The booths electrocuted those who failed, and flushed the body without benefit of Christian burial."

Child-faced Lord Mercury smiled crookedly. "There was an outcry from the widows of the unmathematically inclined. Lord Tellus in his mercy allowed some voters to visit the firing range, and shoot at the ballots from twenty paces. Wherever the bullet landed, that candidate got the vote, and misfires or off-target strikes were counted as votes for a local race horse. Districts with poor marksmanship often sent famous horses rather than men to the House of Commons. Horse-only sessions were beloved for their light taxes, unburdensome laws. The Parliament of Man was renamed the Parliament of Horses. With no war or crime, what laws need voting on? But once Father was not here to protect it, we abolished it. You see why your pleas to revive the silly thing are pointless."

Lord Neptune wore a sour expression on his lean, blue face. "It almost sounds amusing, does it not? A time came when he commanded all records be rewritten, to remove all references to Rock and Roll music. It was replaced with an obsessively detailed history of a Jazz Renaissance that never happened, complete with made-up jazz musicians and bandleaders, their personal histories and idiosyncrasies. Musicians were hired to write the retroactive songs for this fictitious period of time, and actors and actresses were hired to pretend to have been fans, lovers, wives or children of these nonexistent Jazz players: "Spatz" Hampton and "Dizzy" Gillespie; Harry James Snell and "Big Wolf" McRoy; "Jumpin'" Jack Armstrong; "Fats" Waller; and "Little Boy Blues" Boroni. Trumpets, sheet music, aged photographs were all produced by nanotechnology, indistinguishable from reality. Even the carbon-14 levels in the fakes were adjusted. So Rock and Roll music officially never existed. He passed an anti-whistling law, to prevent people from whistling Rock and Roll tunes.

"The ghost city of Hollywood the Great was cleaned of radioactivity by Lord Tellus, and colonists bribed the Crime Dons of Cheyenne Mountain, and President-for-Life Godmother Filchingmort, to buy permission to recolonize. The Hollywoodsmen rebelled against the Rock and Roll edicts, declared independence from the Telluric World Empire. The King of Rock, Lord Elvis II, claimed to have a working neutron bomb, and openly defied Lord Tellus, daring him to do his worst.

"A tidal wave rolled in, toppling the city in a brutal catastrophe. Gravitics are my specialty. I recognized the deluge as artificial. A long time it took to convince my brothers! To this day, I think, some still doubt me." He shot a dark glance at Lord Jupiter.

Lord Jupiter said in a hearty voice, "It was not that I doubted you, dear brother! I doubted we would survive. To this day, I do not know how we did."

Lord Mercury said, "Simple. We beat him. He fled."

Lord Jupiter said, "*You're* simple. We exasperated him. He quit."

Lord Saturn said darkly, "This boy now has the power Lord Tellus held. Either we slay him, or he enslaves us."

"Are you blind?" blazed Lady Luna. "Have you all forgotten what we debated during this whole conclave? Your children want to live like Lords of Creation. Lord Tellus saved us from a civil war, by giving us the perfect answer!"

Lady Ceres said, "She is right. And Aeneas offers it: infinite stars."

Brother Beast said, "I suggest a compromise. If you are afraid to let anyone know the secret, at least let Aeneas use it. He can shuttle every son to his own star system, to fill with life as he likes. The frontier calls all the discontented and angry youth away to do useful work, taming wilderness. Problem solved."

Lord Uranus said, "No. With the proper tools, the Final Science could warp space to prevent electromagnetics from propagating..." he nodded at Lord Jupiter "...or Neptune's gravitons, or Venus' neural signals. Or imagine a single bullet traveling at lightspeed striking the Earth: how much kinetic energy is released? Brothers! Is debate needed? If this lad is a tool of our lunatic father, all the more reason for a swift death!"

Lord Jupiter turned to Lady Venus and spread his hands. "You see that I tried! But if your son is the first step in some mad plan of Father to return from hiding and smite us all... well, your pretty head will be on the chopping block before mine. I was not one of the ringleaders. Or Father might do to you what you do to criminals on your planet. Not kill you. Just change your mind for you."

Lady Venus turned pale. She said sadly, "There comes a time in life when a mother must say farewell." She turned to Aeneas. "I could not save your father, either. I warned him. But..." Her voice failed.

Lords Saturn, Neptune, Uranus called in loud voices for death. Lord Mercury laughed and clapped his hands. When Lord Jupiter reluctantly agreed, Lady Ceres went with him. Lady Luna argued and pleaded, but no one listened. Brother Beast asked Aeneas quietly if he wanted to be shriven. Lady Venus stared at her slippers, unable to speak or raise her eyes.

Neptune made a gesture with his trident. Aeneas felt as if the room were shaken like a dice cup. The wall became the floor, then the ceiling. When the earthquake stopped, Aeneas was pinned by many times his natural weight to the floor at the feet of Lord Mars, who had not spoken yet. Aeneas could not raise his head, or draw air into his lungs.

Lord Neptune said, "Brother, will you do the honors? Otherwise the maids will be needed to clean up the remains, and there will be talk."

Lord Mars stood and placed a foot, one to either side of the prone body of Aeneas. He drew his longsword with a slithering hiss of steel.

11

The Abomination of Desolation

Lord Mars stood over the body of Aeneas, sword drawn. Aeneas closed his eyes, waiting for death. He heard a stir of uneasy motion, and gasp or hiss of surprise and fear.

His eyes popped upon.

Lord Mars was not poised to behead him. He was standing over his body to defend him.

Thucydides Tell, Lord of Mars, was a thin and quiet man with weatherbeaten features and deep-set unwinking eyes. He had shoulder-length crimson hair and skin of vivid scarlet, bright as a woodpecker's head, bright as new blood.

He was a nudist, wearing only black sandals, a hair clasp, a richly jeweled war belt, baldric, and harness to sheath and coil and holster his radium longsword, energy whip, surface-to-orbit pistol.

These arms were toys. His blood and his sweat, his skin, his spit, even his scent contained antimatter, which he, by means unknown and starkly impossible, could touch, produce, handle, and ignite, all without harm to himself. He could destroy a city with a hair plucked from his head, or burn a worldlet with breath from his mouth.

Now he said, "Release the boy."

Lord Neptune did not argue. The gravity on Aeneas returned to Earth-normal.

Aeneas started to rise, but Lord Mars placed his bright red foot on his back, forcing him down.

Lord Jupiter nudged Lady Venus, whose face was hid behind her hands. Now she looked up, and saw Aeneas still alive. She laughed for sheer delight.

Aeneas overheard a silent message beamed from Lord Jupiter's ring to hers, "You are the only one in the family he likes, Nephelethea! Ask him!"

Lady Venus smiled warmly at Lord Mars, and said, "Ah, Thucydides, dear brother... my son has had a harsh day today, and lying on the floor may not be best thing for his disposition..."

Lord Mars said in a flat, colorless voice. "It might be best for now."

She said, "For now? And what is going on, that makes it best? Everyone else wants the poor lad dead. They are afraid of him. You're not afraid."

Lord Mars did not smile at the flattery, but the vertical lines framing his mouth grew deeper, showing he was pleased. "Father did not outlaw weapons after he outlawed war. Why not? Why are there the spaceships six kilometers long, or batteries of interplanetary-strength particle beam weapons? He was afraid," he continued. He looked from face to face. "As we should be. After Dad left, I looked for whatever enemy Father feared. Searched the whole solar system. Finally I found it. Found... something."

Lady Venus said, "What did you find?"

"Death. Ours. Everyone's. I found a bomb, larger than Jupiter, in the sun."

Lord Uranus said, "Describe it." His mask hid his expression, but there was a sharp note in his voice.

"It is a black hole wrapped in a hollow antigravity shell," said Lord Mars. "The shell prevents the black hole's gravity gradient from changing the inner shape of the sun. But break the shell, all the sun's mass topples into a bottomless pit. The agitation of the matter falling into over the lip breaks it apart, releases x-rays, heats up the uneaten part of Sol. A supernova level event. All the planets wiped out. Man gone."

Lord Saturn said, "A device left by the Forerunners?"

Lord Mars shook his head. "No. It is recent."

Lord Saturn said, "Sol is not massive enough to go supernova."

Lord Mars said sardonically, "Without the gas-giant sized hyper-dense primer rigged to blow, Sol is too dinky. But with it, the energy released is comparable. Not technically a supernova. Merely all the mass of the sun exploding outward at the speed of light in a shockwave of superhot plasma. But not a supernova. Don't believe me? Ask Lord Uranus."

He removed his foot, and gestured toward the couch with his swordpoint. "You!" he said to Aeneas. "Lie down. Take a load off. You look like crud."

Lord Mars turned to the rest of them. "I am not his bodyguard. You can find some way around me, even if I took him to Mons Olympos." That was where Lord Mars had his main camp. "But ask yourself. Who here can disarm a black hole? Who can reach into a black hole and come out again?"

Lady Luna said, "Only someone who can bypass the speed of light."

He said. "Nope. Close. Guess again."

Lady Luna pouted. "My answer was good! So who *can* disarm a black hole?"

Lord Mars put his sword back in his sheath. "That kid on the couch. No one else. Kill him, we die."

Silence gripped the room. Aeneas sat up, and put his feet on the floor, waiting to see what his fate would be.

Lord Uranus turned his mask toward Aeneas, "So Lord Tellus himself is your patron! He is willing to slay everyone everywhere merely to keep you alive. Feel smug now, if you like. But now you understand how unbalanced he is."

Lord Mercury had drained his winecup and was using it to toss and catch a small golden ball in the air. With his eyes on the golden ball, he said casually, "I suppose we should make sure Lord Mars is telling the truth?"

Lady Ceres rolled her eyes and spoke. "Mars has no interest in family squabbles. He could have made himself Emperor by sheer brute force, had he wished it. Had he wanted to save Venus' youngest child, he could have simply demanded it."

Lord Mercury did not look at her. "But one of us could assassinate Aeneas without Mars being the wiser. Do try to keep up! What say you, Lord Uranus? What does your peculiar superscience tell you?"

Lord Uranus spoke bitter words, but in a toneless, matter-of-fact way, "It tells me Father cheated me. You all know that. Well—I suppose our niece Penthesilia does not know, does she? And I suppose I have to get used to calling her Lady Luna. She does not know about me."

Lady Luna said, "I don't understand. Lady Venus told me your field of study was astrology."

The mask raised one eyebrow. "One of her little jokes. But stars issue psychic waves which I can read. Psychometry of the stars. I can read their dispositions, but not their minds. They have none."

Lady Luna said, "How can a ball of nuclear plasma have a disposition?"

Uranus answered, "How can numbers be rational, or musical chords be passionate? Neuropsionic particles radiate from each sun in particular waveforms that carry meaning: the light of our sun is holy."

Lady Luna said skeptically, "Your science can measure holiness?"

"I am using a human word to express a concept of nonhuman Forerunner science. Certain symbol-forms embedded in the information layer of the cosmos are equal in data-radius to the entire sidereal universe. Those in rational proportion with the universe are holy;

unharmonious are unholy. Forcing the sun to kill all of her children would register as unholy, since it is against her nature."

Lady Luna was bewildered. "But what does it all mean?"

Lord Uranus said, "It means the universe is stranger than we know. Also, it means my superscience has no useful technical applications. Dad gave it to me because he hated me."

Lord Mars said, "Your science is useful to me, now. Can you confirm my report?"

Lord Uranus held up his signet ring. Aeneas sensed activity on several bands radiating from small instruments in the buttons of Lord Uranus' uniform. This activity was mated to matching signals issuing from a certain machine with a metallic radar-shadow sitting half a mile away in the wing of the palace complex occupied by Lord Uranus and his staff.

After a time, he lowered his ring. Lord Uranus said, "No alien enemy left a nova bomb in the sun."

Only Lady Luna breathed a sigh of relief. The others knew Uranus too well.

Venus said sweetly, "Yes, brother? We're waiting…"

Lord Uranus said, "It is not alien handiwork. Sol recognizes it as our father's. He means to obliterate everything in the solar system. An observer standing on a planet one hundred lightyears away a century from now will see their night sky turn bright as day. The purity of the sun is offended by the abomination of desolation inside her." The mask of Lord Uranus was expressionless, but he shook his head in wry amusement. "Father never ceases to surprise me!"

Ceres said, "This time, we must find Father and kill him!"

Lord Mars said, "And put a bell on the cat while we are at it. What about the lad? I want you all to agree to keep him alive, so he can save us."

Neptune said, "I don't agree. He will make us slaves."

Mars gave him a withering look. "Life is short and full of pain but death is full of nothing, and lasts a hell of a lot longer. Pick one."

Lady Venus suddenly brightened up and laughed. "I can save him, and you, and all of us!"

Lord Mars said, "Now *you* are keeping *us* in suspense, sister. Out with it."

She smiled sweetly and horror came out of her mouth. "I can lobotomize his free will, leaving the rest of his intellect and memory intact. The warptech will be known to him, not to us. We order him to defuse the nova bomb."

Lady Luna was looking at her with revulsion. Lord Neptune looked on with newfound respect.

"It saves his life, doesn't it?" Venus spread her hands, and shrugged, "And I can reinstall a new personality later, one less willful. Will you all agree to spare his life on these terms?"

Lord Jupiter said, "All in favor, say *aye…*?"

There were no objections. Not even Lady Luna disagreed.

Aeneas, lying supine with his eyes shut, heard all this. He was too weary even to feel disgust or despair. He was prepared to die fighting. Despite the lethal damage it would do to his wounded organs, Aeneas charged his internal weapons.

Or tried to. He could not. He tried to rise, to move, and could not. He could not open his eyes.

His echolocation detected the silhouette of a tall man standing silently by the windows. Magnetic resonance showed he wore a helm.

His was the heat signature and energy aura of Lord Pluto. Between eluding the lunar beam weapon, the flight aboard the aerospace plane, the talk in the garden and trial in the library, hours had passed. It was enough time for a space contortion wave to have arrived here from Pluto. He had been standing in the room, undetectable, unseen, perhaps for a long time.

"You are careless, brothers. I have suspended the voluntary motions of the lad, who was preparing to flood the room with lethal radiation," Lord Pluto said in his cool, dispassionate voice.

Lord Jupiter said, "I would have been safe!" And he laughed.

Lord Pluto said, "He used a spacewarp to travel here from my sanctum on Pluto, in excess of lightspeed. Any report that he lacks memory of the warptech implant is false."

Lady Venus said, "Then he is more dangerous than I thought, for apparently he found a way to use the warp science to distort my readings."

"Did he?" said Lord Pluto coldly. "Did he indeed?"

"Come!" she said sweetly, "One of you move the couch under the isolation cage, so I can establish the thought-surgery field. We are a suspicious lot: would any of you care to synchronize your ring with mine, and watch what I am doing? I would hate anyone to think me so sentimental that I would put the good of a disobedient child above the good of the family. Who wants to watch?"

Brother Beast said, "Such arts are an abomination. I will not watch."

Lord Mercury said, "If sister is going to warm up her thought-control gear, I want to be well outside of its range. Who knows who will end up as a puppet of hers, if you stay and watch? You must excuse me."

Mars said nothing, but he left the library with Mercury and Brother Beast.

Aeneas felt the mind-destroying cap settle over his scalp.

12

DEFUSING THE
SUPERNOVA

From the remote safety of his secondary brain, Aeneas watched as his mother patiently carried out the inhuman thought-surgery on his primary brain, reducing its free will to nothing, killing it while keeping it alive.

"You may restore his voluntary nerve use, Lord Pluto," said Venus. "He now has no ability to do anything voluntary."

Aeneas opened his eyes. Lady Venus gave her son a wink, and put his signet ring back on his finger. Control of the molecular engines systems allowing him to reorganize his body at will was restored to him.

Aeneas stood when told to do so. He did not need to playact or pretend to be an automaton. All he had to do was not interfere when the primary brain, which was an automaton, acted.

Lord Neptune said, "What is this? You returned his signet?"

Venus said, "To defuse the nova bomb ticking in the core of the sun requires the authority of the Lords of Creation. Besides, I never taught him how to read."

Lady Luna said, "If the family realizes you Elders lobotomized one of us, all your children would rise up to overthrow you."

Lord Jupiter said sardonically, "It is a family tradition, isn't it?"

Lady Luna did not laugh.

Jupiter scowled. "That does not include you, does it, daughter?"

She said, "I cannot forgive what you have done to Aeneas! You said he would be unharmed!"

He laughed heartily. "Well, there he stands! Fit as a fiddle!"

She turned her back on her father and said to Lady Venus, "Can it be reversed? Once you are done with him?"

Lord Neptune, who was nonchalantly inspecting the fingernails of his blue, webbed hands, answered instead. "Once we are done with him, Penthesilia, we are back to square one. If we let him live, he enslaves us, whether he wants it so or not."

Lady Venus said stiffly, "If...?! You agreed not to harm him. That was our deal."

The masked lord, Uranus, interrupted, "How long will it take him to defuse the dark mass? Can Aeneas answer questions?"

Lady Venus said, "I have established the nerve paths so that he can answer direct questions on any topic, even explain what he can do with his warptech, except he will not teach anyone else specifics. None of us learn his arts! That is as we agreed. He will obey direct commands from a family elder in a flexible, even in an imaginative, fashion. If you ask him to make suggestions, he will do so, but not if not asked."

Aeneas heard his voice answer: "I don't know how long, or even if defusing the sun can be done at all. I have not inspected the singularity bomb, nor been given any tools. To reach into a singularity, I must have a warpcore twenty thousand cubic centimeters in pre-collapse volume."

Lord Pluto said, "I can estimate. Months. A year. Longer. As for resources, each of us must place all the wealth of the worlds we rule at his disposal."

Lady Ceres said, "You're joking!"

Pluto turned the cyclops-lens of his faceless helmet toward her, "I never joke. Aeneas just said the human race has to produce a sphere of neutronium is roughly the size of Halley's Comet. Given the mass per cubic centimeter of neutronium, this is eight million trillion grams. It must be collapsed it into a singularity in a controlled fashion, and then rotated it at lightspeed to produce the Tipler frame-dragging effect. So the expense is the same as accelerating Halley's Comet to ninety-nine percent of lightspeed. The method is something only Aeneas now knows. When Japan built a modern surface navy able to defeat the Czar, or the Americans built the atom bomb, or the Soviets enacted a space program, it required a major commitment of their available resources. Our task is proportionally greater. Whether the Solar System civilization has sufficient resources or not remains to be seen."

Lord Saturn said, "It is our good fortune that ours is an autocracy ruled by one family, or otherwise coordinating such an effort would be impossible."

Lady Venus said, "Aeneas is to be released to me afterward! That was our deal!"

Jupiter smiled a genial smile, and said, "Not to worry! I'll keep an eye on Lord Neptune, and make sure he tries nothing to harm the boy."

Lord Neptune said, "And who will keep an eye on you, brother? I do not wish you to winkle the secret of the Final Science out of him! There should be two watchmen, so that they can watch each other as well as you. I nominate Lords Saturn and Uranus." He turned to the white-bearded Saturn and masked Uranus. "What say you?"

Saturn and Uranus were members of Neptune's faction. With Mercury and Brother Beast missing from the discussion, Jupiter was outnumbered. The family vote went against him. Saturn and Uranus were assigned, along with Jupiter, to watch Aeneas.

The Empire of Man often employed the lifeless or the mindless for manual labor or routine intellectual tasks. Some were abioforms, that is, vat-grown pseudo-organisms existing in the shadow condition of unlife that had never been alive. Others were necroforms, that is, felons guilty of capital crimes who, after execution, were trapped in unlife and required to make restitution. A third group, like Aeneas, were anthroforms, that is, living men whose minds had been neuro-electronically lobotomized to non-volition.

The treatment of such human-shaped tools was routine. Aeneas had a medical closet where he was stored, a nutritious diet, and an exercise regimen. Brother Beast, who understood more biotechnology than even Aeneas, was called in to help with the diet and conditioning of the various organs in Aeneas's nine foot tall body no one else understood.

He often smiled strangely into the dead face of Aeneas, and took special care to see to his bodily comfort. But if he suspected anything, he said nothing.

Weeks turned into months. Aeneas lived as an undead, without leisure, entertainment, conversation, or distraction. Ironically, it was less strict than what Brother Beast might endure in a monastic cell, or Lord Mars in boot camp. And the intellectual problem of organizing the whole solar system in a massive campaign was the first real work Aeneas had ever done in his life. He was fascinated.

The work was as slow as Lord Pluto had warned. Aeneas needed tools and materials unknown to human technology, which could only be built out of unknown materials with other unknown tools.

It was as if Piltdown Man knew how to build a space rocket, but he had to explain how to make iron axes and shovels to his tribesmen, so they could start felling trees and digging ore needed to erect a Bessemer furnace needed to smelt alloys needed for drill heads needed for oil rigs needed for rocket fuel. But iron axes needed bronze tools to make them, which needed copper tools.

The earlier parts of the project took longest. Building a supercollider that entirely circumnavigated the sun just inside the orbit of

Mercury, for example, required the countless mountains and icebergs of the Oort cloud be hauled inward, and atomically reorganized.

It was the largest scale structure the human race had ever engineered.

Not new elements were to be constructed in output mouths of this monster, but new subatomic particles. Spherical particle shells were recombined into cylinders, cones, or cubes useful for building new fundamentals. These fundamentals were not elements: a cone containing a proton at the apex and a skirt charged with one electron is not a hydrogen atom, nor a cylinder with one antigraviton for an axis with one graviton forming the surface.

The fundamentals had to be combined into Dark Energy Materials, neutrino chains and antineutronium lattices and more exotic formations, with electrical and gravitational properties impossible to normal matter.

Due to the neuropsionic particles given off by Sol, necroforms could not be used anywhere in the inner system. Automatons lacked imagination. Thus, living human beings had to do the work. So a vast work force had to conscripted and motivated.

In this post-scarcity economy, work was never done out of necessity. The three hundred separate races had been designed each to serve one family member alone. Now all must work with discipline and unity toward a larger goal.

Over these months, Aeneas attended many a family meeting, propped in a corner in case a technical question arose. He heard his two hundred cousins discuss what threat or lure could motivate so many to do something so much against their nature.

It was Lady Luna who offered the answer. Only the truth would serve: all must be told that the solar system was about to be obliterated. All would work together or all would die together.

Aeneas was pleased with her, but only at first. She packaged the emotional import of her message as dreams, and gave out dream-broadcast units for each cousin to force into the subconscious minds of his servant population. It was irresistible propaganda.

The truth worked, or the mesmeric dreams did. Aeneas, from his hiding hole inside himself, watched with grim satisfaction as a spirit of camaraderie inspired the solar system. Human beings were still pets, and that galled him. But like sheepdogs rather than lapdogs, now Man had work. The hopelessness was gone.

The Mercury-crossing asteroid 5786 Talos, a flying mountain half a mile wide, was hollowed out, set with gravity amplifiers, and filled with spaceman's fog. This green fog was one of the more useful inventions of pantropy: a cloud of microscopic plantlife programmed to scrub and scent the atmosphere, and maintain the oxygen balance.

The warpcore rested in the middle of the workspace and laboratory of Talos. The warpcore occupied an armature of intersecting Tipler rings which, from an outside frame of reference, measured fifty yards wide.

Lords Saturn, Jupiter, and Neptune were there. The army of technicians had gone, teleported by contortion pearls back to their worlds and moons. The three were alone with dead-faced, dull-eyed Aeneas on a gravity-opaque catwalk overlooking the warpcore.

Uranus said, "We are agreed? Only the combination of our three powers could have set up this deathtrap. I have altered the orientation of the matter inside Aeneas' body toward the neuropsionic solar output; the matter will react when the Sol psychic rays return to normal, releasing Jupiter's trigger, which has set the electrons to ionize. That ionization will power Saturn's chronic particles to release and trigger proton decay. Every atom in his body is therefore a bomb. Any one of the three of us could disarm it, so we must be agreed."

Aeneas of course had seen his uncles subjecting his body to what he had thought were medical tests, but no sense of his could detect what they had done. Dread grew in him: the trap was thorough, and he knew no way to undo it.

Saturn said, "Ghoulish to talk about it in front of him! What if he hears, deep down?"

Lord Jupiter said, "No matter. What could he do? We tell him to throw the switch. The warp field changes the black mass inside the sun to unrotate its polarity from antimatter to matter, and unfold its event horizon. The mass returns to normal. The solar output, including the psychic radiation, changes accordingly. When it passes through him, the radiation disintegrates his body atom by atom. No clues for Lady Venus to find."

Lord Uranus said, "Brothers, what is the harm? If, for any reason, the sun is not cured, the solar output remains unchanged, and we command him to try again. But the moment he cures the sun, the sun obliterates him."

Saturn stroked his beard. "What if he stands in the shade?"

Uranus forced his mask to smile. "No physical object blocks neuro-psionic waves. Thought-screens such as those Lady Venus builds cannot block out these frequencies and magnitudes. It would be like trying to block cosmic rays with a silk parasol."

So the three were agreed. Without looking at Aeneas, they shook hands and vowed vows.

Lord Uranus told Aeneas to proceed. Aeneas held up his ring. The Lords, watching carefully through their own rings, saw the orders given to the warpcore. None of the three could understand the meaning of the multidimensional topology symbols Aeneas fed into the servominds in the control board, but none fretted. A mindless man could not form the intention to deceive them.

Lord Jupiter smiled in good humor; Lord Saturn's tired and old eyes were filled with malice; Lord Uranus' mask hid his expression. But each, in his own way, was savoring the sadistic irony of having Aeneas mindlessly giving the order that would save the sun and kill Aeneas.

There was no hesitation. Aeneas gave the execution command.

13

Ripping the Fabric of Reality

Aeneas gave the command to the warpcore. The great dynamos feeding power to the warpcore throbbed. The armature spun into a spherical blur of silver. The red light of Doppler shift lit the warpcore as it came alive, sullen red as a coal on the floor of hell.

The singularity was hollow. The ultradense substance called hypermatter formed an empty sphere of black hole material, but it surrounded a node or oasis of unwarped space at its heart, like a miniature continuum whose lightcone could be tilted in any direction.

Because an event horizon surrounded the inner micro-continuum on all sides, the volume, diameter, density, and time relation of the inner to the outer universe was indeterminate, held perpetually in Heisenberg uncertainty. A faster-than-light effect of quantum entanglement allowed one half of a particle pair outside the inner continuum to establish or edit the spacetime metric of duration and distance between the two. This enabled Aeneas to tilt the lightcone of any object within the operational range of the warpcore and orient it to the metric of the inner continuum, along with whatever fundamental physical constants (most importantly, the speed of light) he desired.

There was no theoretical upper limit on how large the warpcore field could extend; there was a practical limit, however, based on the mass of the warpcore itself. With a warpcore at his command, Aeneas had enough mass to established a warp field around an entire planet.

The dark mass in the sun was equal in size to a gas giant. It filled almost half a percent of the sun's unimaginably vast volume. How Lord Tellus, acting alone, had constructed and placed it there was incomprehensible. Whether Aeneas could match the feat and reverse it was unknown.

A robotic voice announced, "Warp executed. The dark mass has returned to normal timespace in a positive matter state. Success!"

But Aeneas stood there, healthy and motionless.

Saturn tuned a vision plate toward a gravity-image of the sun. In the image, the dark mass of antimatter was still present at the solar core. "This is some trick!"

Uranus said softly, "You forget that we are nearly three lightminutes away from Sol. The warpfield acted instantaneously, but the news will not reach us for another half minute... ten seconds... five seconds... Aeneas dies... *now!*"

Screams filled the workroom. But they were not human screams.

Several things happened at once. The environment alarms screamed. The hull integrity alarm screamed. The gravity failure alarm screamed. The force-field alarm screamed. The high pitched whistle of pressurized air escaping into space screamed.

The Lords Uranus, Saturn, and Jupiter, were flung headlong as were all stray objects in the chamber. Their personal security alarms were screaming, and Lords Saturn and Jupiter screamed in fright as well, while the eyes of Lord Uranus, behind the eyeholes of his mask, narrowed slightly.

A blue-white light appeared around Lord Saturn as he slowed the local time-rate and sped himself up. Electricity gushed from the fingers of Lord Jupiter as he anchored himself in place with a powerful magnetic beam.

Small personal force bubbles, such as every Lord of Creation carried, appeared around Uranus, Saturn, and Jupiter. Their motion halted.

Spaceman's fog was not just a convenient green gas cloud that converted stale air to sweet. It was also programmed to turn bright red when under sudden pressure loss, as when it whistled out through a microscopic crack. This was meant to make the location of the hull puncture obvious.

In this case, the breaks were much larger. All the bulkheads of the workchamber equidistant from the center of the warpcore had been sheared off along a mathematically perfect curve, without rubble or debris, exposing the workchamber to the vacuum of space. Hence, all the air was bright red.

Large concentric fields of force snapped into existence around the whole workchamber, preventing the further escape of atmosphere.

The self-repair circuits, hissing and straining, took material from the still-solid segments of bulkhead and re-formed it into a nanomachine paste. This mud-colored paste reached pseudopods toward gaps to patch them.

The smaller punctures were sealed at once. The larger were bandaged only with transparent fields of force, but their writhing edges were slowly contracting.

The largest opening was the farthest part of the workchamber. This had contained security lenses, self-destruction charges, and internal weapons. That expanse of bulkhead was entirely gone, leaving the wide panorama of naked space visible to the eye.

Gravity returned. Automatic force rays returned each flying bit of flotsam to its proper place. The Lords of Creation stood in midair, each anchored in place with his force rays under his command. All three stared out through the wide gap in the far bulkhead.

Two suns, an orange and a yellow, were blazing against the night sky, and a third sun, smaller than a full moon, burned like a dull red coal in the remote distance. Dozens of crescents, brighter than Venus seen from Earth before dawn, hung to either side of the twin suns, their horns pointed away. Many were ringed like gas giants.

In the Lagrange point directly between the twin suns was a spherical cloud of scores of giant and supergiant planets, looking like a cat's eye with slit pupils, for their western and eastern hemispheres were bright with orange or yellow day, their central meridians dark with night.

Three vast rings, huge beyond description, hung between the two suns and encircled this cloud of supergiant planets. Each ring was at right angles to the other, and it was not clear whether these rings were solid, like the Mercury supercollider around Sol, or particulate, like the rings of Saturn.

The rings were eight times the radius of the orbit of the Earth. A ray of light would take an hour to cross the distance. It was manmade, unnatural, impossible to grasp.

Lord Saturn's beard was quivering. Sparks danced in the astonished eyes of Lord Jupiter, and the golden cup had flown from his fingers. Lord Uranus tapped politely on the personal force bubble surrounding Lord Saturn, and pointed to the catwalk.

He pointed to where Aeneas was lying prone. Now Aeneas rose to his feet, gazed out at the strange, alien, foreign solar system never seen by man before. And he smiled.

Lord Uranus reacted more quickly than his brothers, and vanished. He was carrying a space contortion pearl on his person as an always-ready escape route, and he used it. Aeneas felt the ripple of timespace as Lord Uranus turned himself into Schroedinger waves and fled away at the speed of light to the pearl's mate hidden back near Sol.

Lord Saturn was saying slowly, "Wait a moment... who told Aeneas to stand? He could not move under his own volition... unless..."

Lord Jupiter discharged an electrical bolt of thirty thousand amperes and ten thousand of degrees Fahrenheit into Aeneas. Instead of striking the young man, the channel of plasma encountered a zone of warped space Aeneas erected like a shield between himself and Jupiter.

Here the speed of light had been slowed to one hundred meters per second rather than three hundred million.

The stormbolt entering this area grew redder and dimmer. It shrank along its axis of motion and grew more massive. The bolt, now a dull ball, dimmed to infrared to microwave to radiowave and was halted.

Lord Jupiter, seeing his weapons useless, now popped out of existence, using a pearl of his own.

The need for pretending to be an automaton anthroform was past. Aeneas recycled the segments in his primary brain his mother had lobotomized, and grew fresh nerve cells from his supply of totipotent cells, imprinting them with memories, tasks and habits from their analogous cells in his secondary brain.

This created a wash of heat and steam from his scalp. Hair smoking, Aeneas turned and said, "Uncle Saturn, forgive me for abducting you, but, actually, it is your own fault. I had to remove myself faster than lightspeed beyond the reach of Sol..."

"Where are we?" screamed the graybearded man.

"Alpha Centauri. Please do not...."

But it was too late. Saturn was also gone in a wash of Schroedinger waves.

Aeneas sighed. "... do not use your pearl to teleport away, because we are four lightyears from Sol, so it will be four years before you arrive."

Alarms, one after another, were falling silent as automatic systems cured and repaired the damage. Aeneas had calculated the shearing plane of the spacewarp precisely, using an infinitesimally thin event horizon effect to chop away any parts of the half-mile wide asteroid-lab containing any mechanisms Aeneas regarded as a threat. These were left back at the solar system. The parts of the asteroid containing robotic guards, for example, were gone. The parts containing the power supply, gravity amplifiers, neutron antennae, and banks of dynamos to power the warpcore were still present.

It had been done carefully, but not perfectly. He had enjoyed hours of uninterrupted sneaking and snooping while he was allegedly parked in his closet or kicked under a workbench. But even then there were places he was never able to enter.

Now nothing hindered him. He inspected his lonely, half-mile in diameter kingdom. Anything he did not recognize (such as a sphere of pure energy standing in the middle of Lord Jupiter's private wing, or a red dome of Doppler shifted light in Lord Saturn's, or a pyramid-shaped machine humming in Lord Uranus') Aeneas simply spacefolded directly into his tame singularity roaring at the core of his lab.

His uncles knew dangerous supersciences he did not understand, but Aeneas knew that none of the slower-than-light phenomena they commanded—even if something as dangerous and swift as an exploding nova—could escape an event horizon.

There were certain locked circuits whose commands he did not know. But, now that the warpcore was his, Aeneas could establish a faster-than-light energy channel to break open the locked circuits from within, before the electric brains, acting at the speed of light, could react.

Aeneas quickly took control of the asteroid.

The next issue was power. The amount of energy needed to accelerate the warpcore's worldlet mass of collapsed hypermatter up to nearlightspeed was astronomical.

The larger a gravitating body was placed at the focus of the warpcore, the larger an area of timespace could be warped, and over longer distances. The current warpcore was the mass of a Halley's Comet: it had been sufficient to move the half mile wide mountain of Talos instantaneously through a closed timelike curve across the four lightyear gap to Alpha Centauri.

Fortunately, the active warpcore itself could be used to create a gravity-differential turbine that would draw power out of the gravity gradient of local space. Hence the warpcore's own mass could be used to create the gravity well used in turn to power it.

Aeneas rapidly gave orders to the warpcore to create the gravity turbine, and issued commands to the robotic tools, man-sized or microscopic, to design, drill, erect, seal, and pressurize a gravity-differential turbine adjacent to the powerhouse. He adjusted the gravity amplifiers so that this chamber would not be reduced to Earth-normal acceleration. The turbines themselves would take roughly thirty hours to accumulate energy into a useful form.

A normal storage battery could not hold such immense power: Aeneas established a warped zone of space between the upper and lower chamber to act as an accumulator. Here he slowed lightspeed to a standstill, so that power fed into it, from an outside frame of reference, would seem timeless and motionless. He could draw power out of this accumulation zone at the voltages he could later choose.

Aeneas was impressed. In a day and a quarter, he alone, armed with the Final Science, could generate an amount of energy equal to the full output of all the powerhouses of all the planets and moons of the solar system.

He murmured to his signet ring, "Sig, I wonder if maybe I am too powerful to be trusted! I wonder how Grandfather dealt with it?"

I cannot speculate, sir, came the answer. *But I will point out that Lord Tellus did go insane. Perhaps you could experiment on your own brain chemistry to reproduce the effects.*

Finally, the asteroid Talos was sealed and repaired, and the energy needed to form an interstellar spacewarp was in the accumulator.

Aeneas, rather than sleep, flushed his body with stimulants and returned to the workchamber where the warpcore roared like a waterfall. He was eager to inspect the alien star system.

Book 2

The Space
Vampires

01

STRANGE FIRES OF STRANGE SUNS

There was no astronomical equipment aboard, but his implanted knowledge told him how to capture various wave and particle images in a gravitationally biconvex aperture via a wormhole into an analytical screen.

He returned to the catwalk above the warpcore. His only concession to fatigue was to tell his ring to have a chair large enough for his nine-foot tall body built in a convenient spot. He sat, and gave the silent orders.

An analytical screen constructed itself above the red-gleaming core in its shining silver armature. Information beams were established between screen and core. The wormhole itself was anchored to the hollow singularity, but its aperture could poke itself into three dimensional space anywhere within a lighthour radius.

The yellow sun was larger than Sol; the orange sun smaller. The cloud of giant planets gathered at the barycenter of the system betrayed no Doppler readings orbital velocity would have shown. They were motionless relative to the two suns.

The analytical screen detected traces of space contortion harmonics in the titanic rings surrounding this cloud of supergiant planets. There was also a black hole right at the barycenter of the system, in the heart of the cloud of planets.

This meant the whole solar system was one vast warpcore armature. But what powered it?

Aeneas drew his eyes from this view down to the human-made warpcore which was gleaming dull red beneath his feet. It had taken all mankind months of the utmost effort to construct it. Seen next to the alien handiwork, it was a child's kite next to a starship.

The screen detected hundreds of singularity engines in and around the cloud, planetary components of the greater system-wide warpcore.

That was the first shock: whatever superior civilization occupied this great star system freely used the warp technology.

Elation filled him. "These creatures, whoever they are, are not fearful and jealous like my uncles! We are looking at a free people, enlightened, who share their knowledge with each other freely!"

As to that, I could not venture a guess, sir, replied his signet ring dryly. *But I will caution you not to leap to conclusions. We know nothing of the conditions of civilization here, assuming there is one.*

"Assuming… what do you mean?"

Note the energy readings.

None of the hundreds of warpcores were active, not one. Spacetime was flat and smooth as a mill pond.

He added more capacity to the screen, so that different threads of data could be combed out from the incoming flood of particles.

The results gave him a second shock. On no world of the triple star system, large or small, was there any artificial light or infrared radiation, atomic energy use, or electrical flows. There were no signs of industrial activity, no vehicles in motion, no communication broadcasts.

Spectrographic analysis showed no oxygen-breathing animals or carbon-dioxide absorbing plants were contributing to the atmospheres of any of the two hundred worlds of this incredibly crowded star system.

Life energy sensors found nothing in the normal part of the life-spectrum: but there was death energy here, untold quadrillions of units, beyond his measurement capacity. The spike in the unlife band of the spectrum blinded his sensors. Aeneas told the instruments to recalibrate and repair themselves. They did, but the reading did not change.

He moved the viewpoint aperture toward the armature rings. Aeneas had been assuming these were three solid rings, something like the vast supercollider mankind had built in Mercury's orbit, but orders of magnitude larger. No: each was particulate, like the rings of Saturn.

He suffered his third and greatest shock when he saw that these were dead bodies, countless populations of them, each one inside an oblong of ice. Larger icebergs contained families or clans or multitudes, jammed haphazardly under the surfaces.

The numbers were incomprehensible. The screen told him there were one hundred quadrillion people encompassed within the arc of his current view alone, and that was not the whole of even one of the three rings.

They were clearly human bodies, despite being here in a foreign solar system. There were minor variations of facial features, in size, or position or number of limbs. Some had faces more apelike or baboonish, or extra limbs, wings or horns. Here were skins and hair of every color, including some spotted like leopards or striped like zebra. Some were gigantic, others were dwarfish, but all were human. Impossibly, absurdly, inexplicably human.

"I am not hallucinating, am I?"

Not that I can see, sir. All your neurological activity is within normal parameters.

All were nude. A spidery webwork of gossamer fiber radiating from each head had also been embedded in the ice. The most microscopic trickle of death-energy was trickling along each fiber from one skull to its near neighbors. It was only small enough to keep the circuit open. Capillaries, conduits and streams of death-energy were ebbing and flowing slowly up and down the axis of each ring.

The systemwide warpcore was powered by death energy.

"Is everyone here *dead?*" Aeneas said aloud. He brought the aperture closer to the endless river of icebound corpses.

As if they had heard him, all the eyes of the hundreds of dead embraced within the view snapped open, and turned toward him, staring out of the analytical screen.

A heavy hand fell upon his shoulder, and a voice behind him spoke. "They are not dead."

He jumped out of his chair.

"They sense your eye on them. Turn it off."

Behind Aeneas was Lord Pluto, the one lens glinting on the brow of his dark and featureless helm. His armored body was hidden beneath the folds of his night-dark mantle. His metal boots and were visible below the lower hem.

Behind him, her head no higher than her uncle's shoulder, was Lady Luna. She wore a skintight pressure suit of silver, black and green, with gloves of white. Her coppery red hair was braided tight and caught into a snood. Her breathing hood was folded back between her shoulderblades. Her coronet was set with thought projection and thought reception ports tuned to the dream-brainwave band of the mental energy spectrum. She waved her white-gloved hand, smiling shyly.

The analytical screen overhead went dark.

Aeneas looked at them both in astonishment. "How long have you been here…?" He realized that they must have been watching when he thought he was unobserved for quite some time. All his preparations to chop dangerous parts of the asteroid away from the main mass had been completed months ago.

But he looked at Lady Luna with even more astonishment. "Why are you here?" he asked. "You're the one who did this to me! And no one designs spaceboots with high heels! And is that a bow in your hair?"

She scowled. But it was Lord Pluto who spoke. "Lady Luna forced me to come."

Aeneas was speechless. His capacity for astonishment had been exceeded. "She… forced you? *You?*"

"I dreamed something I should not have." Lord Pluto said dourly.

Aeneas stared at Lady Luna, who shrugged and looked both flattered and flustered. It was an expression a cute schoolgirl would wear rather than a cold and ruthless sovereign of the highest rank in the Imperial family. But anyone who could coerce Lord Pluto was no one to be trifled with.

Lord Pluto continued in a dry voice: "It is fortunate for you that she did. I have placed negative information broadcasters on the cardinal surfaces of the asteroid. I had meant to turn the whole asteroid invisible, you, your captors, and all. By good happenstance, this saved you from enemy observation. Heretofore."

A gush of questions rushed out of Aeneas. "How can you know what type of sensors these creatures might use? Why do you call them an enemy? An undiscovered race of utterly alien beings could have no quarrel with us! And… who? Who is the enemy? Everyone here is dead!"

"To answer your questions in order—" came the voice from Pluto's helmet. "First, the stratonic superscience Father gave me does not block or redirect the waves carrying sense impressions. The visual information is removed from the information stratum of the universe itself, below the level of matter and energy phenomena. It does not matter what form of sensor is used: the information will not be carried. Second, they are enemies of all that lives. We are their natural prey. Third, they are necroforms, existing in the shadow condition.

Their cellular motions mock organic life, but are not life. This is an empire of vampires."

Aeneas said, "Are you saying you remove the visual information from the cortex of the viewer? Even my mother could not do that, not to a crowd."

"Nothing like that," said Lord Pluto impassively. "There are levels more fundamental than the mental or physical. Human science has barely scratched the surface of the enigma called the universe. The Forerunners penetrated to the core."

"Why should I believe you? You want me dead!"

Lord Pluto said, "My words fit the available evidence. Your trespass onto my world's secrets is a moot point. Your death now would be counterproductive."

Aeneas looked up. "How did you turn off my analytical screen?"

Forgive the presumption, sir, said his signet ring, speaking aloud through an annunciator. *I did that. It seemed wise to assume the danger real until you had time to assess.*

Lady Luna said, "Wise indeed. The necroform horde detected your spy ray."

Aeneas said, "Not a spy ray: I was using a gravity lens to feed photons into a topologically linear timelike curve segment...."

He saw the blank look on her face.

"... It is a periscope I can place anywhere within a lighthour radius."

Lady Luna smiled. "Whatever. The lens of your periscope is beyond the reach of Lord Pluto's cloak of invisibility. They saw it."

Aeneas said, "How do you know?"

She held up her ring. "Even though they are dead, the subconscious parts of their minds are still active. It seems to be part of a general command and control circuit. The vampires may be unaware of who is commanding them. I can show you, but you would have to trust me, and form a mindlink through our rings."

"And why should I trust the girl who sicced the family on me?"

Her eye flashed like green fire. "I was trying to save your life. If you shared the secret of the Final Science with the family, no one would be in any hurry to kill you."

Aeneas said, "Did you hear what Jupiter, Uranus, and Saturn agreed? They would rather nobody have the secret than let any brother have it."

She said, "I know that now. I hope you are honest enough to admit that it was worth the risk. Because now there is only plan B."

"Easy enough for *you* to risk *my* life." Aeneas said sourly, "What's plan B?"

She said, "Crown you Emperor."

He said sarcastically, "Time to flatter me and fawn on me, since I am the next rising power, is that it?"

She sighed a sigh of disgust, and held up her ring. "No, time for you to thank me. This is now the third time I've saved you. I can hear the vampire dreams. Take a listen."

Aeneas touched his ring to hers. There was a flood of preverbal thought, roaring raw images without words.

Aeneas saw, and heard, and felt a dark deluge of infinite hunger and endless pain.

Then, suddenly, a sharp message came through the dream-minds. It was a command voice speaking into an unconscious level where no one could disobey: AN INTRUDER DRAWS POWER FROM THE GRAVITIC GRADIENT. DIRECT ALL AVAILABLE DEATH-ENERGY THROUGH THE SYSTEMWIDE WARPCORE TO THE FOLLOWING LOCATION...

Since the communication was directly thought-to-thought, Aeneas did not need to puzzle out their map system. It was pointed at him. His gravity-differential turbine, like his aperture lens, had reached beyond what Lord Pluto could protect.

The solar system sized rings instantaneously, without any acceleration or resistance from inertia, were rotating at lightspeed. The hundreds of other warpcores in the planetary cloud fed the unseen singularity at the core of the star system. From this core, a beam

containing the death-energy of quintillions of vampires materialized
instantly, faster than lightspeed, and struck with unimaginable, irresistible force.

02

BLIND JUMP

There was power enough for one interstellar spacewarp, but no time to perform any navigational polydimensional topology calculations: Asteroid Talos vanished into an arc segment of a closed timelike curve in tesseract space, outside three dimensional timespace.

The analytical screen was as alarmed as Aeneas to overhear the necroforms issue their execution order. Of its own accord, the screen activated, and recorded the range and vector of the incoming attack.

The beam was one lightsecond in radius, so it would have filled the circle described by the Moon's orbit about the Earth. Moving faster than the speed of light, it reached five lighthours, roughly the distance from Sol to Pluto. Any living thing, including viruses and growing crystals, caught in that beam would have been instantly destroyed.

So much energy was released that even nonliving matter would have been affected. The beam would have disintegrated a body the size of Earth. A body the size of Jupiter would have had its upper and lower layers of atmosphere and hydrosphere blown away into space, and the remaining core been ionized. It was overkill on a massive scale.

But, fast as it was, Talos was faster. Aeneas, like all in his family, was a frequent target of assassination, and had artificial intelligences, whose reactions were far faster than any biological reflex, standing by at all times. The signet ring of Aeneas, reading the intent beginning to form in the mind of Aeneas to risk a blind jump through the tesseract, had carried out the order before Aeneas could think it.

Because the screen was open, Aeneas, Lady Luna, and Lord Pluto saw the actual moment of passage through the spacewarp: the stars and worlds in the view turned red and then black and fled away from each other and from the viewpoint, leaving them alone in a barren universe.

Then the universe solidified, and a hollow sphere of rock appeared around them. It was not at first clear what this sphere of rock meant, but Lord Pluto pointed at certain metal ports, antennae, and docking rings, and said these were the surface features of Talos. It looked like their own asteroid but turned inside out: its equator was their celestial equator, its north pole was overhead and its south pole underfoot.

As if they were inside a rubber balloon made of rock that suddenly expanded, the walls of the universe moved away at high speed, turning red, then dark red, and then going invisible when the rate of expansion surpassed lightspeed. For another instant they were in a dark and bare universe, and then all directions were opaque with white energy that rushed toward them, but which turned transparent and resolved itself into scattered bright blue stars. The stars came together and dimmed, and then a normal night sky was around them.

Aeneas did not recognize any of the constellations. The analytical screen, however, was able to match the spectrographic fingerprints of certain brighter stars in the view: Betelgeuse, Sirius, Vega. The stars Rasalhauge and Kornephoros were brighter than when seen from Earth. The three stars of Orion's belt, Alnitak, Alnilam, and Mintaka, were a shallow triangle rather than a line.

But the spectrograph for double stars of this system was not in any almanac. It should have been a star visible from Earth, with its characteristics known and recorded. It was not.

"We are within thirty-five to fifty lightyears of Sol," Aeneas announced after scrutinizing the astronomical data for some time. "The bad news is that I do not have an exact location. This spectrographic fingerprints for these two stars appear in no almanac. The worse news is that I cannot return us to Sol with this equipment. It is roughly three or five times outside my operational range."

Lady Luna had prevailed upon servant mechanisms to provide her a chair, not to mention a small luncheon of fruit, salad, venison, and red wine. She sipped the wine from a diamond cup.

Lord Pluto neither moved nor spoke, and may have turned off his own nervous system, since he stood without fidgeting.

Luna said, "By 'this equipment' you mean the warpcore it took a highly advanced technological civilization inhabiting every world and moon of the Solar System over a year of intense effort to prepare, right? So all we have to is, what? Find a civilization roughly three to five times more advanced than the Empire of Man? What is the good news?"

Aeneas said, "We are smack in the middle of a binary system whose suns are roughly the same size. A subgiant yellow sun twice as big as and six times brighter than Sol; its companion is an orange-red main sequence star a hair smaller than Sol and half as bright. Because of this, the gravitation barycenter is not underneath the surface of a sun, but nicely placed about seven AU's from either star." Seven astronomical units was smaller than Saturn's distance from Sol, but larger than Jupiter's. "It might be a trinary system, because that subgiant star is occluding our view of another star-sized gravity source beyond it."

"Why is that good news?"

Aeneas answered, "Because I just found out that this kind of long-range jump lands you in the center of gravity of the target solar system. If this had been a single star system like Sol, we'd have unwarped out of folded space directly into in the middle of a sun. Since about half the star systems in the galaxy are single-star, we just took a fifty-fifty life-or-death gamble without knowing the stakes or the odds. Lucky us. We won the coin toss. Lord Pluto, who the hell were those people, those things, we just ran from?"

Lord Pluto tilted the lens of his blank helmet toward Aeneas. "I have no idea. How would I know?"

"You knew they were enemies!"

Lord Pluto said, "Naturally, we arrived in the Alpha Centauri system with you and knew no more about life outside our solar system than you. The only difference is that my instruments detected the levels of death-energy filling the entire volume of the star system, so I knew no organic life was present, whereas Lady Luna was aware that all the minds of the system were interlinked and formed one uninterrupted mass subconscious mind… the content and character of that mind you saw yourself."

Aeneas said, "And you didn't warn me?"

"As soon as it became clear your activities might attract their attention, I made myself visible to you. Since we parted on doubtful terms, I thought it best to prove my good intentions by waiting until you found yourself in need."

"Your hesitation almost destroyed us."

"Because I did not understand the implications of your technology. I did not know your gravity differential turbine could be detected outside my negative information range. Our family system of not sharing the stratonic sciences has proven insufficient."

Aeneas said, "And somehow you knew they would attack without warning. How?"

It was Lady Luna who answered. "Other predator species suffer a die-back if they over-consume their prey, or outgrow their food source. Not vampires. As long as there is any organic life-energy to consume, they have no need not to multiply. The Alpha Centauri system civilization must have consumed all local life millennia ago. And been suffering agonies of starvation since then."

"Why did they look like people? Human biology is so exactly adapted to the environment of Earth, we could not possibly have evolved anywhere else."

Lord Pluto said, "Lady Luna peopled the Moon with humans and other primates, as well as hounds and harts and various game animals. The relation of species in that case was a product of engineering, not evolution."

"Are you saying Earth was created artificially?"

"Perhaps only the Cenozoic ecology is artificial, once the Cretaceous Extinction cleared dinosaurs out of the way."

Luna said, "If Earthlife is designed, the Forerunners do not look like us: we look like them."

Aeneas said, "Were *those* the Forerunners?"

Lady Luna said, "Unlikely. Subconscious minds like those we saw are incapable of speculation or imagination."

"They have warptech."

Lady Luna said, "And their dreamtech network was bigger than anything I could dream up. But wherever they got it, they did not invent it."

Lord Pluto said in his calm, undisturbed voice, "It disturbs me that the Space Vampires have warptech. How far did they spread?"

Aeneas said, "We had better hope they are not here, because we need native materials and help."

He gazed at the screen. "Odd. This star system also has planets in the hundreds, not eight or nine. I wonder if that is a commonplace feature of multiple star systems. We may never know. The trove of Forerunner science Grandfather found did not include the answer to that question. And human science has since lost all curiosity."

Nearly all the worlds had some trace of cities or roadways under oceans of liquid or glaciers of solid nitrogen. This system had been civilized when the orange sun had been hotter, geological ages ago.

Only one small planet was close enough to the subgiant sun to have water. A single ocean formed the southern pole. The rest of the globe was one supercontinent entirely crisscrossed with a web of canals and reservoirs. A single vast mountain rose from the north pole like the horn of a unicorn, reaching above the atmosphere.

It was surrounded by six large, close moons, whose shadows coated part or all of the small globe every few hours at irregular intervals.

It would have taken minutes to drop space contortion pearls to the likely locations on the surface and then teleport down. Instead, Aeneas equipped the asteroid with gravity-drivers, disinertia fields, impellers, and all else needed to transform the mountain into an interplanetary vessel able to land. He was unwilling to leave the warpcore too far behind him, and even more unwilling to be left behind while the others explored.

The asteroid, now a three sided pyramid coated with silver ablative, descended on negative-gravity beams from the cloudless purple sky above trees that looked remarkably like feather dusters. It landed next to a native city near the foot of the north polar mountain, crushing a square mile or so of this lacy forest beneath its base.

The towers of this city were thin stalks in the low gravity, wider at the peak than at the base, like trumpets standing on their mouths. At ground level were domes and spirals. All the cobblestone streets were curves. The doors and windows were tall and thin, as if meant for a race of wraith-thin giants.

Other than some architectural oddities, it might have been a city of Earth. An airport held craft of many fanciful designs, triplanes, ornithopters, and helicopters woven of silk and gossamer. There was a spaceport with a monorail launch-catapult. There was a power plant, with the characteristic cooling dome betokening atomic power.

Lady Luna cautiously sealed her breathing hood before exiting the airlock.

Lord Pluto was more cautious. He surrounded his armor with several defensive fields and energy shells, and vanished from their sight.

Aeneas was confident he could not be harmed by any combination of gasses, or biological or chemical agents. He wore a purple-hemmed white tunic and white sandals.

An energy ramp reached from the airlock to an oval fern-garden, intersected by canals, in the center of the city. Down the two walked.

Above the doorway of every building were hanging one or two or a dozen yard-wide globes of material whose surfaces were opaque to Aeneas' instruments. These did not seem to be lights or weapons or energy supplies. Perhaps decoration?

The walls were likewise impenetrable, but clearly the native eyes could pierce their substance, because their windows were made of it also.

It was for this reason they had landed and drawn close. Lord Pluto's power could not be broadcast over large distances. Aeneas said, "Lord Pluto, I assume you are still within earshot?"

He was. Suddenly the walls became clear as glass. All the buildings and towers were empty of any living thing. The gear and artifacts of the native peoples were all folded or stowed neatly, with no signs of panic or haste.

"That is eerie," said Aeneas. "I've just noticed how quiet it is."

Luna said, "No insects. No songbirds. My instruments detect no bacteria."

The yard-wide globes hanging, either singly or in clusters, before the doors, now turned transparent as well. They revealed their contents. Lady Luna screamed in shock.

They were filled with corpses. Some held one. Some held many. They were long-limbed and long-necked men, all crushed or compacted together. All seemed to be of the same race, but the mangled conditions of the bodies made it hard to tell. All were in postures of frenzy, as if dying in mid-struggle, in torment.

Aeneas, meanwhile, bent over and touched one of the ferns of the thick garden in which they stood. The lacy leaves seemed oddly pale and motionless. The plant stirred and chimed like glass at his touch, and his hand went numb.

"These plants are undead," he said in a voice of quiet horror to Lady Luna.

The whole garden rippled as the lifeless leaves unfolded, spread, and turned toward them hungrily.

03

THE GREAT EYE OF ZETA HERCULIS

Lord Pluto's voice issued from a point in midair. "I have rendered us invisible to the life-absorbing plants. They are still a danger should you touch them: step on no grassblade, let no leaf brush you."

In the distance was the north pole mountain whose base was hidden behind the too-near horizon. It rose into the purple sky like a column, made ghostly by distance. Its peak had the crisp clarity and sharp shadows of an object in hard vacuum, and the crown had the typical antennae and dishes of an astronomical observatory. Aeneas said, "Let's go there. We can use the equipment to search for any living worlds in this system, or to discover our precise location, which I need before I can calculate a warp-path."

A kinetic ray placed a contortion pearl on the peak, teleported a mass of molecular engineering microbes as well as larger robotic tools, and a set of servile automatic minds to run them. The servominds built and pressurized an atrium fit for their humans to step into. Then the molecular engineering microbe mass with their escort of tools flooded through the observatory, seeped and pried into alien mechanisms, and began the classification and analysis process.

Aeneas, Lady Luna, and the unseen Lord Pluto contorted to the mountain top, to direct the servominds, and make any decisions requiring ingenuity.

While they waited, Aeneas stood on the balcony and looked at the alien world underfoot. With his amplified vision, he saw flying creatures that looked like autogiro-winged butterflies, but they were pale as ice and radiating death-energy. He also saw myriad wormlike things floating on the surface of the canals, also pallid unlife. And, elsewhere, a swarm of locust-winged things hung on the wind like a silent dust storm over a vast but pale grassland. All were necroforms. All were vampires.

Aeneas could not restore feeling and motion to his hand. All the molecules of the dead cells were present, and in their proper places, but nothing was moving. Aeneas severed his wrist with an energy beam and grew a new hand from raw totipotent cell masses.

The servominds reported: The alien thinking machines were not actually machines, but a set of undead microbes, connected by thought-energy threads in a decentralized network, and held in a blood-red liquid substance that radiated death-energy. This liquid ran through every instrument in the observatory and controlled them.

Sir, milord, and milady, sent the servominds: *Spaceman's fog contains microscopic, positive life. This can be fed into the fluid containing negative life. This will power it, and allow the instruments to activate. To proceed, please give the order.*

Aeneas studied the fluid using his many senses, warping space to bring him remote information or to Doppler-shift unseen frequencies into view. A spike of neutronium reached from the peak along the axis of this super-stratospheric mountain to the long dead core of the planet. Rivers of this vampire microbe fluid flowed up and down this spike, and through the spherical core sea, and up fountains like vertical rivers. These waters circulated through vents and chimneys in the crust to the floor of the southern polar ocean.

Aeneas said, "This planet is all vampires. Their cells are dispersed throughout the hydrosphere, and are carried by the canal system to every part of the globe. I am not sure what the canals are for..."

Lady Luna said, "The canals form their computing network. The natives here have rigorously organized their subconscious minds, their dreams, to carry out both simple and complex mathematical computations. The unconscious minds of everything on the planet are connected to this worldwide liquid mind. It acts something like our signet rings, to carry out routine thought operations."

Lord Pluto's voice spoke out of nowhere, "Let me inspect the astronomical machinery. If I can hide us from any observer, even one inside the liquid mind used to control this facility, I will activate the instruments. Agreed?"

Aeneas said, "If you can mask us, yes."

Lady Luna said, "I will ask my ring to help yours. Since the unconscious minds here are also organized into one system that commands the waking thoughts of the vampires, it should be quite easy for you. But I must also scan the machines from closer range."

Inside they went. Any instruments based on the same principles of engineering as their Earthly counterparts could be understood. Other objects were incomprehensible.

The ceilings and doors were tall and thin, as if built for men on stilts, but Lady Luna could squeeze through them by turning sideways. Aeneas tossed a pearl through any door he could not negotiate, and contorted through.

There were neither ladders nor ramps, merely trapdoors in the ceilings. In the low gravity, it was no more effort to leap thirty feet straight up than to step up a stair.

A trio of alien corpses were arranged on benches in a chamber filled with mirrors. This race differed markedly in shape from the corpses stuffed into glass spheres outside. Perhaps it was a caste or class difference. They were shaped like five-legged centaurs, if centaurs were proportioned like giraffes. The extra leg was designed for prodigious leaps in the low gravity. Their arms and fingers were long and elegant, with more joints than human arms. Their faces were narrow and strong, with philosopher's brows, features expressive even in repose, sensitive lips and nostrils.

A set of carefully arranged glass wands held the dead bodies upright, limbs poised gracefully.

The floor was covered with markings of a writing system. Aeneas addressed the servominds. "Can you translate it?"

Not at the moment, sir. We have as yet encountered insufficient correlatives. We can translate their engineering manuals, and scientific textbooks, because we can correlate any patterns of possible symbols to various possible models of the universe. The writings here have an emotional or religious value for which there is no common ground.

But Lady Luna said, "I can read it. My ring can correlate these shapes with archetypes and symbols encountered in the local dream-spectrum, which is active. I've been recording continuously."

Aeneas said, "Someone is sleeping on this world?"

"The whole solar system is one nightmare."

"So what does it say?"

"This is a suicide pact: these three are servants who, at the last, refused to obey the order to turn themselves into vampires, but who did not wish to die by being fed to vampires. It is a set of poems or musical stanzas praising the goodness of their life they are leaving behind, sunlight and wind and scented ferns, and those stanzas praise the greatness of the master-race who created them, who no longer has need of them."

Aeneas said, "For what reason? Does it say?"

She shook her head. "There is a statement that the master-race was created by an even higher master-race, overlords. The overlords ordered the masters to commit racial suicide. The servant race here was supposed to follow their masters out of love. Except *suicide* is the wrong word. What is it called when one surrenders life, not into death, but into anti-life?"

Lord Pluto's voice came out of midair. "The word you seek is *damnation*. These three killed themselves to find escape."

Lady Luna said sadly, "I do not think they escaped damnation. These sections written here are praises of the wisdom and justice of their masters, and expressions of their own grief and misery for not having the *virtue* to follow them into the endless pain and horror of a zombie existence. Any being who loves and praises his own tormentor is damned!"

Aeneas said, "Any being whose creator made him see evil as good and good as evil would utter such praises. Any creator making slaves to serve him, not children to inherit all the good he can bestow, will create blind creatures."

Lady Luna muttered, "Horrible!"

That annoyed Aeneas. "Oh? Is our family so much better? The Moon Maidens you have made—is it their fate to serve you forever?"

She raised her hand and slapped him sharply on the cheek. He raised one eyebrow and smiled a crooked smile with half his mouth. "Hit the bull's-eye, did I?"

Lady Luna said in a husky voice, "We are nothing like them! Nothing like this!"

At that moment, the alien machinery stirred into life. Aeneas could see ultraviolet and microwave-colored torches ignite, and hear sonar holograms being projected. Fluid containing undead microbes rushed through tubes and capillaries webbing the alien instruments.

Lord Pluto's voice spoke. "We remain unseen. For safety's sake, let us return to Talos, and have the servominds report there."

A mental command sent to their contortion pearls returned them to the pyramid.

The suns were examined.

Aeneas said, "As it turns out, there is a cloud of material between here and Sol, absorbing certain spectrographic lines, messing up human almanacs of this star's fingerprint. We are at Ruticulus, also called Zeta Herculis."

Lady Luna said, "Am I supposed to recognize that name?"

Aeneas said, "No, but you are supposed to be glad I do. Sol can be reached in four warpjumps taking a day and a half each. The only question is fuel: I cannot refuel in deep space. I need to be in a gravity well."

The other planets of the Ruticulus star system were examined. No living things were present anywhere. Beneath their layers of frozen atmosphere, all the unlife was quiet, motionless, torpid. The industrial complexes were still, materials packed, the space vessels grounded and partly dismantled.

Some of the worlds circling the warmer second sun had plantlife, insects, animals. From pole to pole, all were undead.

Through her ring, Lady Luna sent, "I assume the vampires consumed animals, bugs, grass, and viruses. But why did they preserve no food supply? Why not leave a seedcorn-stock of living beings alive to reproduce?"

She had ornamented her quarters with the pools and airborne orchids of her Moon. She luxuriated in a pond of breathable fluid. Around her, the deck was grass. Fawns grazed and puppies sported.

Lord Pluto sat on an iron chair in his unadorned chamber. "The whole star system is in mothballs. The glass spheres hung on every house were feeding troughs. The living were fed to the undead while the undead packed. Then the undead buried the undead."

Lady Luna said, "The buried populations are in endless pain, hungering and famished. Who would do such a thing?"

Lord Pluto said, "I have necroforms on Pluto. They can be stored in compact spaces, and need no life support. I do not kill them, lest their memories and skills be lost."

Lady Luna shivered, despite her warm pool.

Aeneas was pacing. Medical apparatus hung from the ceiling of his quarters, and vats and cells containing growths from the walls. His rib cage hung open, and he was idly fiddling and tinkering with his internal organs as he walked, dripping.

"The problem is that I do not know how to power the warpcore in a way Lord Pluto can hide. But what if all the space vampires stay asleep? Are there any overlords in this system at all? Is anyone looking for us?"

Just then, one of the moons of this world eclipsed the distant orange sun. The near one, the yellow subgiant, was below the horizon.

The third sun, a dark body, was visible in the rays of the other two suns. It was an orb of black, larger than a gas giant, a dwarf-sized neutron star that never ignited. It was hanging a degree beyond the yellow subgiant, as the season when this planet was in opposition was ending.

The neutron star object rotated, and brought into view its other hemisphere. Here was a huge eye, immense beyond measure, with iris and pupil. The eyelashes were longer than space elevators. A layer of atmosphere many miles thick was floating above its sclera. The storm systems, larger than the Great Red Spot of Jupiter, were as tiny to this eye as the microscopic flotsam found in the moist surface of a human eye.

Moons and asteroids would have been dust specks in those eyelashes. The lids narrowed as the eye-shaped artifact squinted, peering.

Luna spoke in a hushed, trembling voice. "I can see into its dreams. It is a weapon designed to consume whole star systems across interstellar distances. Its work is done. All worlds in the galaxy are dead. It is looking for life... it hungers... it knows we are here!"

04

GRAVEYARD WORLD

The neutron star eyeball stared down at the world where the pyramid of Talos had landed. The astronomical observatory went dark, and all communication with the servominds there ceased.

Lord Pluto was sitting on his iron chair in his barren quarters. "It cannot see us."

Lady Luna was half submerged in a floral pool in her quarters. Over her ring, she answered, "Not us, personally. I can see in its thoughts that it is aware of life energy present in the liquid mind of this inner planet. You said you could keep us hidden from any observers!"

Lord Pluto said calmly, "Evidently an overestimation. It was more difficult than expected to make thoughts inside a mental network invisible to each other. I am not familiar with the nuances of dream-frequency thought-transfer, as this is your specialty, Lady Luna. Again, we see the disadvantage of the compartmentalization of specialties Lord Tellus imposed on the Imperial Family."

Aeneas was pacing in his quarters, scowling. "Can you mask the detectable side effects if I erect a gravity differential turbine to power the warpcore?"

Lord Pluto mused, "Assume them familiar with Forerunner technology, Aeneas. From what distance could you detect such a thing?"

"About half a lightyear. Three trillion miles."

Lord Pluto said, "I can influence a volume of about half a mile diameter."

Aeneas grunted glumly. "My warpcore is the mass of Halley's Comet. My ability to warp space is limited by that mass. The longest safe warp I can make is ten to fifteen lightyears, which is nothing on a galactic scale. It is three lightyears from Zeta Herculis to HIP 82003, from there eleven lightyears to GJ 3959, from there sixteen lightyears to Bernard's Star and then five lightyears to Sol. That includes two tesseract segment warps I cannot promise will be stable or safe. So we are not returning home without native help."

Lady Luna said, "But you got us here!"

Aeneas said, "It was a blind, uncontrolled jump, and we were lucky. Longer and unsafer jumps I can make. Let's not."

Lady Luna said, "Can you add mass to your singularity?" She smiled, and let her ring show the smile to him. "Something as large as a neutron star?"

Aeneas said, "Easily. If a warpcore were built at the center of the neutron star, I need not even erect any armature rings around it to control the warp vectors. I could slave the Great Eye warpcore to mine by a resonance effect. The interior of a rotating Kerr singularity does not know or care where it is in time or space. The hard part is getting the Great Eye to cooperate—it is only a death-energy powered interstellar range weapon able to destroy all the planets of a star system in one shot, after all. Are you saying you can—without killing us— mesmerize it? You are a tougher lady than you look."

"I am also older than you and outrank you, Annoyance."

Aeneas said, "Peanut, our uncle Lord Pluto is a cautious man over a century old. Why not convince him it will be safe to do whatever you are planning?"

She said to Lord Pluto, "The Great Eye is controlled through a unified subconscious control network, just as at Alpha Centauri. The overlords did not allow their servants to talk back, suffer doubts, disobey orders, or think for themselves: my instruments show the Great Eye to consist of a completely vacant and unwatched subconsciousness in total control of the conscious but zombiefied mind. I could insert any commands I wished. No passwords. No one is watching. As long as no one attacks it, it will stay half asleep."

Lord Pluto said, "Absurd. Who leaves a weapon of such power lying about unlocked?"

Aeneas laughed. "A society of necroforms with no free will whose nearest neighbor is the star system LP 275-68, three lightyears away. After all, you did leave your tower unlocked and unwatched..." Aeneas scowled. "Or did you? You *allowed* me in, didn't you? And then let me escape? Why?"

Lord Pluto said curtly, "My motives are my own."

Lady Luna said, "So they are, but, not knowing them, why should we trust you?"

Pluto said, "We are trapped on a necropolis world in an undead star system, and cannot escape unless you two perform works of ultralargescale engineering and subversion. Can either of you perform these feats, and remain undetected, without my help?"

Aeneas had no answer for that.

The three selected one small island in the southern polar ocean of the small world Aeneas now christened *Necropolis*.

Lord Pluto's automata surrounded the coastline of the island with units to render the island invisible. A village where undead islanders were stacked like cordwood was flooded with Spaceman's Fog. The tiny plantlife revived them. The necroform giraffe-men had no power to resist commands from their subconscious mind-network. Lady Luna had them mesmerized in short order.

This workforce was set the task of clearing vampire grass from the soil, and replanting it with Earthlife, then filling it with livestock, which they were required to tend and forbidden from consuming.

Forced-growth techniques allowed farms and ranches to reproduce generations in days rather than years. Once the deer population was above a certain threshold, more native undead were revived, but, again, they were only permitted to consume the life-energy of a specific percentage of the herd, not more.

Every undead man, animal, and leaf in the whole solar system would have consumed this tiny island of living beings in an instant, but it had vanished from all their sense impressions.

The islanders were next given the task of building other tools and instruments, including additional invisibility units for Lord Pluto, dream-transmitters for Lady Luna, and gravitational amplifiers for Aeneas.

The first of several battles for Necropolis took place when the islanders loaded up ships and sailed to a city on a peninsula selected for their next prize. Lord Pluto cut sight of the peninsula off from the remainder of the world.

When the necroforms under Lady Luna's mesmerism, filled with life energy, descended on the city, the undead there rose up from below the cobblestones and from submerged graveyards in the bay, and assaulted the ships.

Lady Luna inserted instructions into their dreams, but the hunger and frenzy of the starving monsters overcame all restraints. The battle for a while was fought in an organized fashion, until the first few victories of the city dwellers allowed them to drain the stolen life energy from the islanders, and then other city dwellers turned on the successful ones and drained them, and a general melee broke out without plan or purpose. Meanwhile, the islanders who had been drained rammed their ships into the ships to the rear of the flotilla, whose undead crews still were replete with life-force.

Several nightmarish hours later, with most of the city in ruins, enough of the vampires had fed off each other for their ghastly hunger to be slaked. These contented vampires were once again vulnerable to

Lady Luna's commands, and their unconscious minds once more in control of their automaton conscious minds.

That city conquered others. In a short time, the peninsula was under cultivation, and moon-trees and moon-flowers of the type Lady Luna preferred were blooming. The vampire armies of this peninsula attacked other coastal regions, this time in a more controlled fashion, for Lord Pluto kept the fed and the starving mutually invisible to each other.

Inland manufacturing centers were next, and after that, the careful, tedious process of flushing all the waters of the world free of microscopic vampire life, and replacing it with plankton and krill and an extreme archeon called a thermoacidophile.

Weeks turned into months, and more territory was converted, stirred awake, and brought under their control. Eventually the whole planet Necropolis, from pole to pole, was theirs. None of the hibernating vampire life thronging the other worlds of the system was aware of it.

Aeneas and Lady Luna celebrated with a party of special magnificence, decorating the ward room, and having their rings concoct wines and delicacies out of various fruits and livestock of the small planet's now-living farms. Lord Pluto excused himself curtly, and took no part of the celebration.

Lady Luna held up her wineglass, "Cheers! I must say, stranded with no one but you and he, this has been the most stress-free family outing I've ever been on. I look forward to the bugged eyes and gaping mouths when you return home as Emperor!"

Aeneas said, "No eyes will be more agog than mine. I will have myself crowned Emperor Hypocritus the First, the only antimonarchist monarch in history. Maybe I should also run for the office of atheist pope, eh?"

Luna looked at him sidelong. "You won't do it? Your self-preservation instinct is weaker than I thought."

Aeneas said, "The whole galaxy is undead. Sol is the sole source of organic life anywhere. Do you think the legal gulf we've erected between an omnipotent imperial family and our impotent servile races can stand? Tyranny is a luxury!"

The conversation turned to the pragmatic questions. Luna said, "We are lucky. Some of the vampires we unearthed last week were dream-engineers from a million years ago who worked on the Great Eye. They cannot volunteer any information, but they can construct a program to insert into the Great Eye's mind. It is chief servant here. Once the Great Eye is ours, the rest of the system will fall with no further fighting, and you can finally have the natives manufacture a large-scale warpcore."

Finally the day and hour came. All was ready. Aeneas had set a small, artificial sun to orbit the world named Necropolis and to keep the new Earthlife flourishing there alive once the Zeta Herculis suns were left far behind. This planet and its tiny pet sun were now in orbit around the Great Eye, which was under Lady Luna's control. A hollow singularity at its core was slaved to the warpcore aboard Talos, which was in the Lagrange One position between the Great Eye and the planet Necropolis.

Aeneas said, "The mass of a dead star gives us enough range and precision to return to Sol in one jump. The energy supply in the Great Eye is a treasure trove, and we'd be mad not to take it with us. This will be tricky, for I cannot appear anywhere inside the solar system without dying instantly, but with the mass of a neutron star at my command, I can establish a warp to carry us all to just outside the orbit of Pluto, which should be far enough away for me to survive.

"From there, I can establish a warp around the planet Saturn and summon it.

"Also, I can establish a meter-wide warp around my chair to prevent neuropsionic waves from propagating: nearer Sol it would not save me, but at this distance, it just might."

Lady Luna said, "What if it doesn't work?"

Aeneas said glumly, "I will be dead before I notice that I died."

To his surprise, she kissed him, and so he did not notice when it was, exactly, that he gave the execution command.

His next moment of awareness was that he was alive, in the workspace, still seated in his chair on the gravity-opaque catwalk above the humming balefire-red warpcore. The analytical screen showed their current location: about a light-day away from Sol, far beyond Pluto.

With them was the tiny but bright artificial sun. To one side was the planet Necropolis, infested by vampire-life under Lady Luna's control. To the other side was the neutron star carved into the Great Eye.

"Well done…" said Lady Luna.

The warpcore throbbed and groaned. It was operating at the far edges of its range. Suddenly in the transplutonian space with them, far, far beyond its normal orbit, was the ringed gas giant Saturn, with all his moons and artificial satellites.

Lady Luna looked impressed, and opened her mouth to speak. Instead, she screamed.

The Great Eye blinked. It rolled this way and that, glaring at Necropolis, at Saturn, at the bright and tiny star Sol. It was no longer under control.

Lady Luna and Lord Pluto collapsed, gargling and writhing. Aeneas' personal warp blocked all mental radiation: that alone saved him. His screen showed how storms of mental energy were exploding from the Great Eye in all directions, immense beyond his instrument's ability to measure. The whole population of Saturn and all its moons, including every animal, was jerking in epileptic fits.

But this was no weapon.

It was a shout.

It was a white-noise of neuropsionic energies on the dream frequencies, reaching out in all directions, filling the surrounding space.

The star-murdering weapon now squinted at Sol, and began to build up the death energies needed to obliterate the whole solar system, every world, worldlet and moon.

Aeneas could not use his ring unless he stood and put his head outside his personal thoughtproof warp. But if he stood, he would be struck comatose.

He did not stand. He leaped. Pain and darkness crashed into his brain.

05

THE DEADLY LIGHT OF A LIVING STAR

The headless body of Aeneas fell back onto his chair, so that his secondary brain was safe within the thoughtproof zone of space.

His bioadmantium skull protruding outside the thoughtproof bubble for just a second had protected his primary brain long enough for him to transmit orders through his signet ring to the control board to the warpcore.

Then the cells of every part of his body outside the surface of his protective warp had exploded. Lord Jupiter, Saturn and Uranus had done their work well: even beyond the orbit of Pluto was not safe for him.

Whether what he did was genius or madness, he did not know, then or ever. Aeneas had only two locations in timespace already solved: the location at Zeta Herculis and the location of the planet Saturn. But Zeta Herculis, thirty-five lightyears away, was still within this monster's firing range.

He chose. He moved the Great Eye to the empty spot where Saturn had been.

The Great Eye, a neutron star whose entire mass outweighed all
the planets of Sol, coated and filled with alien weaponry and whose
endless capacitors and banks and batteries, countless cubic miles of
them, were filled with death energy, now materialized between the
orbits of Jupiter and Neptune. Sol, at this distance, was merely a
small star, brighter than others.

But the whole surface of the neutron star grew discolored as some
unseen, unknown energy from Sol disrupted the crystalline structure
of the neutronium, and turned the whole surface a leprous white. The
cubic miles of atmosphere and hydrosphere filling the sclera of the
Great Eye now inexplicably erupted into space, climbing against the
unimaginably steep gravity well. The amount of energy required to
move so huge a liquid mass against so vast a gravity was incalculable,
and seemed to be coming from a titanic internal turbulence.

The Great Eye itself turned wildly left and right, then lost all power
of motion, went dull and blank, was covered over with the strange
white discoloration. The gasses and oceans thrown into orbit formed
a ring of steam around the equator of the neutron star, and slowly
cooled into icebergs, a glittering rainbow.

There was no sign of who or what had so instantly obliterated such
a monstrous sphere. Cracks appeared in the surface, as continent-
sized areas subsided, and gamma radiation began escaping from these
cracks. Matter was turned to plasma by the immense heat escaping
from the interior, so the cracks now had glowing, molten lips. Volcanoes like pock-marks scarred the white surface. Instruments showed
the volume of the star was less than it had been a moment before, even
though the mass remained the same. Material at the core was being
lost into the singularity.

The neuropsionic energy output dropped to zero. The great shout
ceased.

Aeneas recovered before Lady Luna or Lord Pluto. His instruments
showed the populations of Saturn and its moons were stilled stunned.
His head and his right hand were missing, and his signet ring had

fallen a few inches outside the thoughtproof warp. He gestured in sign language for a robot to pick up the ring and return it to him. He grew a hand, filling it with brain cells, into which he programmed a set of commands. He put the ring on that hand, which he removed from his body, and ordered it to crawl outside the range of the thoughtproof warp. The hand also ignited when it passed beyond the thoughtproof warp, but the faster than light circuits Aeneas had established in the surrounding control boards were able to react even faster: the commands in the hand were sent to the ring and then to the warpcore.

Again came the moment of the passage along the closed timelike curve segment of a tesseract: it looked like a hollow looking glass reflecting the distorted image of Saturn's clouds expanding outward suddenly to infinity, and then a starry sky collapsing back inward.

With a sense of relief, Aeneas dropped the thoughtproof warp around himself, and reconnected his headless body through his ring to various instruments and sense impressions. He could see through cameras until his head regrew.

He gave orders that Lady Luna also be looked after. She had not yet recovered from the shock of the Great Eye's mental shout. Aeneas did not bend to pick her up himself for fear of defensive traps or robotic reflexes hidden on her person, or in her accessories. Serving machines carried her gently to her quarters.

Lord Pluto was nowhere to be seen.

The giant planet Saturn, all its ring and moons, the pyramidal asteroid Talos, and the dead planet Necropolis with its bright miniature sun were now in normal timespace. Three bright stars, two yellow and one small and red, shined to one side. These were Alpha, Beta and Proxima Centauri, half a lightyear away.

Aeneas asked the navigation systems to recheck all calculations, and he opened the analytical screen to its full aperture.

The calculations had been precise. Even as he watched, a microscopic red dot appeared in the Alpha Centauri system, swelled up in size, and resolved itself into the asteroid Talos, at that time a smoothly polished sphere of rock with lights shining from gaps in the surface. The light beams were visible because Talos was shedding oxygen snow. A hailstorm of tiny debris was expanding like a soap bubble, being pushed outward by explosive decompression.

The light which had bounced off the asteroid when it first arrived half a year ago at Alpha Centauri was even now reaching Aeneas' receivers half a lightyear away. Lord Pluto's invisibility field took a moment or two before it cloaked the asteroid. These were the images that escaped before that moment.

He saw the flicker of energy as the shattered asteroid surrounded itself in a forcefield to prevent the escape of air. He saw the crawling black ooze of nanomachinery appear at the edges of each brightly-lit hole or break in the hull begin to paste the breaks shut.

There was a twitch in his instruments a moment later. A space contortion wave passed through the area. It was a mass of probability waves, lacking any extension or precise location, roughly equal to the volume and particle count of a tall man.

Aeneas could not smile without a head, but he felt a sense of satisfaction. He turned off the miniature sun, knowing that Saturn and all its moons, as well as the dead planet Necropolis, could survive for a few hours without any incoming heat or light.

And then he had himself carried to his quarters to see about various medical and biotechnical operations to restore himself to fitness.

It was four hours later that the message he had been expecting came. Aeneas went to the wardroom, to find Lady Luna and Lord Pluto already there. Lady Luna had redecorated the room, filling it with slender birch trees, changing the floor to grass, and introducing does and fawns grazing. She sat on a blanket of antigravity half an inch above the grass, with silver bowls of fruits and sweets hovering near to her hand, a decanter of wine and a crystal wine bowl.

Lord Pluto sat at the original wardroom table, except that he had turned the mahogany surface to black iron. There was a pot of hot coffee at his elbow; he had thrown a drinking pearl into the fluid.

Presumably the pearl's mate was in a drinking nipple inside the mouth-piece of his helmet.

Aeneas seated himself at the table. "Why do you never remove your helmet?"

Lord Pluto said, "The human brain has special nerve paths for face recognition, among the first nerve paths children develop. A face is therefore more difficult to remove from visibility than any other visual information."

Aeneas said, "I still do not know your motive."

Pluto said, "It is a simple one, therefore I keep it carefully hidden."

Aeneas turned to Luna. "With what did you blackmail him?"

She smiled and showed her dimples. "A secret that is worthless if not kept secret."

Lord Pluto said, "I see I must prove myself again. Here."

There was an old fashioned upright phone in the center of the wardroom table. It rang with the sound of a bell. Aeneas stared at it blankly, wondering how old Lord Pluto really was. Lord Pluto pushed the phone toward Aeneas. "Geras is on the line."

Geras was Lord Saturn. Aeneas said, "You did not speak to him?"

Pluto said, "There is no advantage to revealing what he cannot suspect, that Lady Luna and I were stowaways on Talos during the entire construction phase of the warpcore."

Aeneas took the phone in hand. "Hello? Is this one of my uncles who tried to kill me in cold blood?"

Lord Saturn's aged and creaking voice replied. "Well, so it seems young Aeneas has gained control of the Final Science, and can abduct whole planets. You have the upper hand. What are your demands?"

Aeneas said, "You have made it so that I cannot be exposed to Sol. Reverse the process. I cannot bring you back to Sol until I can go back."

"Suppose I say no?"

Aeneas said, "That would not be in your best interest. I have made first contact with an extraterrestrial civilization. They are entirely composed of necroform vampires, their entire ecology down to the microbe level. Apparently every star in the galaxy has suffered the same fate. Organic life no longer exists, except, for reasons unknown, around Sol. Hence, there is no other star around which I can put your planet. We return to Sol together or not at all. There is no other star."

"You expect me to believe such an outrageous lie? Is this how you chose to abuse the despotic power you've obtained—threatening a trillion innocent lives with slow, freezing death?"

Aeneas stared at the ringed gas giant. It was streaked with gold and green. The upper atmosphere was streaked with storm bands. Below this, artificial supercontinents, greater in surface area than all the lands and seas of Earth combined, hung at various levels in the gigantic atmosphere. Each was surrounded by layers of Earth-like air, and floating buoyantly on strata of denser materials. Archipelagoes of floating islands drifted between the flying continents, minnows among whales. The population was a hundred times that of Earth's ten billions, and yet the population density was far less.

Aeneas replied, "I knew your escape hatch led somewhere on or about Saturn, its rings, its moons. I did not know where, so I brought it all. There is no threat. I desire no power over you. I merely want my life back."

Saturn said, "You would have to trust me as a man trusts his surgeon: you must bring me to where you are, personally."

Aeneas said, "The pearl from your quarters is still here with me. Come ahead, but come alone."

Saturn said, "What if you mean a trap for me?"

Aeneas said, "You are already in a trap, one you set for yourself. I am offering you escape."

Aeneas tossed the pearl into a corner of the wardroom. Lady Luna stepped close to Lord Pluto. Both faded from sight.

The pearl turned blue, and a line of distorted space unfolded from it, became a cylinder, and a thin, bright and stretched version of Lord

Saturn stepped out of it, his face and limbs growing and dimming as he did so. By the time his foot touched the grassy floor, his proportions and color were normal. He was dressed in a gray cloak, the same hue as his beard. He leaned on the wand of his phimaophone.

His eyes darted to the trees, the startled fawns, the nine-foot tall Aeneas at the table.

"Where are your guards?" asked the old man.

Aeneas said, "Think of this as a test of your fitness to live among free men as an equal."

The old man nodded, and then blurred into motion too swift to see. The room grew blindingly bright. The air was hot and thick around Aeneas like settling concrete.

His special senses told him it was a time distortion, but not a spacewarp: he was in a lower energy frame of reference from the rest of the asteroid.

Aeneas was dumbfounded with surprise, and blushed with shame. He had no idea Lord Saturn had controlled such a power as this.

Here, seconds had been expanded to hours or days. Outside, Lord Saturn had time and leisure enough to replace all Aeneas' servominds and instruments with his own, bring any number of people needed up from the nearby moons. It would all be over before Aeneas could blink.

06

THE SURRENDER OF SATURN

Lord Pluto's voice sounded in the ear of Aeneas. "Lord Saturn, this is your brother, Darius. I am using my power of negative information flow in reverse, so that, no matter where you are on this asteroid, or in what time-frame, you cannot help but hear me. Your powers of time-acceleration are worthless. I have rendered all exits undetectable by any means. Your mind has already been contaminated by Lady Luna, who is here with me. She has introduced nightmare-level thought disturbances into your unconsciousness which will expand until you go insane. Only she can reverse the process. The longer you wait, the worse it grows."

The world of normal light and motion returned to Aeneas. A blurring, twitching version of Lord Saturn came into view, and slowed to ordinary speed. Aeneas scanned the fabric of space with his ring, but, despite what it seemed, this had not been a spacetime warp.

Lord Saturn was disheveled, his clothing tattered. The deer in the chamber were gone, as were most of the trees. A pile of bones was in one corner, and burn marks from where the trees had been chopped into campfire wood.

"You could have left me with something better than water to drink, you know…" Lord Saturn pouted. The bags under his eyes showed he had not slept in days, perhaps weeks. "I have this nightmare of walking down corridors and having the doors vanish behind me. I cut through the wall with a weapon, and there is nothing behind. I look in the mirror, and there is no one there. Each day one more corridor or cabin has vanished, until only this room is left! I could have killed you a dozen times over, Aeneas!"

Aeneas recognized the handiwork of Lord Pluto. The growing insanity inside the old man's subconscious would have made the mystery of the ever-shrinking and ever-vanishing satellite impossible for him to solve. Neither his senses nor his mind had been trustworthy.

Aeneas said sternly, "I said this was a test to see if you were fit to be a free man. You have failed. Do you surrender?"

Lord Saturn fell to his knees, weeping. The old man clutched the long, dangling white locks of his hair. "Yes, yes! Anything! Only stop my mind from disappearing… I can feel it going… my thoughts coming unraveled…"

Aeneas said, "I have Grandfather's power. I am the new Lord Tellus. I am Master of the Empire of Man. Do you agree?"

"Yes! By hell and perdition, yes!" screamed the old man, clutching at the knees of Aeneas.

Aeneas knelt and lifted Lord Saturn to his feet. "I receive no fealty in those names, or under duress."

Louder, he said "Lady Luna, if you please…?"

Aeneas detected a throb of power in the lower parts of the thought-energy spectrum. A light of sobriety, and sanity, came into Lord Saturn's eyes then.

Aeneas said aloud, "Lord Pluto, if you please, let the doors and corridors between here and Lord Saturn's apartments be visible to him. He may need rest. Also, let the servominds hear his requests for food and drink."

Lord Saturn stood, leaning on his wand, and took a few unsteady steps. "My people are not frozen, are they? It's been weeks for me, trying to find a way to escape. But it's been less than a minute here, hasn't it? And the nightmares came while I was awake…"

Aeneas steeled himself against pity. "As soon as you remove from my body the trap that makes Sol's light deadly to me, your world will return with me to the Solar System."

Lord Saturn blinked blearily. "Done, my boy. Done long ago. The influx of chronic particles I used to slow your personal time would have washed away the energy structure I erected inside you. I can double check and remove any trace elements in the morning… must sleep now…"

Lady Luna faded into visibility, scowled at the bones of her deer, but then smiled and put his hand to Lord Saturn's elbow. "Come along, Uncle!" she cooed, "I'll tuck you into bed. Tell me what dreams you want to have?"

"Ones without vampires… no more vampires…"

She and he departed the wardroom.

Aeneas turned toward the table. Lord Pluto was seated there.

Pluto said, "Have I proved myself sufficiently?"

"You let me escape from your tower, didn't you?"

"Yes."

"Why help me?"

"You need help. You are unalert and unsuspicious. I took the precaution of installing invisibility broadcasters on every exit and bulkhead. Even though I was excluded from Saturn's high-speed temporal imbalance field, my preparations acted automatically. They removed the visual information from the universe, so that Lord Saturn could see no exit."

Aeneas said, "Why didn't I see these invisibility broadcasters…? Um… never mind. That question answers itself…"

Pluto said in his cold, ponderous voice, "Lady Luna also set up her equipment in this room, hidden inside her trees. You failed to look for an ulterior motive to her love of redecorating. Was she not seated in a garden when you were caught by her?"

"Are you saying not to trust her?"

"I am saying treat your allies wisely. Know their capacities. Lady Luna's power over dream may seem slight, but she uses it well. Lord Saturn suffers dreams to make him more amenable to the task of fighting the space vampires. Obsessions are also a lunacy, and within her purview."

Aeneas said, "You insist on being mysterious."

Lord Pluto said in an icy voice: "Trust given, not earned, is worthless."

"You call me untrustworthy, then? I have been…"

"Inconstant. You decreed yourself Emperor of Man, a thing you swore not to do. Either you vow rashly, or break vows lightly."

Aeneas thought of several sharp replies to this, but before he could pick one, Lord Pluto vanished.

Aeneas moved the planet Saturn and its fifty-three moons and countless moonlets, smaller bodies, space icebergs, satellites, flying palaces, gardenhouses, and ring system across the lightyears from Alpha Centauri to a position not far from Pluto, with Talos and Necropolis placed in orbit around the gas giant.

He was pleased when the sunlight did not destroy him.

Here was the ninth planet and its moons, Charon, Styx, Nix, Kerberos, and Hydra. Charon was a world of snowy pine groves free of animal life, a silent monument to Lord Pluto's dead wife Cora. The other four had been terraformed into gardens and plantations by his two sons and two daughters, peopled with slender, solemn races.

Aeneas, Lady Luna, and the Lords Pluto and Saturn were in the wardroom, which had been restored to its sylvan beauty.

Aeneas said to Lord Saturn, "Pluto may have a small gravitational effect, but any orbital corrections to your moons and rings can be made once Saturn is back in its proper place."

Lord Saturn wore a guarded expression as he sat. It was the same look he wore when near his brother Lord Jupiter. Aeneas did not like what this implied.

Lord Saturn said, "I do not expect my world, or any human life, to mean a great deal to you, youngster. Power over men and compassion for them are mutually exclusive."

Aeneas smiled without mirth. "My newfound power opened the stars to all mankind: but in the stars is a danger beyond belief. Compassion says you must help me fight it. Power over men I do not crave, nor need."

Lord Saturn said suspiciously, "So speaks the new Emperor! Why bother to convince me? I am your prisoner; my world is your hostage."

Aeneas said, "Your world is here to put any materials you need at hand. You have a machine for seeing into the past, or so I have heard. I want you to inspect planet Pluto. Do you have such a machine?"

Lord Saturn's eyes flicked to Lord Pluto's helmet. He sighed. "The science is called Palaeoscopy. Lord Tellus instructed me in it, no doubt as one of his cruel jests. He thought it fitting to teach me a superscience with no military use, so that I would always be helpless before my brothers—and now, it seem, before my niece."

Lady Luna smiled as if flattered.

Saturn said, "The first thing I did with it was examine the past of the Forerunner cache Father discovered, or try to. Something blocked my attempts, and turned the location invisible including backward through time. If that is why you rescued me, the secret is protected."

Lord Pluto said, "It will work now."

Saturn raised an eyebrow. "So it *was* you!"

Lord Pluto said, "Not I."

Saturn turned to Aeneas. "I need to make contact with my people in Lesser Chronosopolis, and on Janus and Iapetus."

Aeneas said, "I have not tampered with your signet ring. You may broadcast commands to anyone you wish."

Lord Saturn was puzzled. "What if I command them to turn weapons on this asteroid?"

Aeneas sighed impatiently. "You never wanted to be a Lord of Creation. It did not suit your artistic temperament. But you *had* to be one, to defend yourself against your brothers. Now you put me in your shoes! I decreed myself the new Lord Tellus! Your choice is to keep attacking me, or to allow me to abdicate. You are no prisoner, because the choice for peace must be free and mutual. Come: I must discover the origin of the Infinithedron, if we are to defeat the enemy."

It did not take long. Cone-shaped satellites teleported into orbit around the planet Saturn focused strange energies on the icy orb of Pluto.

Lord Saturn said, "The data from any event must settle from the information layer to the memory layer of the universe, where time particles are produced, before this method can read them. The more current an event, the more difficult it is to read. Let us start with five million years ago. Lord Pluto will have to direct me."

Lord Pluto said, "Look to the foot of Mons Wright."

The image was carried through all their signet rings directly into the visual cortex of their brains. At the location named was the many-sided orb of the Infinithedron, half-buried in the oxygen ice, as complex as a human brain. It glowed orange-gold.

Even as they watched, the orb wrinkled, and its many surfaces divided and divided again.

A cry of alarm escaped Aeneas. "Impossible!"

Lord Pluto said, "It is made of Schroedinger matter. The act of observation collapses the probability clouds of which it is composed."

Lord Saturn said, "This is five million years past."

Aeneas said, "How is the Infinithedron able to react *then* to the event of us here seeing it *now*?"

But Lady Luna snapped her fingers, "Another observer must be alive, then and there." Now she frowned, looking spooked. "In the Neolithic. On Pluto."

To the near horizon a mile away, a level expanse of oxygen ice beneath a layer of hydrogen snow reached, motionless, silent, dead.

Saturn said, "The palaeoscope picks up life energy as easily as light waves. There is no living thing on this world."

Aeneas said softly, "Then who is looking?"

Saturn said, "I can probe further back... five million years... seven... ten..."

Glacier-mountains shrunk and craters vanished as the planet grew younger.

Suddenly, at the ten million year mark, the planet was covered with a hellish city from pole to pole, dark with factories and torture cages, armories, slave pens, cannibal feast halls, weapon vents. Despite the lightness of the planet, the architecture was squat, ugly, asymmetrical. It had a similar architecture to Necropolis: the buildings were wedge-shaped, wider at the top than at the base, and gates and windows likewise.

"Where are the natives?" asked Lady Luna. For the city was empty and dead.

The planet moved. At eleven million years, Pluto was moving through the Oort cloud, the outer asteroid belt surrounding the solar system. At twelve, it was in interstellar space.

Lord Saturn said thoughtfully, "Our idea of history must be revised. Father was not the one who murdered the three hundred officers and crew of the *Cerberus* and changed them into necroforms. Unlikely he could have created the complex equipment needed to induce the shadow-effect into the cellular life. He had not the means."

Luna said, "Then who did?"

Saturn said, "The natives. The Plutonians."

The world-city of the sunless interstellar planet was now filled with moving things, manlike shapes. The narrow streets were filled with hot-eyed and pale-skinned hominids, moving with the jerky, unnatural energy of creatures whose dead limbs are animated by superhuman force. There were throngs. It was a vampire world.

07

THE FEAST OF
VAMPIRES

Aeneas, Lady Luna, and the Lords Pluto and Saturn stared at the long-dead past of planet Pluto.

Lord Saturn said, "Why do they look like people?"

Aeneas said, "We wondered the same thing. Forms like this are also at Alpha Centauri and Zeta Herculis."

At twelve and a half million years ago, the planet changed: now there were green plants and trees on the interstellar world, despite the absence of a sun.

Aeneas said, "Their terraforming was equal to ours. They have an artificial envelope of atmosphere, at least at that time. What happened?"

Lord Saturn said, "My method crosses time, not space. More than half a lightyear outside the Solar System, I cannot see. The oldest image layer is here: thirteen million years ago."

The dark fanes and pillared temples were filled with living men, huge in the low gravity, but too large to pass between the pillars. The pillars were not pillars, but bars. The hot-eyed vampires gathered from time to time on the shining plaza grounds and esplanades to feast on them, but they never smiled at the lingering torment inflicted on their victims.

Through the transparent layers of ice, the woebegone faces of the trapped giants could be glimpsed in agony as their life energy was drained from them.

After each feast, the vampire creatures marched silently along the crooked roads of the world-city. They gathered into an arena. In the center, buried up to the neck, was a gigantic monster so huge as to make the giants minnows. To this half-buried head the vampires bowed and prayed. The skull was a dome. Its face was horrible, its mouth a gaping pit, its eyes filled with pain and pride. From out the ghastly mouth would reach a score of tongues like tentacles, yard upon yard, and eat his own worshippers.

There was another, larger arena to the south, with an even larger twin to this monster there, and another after that, in every district of the world. The further south the monster was buried, the larger it was.

A monster at the south pole, far larger than the others, whose crown extended beyond the atmosphere, would reach out with mouth-tentacles miles in length. Vaster than dark rainbows, the dripping tendrils stretched across horizons. It raped the lesser monsters of their stolen life, torturing them, but leaving the rest of them mostly intact. Its eyes glared with ecstasy, and temblors shook the small world as its buried body writhed, but soon it subsided and wept, and closed its eyes to sleep again.

Lady Luna said, "Where do they come from?"

Aeneas looked at the orbital elements in the image. "They are from Gamma Crucis, eighty-eight lightyears away. The nearest red giant."

Lord Saturn said doubtfully, "Are these the Forerunners?"

Aeneas said, "I doubt it. Where is the Infinithedron?"

The image changed to roughly nine and a half million years ago. They saw a black cube hanging in space. It was the Infinithedron in its simplest form, with no observers. The cube fell through black space, approaching Pluto.

The black cube made a soft landing on Pluto, in the snow at the foot of the mound which later would grow into the ice volcano of Mons Wright.

Lord Saturn said, "All my life, I thought the Infinithedron was a library, a repository of knowledge, that Father found on Pluto. What is it, really?"

Lord Pluto said, "More than that."

Lord Saturn focused on the cube and ran the images backward, as the alien object crossed the billions of miles from the inner system.

It came from Earth.

The cube had lifted off from Antarctica. At that time, in the Late Miocene, Antarctica's northern peninsula was a tundra. Lord Saturn found an image of the black cube resting silently on a knoll covered with pine trees, while dire wolves and woolly mammoths prowled the snowy wastelands in the near distance.

Luna said, "So the Forerunners are *Earthmen?*"

Aeneas said, "No. This is before Homo sapiens."

Lord Pluto said, "Brother, please go back to the Cretaceous extinction."

Fifty five million years earlier, the cube was in the same location, except that Antarctica was a tropic land.

The Infinithedron was glowing with blinding, unearthly energies. Particle energy beams of immense force and range were shining into the sky like searchlights, disintegrating incoming meteors, or forcing them aside to miss the Earth. There were dozens, scores, hundreds.

The desperation of the cube was obvious: its beams stammered, flickered, and failed.

It was a very near thing. One and only one enemy meteor made it through this magnificent defense, and even it was disintegrated to half its original size.

This meteor struck the Yucatan Peninsula at Chicxulub with a force two million times more potent than a fifty megaton atomic bomb.

The crater was twelve miles deep. Tens of thousands of cubic miles of sediment were displaced: superheated dust, ash and the steam from the boiling waters of the newly-formed Gulf of Mexico smothered half the globe. The largest megatsunami in Earth's history reached to Texas and Florida. Shrapnel thrown into orbit by the impact reentered the atmosphere as incandescent fragments, igniting wildfires. Shockwaves triggered earthquakes and volcanic eruptions in the other hemisphere. A black cloud covered the world for a decade.

Lady Luna said, "Lord Saturn, with your machine, you never looked into the extinction of the dinosaurs before?"

The old man said, "Many times. I encountered blank spots which I thought were some natural failure of the record layer. There were no images of the Infinithedron shooting multimegaton power beams into space."

Lord Pluto said, "We are allowed to behold what was formerly hidden. Trace the Chicxulub impactor to its source."

Lord Saturn gave his brother a curious look, but asked no question. The viewpoint backtracked the incoming meteors. Earlier, they had been a single hundred-mile wide worldlet headed toward Earth. It was severed by a beam issuing from Earth, forming the Baptistina family of asteroids. The family then accelerated, only to be deflected or disintegrated by the Infinithedron. All but one.

And the Baptistina worldlet, in turn, came from the Oort cloud. Before that, it was in interstellar space.

As with Pluto, at a certain point in the past, suddenly the worldlet was covered with a worldwide city. The hellish architecture was the same, the crooked streets, the buildings wider at top than bottom, the giants trapped in feasting cages, and the buried monsters with their multiple tongues.

Aeneas said, "As with Pluto. It comes from Gamma Crucis."

Lord Pluto said, "Brother, can you find the exact moment when the vampires were wiped out on both worlds?"

Lord Saturn said, "The Plutonians of the Miocene were destroyed when Pluto passed inside the orbit of Neptune. The Baptistina worldlet of the Paleocene was much closer before the vampires dissolved, about halfway between Neptune and Uranus." He turned to Aeneas. "Speaking of which, you need Lord Uranus, so you will have to go into deep space and recover him, just as you did me. The neuropsionic solar radiation properties that destroyed these necroform creatures were different during the two different eras. It is his area of expertise: I know nothing of it."

Aeneas said, "I take it you believe my wild tale of space vampires now, Uncle."

Saturn said, "These images can be blocked by Lord Pluto's science of invisibility. I doubt they can be faked." He turned to Pluto. "Why did you block me before, brother?"

Lord Pluto said, "Not I. Father knows all he taught us."

Lord Saturn said, "Father! He yet lives? Why is he letting us see these things now?"

Pluto said, "For the same reason the Infinithedron sent the signal to Earth when it detected evidence of space travel: to prepare us for the next battle. Come! Let us see more. Where did the Infinithedron originate? Where are the Forerunners?"

At four hundred fifty million years ago, during the Ordovician Period, the cube splashed down in the seas of the Southern Hemisphere.

Lord Saturn said, "This is the Silurian Extinction. It is a period I have never studied. Roughly half of the marine families were wiped out…"

The sea bed was a phantasmagoria of primitive life. Clams, mussels, scallops, large and small, ranged the sea. Echinoderms, starfish either five-armed or seven-armed, stone lilies, and sea cucumbers stalked the watery wonderland. Bryozoans like soft, fantastic fronds of lace grew everywhere, and coral in crooked horns like witchy towers wearing gem-studded armor.

Resting in the middle of an active volcano at the bottom of the polar sea, the black cube seemed to do nothing for at time. Then, at forty-four million years ago, particles left the cube. A cloud spread like ink through the seas. Roughly half the life in the sea was changed. Brachiopods and bryozoans were affected, along with trilobites, eel-like conodonts, and wormy graptolites.

Not destroyed, the sea worms and plants rose to the surface, and were washed ashore. Like some cursed maiden in a Greek myth, the organisms transformed, putting down roots, or burrowing into the sand.

Green plants spread across dry land, forming extensive forests. It was a primordial garden of ferns. No flowers, and no animal life was anywhere in them.

They all recognized what they were seeing. "Pantropy," said Luna. "It was not an extinction at all. Why?"

Lord Pluto said, "Earlier, please."

The Infinithedron came from out of the sun. They watched the black cube rising up from against the immense gravitational pull of the star, untouched and unharmed by fires able to melt any object made of matter, serenely move through space, and going into orbit around the Earth.

Saturn said, "Either the Forerunners live in the sun, which I doubt, or the cube entered Sol earlier for some purpose. That event I cannot find. My instruments cannot read inside solar plasma."

Lord Pluto said, "Let us inspect the destruction of the plutonian vampires. Have all the sensors of all bands trained on the image. I want to see what becomes of the death-energy accumulated by an entire civilization of necroforms over millions of years."

Saturn returned the viewpoint to the Pluto of ten million years ago. Here was the hellish torture-city of the vampire race. The trapped giants had all been consumed eons before, and the green life. The atmosphere had been allowed to collapse. As Pluto approached the solar system, the vampires began to writhe and melt, even though Sol was hardly brighter than the morning star in the black and airless skies. Even those on the hemisphere away from the sun died.

Like burning wax, each slumped into a reddish and vile liquid, screaming, gibbering, hands clawing. As each one melted, it tried to consume its melting neighbor, and drain it of its horde of stolen life energy. The buried colossuses of each district reached out across the rooftops with tongues dripping and melting as they reached, licking up the half-fluid half-corpses of their expiring worshippers. The larger colossuses ate the smaller. The monster of the south reached out its tongues many miles long, and consumed them in turn. Then it also melted. Its eyes ran over its flabby cheeks like tears; its domelike skull sagged and cracked and released a deluge.

The waters poured out and out as the extensive body, larger than a continent, liquefied, and was forced to the surface by the collapse of subterranean vaults the once-solid bones of the monster had forced open.

The waters of the monster covered the planet from pole to pole, and froze.

The hundred-tongued monster of the south, even as it melted, used the death energy gathered from its slaves to activate the selfsame warpcore later found by Lord Tellus. This halted its approach toward Sol, and preserved it from further damage.

Though clogged with ice, the muzzles of interplanetary range weapons were readied, trained on Earth, but lacked the energy to fire.

The black cube fell from space, and erected a warp field. A wrestling match began. The cube pulled Pluto closer to the sun; the world-vampire pulled away. Eons passed. Eventually the world-vampire tired and slept. The cube stood guard over it.

And the glacier stirred. The cube became an octagon. The glacier murmured. The octagon became a dodecahedron, then an icosahedron, then…

Lady Luna said in a voice of cold horror, "It is still there, isn't it?"

Lord Pluto said heavily, "In old stories, the seal of Solomon was said to cap the brass bottle in which an evil spirit was trapped. The Forerunners had the foresight to write on their Solomonic seal all the sciences needed to arm anyone who opened it against what might be released."

08

THE BLACK SHIP

Aeneas said, "I am curious about one other thing, Lord Saturn. Someone left a black pearl hidden in my bedchamber, and put its mate on Pluto, in the ruins of the *Cerberus* expedition habitat. I want to see who it was."

"These events were too recent," said Lord Saturn.

Lord Pluto said, "I have records. The visual logs from the expedition."

A mental command to his signet ring presented the images to them.

It was odd looking at the twenty-four year old images of young Evripades Zenon Telthexorthopolis in his political officer's uniform, hauling himself hand over hand down the axis of the *Cerberus*, a vessel of antique design, with no artificial gravity.

They watched the landing, and the erection of the habitat, and the initial months of search. Everything was visible up until the moment when, standing in a circle around the excavation crater, three hundred officers and crew, in their environment armor, waited for the drill-and-grapple crane to bring the newly discovered Infinithedron up a sheer well to the icy surface of Pluto.

Only Evripades Zenon Telthexorthopolis was back inside the ship, watching from a distance. Then the images went dark.

Lord Pluto said, "Events touching the *Cerberus* expedition after this point have always been censored. Father wishes me not to discover all my brothers' secrets, or his."

Aeneas said, "Do you have any record of who approached your world to plant the black pearl in the ruins of the habitat?"

Lord Pluto said, "No. However, it must have been done by ship. Perhaps Saturn can find the image of any recent vessels in the area."

Saturn shook his gray head. "Not so. My machines see things millennia in the past, not hours nor years."

Pluto said, "However, is the rate at which visual information enters the data layer of the universe dependent on the shape of timespace? Basic relativity suggests it is. Perhaps if young Aeneas searched his implanted knowledge, and the two of you worked together, a solution might suggest itself."

Among the Lords of Creation, since all the machinery and instruments needed could be assembled instantly through molecular technologies, and any routine mental operations could be performed by automatic highspeed servant-minds (including batteries of extrapolations and experiments of every possible combination), it was a matter of hours of research and study, rather than months or years, to launch a prototype vehicle: it was awkwardly named the anchipalaeoscope.

The first seventeen returned no information from recent layer of time.

But then the eighteenth trial returned an echo. The first images found were of a squat, gray, unadorned ship Lord Pluto said was his private craft. These were dates, many decades ago, when he was arriving or departing using a vehicle rather than a space contortion pearl.

Next, the view found another shape, slender as a needle, black as jet. The vessel was directly behind Charon, so that the bulk of that barren moon blocked Pluto. The whole vessel was coated in a field that absorbed light, so that neither radio waves, nor infrared, nor any other wavelength rebounded from the hull. It was black with an absolute blackness, and issued no heat, no radiation.

Aeneas looked at the readings. "This image is from twenty years ago."

Lord Saturn said, "An antiphotonic field. I cannot penetrate it."

Aeneas said, "I can. Tachyons trump antiphotons. Allow me."

Aeneas made tiny adjustments to the instruments he and Lord Saturn had made, and the hull of the vessel was visible. It was made of a non-ferrous black ceramic. A ring of space contortion pearls circled the stern of the vessel, and another the bowsprit. A space contortion field transmitted her constantly to the position in front of herself. The inside of the vessel was composed of nothing but engine. Certain parts of the engine, such as fuel cells, blinked into and out of space contortion according to when they were needed. There seemed to be neither crew nor controls. How the vessel was being steered was unclear.

The vessel was moving in a disinertial field. Lord Saturn's machine could not focus on the black vessel at any point in time before it came to rest behind Charon, because it was moving too swiftly.

Lord Saturn said, "That could be Lord Jupiter's technology. He is the master of the electromagnetic spectrum."

Lady Luna said, "Lord Mercury knows the ins and outs of space contortion better than anyone, and I've never seen a setup like that: is the vessel transmitting itself from its own stern to its own bow? That is impossible."

Aeneas said, "It seems to be riding an artificially produced gravity wave, and gravity is Lord Neptune's area of expertise."

The vessel corkscrewed in toward the planet. Lord Pluto said emotionlessly, "The captain knows the location and period of my defensive satellites, and the range and location of my ground-based sensor sweeps, because he is always in the area of least overlap. The timing is impeccable. He has also selected an area to splashdown where I post no watchers, because there is nothing there to guard..."

For the black vessel now darted toward the surface. She moved too quickly for Lord Saturn's machine to track, but he examined the glacier below by tenth-second increments, until he detected a blur of motion, and then he carefully backed the image up by a second. The vessel did not slow as she descended, but instead sent out a fan of heat-rays from her bow. The glacier underneath was turned to liquid. The vessel nosedived into the fluid, but, without inertia, was not hurt. Inertia returned for a moment when the field was shut off. This was the only moment when Lord Saturn's machine could get a clear view. Then the vessel was under the surface of the lake of liquid oxygen, whose surface formed a frost and thickened rapidly into ice.

Lord Saturn said, "Interference is here: I am not sure what is causing it."

Lord Pluto said, "Clever. The spyship knows I post no sentries beneath the glacier surface. He could have rested there as long as he liked."

Aeneas said, "Doing what? What is there to spy on?"

Lord Pluto turned his monocular helmet lens toward Aeneas, "A drill to seek the layer of frozen undead material forming the main body of the world-vampire could be lowered. A neuropsionic broadcaster could make contact with it, and translate its thoughts into words. It is a first contact mission."

Aeneas said, "There may be earlier or later visits. Search for them, please."

Lord Saturn gave orders to his navy. Automatic machinery made a plethora of the new short-range anchipalaeoscope satellites in a matter of minutes. A flotilla of small cylindrical probes, each looking like two cones connected through the apex, now formed a cloud at the Lagrange Two spot, on the far side of Charon. These sensors consisted of two counter-synchronized chronic particle cyclotrons, and were connected through contortion lines to the anchipalaeoscope machines in the time-observatories at the poles of the planet Saturn. The far side of Charon was the only point in space where a clear near-past image of the black ship had been picked up.

The probes sought until they found a second image from twenty-five years earlier, and a third from thirty years, but both were blurred. Neither was clear enough even to be sure if this was the same vessel, even though she was moving at the same remarkable speeds. And nothing closer than twenty years old was possible.

"I suspect," Saturn said finally, "the black ship does not normally turn off her disinertia field when entering orbit, but simply plunges to the surface without slaking her speed. I am not sure why she stopped that one time, but I was lucky enough to pick up the image."

Lord Pluto asked, "What was the date of the first image?"

Saturn said, "24 December, AD 2474, Imperial Meridian Time. Christmas Eve."

Lord Pluto said, "A day I am called to Everest for celebrations. But that year I had increased my sentry satellites. The black ship paused to take readings and calculate an approach. How long was she motionless?"

Lord Saturn said, "Six hours."

Aeneas saw the slight flicker of neural energy in Lord Pluto's ring. He was evidently consulting an almanac, for he said, "Interesting. At that date, Uranus was in opposition, hence more than fifty-eight AU from Pluto. Seven and a half lighthours. A signal from the ship, either a Schroedinger wave or electromagnetic, could have reached and returned from any other world or worldlet in that time, but not from a point on Uranus or his moons."

Aeneas also saw the flicker in Lady Luna's signet ring as her servant mind reminded her of something. Luna looked startled. "Wait. What date did you say? Because today is Christmas Eve. Unless we have lost or gained a day somehow during all these spacewarp jumps we've made. If the spyship is coming precisely on this date, Imperial Meridian Time, every five years, then she is coming here *today*!"

Lord Saturn told his astronomers on various moons and satellites to train their instruments on the Lagrange point on the far side of Charon. They saw nothing. Lady Luna relaxed visibly. "Good! Not here yet. Because if that ship came, and saw all of the remotes Lord Saturn scattered in that area, she'd know we've seen her, and…"

But Aeneas said, "Look!" and sent the image from his analytical screen into all their rings.

The black vessel hung in space. She had struck one of the swarm of anchipalaeoscope receivers at high speed, but, being without inertia, had come instantly to a halt without jar or harm. The various sensor beams issuing from the moons of Saturn were being quietly absorbed into the black skintight field of anti-photons, and returning no echoes.

Lady Luna said, "How long has that ship been there, Uncle Saturn?"

Lord Saturn said bitterly, "My machine cannot see recent events."

Aeneas said, "Long enough to radio home for instructions? Or contort the captain and crew with cabins and lifesupport into vacant places inside the hull?"

Saturn said, "I don't know. I do know that whoever is aboard knows these probes are mine. Their gross structure is the same as a palaeoscope. He knows we are looking into the remote past of the planet. He may deduce that we know the planetary vampire mass is still alive—if that is the word—under the ice."

An open antenna dish appeared amidships on the black vessel, so suddenly that it must have been contorted into place. Powerful signals left the black ship, bent around Charon, and passed across the face of Pluto.

Lady Luna said, "This is bad. All the nightmare wavelengths of the planet just became full: more signals than my instruments can register. It woke up. The planetary vampire mass is awake!"

Lord Pluto said, "Necroform science is my particular area of study. There is no way for such a mass to have come awake again: we just saw how, eons ago, it was drained of the death-energy that sustains it in the shadow condition."

Aeneas said, "The signals from the spyship are not electromagnetic. It is a laser of death-energy. The ship is feeding the plutonian world-vampire."

Lord Pluto raised his ring. "I have sent a signal to my automatic defenses on Pluto. But they were designed to repel warships, not planet-wide undead glaciers."

Aeneas focused his analytical screen on the surface. The dark tower faded from view, and a webwork of paralytic and nerve-destroying energies radiated out from the spot. But the whole valley folded inward on itself and was swallowed whole.

The death-energy readings suddenly spiked. On those wavelengths, the planet glowed like a black gem. Lord Pluto said, "The world-vampire is consuming death-energy from the *Cerberus*. Alas for Captain Lang! Alas for the crew! He and his deserved a fairer fate!"

The readings showed the creature was flushed with power from pole to pole. Aeneas said, "The creature captured the death-powered warpcore intact. It is using the three hundred to control the warpcore. I am now reading powerful gravity waves coming from the core of Pluto."

Lady Luna said, "It knows all the Forerunner sciences. We're doomed."

Aeneas said, "It is folding space and preparing to form a weaponized spacewarp, an area where the laws of nature are twisted. What or how, I do not know—but the focusing striations are pointing directly at Sol!"

09

TERADEATH

Aeneas sent signals to his warpcore, attempting to unfold the space the world-vampire was folding, but it was no use. The reach of a warpfield, its mass and degree of deviation depended quite straightforwardly on the mass-energy the warpcore controlled.

And the world-vampire was more skilled than Aeneas. In the first instant of combat, a field lashed out at the small planet Necropolis. All the vampires, who had been deceived into serving Lady Luna, now received new orders, linked mind to mind through the plutonian creature. They drained the world of life in a moment, and then they were drained in turn. Forests were turned into leafless hulks, and herds of deer to skeletons. Like a candle being snuffed, the whole planet Necropolis fell still, its every erg of vital energy fed into the plutonian world-vampire.

Aeneas attempted to throw a warp around Pluto and toss it closer to the sun; but the world-vampire flattened space in each direction around the icy globe, and prevented any warps from forming. Meanwhile, the gravitational energy in the core continued to grow and grow.

Aeneas said, "It is going to create a zone of space one micron in diameter and six lighthours long and run it through the sun like a spear. It will form instantaneously, traveling faster than lightspeed. Within that zone, the fundamental gravitational relation of mass to acceleration will change, and all the particles inside the sun caught by the field will form a singularity. A very long, thin singularity. If rotated, the warp will also form frame dragging effects, and tilt the lightcone of the sun out of normal timespace and into a closed timelike curve. I have no idea what that would do. Image a doughnut shape of nuclear plasma the size of the sun collapsing inward into a wire-thin black hole. The x-ray emissions alone will obliterate the solar system, not to mention the tidal effects of having a Tippler singularity string sweeping through the plane of the ecliptic. To the crows with it! I'm... lost... I don't have enough energy to stop it."

Aeneas turned and saw the old and careworn face of Lord Saturn. "Well. I resign as the new Lord Terra. If my terrible superluminary science cannot protect mankind, I have no claim to be its protector, do I?"

Lord Saturn said, "I know how to stop it."

Aeneas looked at him in surprise.

"Aeneas, do you have enough energy to place Saturn between Pluto and the sun? Preferably with the ring plane normal to an imaginary line connecting Sol and Pluto?"

"Yes, barely."

"Please do so."

The gas giant planet turned red, shrank to a point, and vanished in one spot, and in another a blue point appeared, swelled up to jovian size, dimming to its normal hue.

Lord Saturn held up his ring, "There are six interplanetary-strength temporal distortion stations at Saturn, which I had set aside in case of Civil War: two at the poles, and four equally spaced in the Cassini Division between rings A and B. I am instructing my servants to erect a graduated time-retardation field."

Aeneas said, "What in the world will that accomplish?"

Lord Saturn said, "Do you know why sunsets are red? Or why straight sticks look bent when thrust into a clear pool surface?"

Aeneas said, "The light rays bend according to the density of the medium."

Lord Saturn said, "Not the density *per se*. Fermat's Principle is that light seeks the path of least time between any two points. By manipulating the time flow at the terminator of Saturn, I can bend the light around my globe, bending those farther more than the nearer, and thereby concentrate the rays like a magnifying lens. A lens, if you will, wider than the rings of Saturn!"

Even as he spoke, the surface of Pluto ignited to dazzling brightness. Sunlight came to the dead world.

Because each element had a different melting point, during the long plutonian winter each element would precipitate out of the thin atmosphere as a layer of snow during its part of the season, and hydrogen, whose melting point is lowest, precipitated last and lay on top, above layers of solid oxygen ice, solid nitrogen, carbon dioxide, and methane.

So, at first, the layers of plutonian glacier merely melted, and the million year old cryovolcanos merely ignited and slumped over, gushing rivers of liquid oxygen, white with vapor, plunging in elfin slowness over cataracts of melting nitrogen ice.

But then the solar beams dug deeper, and struck the layer of methane ice. It mingled with the molten oxygen and the blue-burning hydrogen. There was a heat source; there was oxygen, lakes upon lakes of oxygen bubbling with oxygen gas rushing upward in great clouds. And when the methane began to melt, there was fuel.

The three things needed for combustion were present. The mountains and craters of Pluto ignited with fire. In the low gravity, the tops of the flames reached to the thinnest regions of the humble atmosphere, and the whole canopy of hydrogen gas ignited like the envelope of the Hindenburg.

It was astonishing to see a planet burn. It was a vision of hell.

The continent-sized vampire amoeba reared up in agony, with mountain ranges of melting hydrocarbons sliding off its undead half-liquid hide. Glaciers of solid and lakes of liquid material were thrown into space. Temblors shook the miniature world from pole to equator as the monster writhed.

The sunlight, not the flame, was killing it. The flames merely helped burn whatever semi-solid cubic miles of tissue the sunlight was forcing from the negative-life condition back into being normal, if no longer living, organic matter. Once it was organic, it burned and burned.

The fire was everywhere. The world-vampire recoiled to the dark side of the world, far from the sun, yanking islands and icebergs and plateaus in its wake, and sending hills into space like meteorites in reverse. However, it was not the electromagnetic property of the light-waves which harmed it, but the strange neuropsionic waves, which solid matter did not stop. Even in at the midnight meridian, the creature disintegrated, and the death-energy dispersed. The fires had started at the noon meridian, but the debris falling back through the burning hydrogen layer of air, the roaring layer of pure oxygen, heated up with friction enough, even in that low gravity, for carbon compounds to ignite.

Seen from afar, half smothered in its own smoke, the planet Pluto glowed like a golden coal, with rivers and seas of red flame within the yellow flame, black outcroppings of carbonaceous chondrite, peaks of blue ammonia ice sinking in ammonia lakes, a whole world bruised and spotted with ash and flame. The surface glaciers and oceans heaved and writhed in the low gravity as the world-vampire, a living bedrock of undead material, shuddered and perished.

With one last spasm, the quakes and convulsions ceased. The readings showed the death-energy at zero. The monster was gone. Aeneas saw the stressed spacetime line between Pluto and Sol vanish as the fabric of space returned to normal.

Lady Luna laughed and clapped her hands in relief, and old Lord Saturn smiled wearily.

Aeneas said, "We are still in danger!"

He fed the words his signet ring was sending him to an annunciator: *The plutonian warpcore is still active. The world-vampire must have programmed a final action. Tachyon echoes reveal an immense amplification of local gravitational force. It is asymmetrical, and being used to propel Pluto...*

But they saw it happening. The dark sky behind Pluto, from their point of view, reddened and puckered strangely, while Pluto shrank. The flames turned dark red and ceased to move as time slowed. Any remaining glaciers, hills, seas of burning methane or clouds of burning oxygen now flattened into a smooth, mirror-like surface. Pluto turned black, shrank to a tiny sphere, and vanished from sight.

But as it shrank it darted toward the planet Saturn, accelerating.

Aeneas raised his ring and issued commands to the Talos warpcore, and uttered a ragged cry of horror. "It's not working! The plutonian warpcore is still active—the enemy has established a zone of space I cannot collapse or manipulate!"

They watched in helpless horror as the singularity passed into the gas giant and struck the north pole. The singularity itself was invisible, but the point of impact was visible.

The surface of Saturn puckered and distorted. The cloud bands of Saturn were pulled up as the singularity approached, swirled together in an immense spiral toward a burning point of nothingness.

Then the floating continents of the struck hemisphere were pulled up and toward the singularity in a vast curving archipelago of destruction.

The damage came not from the gravity, for the singularity was only the mass of Pluto, nor from the threat of Saturn being consumed, for the surface area of the event horizon was only a few acres. The damage came from the matter of Saturn being disintegrated under tidal stress as it was pulled into the pinpoint of superdense nonbeing, heated to plasma, and released as x-rays and gamma rays and high energy particles: the atmosphere of Saturn was irradiated and superheated.

Vents of gas erupted in huge arcs up into space and back down again. The hydrogen ignited and burned blue, and then, heated even hotter, began to fuse. An irregular cloud of solar plasma with limbs of fire like a burning kraken erupted into being in the center of the collapsing hemisphere of Saturn.

All the billions of men living on the flying continents near the point of impact were killed instantly as white-hot x-rays passed through the area, ionizing atoms, breaking chemical bonds, fusing atoms. The heat released simply obliterated anything made of matter, including the containment vessels for powerhouses and space contortion fields that were part of modern, civilized life. The ignition of these captive energies, now freed, added fire to fire. The continent-sized habitats in the southern hemisphere which were farther from the point of impact drifted serenely for the long moment before the supersonic shockwave passed the equator and converged.

Nothing on Earth had ever been as large as this semisolid wall of winds. A hundred Earths could have wandered, lost, in the immensity of Saturn's atmosphere, and never been in sight of each other. Flying continents larger than the whole surface area of Earth were upended.

The continents were overturned by the pressure, crumbled under the stress. Seen from space, the lights of famous cities could be seen to go dark, as swiftly as if a cloak had been thrown across a constellation and smothered it. The smaller lights of floating palaces and pleasure craft drifting in the serene cloud-filled abyss were extinguished without being noticed.

For a moment, the planet Saturn seemed to be like a fruit with a large bite taken out of it, or like a small, burning star with a hemisphere of gaseous matter poised like a shell over the southern half of it. Then the edges of the globe collapsed inward toward the burning star, pulled by the mass, which, albeit compressed, had not disappeared. Like a cresting wave breaking, the rim of matter overhanging the bottomless bright well of the singularity fell inward. The violence of this fall, the tidal stress, and the agitation from the accretion disk broke the atoms into their subatomic constituents. As the singularity ate further and further into the boiling liquid heart of Saturn, the collapsing rim ignited into atomic fire.

Aeneas, his face white and sweat-slick with stress, tried again and again to warp the timespace and hinder these disastrous effects. He tried to set warps around the moons and pull them away, or change the rate of propagation of light to preserve them from the gamma ray and x-ray bombardment. Nothing worked. The moons were scalded like cinders, and their artificial atmospheres blown out into space by the sheer radiation pressure issuing from the dying world.

Each cubic mile of Saturn's immense ocean of atmosphere could sustain many more people than Earth at her most overcrowded. Aeneas was appalled, for he was unable to imagine, unable to grasp, the numbers who had just died: husbands, wives, children, caught without warning in the midst of work and play.

10

HATRED FOR ALL LIFE

Aeneas said, "If I can figure out how the enemy folded the space here, I can undo it, and maybe I can warp some of the flying continents on the farther hemisphere to Uranus or Jupiter... a chance to live..."

But Lord Saturn, his face as motionless as the face of a dead man, said, "Leave them."

Aeneas jerked, and stared at him in wordless wonder.

"Abandon them," said Lord Saturn. "The singularity was not meant for my world. It was sent toward the sun, and it is accelerating."

Lord Pluto said, "Once it passes lightspeed, you will not be able to see or stop it. You must stop it now."

"How?" shouted Aeneas. "A protective zone of flat space prevents me from forming a warp anywhere near!"

Lord Saturn said, "Then form one far away. Pick up the neutron star called the Great Eye and place it in the path of the singularity before it strikes our sun, and completes the work of obliterating all my brother's worlds as it has done with mine."

Aeneas said, "But if any of your people are still alive..."

"The remnant of Saturn will not outlive the death of our star."

Aeneas said, "I am drained. I don't have the power to move the Great Eye."

Saturn said, "I am turning over to you control of the remaining energy production stations, space contortion dynamos, and power-houses through the rings and moons and satellites. They will not last long. Use them wisely, my lord Emperor." He drew a deep and ragged breath. "Save the people!"

This amount of energy was not negligible: the original warpcore had been powered by the output of the four gas giants, and the contributions of minor planets, worldlets, and moons. This was roughly an eighth of that.

But it was enough.

Aeneas, his face grim, issued the orders to the Talos warpcore. Signals issued to quantum entangled particle-pairs inside and outside the spherical singularity altered their mutual frames of reference. The Tipler rings raced. The lightcone of timespace in the immediate area was tilted by the frame-dragging effect. A closed timelike curve segment was formed between the Great Eye, and a point just beyond the dying Saturn.

A blue-white dot emerged, dazzling, and swelled into the immensity of the Great Eye. The invisible singularity must have emerged from the far hemisphere of Saturn, for the burning mass of its accretion disk, and the immense gravitic distortion glowing like a dull coal, reached out from the ruins of Saturn and struck square into the center of the Great Eye.

The surface distorted and puckered when the unseen pinpoint of nothingness intersected it. Concentric rings of fission and tidal stress ignition surrounded the point of impact. But the neutronium was not so easily pulled into the event horizon as the high-pressure liquid atmosphere of Saturn. The neutron star formed a crater for a moment, with a momentary mountain of neutronium lava midmost, but the immense gravity pulled the surface features flat again.

And the great scream of the Eye came again. Anyone left alive on Saturn's moons or orbital space stations no doubt was writhing on the floor. The plutonian vampire must have preset the warpcore of Pluto to catch and amplify it, because the tachyon sensors detected a faster-than-light signal carrying that shout of alarm toward all the nearby stars.

His signet ring, without waiting to ask, had the warpcore establish a thought-free zone around Aeneas, but hollow rather than solid, so that he could still give commands to his ring, which could send them out electronically.

On the analytical screen, Aeneas could see the gravity well of the singularity at the center of the neutron star. He made slight adjustments. Aeneas placed the singularity at the neutron star's burning center at the correct distance to pull the plutonian singularity's path into a parabola, then into a circle, then into an ever-narrowing spiral.

The two event horizons in the middle of a mass of molten neutronium spiraled together, and merged. The combined singularity spun faster and faster, like a spinning iceskater who draws her outflung arms together.

He turned his attention back toward the dying gas giant. Wherever he could detect life-energy, he formed a warp, and teleported the land mass involved to the corresponding depth in the atmosphere of Jupiter, along with a generous volume of the specialized oxynitrogen clouds terraformers had designed to grant the floating landscape Earthly temperature and pressure, and to protect Earthlife from the surrounding ultracold high-pressure helium or methane.

Tears started leaking, unnoticed, along the cheeks of Aeneas' stern face. It was so few. Out of the countless trillions who once had lived in the immensities of Saturn, so few were left. Perhaps the miraculous superscience of the present age could save bodies horribly burnt by x-rays and gamma rays, but perhaps not, not if the damage were too severe. There were a few more left alive at the outer moons. Aeneas left them where they were, for the mass of Saturn was the same. Despite the magnitude of the disaster, the orbits of the moons had not been disturbed.

Gently, he returned the broken corpse of the gas giant to its proper location in its orbit, the right distance from the sun for surviving terraformers on the half-burned and blasted moons to restore their environments.

Lord Saturn said, "My wife, my children… they had contortion pearls. Security insisted they carry them at all times. Many of my officers, courtiers, friends… and there were public teleportation circuits for the common people…"

Aeneas said, "The enemy flattened the space and prevented the formation of any contortions. I could have counteracted it, if I had only had enough power, enough mass. But I was using the power from Necropolis, and that was stolen, turned against me…. Sir, I… no one could have used a pearl to escape. The way was blocked."

Saturn sobbed, "But why? Why, even as it was dying, would the monster bother erecting such a block? Merely to prevent victims from escaping? There were no military targets! It is so malign, so pointless, so…"

Lady Luna, who had watched the whole disaster wide eyed, now laid a gentle hand on Lord Saturn's shoulder. "I have seen their dreams. They are consumed with a hatred for all life. They need us and despise us. Perhaps, at one time, in ages long ago, they kept alive certain living things as food sources. But always, sooner or later, their hatred and jealousy of life overcame them, and they consumed and destroyed it all, even what they needed for themselves. Ours may be the last living star in the galaxy."

Lord Saturn sank down on one knee before Aeneas. "What you compelled from me before, my sovereign lord, I now freely offer. Lord Tellus passed his knowledge to you. It must have been him: there is no one else who knew the superluminary science! Let not my people have died in vain!"

Aeneas felt the pull of temptation. The splendor and pomp that could be his for the asking! No, he did not need to ask. It would be pushed into his hands. Then he could command his uncles, or step on the neck of Lord Mars! Any of his fair cousins, he could ask to be his queen... or, following the lawlessness of Lord Tellus himself, he could gather as many wives and concubines as Solomon...

Raw self-loathing shocked him back to his senses. Is this what drove Lord Tellus mad, in the end? When even a sober man is given so much power, power to escape all punishment, all retaliation, will he always lose the ability to tell right from wrong?

There, in his eye, was the burning wreckage of a world, collapsed to half its former volume, bright with burning fires in its methane layers, its core now a neutronium ball mere yards in diameter. Saturn had been one of the brightest jewels in the Solar System, a center for art, contemplation, and culture unparalleled in history. There were not even bodies to recover! All obliterated, now, due to the dying malice of a sick-minded undead creature. That was what evil looked like, when let free of the cage of conscience.

Aeneas said to Saturn, "To your feet, Uncle Geras! Do not bow to me! I will teach everyone my art. We will *all* be Lord Tellus!"

But Lord Saturn did not stand. "To whom will the secret be given?"

Aeneas was puzzled. "What do you mean?"

"That black stealthship! Who was aboard? Whoever it was, he is in league with the space vampires, and has known of them for over fifteen years."

Aeneas shook his head. He could not truly grasp the idea that someone would betray his family, his species, his kingdom, his very condition of being.

Lord Saturn stood up. "Each of the Twelve controls a supertechnology known only to himself. Moreover, you have nine brothers and four sisters, and Hermaphrodita, who is both. You have two hundred cousins and twenty nieces and nephews. Then there are the five Empress Dowagers. All of the second and third generation are armed with the basic stratonic technologies we keep within the family, including enough photonics, kinetics, and contortion science to have made that black stealthship. Any of them could have been aboard. So who is the traitor? Who can you trust?"

Aeneas said, "You, Lady Luna, and Lord Pluto were here with me the whole time."

Lord Pluto spoke up. His voice was cold and remote. "I could have arranged all this, or operated the ship by remote control. Lord Saturn likewise. You have not learned the lesson of mistrust I imparted earlier. The family is not to be trusted."

Lady Luna looked shocked. She said sharply, "Lord Saturn is above suspicion! Not only has he lost friends and family this day, but if he were the captain of the stealthship, he could have hidden the ship from us by merely *not* finding her with his machine, which only he controls! Absurd to suspect him!"

Lord Pluto said, "The human heart is dark. It is not impossible that men should slay wives and children, or kill a thousand billion of souls, if the goal was to obtain immense and untrammeled power over all other men. Before Lord Tellus imposed peace by terror on mankind, this was commonplace."

Lord Saturn, standing, was tall enough to look the seated Aeneas straight in the eye. "Imperial Majesty, you must not abdicate the power which the madness of fate or the madness of Lord Tellus has imposed on you. I saw you act with speed and compassion, and save all mankind this day. If you lead, I have some hope of vengeance and retaliation against the foe. If you give your knowledge to the traitor, there is none. And you dare not share your knowledge until the traitor is found. The only way I can prove that I am not he is to insist that I never learn the secret of the superluminary science!"

Lady Luna said, "It will have to be shared eventually. But I think Lord Saturn speaks reason. Teach me last, after everyone else in the family." Suddenly she looked woebegone. "I mean Uncle Geras. I– I suppose he cannot be called Lord Saturn, now that the planet is destroyed. And as for how many cousins you have—we don't know." She began sobbing.

Lord Pluto said, "It is a smaller world, but of the same mass. Saturn can be terraformed."

Lady Luna gritted her teeth, angry beneath her tears. "Uncle Darius, sometimes you are heartless! Now is not the time to speak of that!"

Aeneas said, "Not just the family."

Lady Luna said, "What?"

Aeneas said, "I intend to give this secret to each and every man of every race of mankind, on every world, worldlet, moon and asteroid of the solar system."

Lord Pluto said, "In our family, perhaps, with risk, you could bestow the power to slay worlds without mankind being slain. But on all mankind, wise and foolish, sane and mad? You saw what one creature armed with warptech did. Extinction is sure."

Lord Saturn said, "No matter the numbers: if you make the secret public, the traitor knows it."

Lord Pluto turned his lens toward Aeneas, "Can you recover the plutonian warpcore from the center of the Great Eye?"

Aeneas turned his screen toward the dead sun, and Lady Luna stiffened. She spoke in a trembling voice kept level by an effort of will. "My instruments detect something—a ghost, a fragment—the scream the Great Eye sent is being answered. It is but a single concept, but it hangs in the dreams of the dead sun like a word echoing in an empty hall. Reinforcements."

She turned to Aeneas. "The vampire lords of the nearby stars know that life still lingers here, in our solar system. They are stirring from their sleep. The darkness is rising!"

11

THE THREE-HEADED THRONE

To Aeneas's surprise, both the plutonian warpcore and that hidden in the Great Eye were salvageable. The measurements of the distortions to the fabric of space tachyonic sensors provided could locate the vertical gravity wells of the two hollow singularities orbiting each other at the superdense neutronium-liquid core of the neutron star.

Thanks to the bizarre disjunction possible between two frames of reference with no common elements whereby one could measure the mass, volume, or location of the other, Aeneas was able to form a warp which moved the two working warpcores into the very center of his. The singularities were nested, one within the next, all balanced precisely at the barycenter of his Tipler rings.

Aeneas said, "If we park Mercury, Venus, Earth, and Mars in orbit around the Gas Giants, the three warpcores may be enough to move Jupiter, Uranus, and Neptune."

Lady Luna asked, "Move them... where?"

Lord Pluto stood up from the wardroom table where he had been sitting. "Father must have known. The reason he never revealed the secret of faster-than-light drive to the family was this: the stars are filled with vampires. Yet space is immense, boundless, infinite. There will be a place to find."

Lady Luna said, "…a place…? For what? You are kidding! The light of Sol keeps them at bay. Even the Great Eye was instantly obliterated!"

Aeneas said, "Our position is known, and indefensible. Vampire planets and stars placed in the Oort Cloud, beyond Sol's reach, could bombard us with waves of worlds like Pluto once was, or Baptistina. We have to abandon the Solar System. We are fleeing, and taking all our worlds with us."

Lord Pluto turned to Aeneas, and said solemnly, "I also accept you as my Emperor and vow my fealty to you. You are the protector of the people. What are your orders, Majesty?"

Aeneas said, "My first command is that you tell me how Lady Luna blackmailed you."

The blank, one-eyed, dull gray helmet nodded slowly. He held up his signet ring. "Lord Saturn and Lady Luna can neither see nor hear us."

Aeneas looked around. There was no difference in sight or sound, he still seemed visible to himself.

Lord Pluto said in his cold voice: "Lord Tellus is alive. I do not know where he is or how he stays alive. He communicates orders to me. I obey him."

"W–What?!"

"Lady Luna saw me dreaming in Everest, when Lord Tellus sent a message into my sleeping brain to wake me, to warn me you were being attacked. He told me of other events to come. I retreated immediately to my world, to await your advent and do his will."

Aeneas said, "Then the voice I heard on Pluto…? The one telling you to spare my life?"

"Was his. He was there, unseen."

For a moment, Aeneas was speechless. "Everyone thinks Grandfather flew off to the stars."

"Perhaps he did. You now know what he found."

"Why make me his heir? Why save me?"

"I do not know. But when a body charged with death-energy, like a vampire is, entered your room, the pearl meant to cover your escape became visible to you. Thoon was still alive beneath a layer of vampire cells embedded in his skin, and so he could exist on a planet so close to our sun. But the amount of vampirism was enough to trigger automatic defenses Lord Tellus long ago established, and set all things in motion."

Aeneas sat, frowning in thought. "Do you mean Grandfather meant to provoke a war between the Empire of Man and the space vampires?"

Lord Pluto said, "Because the war had already started, albeit in secret. Whoever seduced Thoon away from your cause is in league with the vampires, for he used vampire technology more advanced than anything I know, and I am lord of the dead."

Aeneas said, "Your brothers would kill you, if they knew you served him. Grandfather is insane. You still obey him? Why do it? Why risk it?"

Pluto's helmet turned left and right as he shook his head. "My motives are my own. Leave them be."

Aeneas said, "Did you know about the space vampires?"

"Only the one on Pluto. Year upon year I stood guard alone. My mission was to prevent its reanimation. I failed."

Aeneas said, "Very well. I trust you: I accept your fealty. Make us visible again."

Lord Saturn and Lady Luna both flinched, startled, at the reappearance of Aeneas and Pluto. Aeneas said to them, "Time is short. We have visited two star systems. Both had arms and armaments enough to crush the Solar System easily. Both had warpcore technology to allow them to travel here instantaneously. However, both were comatose, entirely drained of the death energy which powers their civilization. Evidence suggests that higher overlords seated at other star systems drained them. Therefore, it is safe to assume the invasion will require time to organize, but unsafe to assume it will take long. We must organize the whole solar system for exodus."

Lord Pluto said, "Majesty, the family will oppose you, and seek your death."

Aeneas stared at him in wonder. "Impossible! The solar system just saw two worlds destroyed!"

Lady Luna said, "It will be five and a half hours before the inner planets see the battle. And any gas giants on the far side of the sun, forty minutes to four hours longer yet."

Aeneas said, "Then let us visit Venus first. Mother is persuasive."

Lord Saturn said, "Too persuasive, Your Majesty. She will take over your mind and take your power for herself."

Aeneas said incredulously, "Her own son?"

Saturn said, "She can always have more sons. There is only one throne."

The planet Saturn had lost half his volume but none of his mass. Heat from the cataclysms still burned and glowed through the immense cloud layers. Since the black hole had passed through the globe from north pole to south, the ring system was untouched. The burnt and blackened orbs of the many moons retained their old orbits, and now the four inhabited moons of Pluto were placed in orbit around Saturn, as well as the asteroid Talos. Saturn and the undead planet Necropolis were placed in orbit about the Great Eye and parked in the orbit Saturn once occupied.

Charon, that silent monument to Cora, Lord Pluto's dead wife, was left in place in orbit, a marker for the vanished planet Pluto.

Aeneas gave the command. Saturn and its moons vanished from normal timespace and reappeared next to the sun, in the Lagrange Two point, with bright Venus in transition before the bright, burning face of Sol.

The planet Venus was the only world that, from space, retained something of her original appearance. All other worlds and moons in the solar system were the white and blue of Earth. Venus had been terraformed differently, with countless swarms of tiny flat motes, black on one side and mirrored on the other, that hovered in the cloud layers, reflecting or absorbing solar heat, and producing a layer of Earthly cool beneath the hellishly hot Venusian cloud layer.

Aeneas lowered the asteroid Talos quickly through the cloud layer. A mist of vapor hung about the flying mountain as it flew down, clouds about its peak. Beneath, as a walled garden in the midst of a hot desert, were the flowering mountains and purple seas of Venus.

The floating city of Cyprianople, like a jeweled crab, was submerged in one of her shallow oceans at the moment, and many jeweled towers, outbuildings, and coracles of the suburbia outside the city dome were either sailing the surface, or hanging in the perfumed air above the gleaming capital city.

Decorative flowers the size of freighters floated on the purple waves as well, and mermaids and sea serpents sported in the waves. The sun was a vast, blurred, bright shadow igniting the cloudbanks that hid it. The reflections from the restless waves formed a moving web of light flicking on the bellies of the clouds above, like the reflection seen on the ceiling above an indoor swimming pool.

Mermaids on the backs of dolphins blew on horns and called up to the floating mountain of Talos, demanding of the intruders to declare their business. Aeneas grimaced with impatience. He asked his ring to call her ring, but there was no response. "Lord Pluto, didn't you have a telephone or something to talk to my mother, without going through her footmen and press secretaries?"

Lord Pluto said, "Your Majesty, if I knew where she was, I could take you to her, unseen by all her guards."

Lady Luna said, "Remember, your mother does not know if you are alive, or are a puppet controlled by someone else, or whether you mean her harm."

Aeneas established the parameters needed to fold space and fling the planet Venus into the orbit of Pluto. He gritted his teeth and fought back the temptation to give the command. He said, "Are you afraid of my mother taking over your brain?"

Lady Luna said, "No. I sometimes worry she did it long ago, when I was her apprentice. Do you want me to go down and act as your minister plenipotentiary, and negotiate arrangements for you to land?"

Lord Pluto said, "You must assume that the Lady Luna who returns will be under your mother's mind control, and treat her accordingly thereafter, as a threat or sleeper agent."

Lord Saturn said, "Majesty, your mother has led a very sordid and dissolute life, and I have gathered from nights long past an extensive file of her indiscretions. She would not dare move against you. So, if you wish…"

Aeneas said, "I wish you not to finish that sentence. My first decree as Emperor Hypocritus the First is that this insane family squabbling, backstabbing, and mistrust must cease forthwith, *post haste*, *in toto*, and *ad infinitum*!"

Lord Saturn blinked in confusion. "Is– is that really to be your official name, Majesty?"

Aeneas waited no more. He ordered a pearl thrown down from Talos, and contorted into the sea. He landed in the water, and found himself surrounded by mermaids and tiny gem-sized robotic insects. "I am Aeneas, Emperor of Man. My mother wants to see me. Take me to her."

With the mermaids was Beroe. She had been designed in the womb to be the most beautiful of women, but she wore no ornaments nor make-up, and never studied herself in a mirror. She said, "Little brother, Lady Venus says it is not meet that the emperor should come to his handmaiden. She will come to you. While you were gone, she built a palace with a roof of coral and pillars of nacre atop Mons Metis and there placed a throne to await your coming. Will you go?" And she offered him a pearl.

The voice of Lord Pluto spoke in his ear: "Majesty, it is folly to trust an untried pearl. You could be sent into a jailcell or execution chamber." But Aeneas took the pearl in hand. The universe dwindled to a point and expanded into a new scene. Beroe stood in an immense bright and airy space, beneath a dome upheld by antigravity beams, like a sky of gold. Countless acres of windows looked out upon the heavens of Venus, a larger sky of silver. Stairs of blue chalcedony and iridescent silver-blue corborundum led up to a dais of red coral and pink tourmaline. A semicircle of slender pillars stood behind. Atop was a throne of black onyx whose capital was carven with the heads of three wolves. One head bore a coronet, one a miter, and one a mortarboard.

Standing to either side of the stairs were nymphs and graces, dryads and hamadryads, puttoes and genii, nereides and oceanids, who were of the various races created by Lady Venus. All the ladies curtseyed, and each putto or genius bowed.

"The throne is yours, brother," said Beroe softly. "Be pleased to sit. Lady Venus is summoned."

Aeneas looked up the long staircase with a sigh of annoyance, and seated himself on the lowest step, elbows on knees, frowning down at his feet.

12

THE LADY OF LOVE

Lady Venus arrived in a sedan chair carried by swans. She landed, and curtseyed, putting her crowned head very low to the shining floor, but her maidens put their heads lower yet. Her face was serene, but Aeneas could see the glint of anger in her eyes.

"Freely I offer my fealty, my lord Emperor. Yours is to command, Imperial Majesty, and mine to obey," she said.

Aeneas did not rise from where he slouched. "And what of democracy?"

Venus rose. "This moment is historic, and you sit like a sack of potatoes. I will have to erase the memories of all my servants and rewrite them, if history is not to mock us."

Aeneas stood, his face black with wrath. "You shall never do so! You will not touch a single brain cell of any soul here!"

Venus smiled her winning smile. "Do you protect the people? That is the task of the Emperor."

Aeneas said, "We are in the midst of an emergency. A nightmarish horror from the stars has come to obliterate us with overwhelming force. We have no chance of fighting them, and only a slender chance to survive. We must move all our worlds to another star system."

Her normal self-control slipped. A look of wonder was on her face. "You— you have such power...?"

"Yes, and more."

"But I thought Father's secret only was to build starships!" She shook her head and shivered. "But I am glad it is you who have it. You are foolish, but not wicked. You will make a fair and stern Emperor."

"I am not Emperor! Aren't you listening? There is no time to debate!"

Venus said, "If there is no time to debate, then there is no time for democracy. Who will dictate commands in the meanwhile? You are emperor whether you say so or not. You might as well say so."

All the ladies in the room cheered. It was a high-pitched, sweet sound, and it rang from the golden dome above. Many voices hailed him as Emperor.

Aeneas shouted at them, "Stop this nonsense!"

The ladies were of many ages, but in appearance were in the first bloom of maidenhood. These maidens quailed, blushing with shock, bowing their heads nervously, faces hidden behind fans, teary-eyed.

Lady Venus held up her hand, "My ladies, if you would give us some privacy, please?"

It took several minutes for the lovelies gathered there to curtsey and walk away, graceful as dreams in their shining peacock-bright gowns, glittering in gems. Beroe, his sister, more beautiful than all the others, unadorned in her plain white dress, also curtseyed and departed.

Lady Venus strode with dignified yet graceful step up to the black three-headed throne. Aeneas, unwilling to shout after her, perforce rose and walked after, taking two steps at a stride with his long legs.

She said, "I had this throne spirited away by stealth from Ultrapolis and brought here to await your coming, and this palace was built as a sign of my faith that you would return, to claim your rightful place, and set the Empire to rights. Turn, and look out there!" She pointed behind him.

He turned. "I see the purple sea strewn with flowers and the silver sky. I see towers floating in the heavens of Venus, and mansions shining in the sea."

She reached up to put her slender hands in his chest, and pushed. He was taken by surprise, and sat. Now he was in the throne.

Aeneas said, "Mother..."

She curtseyed, and then backed away, so that her feet were on the top step, not on the dais itself. She said, "Son, listen. This is the last time you will obey me as a mother! After today, I am your vassal and handmaiden! But listen. Do you know what happened while you were gone? Everyone but me thought you were dead, destroyed in some mishap of your terrible warpcore. Many suspected Lord Neptune had arranged your death in order to slay Lord Jupiter."

Aeneas squinted. "How could anyone believe that? Lords Uranus and Saturn support Neptune in every family gathering! And Lord Neptune would be outnumbered..."

Lady Venus said, "Yes. With those three gone, Neptune is alone, but he is opposed by three women, a child, and a monk." She meant herself and Ladies Ceres and Pallas, Lord Mercury, and Brother Beast of Earth. "Do you think the family would support Lord Mercury over Lord Neptune as emperor? Everyone hates the little pest. So Neptune had no support, but also no one who could stop him. He has placed gravitational amplifiers in orbit around every world, and threatens deluge and earthquake to those who will not bow."

Aeneas said, "Excellent!"

She said, "What?"

Aeneas said, "Those amplifiers should be able to create gravity wells deep and steep enough to allow my warpcores to grasp. Otherwise, I might not have the resources to needed to encompass the exodus of man."

She said, "And his claim to be next Emperor?"

Aeneas said, "It is nonsense for which there is no time. Besides, Lord Tellus is alive. I heard his voice on Pluto before it was destroyed."

She blinked. "What? Is Lord Pluto dead?"

"Pluto is dead, the planet. The man is still alive. Pluto the planet was a weapon, launched in the dinosaur age, but wounded by too close an approach to our sun, and the race of space vampires inhabiting it were all eaten by their leader, who melted, turned into an amoeba that covered the entire surface, and then froze. This planet-wide glacier amoeba space vampire then woke up when a traitor in the family fed it, it turned the planet Pluto into a black hole, and shot through planet Saturn trying to shoot the sun, killing a trillion people. But I stopped it before it struck the sun and killed us all."

Lady Venus took another step back from her son, and now stood a step lower on the stairs. She was breathing heavily, and her fingers were at her lips. She trembled. "Oh… my."

"Do you see why I have no time to debate Lord Neptune's silly claims? He wants to be cock of the roost and lord of the chicken coop, but the farmer with his ax and his dogs is about to enter the coop and kill every last bird."

Lady Venus touched one of her thought-ornaments and made some adjustment to her own brain. Calm returned to her face, and her eyes grew bright and forceful. She said, "If you are the only man in position to save us, then you must do what is necessary."

He said, "I would rather do what it right."

She said, "The idealistic and the pragmatic always wrestle in the minds of the young, but an ideal is like a blueprint, or a gene sequence. If it is not thought out correctly, you can build nothing real on it, nothing that lasts."

"What does that mean?"

"It means that like it or not, human mob psychology is what it is. It means you cannot lead all the people unless you act the part of a leader. These signs and symbols of authority, our titles, that throne, were not made by us to glorify ourselves. They were made by the people to glorify the leaders and saviors of the people. They were made by tradition, by all the normal folk who need to be reassured that the man they trust to save their lives is more than a mere man. The insignia of royalty are not irrational, not meaningless, not signs of power."

"What are they signs of?"

"Hope! The hope that the high command knows what it is doing, and can dig you out of hell!"

Aeneas scowled, but he had no answer. The idea was new to him.

She said, "Do you understand now why your talk of democracy and voting must cease? Nothing can be built with that blueprint, not at this point in history, not with the raw materials and tools available. I myself, just with the pantropy cells in my own palace, could give birth to ten thousand voters a month! The population of Jupiter's globe outnumbers all the rest of the planets together. How many voters could he build? And here are you, who apparently has the power to toss planets across the abyss like juggler's balls to other stars. Do you see?"

Aeneas said, "I see a tyranny that cannot last."

She said, "Politics is based on power. Whoever has the power picks the leader. Any era that picks a leader no power backs, the power will rise up and destroy.

"In some ages, the common man, because of his numbers, his common decency and common sense, had the power: democracy was for that age. In others, only the military had power, the Praetorian Guard, and who they picked to be commander in chief became emperor. In others, the wealthy families had the power, and the aristocracy selected the rulers, or selected a ruling family to pass the rulership from father to son. In more ancient times, in China and Mesopotamia, India and Egypt, the ruler was also worshipped as divine, and the priesthood had the power, because the conscience of the nation was in their hands.

"But the Forerunner supersciences changed all that. Now only one family has the power: the House of Tell. Our powers are indistinguishable from magic. We are a family of witches and warlocks, of demigods and demigoddesses. It is us you must convince to follow you, if you want to lead mankind to life! Us!

"If you don't act the part of Emperor, the empire will break and scatter. No one, no one, will trust one of my bastard children, a crazy boy who experiments on his own brains and fills his organs with geegaws, to carry his family and world to safety! They will only trust an Emperor!

"Emperors have dignity. They act with strength. They command.

"You are the one who called the human race chickens: …well, then? If you cannot get the chicks to line up in order and stop the hens from cackling, all the birds will be scared and will scatter, and the farmer will find them one by one. You need the family behind you! Therefore you must be in front. Be Emperor! Otherwise, the worlds will lose hope, and panic."

Aeneas shook his head. There had to be something wrong with what his mother was saying, but he could not put his finger on the error.

She said, "Did you not demand the family not to be ruled by fear when they were debating whether to kill you? Were you not right to make that demand?"

He said, "And you told them that I did not have the warptech imprint. And then you told them you would make me into a zombie!"

She shrugged. "The first was a lie, the second a half truth. They were trying to kill my son! You might be an idealist who thinks it better to watch one's child die than to sully one's tongue to tell a lie, but I am not."

He said, "But you are the boy who cried wolf. Now that there are real wolves out there, among the stars, thirsty for our blood, who will heed you?"

She smiled and her eyes twinkled. It was a look he recognized, a look of love and romance, and so he groaned. She said brightly, "Lord Mars will hear me! I will call him here to swear to you! He has been neutral until now. But if he hears and believes your word, now that you have killed Lord Jupiter—that is a show of strength from you even I did not expect!—then Lord Neptune will have no choice but to be cowed!"

"He's not dead."

"Imprisoned? Even better. You are daring."

Aeneas rubbed his temples. "Please call Lord Mars. How long will it take?"

"Less than half an hour."

"Time enough. While we await him, I will move Earth, Venus, Mercury and Mars into orbit around Uranus, Neptune and Jupiter. Call the terraformers on each world stand by to adjust the atmospheric temperature as the distance from the sun changes."

13

THE EXTINCTION OF SOL

Thucydides Tell, Lord Mars, was as naked as a jaybird and as scarlet as cardinal. He wore black sandals and a diamond-studded weapon belt. Pistol and longsword hung at his hip. His torch-red hair was clasped at his neck in a short tail. His eyes were deep-set, unwinking, cold as painted orbs of glass.

He stepped out of a contortion pearl, came into the gold-domed presence chamber Lady Venus had erected. He looked up at Aeneas on his black throne, and his expression did not change or flicker, no more than a face of carven stone would have.

Lady Venus started a flowery and formal greeting, calling him by several titles, but Aeneas interrupted her to speak of the approaching enemy. Lord Mars interrupted him in turn, holding up his thin, red-colored hand.

"For many years, I knew Father had an enemy he feared, and knew it to be extrasolar. I knew using the faster-than-light drive would trigger a war, because, otherwise, he would have shared the secret with one of us. Majesty, I await your orders."

He knelt and drew his sword and tossed it to the bright floor, where the blade rang like crystal chimes.

Aeneas said, "Just like that? You just declare me emperor, and vow to serve me? Don't I get a vote?"

Lord Mars said, "No, Majesty. No vote for you. None for me. I await your orders."

"And if I order you into jail for having assaulted me, stepped on me, and conspired with others to erase my mind?"

"Then I obey and go while you waste a needed vassal," said he, still on one knee, speaking without a smile. "Your Majesty."

Aeneas said, "Very well, but you don't need to bow and scrape to me."

"No, Majesty. I do. That should have been explained to you by Nephelethea." He nodded toward Lady Venus, a fond look in his eye.

Aeneas realized that these two must have long ago planned out what they would say to him when he reappeared.

Aeneas leaned back on the throne, noting how uncomfortable it felt. "You two have some plan to bring the other Lords of Creation to accept my leadership?"

Lady Venus rolled her big, long-lashed eyes toward the golden ceiling overhead, and looked innocent. "No, not really… not a *plan* plan…. Just some ideas really…"

Lord Mars said, "We have a plan. Did you kill Lords Saturn and Uranus? Both disappeared when you vanished. What about Pluto? And the new kid?"

"No. Saturn and Pluto support me. Lady Luna also."

"Have them stand to either side of your throne when you summon Lord Mercury to come and bow. He fears Lord Saturn. Pluto, too. Once Mercury swears, Lord Neptune will be alone. Have you killed Lord Jupiter?"

"No."

"Kill him."

"No."

Lord Mars shrugged. "It is your battle. If you want to fight with one arm broken, it is your funeral. And the funeral of everyone who follows you."

Aeneas templed his fingers. "You have always before stayed aloof from family politics. Why?"

Lord Mars said, "I don't step into family squabbles for the same reason I don't step in quicksand."

"You are aware that Father knows of some terrible outside enemy?"

Lord Mars nodded. "There are no radio signals of intelligent life ever heard from any stars. Something happened to them. Father fears that something."

Aeneas said, "I have met that enemy. They are vast and terrible, and we have very few ways to fight them, and little time. Do you think mankind has a better chance with Lord Jupiter in the battle, or in the quicksand you mentioned?"

"And if he kills you first?" asked Lord Mars.

Aeneas said, "Then you are free from an inexperienced and reluctant Emperor. I will send Lord Saturn to collect Lord Mercury. You go bring Lord Neptune to me. They may both be willing to answer the summons once they realize their planets are now all gathered into the shadow of the undead neutron star." And he sent pre-arranged thought signals through his ring to Talos, and the warpcore there. The twin cores inside the neutron star responded.

The silver-white sky of Venus suddenly blazed white, turned red as a coal, and then went black, as it passed through a closed timelike curve and took up a new position. The silvery light of the sun seen through the swaddling cloud layers returned, but much dimmer.

Lady Venus looked startled for a moment, and then smiled a small smile of motherly pride.

Lady Luna next arrived. She apparently intended to make an impressive show of her entrance, for a great escort of moon-maidens, hounds, and antlered stags from the moon, as well as anctitones and acephals, lunarians and selenites and fierce centaurs called Vagas flanked and followed her, and the music of lute, flute, silver bells, and clashing cymbals preceded her.

Aeneas asked her to stand to his right by the black throne. When he turned to his left, the second place of honor, he saw that Lord Pluto, who had arrived alone and without a sound, was already standing there. A black cloak hid Pluto's unadorned armor. The single lens in the brow of his unadorned helm glinted.

Lord Saturn, gray and old, garbed in silver, arrived with his surviving children in his entourage: the Lords Janus, Mimas, Encledes, and Iapetus, and the Ladies Tethys, Dione, Rhea and Phoebe.

He escorted a sullen Lord Mercury, chubby and childlike, dressed in lace and livery. With him were officers and dukes of the two dominant races of Mercury, the first called demons, for their stubby radio horns they grew from their skulls, the others called witches, for their miter-shaped skulls, hooked noses, pointed chins.

Lady Venus returned in state with all her maidens, doves, and winged children. She brought the news that Lord Neptune would not remove himself from his citadel at Aegei. This was his armored palace resting on the ammonia ice bed of Neptune below the miles of unthinkably cold and unbearably pressurized oceans of liquid helium, water, methane, and ammonia: ocean below ocean, each according to its density and freezing point. However, Amphitrite Lady Naiad, his wife, had come in his stead.

The Neptunian queen was dressed in silver and blue. The bodice and skirts of her garb was liquid water bound with gravitational microfields so that it flowed and fell about her shapely limbs like a fabric of silk.

Aeneas said to the court, "I have placed Earth in orbit about the fragment of Saturn, Venus around Uranus, Mercury about Neptune, Mars about Jupiter."

The courtiers stirred uneasily, albeit some smiled. All in the chamber clearly saw the political overtones to this division of worlds and moons: Brother Beast, Lady Venus, and Lord Mercury were loyal partisan favoring Lord Jupiter, whereas Lord Mars was not. The outer gas giants now each had a hostile moon keeping an eye on it.

Aeneas continued: "All four gas giants are in the umbra of the neutron star, to shield us from the nova long enough to form a warpchannel to our next destination. The three working warpcores, I have placed at the centers of three of the three undamaged gas giants. I would have preferred to ask Lord Neptune for his permission, but if Lord Neptune wishes to perish, such permission is not necessary."

Aeneas nodded gravely to Amphitrite. "Lady Naiad: please inform your lord husband that both his fealty and the use of the gravitic amplifiers he has thoughtfully placed in orbit around the planets of the Empire of Man are required here."

She blenched. "Are you saying…"

Lord Mars said, "That is not the proper form of address!"

Lady Naiad curtseyed, gracefully, hands lifting her shining skirts of living waters, one foot behind the other, bending the knees, bowing her head. "Is Your Imperial Majesty saying he is going to destroy the planet Neptune?" She swallowed. "Sire?"

"I suppose I should speak in the plural when I speak on behalf of the empire, shouldn't I? *We* will not protect any world which does not need *our* protection. How does Lord Neptune plan to deal with the nova?"

Lady Naiad said, "How do you have such powers? It is madness!"

Aeneas clutched the black arms of the imperial throne. He grimaced. There was no seat less comfortable in any world. "A madman bestowed the power. We do what must be done to protect the people."

Lord Pluto raised his gauntlet. "Majesty, look to the skies. Alien forces are materializing."

The Lords of Creation looked to their signet rings and made mental contact with the various machines that served them. Dukes, counts, and others in the chamber opened bracelets or ornaments which hid phones.

Lady Venus said, "My orbital telescopes detect nothing!"

Aeneas said, "The light will not reach here for four hours. They are in the Oort Cloud, beyond the solar system. I will project the image for you."

The golden dome above lit up with an image. Here was the stark blackness of the fringe of interstellar space. There were comet heads and icebergs floating in the endless night. The cloud of icebergs formed a rough globe around the sun.

From the nadir to the zenith of that cloud of ice fragments, now appeared objects. First they seemed blue-white dots, but then they faded and swelled up to their real size. Neutron stars were here carved into staring eyeballs, or brown dwarves covered, as with oozing sores, with crevasses and volcano cones leading to interiors of still-active solar plasma. Here were magnetars spinning, with twin x-ray arms like turning scythes or beams from a lighthouse, ready to destroy whatever was in their path. Here were dark and cold gas giants, blue with methane, or ribbed and tiger-striped with storms.

As belts at their equators, many gas giants had a ring of iron moons, armored and roofed with weapons, or the severed heads of undead monsters of prodigious size. Of ringworld armatures coated with quadrillions of corpses, there were only four, equally spaced around the solar system at the points of an imaginary tetrahedron.

The great eye of Zeta Herculis would have been lost in the swarm of dark and mighty planets. Perhaps there were also orbital fortresses, superdreadnoughts, battlewagons, battleships, and war-moons scattered among the suns and gas giants, but, if so, they were like dustmotes lost against a mountain-range of countless peaks.

The signet ring of Aeneas sent: *Sir, the enemy is preparing to fire. The death energy build-up in the various neutron stars and brown dwarfs exceeds the total energy output of all planets in the solar system. Once those beams fire, no living thing will be left.*

Gasps of horror ran through the chamber as the great and staring eyes of the neutron stars, larger than worlds, larger than suns, opened their massive lids. An inner heat, doubtless caused by internal volcanic processes preliminary to firing, boiled the oceans filling the sclera of those eye-shaped weapons into space. Stream clouds larger than worlds achieved escape velocity, despite the immensity of the gravity of the dead suns. Black gas giants and superjovian bodies with belts of corpses orbiting them spun their armatures up to speed, vanished, and reappeared millions of mile closer. In the image, these faster-than-light motions made a gas giant appear at its destination before the light-image showing it vanishing in the distance reached the viewer, so that, for a moment, the number of space vampire battle worlds seemed to double.

Aeneas raised his hand. "I set off the nova hours ago. I am also flattening space in a fashion around us I hope will prevent the enemy from establishing a faster-than-light periscope of the type I am using. We may depart at our leisure. Lady Naiad, please ask Lord Neptune if he wants his world to accompany us? Lord Mercury, the same question is yours?"

Lord Mercury drew a black dagger and laid it carefully on the shining floor. "I am your vassal, Imperial Majesty."

Lord Neptune appeared out of a pearl in Lady Naiad's hand. With no word, but with his eyes blazing and his teeth clenched, the blue man slowly knelt to one knee. He cast his trident angrily to the floor, ringing.

Aeneas said, "Take up your blade in my name and in the name of the law, to preserve life against death."

The four gas giants with the lesser planets orbiting them vanished, a fact that the black fleet would not see for several hours. When they did, another sight would greet their eyes.

Sol reddened, grew lopsided, and, with the horrific slowness of vast disasters, began to expand, growing ever brighter as it did.

But by the time the light image of the nova was seen, the wavefront of neuropsionic particles deadly to unlife was already passing through space.

And the world fleet of the space vampires in their countless myriads fell silent, and all their dark suns.

14

THE OVERLORD OF UNLIFE

The heart of the galaxy was dark indeed, and burning with hellish fire.

The supermassive black hole at the core of the Milky Way galaxy was on the order of a billions times the mass of tiny, tiny Sol. Star systems venturing too near the unimaginably titanic gravity well slowed, reddened, shrank, and vanished from the frame of reference of outside observers, and no light nor radio signal escaped to tell their fate.

Human astronomers named this dark galactic core *Sagittarius A*. Most black holes are miles wide. This boasted a Schwarzschild radius the size of the orbit of Mercury.

Above the event horizon was the accretion disk, a smeared ring of plasma and shattered atoms. Above this was a globular cloud of rogue planets, giant and dwarf, torn from the grip of shattered solar systems unfortunate enough to have wandered too near the unseen galactic heart.

To behold a waterfall of gas giants toppling slowly into the red-burning accretion disk, pulled into the shape of eggs, teardrops, spears, as they fell, was a sight of sublime and awe-inspiring destruction. The stars falling were a vision more terrible, blushing red under the

Doppler shift. They grew oval and were torn into thin, fantastic rainbows of nova energy.

High above all this hellish burning were ten million stars of the galactic core. Between the two was a gap not unlike the Cassini division in the rings of Saturn, created by shepherd stars.

This division was occupied by a mighty work of engineering. Here was a spherical latticework two lightyears in diameter, surrounding the supermassive black hole like a cage. Hundreds of ringworlds and Tipler rings formed the cage bars, set apart far enough to allow falling solar systems to pass between.

The interstellar tractor beams which arranged a regular diet of such starfalls had long since gone dark. Lower ringworlds within the structure, long abandoned, were tattered and peeling, slowly being dismantled and fed into the accretion disk underfoot. The black core glowed like a red coal.

Had it been unbroken, the great sphere's surface area would have more than twelve square lightyears. Nonetheless, the ringworlds from pole to pole comprised one city, an astronomical super-megalopolis. Had the galaxy been filled with life, only such an absurdly vast structure would have been able to house overseers sufficient to bring order to so many stars.

No longer. The great sphere now was dark and cold. The empty apertures, gateways, and portholes of the airless buildings stared hungrily in all directions. The empty space elevators rose like weeds. Carriages and payloads hanging in linear accelerators meant to circle the meridians of the great sphere at near lightspeed were motionless.

No ringworld turned. No trace of air and ocean clinging to their inner faces remained. There was nothing to break the bleak monotony of fastnesses and fortresses, torture pits, feasthalls, slaughterhouses, storerooms, shipyards, workrooms, absorption temples, broadcast towers, powerhouses, observatories, archives, arsenals, energy stations.

At the north pole, a thicket of space elevators rose up in a tangle like thorny vines. At the peak, where all the conduits and paths converged, was a tower with a window. Here was the sole inhabitant of the dead astromegalopolis. Here a lamp burned. What it shed was not light.

The window was so large that visiting worlds, all gravity absolved, in times long past, once passed into the audience chamber without their rings and moons brushing the lintels. Now, crater impacts and radiation damage marred and discolored the frame.

In this window hung a servant in the shape of a mirrored sphere: Spherical, to conserve radiant heat loss; and mirrored, to reflect back to his master's eye only his master's own visage. No servant would boast he displayed his countenance to the Uttermost Overlord.

A beam of death energy from the interior of the chamber was shining on the sphere like a spotlight, pinning it in place.

The Overlord spoke not. Vampiric energy entered and extracted any desired information directly from the underling's brain, not without pain.

Had the communion been in words, it might have run like this:

"Your manservant makes obeisance, Uttermost Overlord. All souls are thine to consume."

"Let Warlord Rhazakhang, called the Initiator of Obliteration, be recognized. Let the matter of the star-system of Sol be discussed. Biological life was detected there. The planet Pluto was dispatched from Gamma Crucis ten million years ago to put an end to the matter."

"Overlord, Sol emits neuropsionics incompatible with anti-life. It is a holy star."

"How? All such stars were destroyed long since."

"Two possibilities, Overlord: a rebel element among us created Sol as an act of defiance, to secure to himself a food source for his gluttony; or else some lingering weapon of the Forerunners, forgotten in an ancient crypt in some dead star, stirred to life after eons, and created Sol as a sign of the downfall of us all."

"The name Evripades Zenon Telthexorthopolis, who styles himself Lord Tellus, intrudes itself into contemplation. There are one hundred billion stars in the Milky Way galaxy. Of those, how many do not serve, do not offer the tribute of souls? How many claim a lord of their own?"

"Only one, Overlord."

"As of last report, Lord Tellus had eliminated all life in the Solar System and reseeded and restocked it with creatures of his own devising, whom he told were his children. But his own origin is unclear."

"No new information presents itself on that matter, Overlord."

"The worlds of Sol are filled with life. Yet my feast table is empty."

"Vsasrhazing the Exsanguinator and Dzazanang the Ineluctable, whom my Overlord pleased to place within his manservant's larder and chain of command, carry the Uttermost Overlord's image and likeness of thy Malefic Visage against the prey animals of Sol."

"Why? What became of Ksthathranang, called the Expunger, and Gorgorthrog, called the Gnawer of Souls, who commanded the expedition? Where is Ylrm Ylrng the Mighty?"

"Lord Tellus, or one of his creatures, ignited Sol to a nova, while flattening space to prevent any faster-than-light readings from forewarning the vanguard of the Black Fleet. Ylrwm Ylrng, mistrusting his fighting slaves, was in the vanguard, and destroyed."

"Was any of his store of life energy recovered?"

"No, Overlord."

"The loss is mourned."

"Yes, Overlord."

"Such energy is irreplaceable."

"Indeed, Overlord."

"What of Ksthathranang?"

"He was more cautious, and hid from his slaves, that he might better detect and consume any who housed untoward thoughts against him. When the forward elements of the fleet were wiped out, however, his underlings in the rearguard discovered his hiding place and consumed him."

"Did you consume them in turn? Where is their energy?"

"Lost. Lord Tellus, or one of his creatures, rather cunningly erected a set of closed timelike curves around the expanding wavefront of the Sol nova, so that parts of the deadly light were teleported to points in space faster than light can naturally propagate. The underlings of Ksthathranang were taken unawares."

"And Gorgorthrog?"

"He was clever enough to send automatons into the light-sphere of Sol, hunting for the gas giants. Due to the space-flattening interference, no faster than light observation and communication near Sol is possible, and the flying gas giants must be found by sight."

"And the result?"

"The machine-life reported success and rendezvoused with Gorgorthrog's fleet, which then immediately vanished. He has not reported back. Fearing that he had betrayed me, and was hoarding and feasting, I signaled the loyalty-worms implanted in his brain to slay and drain him."

"Was any of his energy recovered?"

"A moiety. It was placed into my Overlord's storehouses."

"It is well. For that, you will not be slain at this time."

"My Overlord is indulgent."

"Is that why you allow factionalism among your ranks?"

"Yes, Overlord. Since my slaves know the least among them will be consumed by the foremost, all yearn with eagerness to be foremost."

"Allowing your slaves free will interferes with efficiency."

"This was an unexpected occasion. Coming so nigh to the living beings of Sol, my slaves grew gluttonous, and gave into the starvation madness. Precautions have been taken to prevent recurrence."

"What precautions?"

"Vsasrhazing and Dzazanang have had selected portions of their memories excised. They falsely believe that life energy is plentiful, and that this is merely an expedition to punish a minor disturbance."

"You grow arrogant. Whatever punishment I inflict on you, you will simply pass on to your servants in turn."

"The life of your servant is food of my Overlord, as are all lives. The arrogance of your servant is unfortunate, but may yet serve my Overlord."

"Because you will be too proud to allow defeat?"

"Because that arrogance lures your servant to hope that when the life energy of the living creatures of Tellus is divided, my Overlord will be generous to his most efficient servant."

"Your efficiency is not yet in evidence."

"The matter is under control, and will soon be concluded."

"How?"

"Lord Tellus, or one of his creatures, controls three gas giants with anchored warpcores. Whenever one of the Black Fleet approaches, the gas giants retreat behind the shockwave of Sol, which is expanding at the speed of light. However, the volume of space where they are protected is so small, and the speed of light so slow, that they have no chance of escape. They dare not leave the light."

"A siege."

"A temporary siege. Their warpcores lack the power to drive their worlds anywhere beyond forty lightyears. Within that volume the Black Fleet can detect any warp fissures as they form. Meanwhile, the neuropsionic radiation from Sol grows less in energy as it expands. Within twenty years, it will be no longer deadly to us."

"Twenty years?"

"Unliving beings have no need to be impatient. It has been four years since Sol ignited. The Tellurians live as vagabonds on flying worlds. They are alive, and will grow weary."

"And the nova? It is holy light."

"It is too small to be of concern. In all that time, only the nearest star system, Alpha Centauri, has been exposed to the deadly brightness."

"Was it evacuated?"

"No, Overlord. Alpha Centauri was drained of all life long since. Nothing of value was there."

The searchlight beam focused into a tighter, brighter line, and began to burn away the outer shells of Rhazakhang's substance. "My slave, you are mistaken. Your underling at Alpha Centauri had kept for himself a small horde of life energy. When he detected living beings from Tellus spying on him, he struck, and attempted to absorb them. This hoarding took place in your jurisdiction."

The pale sphere hovering in the window, trapped in the beam of light, radiated fear.

Rhazakhang emitted: "Alpha Centauri will be punished!"

"No need."

The Overlord now drove thoughts like red hot needles into the brain of Rhazakhang, showing him images from Alpha Centauri.

In four years, the shockwave of light from Sol crossed the four lightyear gap. In that same hour when Sol blazed bright in the night skies of the worlds of Alpha Centauri, the World Armada of Tellus arrived, to find all the vampires dead, all their equipment intact. The Tellurians spun the rings up to speed, and formed a timespace fissure reaching across ten thousand lightyears.

"Fool! In twenty years' time, while your fleets still searched within forty lightyears of Sol, they would be fled beyond reach."

Rhazakhang protested. "But– but– The Tellurians have no equipment, no resources! How did they impel the Alpha Centauri rings to motion?"

"The automaton battleworlds sent into the light by Gorgorthrog were compromised. He was lured into a ray from Sol, and the light dissolved him, leaving his worlds and all their cities intact… and power enough to work the rings of Alpha Centauri."

Rhazakhang released drops of life into his undead brain to sharpen his wits. "My Overlord has a betrayer among the Tellurians, who has told him all these events. If so, the betrayer surely told my Overlord the direction of the warpfissure! They cannot emerge into truespace save at some point along that line! All dirigible worlds and battle Dysons can scour the path of escape of the Living Creature World Armada. Let it be a cylinder forty lightyears radius with the warpfissure as the axis: no farther could the three gas giants depart the line."

The searchlight softened. "Now the efficiency of my servant is seen! You deduce correctly."

"What vector?"

The answer described a line reaching from Alpha Centauri and going toward the Ara Cluster, in the Zone of Avoidance.

Rhazakhang was impressed despite himself. The World Armada of Tellus was heading toward the core, where the power of the space vampires was greatest. It was the last direction any rational leader would have selected.

While it was true that the World Armada might drop back into normal spacetime at any point along the ultrathin line of warped space, it was also true that warpchannel reach was increased when a massive star was its endpoint. The Ara Cluster was a super star cluster, an open cluster of young stars, including half a score of yellow hypergiants and red supergiants.

Rhazakhang said, "Westerlund 1 is the destination, called Ara A." It was a red hypergiant star, one of the largest known, massive enough to quintuple the range of the modest Alpha Centauri rings. "We can arrive first, and trap the prey."

The searchlight beam displayed the Overlord's pleasure by feeding life energy into Rhazakhang. New strength poured into him.

And with it, a command: "Go! Display the Malefic Visage. Let all life cease. Let my feasthall again be full."

"All souls are thine."

15

THE UNHOLY LIGHT OF ARA A

Even among monsters, this star was a monster.

Over eleven thousand lightyears from Sol, Ara, the constellation of the altar, was between Scorpio and the Southern Triangle and held the Westerlund 1 super star cluster. The cluster held a large number of rare, evolved, high-mass stars, including two dozen Wolf-Rayet stars, a luminous blue variable, many O-type supergiants, and at least one symbiotic forbidden-emission B-type shell star.

Here was Ara A, also called Westerlund 1-26, a red hypergiant star.

Ara A was equal in radius to seven AU's. Had the old solar system been placed in its center, the orbit of Jupiter would have easily fit within. It was hundreds of thousands of times more energetic than Sol, albeit dimmer in the visible band, and stood at the center of a three-lightyear wide nebula of ionized hydrogen.

The hypergiant was writhing with endless dark ripples of sunspots. The corona was erupting with streamers, plumes, flares, and loops so large Sol could have passed beneath them with room to spare.

Here also, appearing as a dot of blue-white light, and swelling suddenly to its full three-dimensional volume, came the World Armada of the Tellurians.

An impossible sound reached the ears of Aeneas Tell. It sounded like a scratching of rats in the roofeaves. He straightened on his throne, and called on all his myriad senses. So many circuits answered and sent so much information into his optic nerve that the waste heat made his eyes to glow and smolder.

"Something is wrong!" he said, even before battle klaxons began to ring.

The four years had drained, grayed, and hardened Aeneas Tell. While the science of the day could erase all physical signs of age and stress from face and hair, the change to the cast of his features, the eagle-harsh look in his eyes, could not be hid.

Aeneas was seated on the black triple-wolfheaded throne of Man. He sat in the long unused throneroom atop Mount Everest, where his grandfather sat of old.

Into the brain cells of Aeneas from a myriad of instruments posted throughout the World Armada came visions and views. Some were sent directly into his cortex, others were first analyzed and simplified by experts, human or artificial.

The star Ara A filled in his view like a vast wall of boiling scarlet and sullen red.

He checked for re-entry damage first. Like a miniature solar system, the World Armada consisted of three gas giants set in an equilateral triangle. Equidistant from them were three captured gas giant planets of the enemy. These had been stripped of useful cities and materials then ignited by to serve as miniature, temporary suns. Together, the six bodies formed the stable hexagon called a Klemperer Rosette. The inner planets had joined the myriad moons of the gas giants.

Timerate, mass, and metric readings for all the worlds and moons of man showed normal. All were correctly oriented into an unwarped frame of reference, congruent with surrounding timespace.

Three battle alarms were ringing, from observers on Mars, Venus, and the Moon. But he saw no sign of the enemy.

"Report!" snapped Aeneas.

Lord Mars was nude and scarlet. He shut off the first alarm. "The old temple battlecomputer Father gave me is programmed with pattern-seeking intuitions human reason cannot follow: it reports that the enemy is here."

Aeneas said, "Sound general quarters. All planets assume battle stations."

Lord Uranus wore a mask that mimicked the face beneath. "Sire, it may be a false alarm."

(Aeneas hid a scowl. Even after all this time, the title still grated.) "Speak!"

"My psychastronomers have analyzed Ara A. There is a reciprocal effect that changes the star when its light shines on unliving beings. None is present."

Lord Mars said, "Sire, the space vampires might be hiding from the light."

Lord Uranus shook head. "Neuropsionic waves pass through planets without slowing. And this sunlight here is unholy, sire. Harmless to them."

Lord Pluto wore a featureless helmet and black mantle. "The mass of the supergiants and hypergiants is an aid to warpcore weapon range. The Ara Cluster would be prime real estate for building fortresses. Best to assume the foe is near, sire."

The throneroom was a cone whose sloping walls were cyclopean black blocks, adorned in massive gold. Aeneas had the old table chopped to kindling, and installed a round table, to gave his quarrelsome uncles no excuse to quarrel over who sat above whom.

Whether the Lords of Creation were physically present at the great round table or not was unimportant. The Klemperer Rosette was lightseconds in diameter, so any Lord could use a pearl to send his throne to his world and back in an eyeblink, leaving an image behind to continue the conversation while he consulted his experts. The wing of the palace where the Lords' personal servants waited was a longer journey away.

Their twelve insignia hung in a circle from the ceiling above the thrones: the Caduceus, Mirror, Trident, Sickle, and so on. The thrones were adorned in precious stones of their heraldic hues, save for the seat of Darius Lord Pluto, which was gray iron. Anargyros Tell, Brother Beast, who spoke for Earth, had no seat, but his legs could not grow weary.

Lady Luna's was the first new throne ever carved. It was silver and set with moonstones and agates.

"I do not concur with Lord Uranus," Lady Luna shut off the second alarm. "My oneiromantic engines of the Moon detect hostility and hatred in the dream-aura surrounding Ara A."

"Can you pinpoint a location, Cousin?" he asked her.

"Dreams are from nowhere, sire."

Aeneas looked again. The remnant of Saturn was half its former diameter, but with rings and moons unharmed. It was no longer a gas giant, but only a superterrestrial. The atmosphere of Saturn was a dusty, mottled amber. In four years the atmosphere had not settled. No lamps shined here except for the running lights of graveyard diving craft, still attempting to recover bodies. The superterrestrial world was used as a scout, and sent in a wide orbit outside the Armada. Earth was its outermost moon. Aeneas noticed that Earth was blazing white, as were all the planets.

His mother, Lady Venus shut off the third alarm. "The Armada is taking on heat, more than our terraformers can deflect, sire."

Instantly, Aeneas established a dark zone around the whole armada. Within this globe of warped space half a lightminute in diameter, lightspeed was now measured in miles per hour. Radiation from the edge of that diameter would not reach them for nine years or more. To all the eyes limited to lightspeed, the skies went black.

Now Aeneas scowled, puzzled. Ara A, though larger, was half as cool as Sol. At three lightminutes from the surface, the temperature should have still been less than Mercury received. The atmospheric shields there supported Earthlife easily.

Information poured into his blazing eyesockets. The heat afflicting the planets was not from Ara A.

There was an oddity at Ara A no Earthly astronomer had suspected: a disk of fiery plasma circling the equator of the hypergiant sun. It was a ring of burning fission. The inner bands orbited faster than the outer, and the swirled turbulence caused massive lumps to form, like miniature suns. One was nearby: this was the source of the heat.

The fugitive worlds of man had appeared in a gap between these rings of fiery plasma. The momentary blister of antigravity that intruded the World Armada back into normal spacetime had, by unforeseen luck, pushed back the nearest streamers of burning material.

Aeneas, staring at the hellish rivers of fire circling the monster star, shivered and ground his teeth. He had landed the armada as close to the star as he dared, to let the vast mass block the warp-detectors of the enemy. He had not imagined this possibility: he had almost destroyed everyone, everything.

Alarms yet rang. Hammering and scraping came from the ceiling overhead. Aeneas rubbed his finger and thumbs into his burning eyes and had them repair themselves. "What the devil *is* that noise? Whose alarm is that?"

Brother Beast stood nearby, barefoot. "It is not a military alarm. It is the palace servomind. Storm warning."

During the four years of continual emergency and battle, Brother Beast had ordered the upper atmosphere of Earth frozen. A solid sheet of ice coated the globe from pole to pole, resting on many mile-high columns of antigravity or artificial mountains raised for that purpose. The air at sea level was kept at its wanted warmth. It was a defensive measure, but it also prevented vertigo in the skyward-looking multitudes on Earth as their world was spun through multiple jumps from point to point in space during combat maneuvers.

Everest itself extended above the ice layer into naked outer space. It should have been silent as a tomb.

Brother Beast said, "The ionized nebula, and the atmospheres surrounding the disk, are dense enough hereabouts to carry soundwaves, sire. That rattling noise is the collision of micrometeorites and particle winds against the Ultrapolis force shells. Not an attack."

The final alarm vanished.

Aeneas said, "Then where is the enemy?"

Lord Saturn said, "I have something. Four million years ago, there were megastructures here, hundreds of them, orbiting the star. As this sun aged and expanded, some of the structures fell below the surface, apparently unharmed. There is no evidence of debris. I assume they survived, somewhere down inside Ara A."

"Dyson Spheres?"

"Each is a spherical shell six lightminutes in radius. As wide as the orbit of Venus once was. Inside the volume of Ara A, sire, and surrounding no star, I would not call them Dyson Spheres, despite their size. Here, I would call them submersibles, lost in a sea of fire."

Aeneas said, "Inside the sun?"

"This is not a dense, small sun like ours. It is a vast cloud that happens to be burning."

"Were they warships?"

"Yes. The equators and meridians had the contours of a Tipler Ring armature."

Aeneas said, "Is there any more recent enemy activity?"

"Near-past probes show nothing within my range." Aeneas had modified Lord Saturn's probes to see events as recent as twenty years ago.

Aeneas said, "Lord Mercury? Have you any more recent news for me?"

The way around the twenty-year blind spot in Lord Saturn's probes was one Aeneas and Lord Mercury had found. A series of ultralongrange orbital telescopes, connected to base by contortion links, had been dropped out of the warpchannel twenty lightyears away, then ten, five, two, and so on, with the nearest tailgating merely a few lighthours behind. The light passing through these points in space carrying images of events at Ara A from years ago could be intercepted now.

Aeneas could adjust the contortion entanglement to introduce a tachyon stream so that the information gathered by the scopes could be transmitted instantly across the lightyears. They were called tachyscopes.

"My people report nothing odd, sire." Said the dwarf-sized, child-faced man, grinning. "There is no evidence of communication or energy use, not that this absurdly oversized sun does not blot out, that is, at any point in the past twenty years. No fleets arrived."

"What of other sensors?"

"If the enemy are here, sire," Lord Mercury smirked, "They are not using any zero-point inertial energy. We detect no contortion stress, no disinertia fields, no ships, no planets, no asteroids. The whole solar system is empty." He scowled. "Except for this ring around the sun. What *is* that?"

Lord Jupiter said heavily, "An impossibility. A ring of material this dense should have fallen back down to the sun here long ago. The solar magnetosphere would degrade the orbit of any particles in a few thousand years."

Lord Saturn said, "It was not here twenty years ago. It is recent."

Aeneas said, "How is that possible? What could cause such a…"

Sig, the signet ring of Aeneas, was trying to calculate for him how much energy it would take for a star of this mass to throw so many solar masses worth of material into orbit, and was getting numbers that perturbed even its wonted calm. Aeneas shushed it.

Lord Pluto said, "It may only be a few days old, sire. When you formed the warpchannel here, it was your first attempt at using the Alpha Centauri armature rings at beyond their operational range."

Aeneas nodded. He has selected a hypergiant star because he knew that if the enemy searched within the normal range of the Alpha

Centauri rings, no one would look so far away. He said, "Shame we could not figure a way to bring that armature with us."

Lord Pluto said, "Forming the warpchannel may have temporarily altered local gravity conditions, and disturbed the starcore. This disk of fire may be very recent ejected material, thrown into space during the days while we passed through the warpfissure."

Lord Mars said, "Good to know. We can use warpfissures as weapons, then."

Lord Pluto turned the lens of his helmet toward Lord Mars, "As can they, and no doubt have for countless years."

Mars turned to Aeneas, "Sire! I trust the hunches of the battle-pattern computer. The enemy is here. If, as Lord Pluto says, this disk of plasma was thrown up from the hypergiant when you anchored a warp here, that may have forced them back, or forced them to regroup."

Aeneas said, "Lord Mars, suppose you were the fleet commander stationed here, preparing to ambush us, and you knew such a long warpfissure would produce a catastrophe. Where would you position your forces?"

Lord Mars said, "If they are not in the unholy light of Ara A, and if there are no worlds in this star system, then they are in the only place light does not reach: inside Ara A. Star interiors are opaque."

Lord Neptune said, "Opaque to light, but not to gravity. I will have my people search for any density variations inside the volume of the sphere. But this volume is immense! Over eighteen hundred cubic lighthours! It may be weeks, or months. I–" He interrupted himself with a fervid oath, leaping to his feet.

Lord Pluto said in a calm, disinterested tone, "They used a Schroedinger technique to detect being seen. They felt Neptune's gaze. Our position is betrayed. I sense we have just been seen."

Aeneas ordered the warpcores in the three gas giants to fling the World Armada into evasive faster-than-light maneuvers. There was no response. He tried to reopen his hyperspatial periscopes, and gain a realtime view of the battlespace. He was blind. Some power immensely greater than his was flattening space in a wide volume all around, preventing any warps from forming.

"We're trapped!" Aeneas shouted.

Lord Neptune shouted, "I see gravity point sources being formed! From gigantic structures, larger than worlds, buried in the star plasma! They are crushing solar volumes of star matter to form nova beams!"

Lord Jupiter said, "Don't panic, dear brother! The sun is three lightminutes away! We have time to…"

But there was no time. The gravity waves Lord Neptune received traveled at lightspeed. This meant the image seen of the enemy firing and the fire itself arrived simultaneously.

Of million-year-old War Dysons, forty were still operational, and hanging just below the tumultuous surface of Ara A. Blisters of reddish solar material lifted and exploded outward into space as the beams erupted. Each War Dyson had swallowed and collapsed a vast volume of star-plasma into a gravitic singularity, and focused the supernova force thus released into a lased beam of death-energy heterodyned on an electromagnetic carrier wave.

The monster star was so great that thousands of Sol-sized volumes of substance could have been scooped out of the middle of Ara A without noticeable loss.

Thousands were not needed. Forty nova-beams projected from below the stormy surface of Ara A, transfixed their target, and obliterated all matter utterly.

16

WAR DYSONS

The violence was unspeakable. Each War Dyson of Ara A gathered the semisolid plasma of the star inside it, a sphere the radius of Venus' orbit. Potent fields crushed the substance into a point source, and the resulting energy was polarized and released through a surface emitter as a solid beam with the power of a nova. So vast was Ara A that thousands of such bites could have been chewed out of its interior without noticeable change to the star. The Black Fleet took but two score.

Each beam carried the energy equal to the nova of a large star across the three lightminute gap separating the Tellurian World Armada from the buried Dysons. This was roughly the distance that of old separated Sol from Mercury. As interstellar ranges went, it was point blank.

Missing a target at that distance was unimaginable.

As for the violence of each shot, by way of comparison, it must be noted that a fifty megaton hydrogen bomb yields hundreds of quadrillions of joules, that is, a digit followed by seventeen zeros. A solar flare yields a destructive force equal to a billion such bombs. The total yearly energy output of a small star like Sol is equal to a billion such flares. A nova releases in one moment a yield equal to ten thousand times that yearly amount. A nova eruption is one duodecillion joules of energy altogether; a digit followed by thirty-nine zeros.

The whole barrage was forty times again that. In no war in man's history had there ever been such extravagant overkill.

Even gas giant sized bodies caught in the beam were not large enough to burn from surface to core. Instead they winked out. Everything made of matter caught in that beam was reduced to its constituent subatomic particles instantly. Each electron of each atom jumped to its highest energy state, and then jumped free, and the ionized protons left behind were reduced into pions, leptons, mesons. These leaped outward, destroying any additional sub-particles of matter they encountered.

And here was something that could not exist in nature: energy conditions so ferocious that even electrically neutral photons, particles incapable of decay, broke down into constituent neutrino-antineutrino particle pairs. The propagation of light ceased in the center of the primordial effect: the explosion was a swelling axis of darkness, neither energy nor matter, surrounded by concentric cylindrical shockwaves of ultrasolid stratonic condensate, surrounded in turn by a mere hellfire of radiation, gamma ray bursts, and electrostatic discharges.

Explosion? The word is inadequate. This was annihilation.

Surviving even one such a shot was beyond impossible: it was unthinkable.

The Lords and Ladies of Creation sat motionless on their thrones in the great council chamber, watching through their signet rings the vision of the forty rays of infinitely destructive enemy fire in the heavens above heading toward the World Armada.

But the rays were not straight. They curved.

The Lords of Creation were on their feet, silent with shock to find themselves alive, staring, startled, open-mouthed at the vision, the glorious, impossible vision of the nova-fire going wide of the target and missing the World Armada entirely.

They were more shocked when Aeneas, who had grown quite grim and sober in the last four years despite his young age, was pounding the arms of the three-headed throne, and laughing like a madman.

The bend was slight but visible at two lightminutes away. The bend became more pronounced as each beam elongated. Each beam was like a white-hot rainbow, bending further the farther it reached. The beams at their point of origin were white hot, but with the bending, each beam spread, and separated into a spectrum. The lower energy reddish light bent the most: blue the least.

Aeneas laughed. Tears streamed from his eyes.

For the beams were not passing through empty space. The ionized nebula cloud that thickly swaddled the sun was a medium dense enough to carry sound. The disk of burning nuclear plasma was in the way of the shots. The space vampire commander had directed the fire directly toward the visual image. Lightwaves, however, even the unimaginably ultrapowerful lightwaves of a nova-strength interplanetary-range beam, do not travel in straight lines when passing from denser to rarer mediums, but suffer refraction.

Over such distances as this, small as they were, shoving a beam through a disk shaped cloud of plasma bent it, in the same way and for the same reason that the rays of the sun bend at the sunset horizon, turn red, and rob the sinking sun of its power to dazzle the eye.

The nova-beams bent, each one passing tens of thousands of miles to one side of the Armada, ignited a cylinder-shaped shockwave of expanding primordial annihilation through the substance of the plasma disk where it punctured it, and sped away out across from Ara A into deep space.

They missed.

And Aeneas lost all dignity and laughed, lolling this way and that beneath the three menacing wolf-skulls of his dark throne, unable to catch his breath. He did not wait for his body to recover its composure. While still breathless, he sent thoughts through his ring.

"Lord Mercury, render the World Armada disinert. We are about to be hit with a shockwave. All stations, prepare planetary drives! Lord Neptune, I need your every gravitational engine at full power, and Lord Jupiter, I need you to give him more power. Instruct the self-aware factories to begin turning the matter of one of the captured gas giants into power cells and gravitic engines and put them in orbit as tugs. We only have a few minutes, and we will need roughly two hundred billion more ships in the navy in the next fifty seconds."

Lady Luna said, "I hope, cousin, you will have a moment to explain why we are not all dead."

Aeneas said, "Give me a moment. The enemy has flattened the contour of spacetime, so I am limited to lightspeed or slower. So are they. The closest Dyson, very near the surface of the sun, will not see the light image of us still alive for at least three minutes. If Lord Mercury has rendered all the worlds free of inertia?"

The childlike Mercury said, "The contortion engines controlling moons and worlds at the lee edge of the Armada have not yet reported in. Lightspeed limits, sire. But so far, my sons tell me any inert worlds are being rammed by disinert worlds, to bring them inside the shadow of their inertia-nullifying fields."

Without inertia, of course, no kinetic energy of any kind passed from body to body, so one moon rushing toward another would come to an instant halt, without jar or deceleration, upon touching the rarest outermost molecules of the atmosphere of the body with which it collided.

Mercury said, "Less than three percent failure rate so far. Also, the self-aware factories are creating new disinertia engines by the dozens per second wherever there is a failure. What are we expecting, sire?"

Aeneas said, "A near miss by forty nova's worth of energy just turned all matter in the area into an explosion of the same kind, albeit smaller, as was last seen during the Big Bang. I assume they will maintain flatspace, because I have the warpcore on the trips, and it will carry us away at superluminary speed as soon as it is allowed. But flatspace means no hyperspatial periscopes. We have to be gone before they see us going. But where? Where, damn it? There is nothing to hide behind! Space is so stupidly empty! Who designed it?"

At that point, the shockwave of the explosion passed through the area. The gas giants, planets and green moons and asteroids of the World Armada were not weightless, but they were inertialess: when the lightest brush of the smallest, fastest moving cosmic ray particles exploding outward from the nova beam brushed against the frailest and outermost layer of a planetary force shell or natural atmosphere, the world was immediately, with no acceleration, moving at the velocity equal to the particle.

Nor did those particles, or lightwaves, rebound from the worlds, because that also requires inertia. So the whole World Armada went utterly black.

There was no physical sensation of vertigo, but the images in their mind which observatories and surface cameras showed them made the Lords of Creation sway in their seats and clutch the arms of their thrones. The supergiant sun, and all the crowded stars of the cluster behind it, rose and fell across every horizon of every moon and planet twice a second as the World Armada pirouetted.

"Where do we go?" shouted Aeneas, all trace of his mad laughter gone.

Lord Neptune said, "I know where. I can save us. Save us all. You doubted my loyalty once. Trust me now."

Mercury said, "Well, I do not trust him!"

Lord Neptune leaned back and crossed his boots on the round table. "Or die, little man. I don't care which."

"Silence your bickering, my lords!" Aeneas snapped, "Where to?"

"Down the barrel of the cannon," Lord Neptune grinned half a grin on his blue, sardonic face. "Along the firing path of the nova beam is the only place where there are no molecules, no atoms, no particles."

Aeneas understood. A disinert body can only move as quickly as the lack of surrounding resistance allows. There would be no resistance along one of those lines: the speed could approach lightspeed.

Lady Venus said, "We'll hit Ara A!"

Lord Neptune smirked. "You should look at the universe using gravity waves sometime. You see things others miss." He sent an image from his ring to theirs. They saw the strange, black-and-white scene of gravitons in space all about them: the vast hypergiant star was shadowy dark gray; their own gas giants were pigeon gray; the smaller worlds an off-white; the pinpoint black holes created at the core of the forty war Dysons were utterly black.

But the path between the Dyson firing apertures, round barrels wider in diameter than gas giants, and the turbulent surface of Ara A was stark white. There were no solid bodies present, not even an atom.

Neptune said, "They will never look for us there."

Lord Mercury said, "Because we will be dead! The column will collapse—! Or has already! Your image is three minutes old!"

But Aeneas, by mental commands cast through his signet ring, had already directed the gravity engines to sling the World Armada around an imaginary gravitational point source and toward the hypergiant sun. The Klemperer Rosette became a line of worlds. The half-sized remnant of Saturn was foremost, with Earth orbiting it; then came Uranus and Neptune, with Jupiter in the rearguard.

Neptune said aloud, "No rush, sire, but why are we not dead now?"

Aeneas said, "You saw them fire. You would not have seen the image of the firing if the fire had been traveling at the same rate. I had erected a slow-light field around the area, remember, as a parasol to block the heat? That is why your gravity image arrived before the visual image, which traveled at the same speed as the barrage. The slow-light zone did not affect gravitons. The foe collapsed my field a moment later by flattening space, but flatspace does not stop Mercury's tech or yours, so we are getting the heck out of here.

"Oh, and the beams missed because when we formed a warpchannel reaching from Alpha Centauri to Ara A, the space distortion caused a starquake so violent that a hundred solar masses worth of substance was thrown into orbit around the star, thick as an atmo-sphere. The necroforms do not take new conditions into account unless ordered to. Vacuum that was no longer a vacuum was not in their orders. So they missed. Like stabbing a fishspear at the spot where the light says the fish beneath the surface is. Refraction. They missed."

In the rear of the column were the three captured gas giants, burn-ing like suns. One was extinguished, and molecular machines were dissembling plasma into crystals and apparatuses to form the gravitic engines previously commanded. The remaining two Aeneas ordered to become inert, resume their full and terrible momentum, and ram each other. The resulting dwarf star explosion would be as nothing compared to forty novae, but it might confuse enemy sensors and slow pursuit. The solar wind from the explosion would also drive back the dense particles from the ring of fire surrounding Ara A.

They needed no heat from such tiny suns where they were going.

The World Armada sped onward into the vast, sullen, hellish wall of solar fire.

Lady Luna said in a tense voice, "Does His Imperial Majesty have a plan for surviving once we enter one of those tubules to avoid letting Ara A collapse on us? Or how we will jump into a cannon's mouth and live? Sir? Aeneas? *Aeneas*!"

17

Down a Dragon Throat

The four gas giants of the World Armada, with the inner planets and asteroids in tow among their moons and rings, raced at ninety-nine percent of the speed of light directly toward the nearest rapidly closing vent or hole piercing the side of the glowering red hypergiant star Ara A.

Saturn was in the vanguard, Jupiter in the rear.

Above the frozen atmosphere of Earth, within the old throneroom atop Mount Everest, the Lady Luna said in a tense voice, "Does His Imperial Majesty have a plan for surviving once we enter one of those tubules of superdense plasma, to not have Ara A collapse on us?"

On the black, three-wolf-headed throne, Aeneas seemed not to be listening. He was frowning, studying the faces present one by one.

"We have overestimated ourselves!" Lady Venus wailed. "We think we can do impossible deeds on the fly, by improvisation! It is like Father all over again. The insanity of power!"

Lord Mercury said tensely, "Disinertia will keep radiant heat from affecting us, but not solid plasma. Great as my speed is, contortion cannot move us faster than they can see!"

Lord Saturn, stroked his beard, and said meditatively, "Three minutes for the light to reach the nearest Dyson and let them see they missed, and three minutes for the return fire, now corrected for refraction effect, to strike us at lightspeed. We have that much time to deduce a means of escape. My ability to see the past is worthless."

Lord Uranus showed no expression on his mask. "My ability to read the psychometry of stars is more worthless. We actually have less time than you said, brother Saturn, for we are moving toward the enemy at near-lightspeed."

Saturn said, "I can speed up our local perception of timerate, if my lords need more time to think."

Lord Neptune said, "The number of gravity engines at my command cannot keep open a tunnel in the sun. Plasma is a fluid, but it is denser than iron."

Each one's signet ring projected images taken from orbital and groundbased observatories directly into his visual cortex. The Lords of Creation seated at the round table could all see the vast and turbulent face of the red sun, like a toppling wall, rush to envelope them.

The War Dysons were hidden in the convection layer. Each point where the immense weapons had discharged was pierced by a whirlpool, and was now the center of sunspots and eruptions. The side effects of their nova-beam fire had thrown helmet streamers, plumes, and coronal loops countless miles into outer space.

Lord Pluto's voice was calm and cold and unexpected, "Lord Jupiter has a solution."

Lord Jupiter had been frowning in his golden beard. He looked up to see the single lens in the featureless helmet of Lord Pluto turned toward him, and started. "Sorry, what? I heard my name come up. Solution, yes, I suppose. My servominds are still combing through the math. Who understands their weird thoughts? But in theory–"

Aeneas said, "Lord Jupiter, no time for theory. I am turning the war department over to you. Call on any resources you need."

Lord Jupiter laughed a hearty laugh, clearly pleased, as thousands of machines, as well as teams and schools of men in high-speed timewarp chambers and high-speed timewarp moons, all made links with his mind. He imagined what he wanted done, and saw it being done.

He smiled in his golden beard. "I can explain easily enough while doing. See those solar flares? Convection current is what creates the sunspots and coronal loops. It is all done magnetically! I don't need any resources."

Lady Venus said, "What do you mean, brother? Our whole civilization cannot possibly have enough energy to erect an energy field to pry open a volume of plasma eight million miles in radius reaching two hundred million miles below the photosphere!"

Jupiter smiled his avuncular smile. "Father never showed me how to reach the information layer or the memory layer of the cosmos, but there is an instruction layer above them which gives the orientation to photons. This layer coordinates the Lorentz contractions between observers and keeps the speed of light constant. How else can a photon passing through one of two slits cooperate with its brother photons to go its right place in an interference pattern? Or get photons to follow Fermat's path of least time for a medium they only just are entering?"

Aeneas said, "I have not yet ordered all of us to swap our secrets, Uncle. You need not explain at length."

Jupiter, despite his blustery appearance, was a subtle man. He understood the implication. Instead of whatever he had been about to say, he said only, "My science is to counterfeit the instruction layer for photons. The energy required is minimal. Like a judo throw, I use the field's own strength against itself. The greater the energy field being manipulated, the easier it is to manipulate."

Lady Luna said, "So, all this time, when you claimed to have one hundred interplanetary strength beam weapons, and we all scrambled to build interplanetary beams of our own—" The young redheaded cousin of Aeneas seemed to have trouble retaining her composure. Her eyes flashed and her bosom heaved with anger.

Jupiter spread his hands, "A trick. I encouraged an arms race. I have the ability to seize control of any electromagnetic beam you might fire, so I wanted you to build a lot. My arsenal consists of a device small enough to embed in a finger ring, which lets me talk to lightning."

Lady Venus said, "Have you ever actually done this before, brother? Driven a tube of empty space into the heart of Sol, for example?"

"Of course not!" roared Jupiter in a joyful, if manic, voice. "Why would I ever drive a tunnel into Sol? First time for everything!"

Lady Venus shook her head wearily, and all the thought-ports and mind-energy emitters in her coronet clashed like bangles. "It is the insanity of power. We are all turning into Father."

Jupiter grinned and winked at Aeneas. "I can hold the tunnel of solid solar fire open while the other worlds pass down the tunnel and ram into the War Dyson's cannon mouth at the far end. What you plan after that, you tell me, lad!"

His grin faltered a bit when he saw Aeneas looking stern.

All the Lords of Creation except, perhaps, the Lords Pluto and Uranus, flinched when their rings showed them the human-occupied gas giants plunge into the eye of the whirlpool of fire. This was the tunnel entrance.

Then they were falling down a well of fire. To either side was plasma, the substance of a sun in flame, a mess of subatomic particles in an environment where the heat and pressure broke and reformed all atoms in a continual storm of nuclear fusion.

The size of the star could not be grasped. Ninety-six billion spheres the size of Sol could have been packed inside this unthinkably huge orb, and forty billion more poured in to fill up the spaces left over between such packed spheres. The gas giants were less than dust specks in comparison.

Even the War Dyson Spheres of the enemy, as wide in radius as the old orbit of Venus, wallowing their titanic bulk through the mudlike opaque fluid of the fiery plasma, were lost in the immensity. Five hundred or more such spheres could have been fitted inside Ara A without crowding. There were only forty.

Yet the interior of the star was opaque. Only at the surface, where the plasma particles, no longer hemmed in, unfolded into photons, was there light.

The channel was a slight curve, reaching from the boiling corona to the inward convection layer. The closest of the forty Dysons was somewhere before them.

Lady Luna said, "You *do* have a plan, have you not, sire?"

"How long before the Dyson can fire again?" Aeneas asked.

Neptune answered. His signet ring displayed into their brains the images his graviton observatories had gathered of the Dyson down whose firing channel they ran. Gravitons could pass through the dense fluid of the solar interior as no electromagnetic wave could. "The Dysons are six lightminutes in radius. Even using contortion technology to render the surrounding plasma disinert, no material thing can move faster than lightspeed. So six minutes is the fastest theoretical maximum for refilling the firing chamber."

Aeneas said, "How would it draw the plasma into its interior?"

Lord Jupiter answered, "Magnetic beams. A field of gravitic and kinetic force crushes the solar masses into a black hole to release the nova-amounts of energy."

Aeneas said to Jupiter, "Can you protect us from such beams when we drive through them?"

"With ease. After preventing the largest star in the galaxy from collapsing on us, you think I cannot hold back a mere Dyson's scoop engines? I should be insulted!" And Lord Jupiter roared with laughter, slapping himself on the knee, and sending his son, Lord Ganymede, for a wine goblet.

The War Dyson loomed in the views from the observatories orbiting Neptune: a vast gray sphere with a sharply defined black dot at the center, embedded in an endless volume of star-substance. The convection swirls of solar plasma rearing and falling to each side formed endless tornadoes, each rotating oppositely from its neighbors, producing smaller whorls, hurricanes and tornados of fire.

Like the arms of a kraken, scores of tornadoes reaching outward and upward had their feet resting on the surface of the Dyson Sphere. These were currents established by the magnetic aura of the solar-system sized engine drawing solar plasma into itself.

The firing aperture of the War Dyson was simply a ring of magnetic engines, less than eight million miles in radius, or roughly as wide as Saturn's outermost ring, embedded into the surface. This was smaller than a pinprick compared to the vast sphere beyond.

The World Armada, along with torrents and rivers of plasma, was drawn inside by a magnetic force.

Suddenly mankind and all its worlds and moons were inside the sphere. The inner surface was a crosshatching of hexagons and triangles, each one a lightsecond in width.

The firing aperture was behind them, hidden in a spreading pool of plasma that entered with them and was ignited into radiance. The radiant pressure drove the disinert gas giants fleets forward ever nearer to the center of the Dyson.

After a minute or two of travel, the erupting globe of plasma rushing in at the Dyson's mouth was behind them, as bright and distant as a noonday sun.

At twelve points evenly spaced about the sphere, but orbiting beneath its roof, were dark stars, carved into the shape of staring eyeballs. It would take a moment for light to travel from the World Armada to the nearest and return with an image of the eye stirring itself to wrath. The farthest would not be seen to turn toward them until a quarter an hour had passed.

In the very center of the sphere was a hole in space, shining utter black in gravitic image, a reddish smear erupting with x-rays in electromagnetic images: the black hole left over from the collapse of the whole volume of plasma which once had been here into a nova.

Lady Luna said, "The dreamlands are filled with images of hunger, despair, and hate. Mounds of corpses eating each other, famished. Pyramids of skulls, all screaming."

Lady Venus said, "Judging from the flow of thought-energy, there are the equivalent of six hundred million civilizations occupying the surface. All automatons. All undead."

Lord Uranus said, "All six hundred million are controlled by groups of master cities at the pole of the War Dyson. The masters are necro-forms, but have free will."

Lord Neptune said, "The surface itself is an unknown, artificial material, possibly a force field dense enough to reflect light. The hull panels are disinert, and held in a latticework of neutronium."

Just then, the whole interior of the Dyson sphere lit up, bright with energy both kinetic and gravitic.

Lord Mars said, "We are under attack, my lords. The compression fields lining the inside of the Dyson have been turned on. The Dyson sphere does not need to be filled with plasma for the firing mechanism to fire. All matter caught in the field is compressed to a mathematical point. The World Armada is about to be crushed. Your orders, sire?"

Aeneas looked from face to face once more, still scowling. He said, "Dive into the black hole."

The uproar of objections and expressions of shock were drowned out by the shrill blast of alarms and sirens.

18

EVENT HORIZON

Aeneas gave the command. Three gas giants and the remnant of a fourth, with all the lesser planets, worldlets and asteroids orbiting among their moons, leaped toward the black hole at the core of the War Dyson. The countless orbital engines of Lord Mercury removed all inertia from these bodies, so they immediately came to the maximum speed without any intervening moment of acceleration.

At the same time, force fields of combined gravitic and kinetic energy began to radiate from each square AU of the Dyson hull. These fields could seize a sphere of solar plasma six lightminutes in radius and compress it to microscopic size, and focus the resulting explosion into a coherent beam. The fields were concentric bubbles of energy, wave upon wave, rushing inward.

The twelve dark stars there to act as gravitational shepherds were obviously not meant to be inside the zone of action when the weapon fired: the kinetic fields overtook them.

One after another, the vast orbs of neutronium were seized. As each dark star was struck by a wall of force, and was accelerated, it lost coherence, became oblate, grew red-hot, then white-hot. Anger and terror shined from the sculpted eyes as each dark star mind realized how it had been betrayed by its masters. Cracks into which a thousand Earths could have fallen with room to spare now broke open in the surface. Each dark star ignited, not into atomic fusion, as objects of ordinary matter would have done, but into exploding clouds of neutrons.

The heat was superconducted instantly through the entire neutro- nium volume of each undead star, destroying the unliving servant minds housed in its crystalline core, and obliterating lesser fighting slaves occupying the cities and emplacements of its surface. Lady Luna winced as the dream-images of their death throes were inter- cepted by her receivers.

Neutrons broke into protons, electrons, and antineutrinos. The fusions and fissions of this storm of particles became an almost-solid wave of high energy cosmic rays.

These spheres of cosmic rays expanded at the speed of light, which was swifter than the inward collapsing motion of the compression fields. Hence, before the compression field could grapple any world or moon of the human armada, the disinert bodies were instantly ac- celerated to the speed of the incoming particles. Like a surfer balanced on a tidal wave, the worlds of man were darted at immense velocity toward the core of the War Dyson.

The distance from the hull of the Dyson to the core was sixty-seven million miles, roughly six lightminutes.

In this place, the inertia-free World Armada could approach the speed of light, but not exceed it, since the interior of the Dyson, after firing, was a perfect vacuum. The oncoming fields of vast, de- structive kinetic and gravitational forces would reach the centerpoint a moment after the World Armada, and their inertialess condition would not save them. Photons bounce disinert bodies up to full speed without any sensation of acceleration, but gravitons do not.

Aeneas guided the course. Straight toward the deadly black hole they raced.

Lord Jupiter dropped his wine goblet and came to his feet, roaring with questions; Lord Mercury leaped to his feet, also shouting in his high, thin voice; Lord Mars, bright red and nude save for his baldric, scabbards, and holsters, also came to his feet, his eyes narrowed in shock.

The mask of Lord Uranus matched his own features beneath, but showed no expressions except those it was programmed for. Yet his voice was also querulous with fear.

Lord Pluto wore a helmet, kept his seat, and kept his silence.

Brother Beast was already on his feet, as he had no seat at the table, but he crossed himself, dropped to his knees, and clasped his hands in prayer.

The Ladies Ceres, Luna and Venus were too well bred to jump up or shout, but looked terrified, annoyed or bewildered, each according to her nature.

Gray-eyed Lady Pallas altered her expression by not even an iota, but, like Aeneas, was narrowly studying the faces of her relatives at the table.

Only Lord Neptune seemed unperturbed. His narrow, sardonic and sapphire face was grinning a small grin.

The mingled voices drowned individual words, but the tone of panic made the message clear: the worlds of man were in the middle of a firing chamber of a star-killing weapon as it was firing. Why had Aeneas ordered the Armada into a black hole, into certain death?

Aeneas leaned back in the three-wolf-headed throne, and heaved a sigh. "A narrow escape, my lords and ladies! I was not sure if the dark stars would ignite into a sufficient number of photons to give us acceleration. Lord Mercury, your engines will continue to remove the inertia from every ship, moon, asteroid, and planet in the World Armada? Even a split second failure would be fatal."

Several of his uncles were shouting questions at him, but rather than raise his voice, Aeneas used the imperial override circuit in his throne to put these words directly into their minds. Being Emperor, after all, allowed him certain privileges.

Aeneas raised his hand. The Lords fell silent, faces red with anger or pale with fear. "We have roughly six minutes, traveling a fraction below lightspeed, before we reach the center of the Dyson, where the black hole is. Shall we take a short break? The store of spirits and liquor for anyone who needs a drink to steady his nerves. Some of us seem jumpy of late. Smoke 'em if you got 'em."

Along with eternal youth, the biotechnology bestowed on mankind allowed all old vices to be indulged without physical harm, and new ones to be invented.

With horror the Lords examined the information from the World Armada observatories. Behind them, Doppler shifted into extremely low frequency radio waves only, came the images of exploding dark stars and the oncoming wave of the compression fields. Ahead, the images were as gamma rays. Only the equator of their motion showed an undistorted picture of the blazing Dyson interior as the firing sequence continued. Because of the distortion, the Dyson seemed immensely flattened in their direction of motion, not a sphere but a hollow discus.

Lord Jupiter said, "Lad—I mean, Your Imperial Majesty—the Twelve would be gratified by the answer of how we are expected to survive falling into a black hole?"

Lord Mercury said, "Retreat is possible! I have had my people drop a planetary-mass pearl behind us we fled. We can contort the whole Armada back to our previous location…"

Lady Luna said sarcastically, "To the spot where the nova beams are aiming?"

A spasm of anger passed across the boylike features of Lord Mercury, and he clenched his little fists.

Aeneas leaned back, folded his arms behind his head, and crossed his legs at the knees. A stared idly at the dark, high ceiling of the chamber. "This Dyson is the size of Venus's old orbit: the diameter of

Deneb. Call it two hundred solar masses. The black hole is formed by the implosion when the outer layers explode outward into a nova. So we are not dealing with anything larger than twenty solar masses. I estimate the Schwarzschild radius of a non-rotating, uncharged black hole of that mass is a tenth of a meter. About the size of a baseball, over a thousand times the mass of all our worlds together."

Lord Mercury said tensely, "The x-rays from the accretion disk will fry us if I release the planetary disinertia engines, and will repel us if I do not."

Lady Ceres said, "And we will be crushed by the gravity!"

Lady Venus cooed, "How are four gas giants all going to fit into a baseball?"

Lady Luna scowled. "Look at him! Aeneas is enjoying watching us guess and squirm! The jackass!"

Aeneas wagged a finger. "Tut, fair cousin! Remember the proper forms of address!"

She rose from her seat, curtseyed, and seated herself again, saying, "Look at His Imperial Majesty! His Majesty is enjoying watching us guess and squirm! The imperial jackass!"

Aeneas rolled his eyes. "Much better. Lord Mercury, please send a second planetary pearl through the first, and have it move at contortion speed to just inside the Dyson firing aperture."

The boy frowned in puzzlement, but saluted. "As you command, sire."

Aeneas sat back erect. "Lord Neptune! You seem placid. You do not fret that the black hole gravity will crush us. Why not?"

Lord Neptune said, "Because we are in free fall, sire. The only thing we have to worry about is tidal effects. When the gravity pulling on the nearside of a heavenly body is greater than the farside, the difference elongates the body. We will be ripped into angstrom-thin spaghetti strands as we approach the singularity. But, hey! No worry about being crushed by gravity."

Aeneas said, "The prospect alarms you not, my lord?"

Lord Neptune said, "You ordered an entire captured gas giant dismantled and reassembled into gravitic control engines. Which were not needed to prop open the plasma tube. By now, I know you plan things."

Aeneas said, "A ring of gravity pulling outward at the equator of any body would distribute the tidal pull evenly, would it not? No matter how massive, the tidal effect is zero if all points on the body are equally accelerated. Do you have enough gravity generators?"

Lord Neptune said, "More than enough."

Aeneas said, "Some of the ladies still seem worried. What happens when we smash into the event horizon?"

Neptune laughed. "The same thing that happens when a sailboat gets her anchor chain snagged on the equator. The event horizon is an imaginary line demarking the point above the singularity at which the escape velocity equals the speed of light. Nothing happens to you when you cross it. Except that the velocity needed to accelerate into a higher orbit happens to exceed lightspeed."

Lord Jupiter uttered a hoarse call.

The view from all the observatories now showed what seemed to be a mirrored sphere hanging directly before them, growing and growing. The mirrored sides reflected distorted images of the metallic skies all around them, the hexagon crossbracing of the endless square lightseconds of the inner Dyson.

It grew. In the middle was a circle of darkness like the pupil of an eye, swelling.

The Lords stirred uneasily. It looked like the oncoming headlamp of an express train in a mirrored tunnel.

Lady Venus asked, "Why can we see it? I thought black holes were, well, black?"

Lord Saturn answered, "We are seeing light left over from the moment when the singularity was formed, I assume when the nova weapon was last fired. Each layer of photons near the event horizon as it formed departed ever more slowly, and the ones we see are still departing. It is a time distortion effect."

Lord Mercury said, "But pursuit will follow us into the event horizon!"

Lord Saturn smiled in his beard, and said, "And never reach us. Our one second headstart will be expanded to infinity."

Aeneas turned to Lord Jupiter. "Lord Mercury expresses concern about the halo of x-rays surrounding the black hole."

Lord Jupiter, with ponderous dignity, cleared his throat and took his seat. "X-rays are electromagnetic. Merely another form of lightning. I speak, and it obeys. The effort is so slight compared to what I just did to create a magnetic tubule protecting us from the plasma of Ara A, I should be affronted. I will have engines constructed to gather, convert and store it, just because I can."

In their view, the mirrored sphere rushing toward them grew, became dark, then darker, became a convex plane surface, a flat plane, and then became concave. Behind, as if seen through a smoky tunnel, came the attacking wave of energy, reddened and darkened and slowed. As they watched it grew slower and slower. The light image dimmed as photons grew scarce. Then, darkness.

Lady Venus said, "Sire, not just the ladies are wondering how will we escape from this timewarp. Are we not trapped forever?"

Aeneas said, "Unless I miss my guess, we will be trapped for twelve minutes exactly. Lady Venus, if you will, coordinate with Lord Uranus to track and locate where all their control thoughts come from. Their setup does not allow for decentralized command. Pass the information to Lord Mars."

Aeneas turned to Lord Mars, "My lord. Are you ready?"

As predicted, the enemy released the flatspace suppressor. Perhaps they wished to bring information out from the event horizon, or shoot weapons in. Only the Dyson interior itself was free: spacewarps could not be formed outside the hull.

Aeneas was amazed to see the black hole unfold. It happened faster than light, depositing the World Armada in one second several lightminutes from its prior position.

No matter. Aeneas had long ago issued the orders. His servominds, the moment their tachyon circuits could operate freely, reacted faster than lightspeed. The World Armada formed a warpchannel to the interplanetary pearl positioned at the mouth of the firing aperture, safely behind the kinetic compression wave, and was there. The gas giants and lesser worlds of man were now in the firing aperture. The fire of the interior of Ara A was before them; the blazing fields of destructive energy of the Dyson interior were behind.

Lord Mars had vanished.

Lord Mercury shouted, "Mars! Where is he?"

Aeneas smiled thinly, "At war."

19

MATTER OF WAR

Thucydides Tell, the Lord of Mars, vanished from the presence chamber of the Lords of Creation.

At the same moment when the flatspace suppression was released, and warp transmission again became possible, Lord Mars was sent through a smaller warpchannel to the location Lady Venus had detected: the hub of all the enemy command lines.

Lord Mars appeared in the authority arena of the alien headquarters. It was vast, dark and cold, an orbicular fortress larger than an asteroid, held in its place in the Dyson hull by the lightest of artificial gravities. Countless other orbs, equal in volume, formed a cityscape larger than Earth, shaped like a cluster of grapes bisected by the Dyson hull. Lord Mars stood on a black floor. He was surrounded by concentric ranks of mountain-sized vampire masses. Some were larger than the plutonian world-vampire had been. This was the first of a thousand fortresses embedded in polar intersection of the armatures of the War Dyson.

The chamber was a mile high and many miles wide. Black stalactites of thinking material, larger than skyscrapers, reached down from the pitted and corroded dome above toward the tiers of the arena below. The mountain-sized vampire masses were huddled like egg clusters beneath each stalactite. Each was half buried into a bowl thousands of feet in radius. The bowl interior was coated with control ports into which they extruded nerves. Each vampire was surrounded by concentric stains of debris and bones, the remnants of feasts consumed geological ages ago.

The monstrosities, at first, had no shape. Some of the nearer ones began to form eyeballs, infrared pits, or microwave horns along their closer slopes of gelid flesh to observe the intruder, or to create trumpets, tubes, and yammering mouths for uttering cries of alarm and anger into the plutonian air. The atmosphere here was helium, thin and barely warm enough to remain as a gas, evidently only a convenience for sonic communication.

The nude and brightly scarlet man, with no word, no change of expression, raised his hand, and all atoms of matter within a two hundred thousand mile radius reversed their orientation in one of the basic matter-energy command layers of the universe Lord Tellus had revealed to him. This was the range of the sensors in his signet ring, one lightsecond and a half.

In the base matter-energy layer, particle polarity was symmetrical. Positive and negative were nothing more than up spin or down spin. Like flipping a gyroscope on its head, these values could be reversed with no change to the form or momentum of the particles in the extensional layer called timespace.

Electrons became positrons, protons became antiprotons. The atoms and molecules all kept their shape: the electrochemical bonds hence chemical reactions of all the molecules in the affected area continued as normal, including those within the undead brains of the vampire beings and their thinking machines, save that they were now antimatter.

Only where this negative matter touched positive was there change. Both suffered total conversion.

The explosions where this negative matter of the fortress-city of the Dyson hull met the positive matter hull began in a doughnut shaped ring four hundred thousand miles in diameter, and expanded both inward and outward. The energy liberated by the total conversion of matter traveled faster than the electronic, gravity-wave, or space-contortion alarms registering the damage: no slave of the vampires had warning, no thinking machine could react in time.

Because the volume affected, compared to the size of this head-quarters, was so large, the quivering vampire lords here beheld the coming destruction via hyperspatial periscope. There was no way to flee: any attempt to contort or warp to a positive matter area anywhere in the immensity of the Dyson surface would have obliterated them. Finding themselves and all their gear now being antimaterial in nature, the monsters did have time to recognize what was happening and send signals to the next in the chain of command, turning over their authority and yowling for revenge to be done in their memory.

These signals were allowed to escape by Lady Venus and traced. Meanwhile Lord Mars turned every other cubic inch of matter within the affected volume back to positive matter, like a chessboard of black and white, in order to speed the destruction. And again he vanished.

The first fortress-city was gone. A circular breach was punched clean through the hull of the Dyson. The burning edges of this breach were not protected by the disinertia and magnetic force fields used to preserve the Dyson hull against the interior environment of Ara A, and so the plasma began melting the neutronium struts and artificial sheets of energy-gathering and energy-projecting material that formed the hull surface.

Compared to the whole volume of the Dyson, however, this dam-age was simply nothing. Solar plasma began pouring into the breach in the hull, but it was a pinprick in a canvas larger than the Atlantic, with a match held to the pinhole.

In the same moment when a new fortress-city received the death signal of the first, and realized it held supreme command of the Dyson, Lord Mars was there, and again the entire volume of the second-in-command fortress-city was reversed and became antimatter. This city sent out dying cries to many locations, not just one.

The ability of Lord Mars to reverse matter polarity had strange side effects. One side effect was that by means of a double reversal, he could make a duplicate of himself, exact down to every atomic particle. These he could multiply geometrically. These he linked through mind circuits using a technique developed by Lady Venus and Aeneas. Aeneas had given the mindlinks tachyon channels, so that the thoughts between all the twin brains of all the bodies of Lord Mars, despite any distance, acted as one.

Led by Lady Venus, Lord Mars followed the command chains of thought. He kept expecting to encounter a false lead running to a trap, but it never happened. Ten thousand of Lord Mars slew one million cities of the vampires in an instant of total conversion; then one hundred thousand slew one hundred million; then ten million slew a billion.

He did this all in a space of seconds, spreading far more damage than all the wars of history combined, and never once did he smile.

At the speed of light, the explosions would not be seen until seconds, minutes or a quarter hour later at any point further along the vast curve of the Dyson. On the other hand, the explosions would have been seen by any slave city that just so happened to have hyperspatial periscope focused on a master city above it in the hierarchy, had any slave dared to spy on its superior.

However, even this damage was as nothing, compared to unthinkable immensity. It was as if one aggressive virus had killed off one billion of the neurons in a man's body, leaving ninety billion untouched.

As planned, at this point, the ten million copies of Lord Mars, acting as one, changed tactics. Now he oriented the atoms of his body neither to the positive or negative, but to a neutral orientation, so that his protons became neutrons, and electrons neutrinos. By what manipulation of the strong nuclear force he could keep the neutrinos flying in the same shape as an electron cloud, and interact with other atoms, was a mystery beyond human science.

But his red body turned jet black, and became as hard as neutronium, invulnerable to any known form of kinetic, physical or electromagnetic damage. Even death energy was slowed and confused by the neutronium based life. (Aeneas, looking on from afar via hyperspatial periscope, flexed the scales of his subcutaneous armor open and shut, feeling paltry and ridiculous.)

When Lord Mars next appeared in a mile-high command arena, he did not obliterate it instantly.

The mountains of undead flesh grew organs and reared up. They were not amoeboid except by choice: each grew limbs, tendrils, claws, manipulator hooks as needed from any convenient surface of its colorless flesh.

Lord Mars signaled to the Emperor Aeneas. Lord Mars saw the distant edges of the chamber suddenly turn red. Aeneas had surrounded this spot, and the ten million like it where any copy of Lord Mars stood, in a warp field lowering the speed of light to just above the speed of sound. Beams and bullets were now useless. Anything traveling above Mach One would find itself outside his frame of reference. And the vampires were trapped with him in the slow-light zone. No signals could escape this event horizon.

The vampire lords formed mouths and roared. Lord Mars drew his longsword in one hand and his pistol in the other. For the first time he smiled.

Then he made a squad of himself, then a company, then a battalion.

As he ran forward he saw all the objects around him flattening slightly in the direction of his motion, slow down like a visual recording played at low speed, and the redness grow darker as its mass increased. The huge hills of undead flesh turned their bellies to a fluid substance that they shed as they heaved themselves out of their bowl-shaped thrones and wallowed forward riding vast slime trails. Towering thousands of feet, the mountains rushed toward him, bellowing, emitting death-energy from their crags and peaks and newly-formed eyes.

Lord Mars slew and slew, wading through undead flesh to slay again.

His pistol was little more than an barrel holding a servomind and a multi-channel reception pearl. Stations on the planet Mars, powerhouses, atomic piles, accelerators, and arsenals were positioned to fire any type of vibration, energy, or solid destruction his gun crews could feed into their transmitting pearls.

This time, what he shot into the lacerated vampire masses heaving and roaring about him were burrowing, nerve-seeking darts designed by Lady Venus, containing thought-reading and infiltration mechanisms.

Some few he spared for a fate worse than death, cutting their brains away from nerve channels. He thrust into the disgusting nerve-mass appliances that prevented the shadow-condition cellular transformations. No cut nerves regrew.

The vampires had all the technologies of the Lords of Creation at their command. When Lord Mars could take them by surprise, he prevailed. In thousands and tens of thousands of battles where they were ready, he died, overcome by energies and forces he could not see or understand.

There were two things that gave him an fighting chance.

The first was that the enemy reacted unimaginatively to the current battle environment. They reached out with death-energy beams or destructive rays or forces which simply could not propagate when the speed of light was so slow. On the other hand, a neutronium sword tip moving at the speed of sound, when that was nine-tenths of the current speed of light, would create a megaton kinetic explosion in any target he struck, or, if he put his back into it, a thermonuclear reaction.

The second was that the enemy reacted unimaginatively to everything. Each underling sent messages during combat to remote higher-ups, but followed unsuccessful tactics until countermanded. Meanwhile, the armies of Lord Mars had no leaders but himself. There was no center, no line of communication to trace or cut. It was all him. Any of him was in command.

After the battle, he reversed the duplication process and gathered himself back into one. That one sat panting atop an undead mountain of pale flesh, teeth clenched, but smiling. As he regrouped, he noticed how many of his selves had committed suicide via total conversion to avoid capture. His smile faltered. The enemy had been fighting to gather captives, not to win. That was not a good sign.

Despite what Brother Beast always said about the damage to his soul, Lord Mars regretted none of his many suicides. Or so he ordered himself to think.

Avoiding capture was necessary. The command-monster on which he sat was proof of that. The vampire mountain had been lobotomized of all trace of free will by the Venus weapons. It was merely the puppet of Lord Mars. All voluntary nerve links were cut. Its identified itself, in its own nonverbal language, as *Xormxragon*, which meant, *the Deceiver*.

That name was also a bad sign.

Dimly, over the mental links, he could see Lady Venus and Lady Luna downloading volumes of memory from the creature's undead brain cells. Lord Mars himself was busy giving counterfeit commands through the brain of Xormxragon. The monster's underlings were prevented from remembering or questioning recent events.

The vast majority was unaware of anything untoward. It was as if Lord Mars had appeared in a throneroom, killed one despot while leaving the empire unaware of the coup.

Lady Venus gave a small scream of surprise and fear. "There is no evidence in any of the surviving brains of any higher officers! There is no galactic empire, no galaxy. In fact, they have no knowledge that any universe exists above the surface of Ara A. They think this red hell is all there is."

Aeneas said, "They shot at us! We were above the surface! They knew we existed!"

Lady Venus said, "Not these. Someone else, by remote control, working through the Dyson-dwelling vampire lords, and made them perform actions meaningless to them."

Aeneas said, "What does it mean?"

Through the brain of Xormxragon, Lord Mars was connected to the control mechanisms of the War Dyson. Through their astroseismic sensors, he now saw the solar temblors heralding the approach of thirty nine Dysons. The vast spheres came wallowing slowly through the plasma of Ara A. They formed a narrowing globe all around. Frame-dragging detectors sensed that the warpcore armatures girdling the enemy Dyson equators were spinning rapidly, preventing any spacewarp, preventing any escape. Gravity readings showed the Dysons were forming black holes at their cores, preparing to fire.

Because space outside the Dyson where he now stood was flat, Lord Mars realized that there could have been no FTL signals sent to these Dysons. The more distant ones could not have yet seen the fact that the first nova beam fusillade had missed. The englobement was prearranged.

The smile of Lord Mars vanished.

Spacewarps were still possible inside the captive Dyson. Lord Mars called on Aeneas and returned to the round table in one step. He threw his useless sword clattering to the floorstones.

Aeneas asked again, "What does it mean?" But now he was staring at the dropped sword.

Lord Mars spoke with no change of expression. "It means, sire, that this was too easy. I have failed you. It means this was a trap."

20

OBLITERATION OF MAN

In an immense dead city that formed a hollow sphere of ribs encircling the black heart of the galaxy, only one window was lit. From it a single beam reached. In the ray of that beam Warlord Rhazakhang the Obliterator was hanging, motionless.

To speak, the Ultimate Overlord thrust into the brain of Rhazakhang the ideas he wished him to possess; to listen, he ripped the thought directly out. Both operations left trails of painful damage.

Had words been exchanged, they would have been like this:

"Let Warlord Rhazakhang rejoice! The matter of Sol is concluded. The Living Worlds have been found, and destroyed, and the horde of their living energy been added to our feast coffers."

"All souls are thine to consume, Overlord!"

"As reward, receive thy portion."

For the first time in countless centuries, Rhazakhang received a pleasing sensation from his master rather than the normal, endless pain. Life energy, golden, sweet and glorious, filled the cells in his body.

Rhazakhang recovered a level of intelligence and opened old memory chains he had not enjoyed in eons.

He remembered the taste of consuming the last survivors of organic life. Their worlds had been found hidden in a nook of this very Great Sphere englobing the galactic core-singularity where the Overlord ruled. He recalled the savor of pain, the smack of fear, the spice of agony and self sacrifice as wives and mothers saw lovers and children shrivel and die in their arms... and this feast had no such scent.

The bliss was interrupted by a lance of pain. As if he had bitten a wasp in the midst of a mouthful, the thoughts of the Overlord stabbed his brain.

"Your doubt is plain. Let Rhazakhang unfold the source of his suspicions."

"The victory was too easy, Overlord."

"How so? The humans acted precisely as you predicted."

"Heretofore, the Tellurians were more erratic. They possess free will."

"Let Rhazakhang contemplate that his swift destruction would please his master, if you are so insolent as to imply that an underling can penetrate a deception that fools his superior!"

"That destruction would also please me, if I am proved wrong. Grant me sufficient energy to travel to the battle scene. If some Living Worlds still live, the trove of their life will pay both for the expense of sending your servant, and will placate your wrath."

The Ultimate Overlord brooded for a time. In some half-buried memory deep in his soullessness, recalled what creatures who possessed free will were like. Having recently fed, his feelings of rage, jealousy, bitterness, and hate were also once more inside him, which he had not for many eons felt.

It was worth any expense to confirm the obliteration of life.

The Ultimate Overlord said, "Go!" The ringworld-sized armatures of the Great Sphere began to spin.

When Rhazakhang arrived at Ara A, some of the other warlords showed signs of insubordination, resistance or self-will. It was a common side effect of feasting. After a series of pitched battles, he killed them and ate their souls. Rhazakhang placed his own trusted servants, Dzazanang the Ineluctable and Vsasrhazing the Exsanguinator, into the places once occupied by the dead warlords. Eventually normal operations resumed.

Dzazanang, his marshal, escorted him to the World Armada of the Tellurians. Neither one, strictly speaking, was in a space vessel. The machinery of propulsion and defense they wore like armor, with lesser servants tucked in convenient pockets in the plates.

Inside Dyson of Xormxragon the Deceiver (a dangerous underling, but one whose involuntary sacrifice brought this victory), were the prey planets. There were punctures from nova-beam fire here and there penetrating the Dyson hull. Some were covered over with force fields. Others simply allowed the plasma of Ara A to flood inside, and spheres of fire were growing there.

The human worlds were orbiting some two lightminutes beneath the hull, surrounded by the eyeball-shaped dark stars that had destroyed them, and countless swarms of battlemoons and combat worlds. Once they had been green. Now all life, down to the last microbe, was gone.

Here were the three gas giants, Jupiter, Neptune, and Uranus, and the shrunken and damaged superterrestrial of Saturn. A crowd of lesser planets, worldlets, and moons of mankind orbited them.

Rhazakhang turned upon the worlds lanterns of various colors taken from stars of various psychologies, and examined the neuropsionic echo. He formed a palaeoscope in his outer flesh and observed the ancient aspects of the globes, using a timewarp to bend their world-lines as he did so, so that the past image did not pass outside his vision range.

Only one had been green a million years ago. The larger of the double planet was the original homeworld of man. The smaller partner of the double planet had originally been gray, waterless, airless. This was called the Earth-Moon system. Rhazakhang expended some store of life energy to allow himself to feel curiosity. He sent flakes of himself as probes to the smaller world. It was the source of all the dreamland disturbances in the area. The ruins of some potent sub-consciousness broadcast system still hung about to the mountain peaks, with wisps of dreams still clinging.

Why would the living creatures bothered to terraform the dead globe and seed it with life? The energy costs of such projects were absurdly high. The population pressures on the homeworld could not explain it: Earth had not, even now, taken the form of a single city reaching from pole to pole.

Rhazakhang altered his shape to match the human norm here. He and his servant created a tube of vacuum through the earthly atmosphere to the surface of the larger planet and plunged down this tube at terminal velocity. At the bottom, they neutralized their inertia, came instantly to rest, and collapsed the vacuum. This created a shock-wave and triggered storms. Flinging a series of contortion pearls from his coat to various points throughout the hemisphere, Rhazakhang stepped from one scene of destruction to another, as curiosity took him.

Finally they stood in the throneroom of the Lords of Creation. Here at the round table, each beneath his insignia, were the dead leaders of the Living Worlds. Rhazakhang stood on two feet as a hulking, faceless biped. Had he not tucked his extra mass into nullspace, he would have been too large for the chamber. Dzazanang was shaped like a tripod, his main mass at the ceiling apex, forming sense organs as needed at the crotch of the tripod, staring downward.

Rhazakhang probed the dead bodies with several energies. Dzazanang did not have as much spare energy in his brain as Rhazakhang, so he could only watch his master's investigations with dull incuriosity.

Rhazakhang eventually stopped moving. "Explain this."

Dzazanang formed a tendril and pointed. "When defeat was certain, the orders given from this one, Lady Venus, went to this figurehead, Emperor Hypocritus the First, who was under her mental control. He ordered all his subjects to commit suicide, in order to deny to us the benefits of their living force. We are fortunate that some disobeyed the order, or else we would not have recovered any life energy at all. It is unclear why she permitted her slaves to disobey her figurehead."

"Did the humans caught alive offer any resistance or defiance?"

"None whatever, master."

"Did their brains show any signs of tampering?"

"Yes, master. Their memories showed that Lady Venus attempted a mind control to compel them to commit suicide, but the population numbers were greater than her broadcast capacity. They were brain-damaged, and reduced to idiocy, but resisted the compulsion."

Rhazakhang reached with a force beam through the walls of the palace, and brought forward a corpse that had been buried in another wing. It was a necroform servant. "They had vampirism technology, but did not use it?"

"Only to create servants, or destroy the free will as a penalty for crime. Records show only the outer worlds, gas giants, used such servants in any considerable numbers. Emperor Hypocritus the First ordered them all sealed away or destroyed when he came to power."

"They had three warpcores of planetary mass and range. Where are they?"

"Lost. The mind records show each was ordered to expel the others from our timespace coordinate system."

"Hm. Lady Venus was the true leader?"

"Yes."

"Where is she?"

"This corpse here. Her name was Nephelethea Cimon, daughter of Ranidaayani. This red colored man is Lord Mars. His name was Thucydides Achilles Apollyon Tell, son of Isabella. He slew all the other lords in the chamber, and came and put his arms around her, touching his lips to her lips before impaling both through the heart with a single thrust from his sword. The meaning is obscure."

"The lip-touch is a sign of affection. Who is this one? Do you know?"

"We know. We captured both thought records and written records intact. That is Lord Mercury. Procopius Tell, son of Filchingmort. Note that he died with hand raised, with only the middle finger extended. Again, the meaning is obscure."

"It is a sign of disrespect."

"Directed at his murderer?"

"No. At us. He foresaw we would stand here."

Rhazakhang now drifted up to perch on the top of the highest of the three heads on the imperial throne. He peered down at the chamber of the dead.

Rhazakhang said, "There is no emotional trace of the agony typically displayed by organics whose loved ones die. They were remarkably placid. Almost bovine. Speculate as to why this should be."

Dzazanang disliked the order to speculate, but, fearful of pain, he released his precious but shrinking store of life energy into higher brain sections.

This brought old memories, emotions, and creative drives out of hibernation. As always, his first sensation was self-loathing, hatred of what he had become.

He said, "From how well they fought, these were obviously a war-like people. Stoicism is common in such races."

"Yet here are signs of affection and there signs of defiance, and other highly-charged emotions of which no trace exists in the cellular residue."

Rhazakhang lashed out with a power ray, cutting the roof of the palace away, reaching across interplanetary space, and severing the planet Mercury in half. The surface of the world turned into molten debris, which a wash of kinetic energy tossed into space as a cloud of asteroids. Revealed was a contortion pearl, grown to be as large as the nickel iron core of the planet. "What is this?"

Dzazanang answered: "A contortion node. It has enough size to move all the planets to any mate, or even a small star. But we found the mate: it was seen hanging near the firing aperture."

"Where is it now?"

"Missing."

"Did the Living Men fire the Dyson beam?"

"Many times."

"Was the missing contortion pearl capable of disinertia? If so, it would have been carried along the beam path without harm."

"Unknown, sir."

"Was the Dyson beam ever fired outsystem?"

"Only once."

"Along what vector?"

"Its first discharge was toward Coma Berenices, the star SN2005ap in the Coma Cluster."

Rhazakhang resumed his full size, spilling out of the broken roof of the throne chamber, coating the city of Ultrapolis, and sending masses of himself, like glacier, creeping down the sides of Mount Everest.

Into each wing of each building of the city, every door and window, vent and chimney, along all plumbing, he protruded substances, leafing through all books, reading all storage crystals, absorbing the brain cell residue from corpses. He prodded and studied.

Rhazakhang said, "In the historical records here, is mention of a law made by Lord Tellus outlawing certain kinds of air vibrations called music, and commanding history to be altered. Let us see the instruments by which this was done."

Dzazanang used a force beam to drive a distortion pearl beneath the crust of the Earth. They both stepped to the spot, changing their bodies to suit the new environment, which was lava. They became streamlined, heavily armored, assuming an aspect of centipedes or sea cucumbers.

Above them was an anti-continent of downward pointing mountain peaks and trenches like celestial domes, reflecting the shape of the seas and mountains flexing the tectonic plates above. Affixed to this roof of boiling stone were gigantic funnel shapes of nanomolecular assembly factories.

Rhazakhang looked at the rows of black funnels. Each one was a half a mile long, with an intake vent to drink in numberless tons of liquid rock, sift it for needed elements, and contort to the surface the goods thus created. A single one could have easily produced all material goods needed for a city. The endless rows marched endlessly into the distance.

Rhazakhang probed the nearest one. It held traces of recent activity. The logs had been erased, but neuropsionic molecular analysis showed that hosts of gravitic engines had been made, or other war materials. But the final strata of traces showed biological material being created. Flesh, blood, bone.

Rhazakhang said, "The records say these are the machines that Lord Tellus built to falsify the history records, and create a Jazz Age where none existed. Speculate."

Dzazanang felt a spasm of hate, and lost more of his dwindling supply. He said, "The falsification of the Jazz Age was a practice run, to train his people how to do the work. The corpses filling the worlds and moons are fake. No mass suicides occurred. The men found alive were also fakes. They were flesh puppets filled with the life energy of cows. The Tellurian wealth is beyond imagining: they threw us a morsel to sate us, and we thought it was the whole."

As he spoke, a second realization came. Dzazanang spoke again. "No palaeoscope will ever reveal their escape route, since the time-record layer is not accessible from inside stars. They allowed themselves to be lured into the Dyson below the surface of Ara A, perhaps knowing it was a trap, for just this reason. It is the only place where the palaeoscope is blind."

Rhazakhang said, "Speculate: How did they make living beings?"

Again, a spasm of hatred stabbed Dzazanang. "Life is made from life, master. Their records show the technique. One needs living matter, even if only a single cell, to go into the matrix of the nanomachinery. It must consume nutriment to build up its life energy, which ultimately comes from the parent star."

"Where did they learn this lore? It does not come from any of the Nine Sciences we take from the Forerunners."

"Master, they grow and live. They do not think like us."

Rhazakhang said, "The Living Beings have escaped us."

And because there was no one else at hand, Rhazakhang began draining life from his screaming servant. Then he forced him to sing flattery while he beat the underling comatose.

Before he slipped into unconsciousness, Dzazanang called out, "Remember, master! Victory is still within grasp. The obliteration of Man is close! There is a betrayer among the Living Beings, who will lead them into our hands…"

Rhazakhang was mollified, and did not kill his servant.

Book 3

The World Armada

01

SECOND EARTH

Aeneas, to celebrate the fifth year anniversary of his coronation as the Emperor of Man, decided to hold court on the surface of Second Earth.

Aeneas set his new throne on the grass beneath a circle of trees atop a tall hilltop on a small island in the middle of a blue lake surrounded by flowering slopes and white mountains. The flowers in the distance reflected pink, purple, white, saffron and periwinkle in the calm mirror of the lake. The new world was sculpted to look as much like Earth as possible: this area was modeled after Heaven Lake, in a peninsula memorializing Korea on a continent memorializing Asia.

It was a beautiful spot. The first time he held court there, however, it was raining, and the miniature sun was at apogee, and was setting, so that the wind was blustery and cold. The seats of the Lords of Creation were set in a circle, each under its proper tree, but there was no table here.

Most of his relatives had erected parasols or pavilions of fabric or energy above their ornamented seats, or lit braziers against the cold, or used a kinetic filter field called "Maxwell's demon" that only let fast moving particles touch their skin. Most, not all. Lord Pluto, in helm and mantle and dark armor beneath his cypress tree, and Lord Mars, scarlet and nude beneath his ash tree, did not deign to notice the wet, or perhaps their nervous systems could no longer register human discomforts.

"Welcome to Second Earth," Aeneas said to the gathered Lords of Creation.

Lady Venus was seated beneath a canopy of living peacocks, who interlaced their wings closely enough above her to intercept each drop. Behind her was her myrtle tree. "Son, why so uncomfortable a throneroom?"

Aeneas said, "Two reasons: first, our business will be carried out with more dispatch if the discomfort of our subjects is reflected in our personal discomfort."

"And the second?"

He said, "I shall answer anon. Lord Uranus, have you good news to report?"

As ever, the mask of Spyridon Tell, Lord Uranus, showed no expression. He was seated before a Rowan tree. "Better than hoped. Urvasthrang the Annihilator was called into the great consultation by the visiting dignitary, a creature named Rhazakhang the Initiator of Obliteration. Urvasthrang was cross examined by direct mind-to-mind contract, as were all the vampire lords, but Rhazakhang believed everything we ordered Urvasthrang to think. There was no sign that he detected the imposture."

Aeneas said, "Does the enemy suspect how we escaped? Or where we are?"

Lord Uranus told his mask to display a thoughtful frown. "I can only speak for sure about my project. Lord Rhazakhang was allowed to discover our manufactories beneath the crust of Earth, and the megascale contortion pearl under the crust of Mercury. He is now convinced we have fled Ara A toward Coma Berenices. He will order a pursuit made."

Lady Venus said, "Sire, the vampire lords who came here to consult with Urvasthrang were lobotomized of their free will, and placed under our control. Two of them have reported back by contortion thought-broadcast. The signs indicate none of the vampire commanders suspect that we had three megascale pearls, not two."

When the thirty-nine War Dysons formed a rough globe about the captured Dyson where the Tellurians were thought to be trapped, their Tipler ring armatures spun to prevent any warp fissures from forming. The armature on the captured Dyson was much larger and more potent than any of the three warpcores of the human race, but it could not out-wrestle thirty-nine.

But this did not stop the Schroedinger particles of space contortion.

Lord Mercury smirked. "The second megascale pearl was disinertialized, then accelerated out of the Ara A system at lightspeed, sire, last seen headed toward Coma Berenices. Once out of visible range (and none of the vampires could use hyperspatial periscopes while they were flattening space) the pearl cloaked itself in an antiphotonic field, and was recovered. I can do that trick with a burst of Sol's holy light two more times and only two. Then the nullspace store is exhausted."

Aeneas said, "None of them suspect we departed the damaged Dyson, leaving our worlds behind? They thought we hid in the fleeing pearl's nullspace?"

Lord Pluto said in his cold, slow voice, "Sire, we should assume the idea has at least been contemplated by the enemy, but, without confirmatory evidence, it would remain just that, a suspicion."

Aeneas said to Lord Mars, "Suppose you were the enemy commander. Would you have seen through this trick?"

Lord Mars said, "Let me remind you of the facts of recent history. Ara A is a globe one lighthour in diameter. The dense, hot plasma prevents the propagation of light. The Dysons, once they flatten space, are like submarines with sonar. Gravitons cannot detect Schroedinger waves.

"During the first phase of the battle, the enemy formation was over twenty lightminutes in radius. Close coordination was impossible. They did not see our first move, which was to rush—well, to lumber slowly through the dense plasma—to the nearest Dyson. When it opened fire, its nova-beam punctured right through us and out the other side. A beam forty-two lightseconds in radius can make a pretty hole in a sphere six lightminutes in radius, but not enough to take us out."

Lady Venus said, "We recall all this, Brother. It was only a few months ago!"

Aeneas said, "Let him speak. He is getting at a point."

Lord Mars said, "Thank you, sire. My point is that each phase of the battle had its own intelligence risks. The beam that struck us cleared a channel that Lord Jupiter held open. We sent back along it the megascale contortion pearl Lord Mercury had readied. I do not see how any outside observer could have seen it."

Everyone smiled at the memory. The pearl had entered the vast volume of the enemy Dyson, too small to be noticed. Then it unfolded.

For space contortion had two uses: the first use was matter broadcast. A pearl could draw a physical body into a condition called nullspace, which created a cloud of Schroedinger waves in its place to bookmark its possible locations in the universe, and when those waves reached the receiving pearl, the waveform collapsed, and the body emerged from nullspace.

But the second use was to draw a physical body into nullspace and store it there.

During the four years of guerrilla war the World Armada had suffered during its long retreat from the expanding supernova of Sol, Aeneas had thought it prudent to return in certain robot-crewed ships insulated by slow-light spacewarp to the site of Sol's ongoing fiery death, and catch some five hundred Earth-masses of solar plasma into nullspace. This was less than a thousandth of Sol's whole mass, but it was the largest Lord Mercury's engineers could store.

There, in a timeless node of nonbeing, the mass waited.

This bit of Sol the size of Jupiter was still was as hot, as nova-hot, as Sol itself, and as bright. The outward pressure of the agitated plasma was the same.

Out it went. In six minutes, the expanding shockwave reached the inner hull of the Dyson. All the fortress-cities of the vampires in their millions and myriads were bathed in the holy radiance. All died before they knew themselves slain. The mass dissipated into an expanding cloud under its own force, cooled, and precipitated into hydrogen.

The single survivor was the lord high commander of the attacking Dyson, named Urvasthrang the Annihilator. He had been found by Lord Uranus, kidnapped via space-contortion by Lord Mercury, paralyzed by Lord Mars, brain-raped by Lady Venus, and deposited in a blind vault, out of harm's way, by Lord Pluto, all in the one well-coordinated second before the wave of light from Sol had struck his empty throne.

Lord Uranus said, "Sire, I agree with Lord Mars. While the opaque hull kept all the visible light of Sol within the Dyson, matter does not halt neuropsionic waves. The property that makes Sol deadly to vampires passed through the hull. The neuropsionic effect was stopped by the unholy properties of Ara A, just beyond our hull. Had we dared do the same trick in open space, rather than inside a star, the enemy would have seen."

Lord Mercury had then used that same megascale pearl again to bring vampire automatons by the millions across from the damaged to the undamaged but now-empty Dyson. Urvasthrang, or his remnant, had been poured back into the cup-shaped throne orb in his master city, and all his staff and his hierarchies replaced, taking up duties of the slain vampires without missing a beat.

Lord Mars said, "From the standpoint of what the enemy could see, the Xormxragon Dyson was struck and holed. The second phase of the battle was a circumvallation. The flotilla of Dysons surrounded us.

Pentagonal force fields were projected between twenty vertices where one or two Dysons were stationed, to create a dodecahedron, with the damaged Xormxragon Dyson caught at the center. The energy planes maintained kinetic and disinertial force sufficient to prevent the escape of anything made of matter. They were also opaque to Schroedinger waves, blocking any space contortion into or out of the dodecahedron. But the two Dysons at the center, both of them under our control, exchanged fire, and this would have masked the space contortion exchanges then underway. Lord Mercury moved us here, and left our deserted worlds back into the damaged Xormxragon Dyson."

It had been a tremendous manufacturing effort to equip each man, woman, and child of the three hundred human races on the many planets and myriad moons of the World Armada with space contortion pearls to carry themselves and a remnant of their belongings, herds and houses, into exile. Even so, without the megascale pearl at the core of planet Mercury, and without the unpredictable genius of Lord Mercury himself to solve the myriad technical and logistical problems, it could not have been done.

"And we said farewell to First Earth," muttered Lord Saturn, sadly. There had been riots among his antiquarians at the loss, and many had been returned to nullspace as punishment.

Nonetheless, certain cities, monuments, and mountains having sentimental value were brought along to Second Earth, their places taken by imitations precise down to the molecular level.

On Second Earth alone the migration faltered. The new populations immediately began to squabble and quarrel, in any places where old disputes still lingered. Aeneas in wrath sent his most terrible servants among them, monstrous things his mad grandfather made: heartless and cyclopean cyborgs with whips of fire and wings of steel, or three-headed dogs with tails of cobras and teeth of iron. The ringleaders were plucked from burning ruins, tortured, and forced each to work to raise new lands from the sea to give to the opposing party as many identical copies to any land in dispute as they wished.

Second Earth had twelve continents, four Jerusalems, three Romes, a New York not far from New Amsterdam, a version of Salem where only witches dwelt, a North America set aside for Sioux, and a Constantinople across the sea from Istanbul.

Aeneas was fearfully severe with the rioters, and executed many, for he held mind-alteration to be abominable. Earthmen baffled him. Venus was a world of sea-nomads in floating cities, where war was unknown, whose histories were lists of festivals and love affairs. Born there, he could not understand longstanding hatreds over land ownership. Nor did he tolerate tumult and murder, not when countless enemies surrounded them.

Lord Mars said, "As before, no foe was in position to detect the space contortion. Then this Dyson, with us hidden inside, took our position, as ordered, at one vertex of the dodecahedron, and erected the proper energy planes. And we are just lucky."

Aeneas said, "Lucky? How so?"

"They want us alive. If they had been fighting to kill, they would have moved faster and struck harder." He shrugged. "The undead crew we left behind in the damaged Dyson, as programmed, spun up its armatures, lowered lightspeed, nullified gravity-waves. This blinded the enemy, and prevented their nova-beams from entering the frame of reference of their target. Like raising a drawbridge. And so the third and final phase, a board-and-storm operation, began."

They remembered those days. Long ago it seemed. The enemy had brought twelve Dysons close enough for hulls to touch, and hundreds of trillions of the undead soldiers began the slow process of migrating into the damaged Dyson, seeking the hidden humans in control of it. The machines and undead automaton crew left behind fought them with suicidal ferocity. On such a scale, what Lord Mars called a board-and-storm operation was a matter of months, not minutes.

Meanwhile, the abandoned worlds of man and their puppet populations had fought back. The puppets were vat-grown creatures, undead, but disguised with layers of living cells to be able to pass for living creatures. Whenever one came near a vampire, it released a man-volume of stored life-energy into special still-living cells set aside for just that purpose, for the victorious vampires to feed upon, and be sated. Upon capture the puppets committed suicide, or seemed to. They had been dead all along, of course, but after death were indistinguishable from any other corpse.

Lord Mars said, "During the board and storm, the puppets we left behind fought with the same level of skill as the person the puppet was based on. Do you remember Father's insane rules about solving math equations and sharpshooting at ballots in order to vote? This was a lucky break for us. All the puppets based on men old enough to have voted under the First Emperor were crack shots. And, as it turns out, those equations are useful for suborbital ballistics. So if real people, ones not programmed to lose the battle, are ever attacked, they can outmatch the zombies of the enemy by ten to one. The casualties were remarkably one-sided. The enemy kept closing to hand-to-hand range. They want to be as close as possible to drain life."

During these months, the humans in the Urvasthrang Dyson began to investigate their new home. Began, but never continued. The size defeated them. But there was space enough to hide all the populations of man and all their cities (which they towed after them) interplanetary distances away from the nearest slumbering corpse-piles of undead.

In most places, the Dyson hull was a solid force field, atom-thin, but wherever the neutronium support beams intersected, clouds of gas or crowds of asteroids had gathered, collected by irregularities in the hull gravity or the eddies in solar wind from the core accretion disk. Some ancient peoples had also built habitats, ranging between the size of a closet to the size of a gas giant, tethered to such intersections like grapeclusters.

Lord Saturn spoke next. "This shipyard—if that is the word for a bay five lightseconds in radius—was abandoned a million years ago. It was not built by the vampires, but by some race that eliminated record of their appearances from the memory layer of the universe. I assume this was the Forerunners. The Great Eye we found half carved out of a neutron star had never been activated. No one knows we are here."

The unfinished eye had been shattered into nine worlds, large and small, and fifty worldlets, by Lord Neptune. Miniature suns were orbited among the moons and asteroids. Terraformers set to work rendering the surfaces habitable, or habitats far below the surface, larger than continents.

Lord Mercury's people deposited trillions of pearls across all the lands and seas and clouds of the new worlds, large and small. The exiled human races emerged from nullspace, and, not without considerable squabbling and confusion, took possession of the newborn planets.

Meanwhile, the puppets in the damaged Dyson, dwelling in the human worlds, in time had been duly overwhelmed and consumed. The battle was over, the human race apparently wiped out, but no new orders came for Urvasthrang.

More time passed. The Dysons stayed in formation, and spacewarps continued to be blockaded.

Lord Mars said, "During all three phases of the action, my battle-pattern computer confidence amounting to certainty is that we have not been spotted. For one thing, we are not dead."

Aeneas clapped his hands together. "Very good! With the advice and consent of the Lords of Creation, I officially call the battle ended. Let all worlds stand down from battle stations. Let the wartime protocols be ended and civilian government resume. The Parliament of Man at its pleasure may sit. The Church of the Holy Roman Empire of Brazil may offer masses of thanksgiving in all worlds, and the Crime Religion of the Syndicates of America may offer bribes to the Crooked

Cosmic Cop they worship. Let all my subjects render thankful prayers for our salvation. Any questions before moving on to our main order of business?"

Lady Luna sneezed, and said, "Yes. What was your second reason for having us meet out in the rain?"

Aeneas said, "When we made Second Earth, New Luna, Second Mars, Second Venus and all these new worlds and moons, I was shocked at how many populations wanted to huddle far underground, leaving these new seas and continents empty. Placing my throne on the surface will show the common people not to fear the open sky."

Lord Mars said, "The foe's weapons would not be stopped by crust or mantle. Putting your head under the blanket will not stop the bear."

Lady Luna tossed her red hair, saying, "It is not fear. It is to get away from the sight of the endless metal heavens! We are trapped inside a Dyson sphere inside the black interior of a hypergiant star. I, for one, am famished for the sight of stars."

Aeneas said, "That time is upon us, cousin!"

He stood. He raised his hand. The clouds parted. The rain stopped. The miniature sun had set. Above were stars, shining bright. They glinted like gems.

He smiled. "Urvasthrang, along with all the other Dyson commanders, were ordered by Rhazakhang to leave Ara A and fly toward Coma Berenices, to search for us. It happened as we sat here."

Lady Luna said, "We are outside the Dyson?"

"We are orbiting it, but still within the warp zone, and are carried along. Our Dyson is currently below our horizon at this latitude." Aeneas sat again. "Now, my Lords, my Ladies, in celebration of our successful escape, of my fifth year as imperial monarch, and, yes, in celebration of the first moment in five years we have not been under a deadly threat of instant death..."

He raised his hand again. The light touching his throne grew dim as a warp field of unknown import surrounded the seated figure, then utterly black, black as onyx.

It was as menacing as if he had suddenly flourished an energy pistol, or commanded a firing squad to surround them. The Lords of Creation, stone-faced and not showing their alarm, touched their signet rings, readying their many weapons, visible and invisible.

The voice of Aeneas came out of the jet-black shadow.

"…let us discuss the fate of mankind. The floor is open."

02

THE GREAT VOID

The Lords of Creation summoned their weapons to their hands, and sat in silence, tense and waiting.

In the hands of Lord Jupiter, his lightning bolt crackled and shined, too bright to look upon. Lord Neptune held his trident, and the eddies of gravity around him made the earth below his throne tremble. Lord Saturn held his sickle. Lord Uranus held his lantern in which was what seemed a star burning. Lord Mercury raised his caduceus.

Lady Luna stood and readied her silvery recurve bow, drawing an arrow of insanity from her quiver. Lady Venus remained seated, but now her mirror was in her hands, in which any thought-rays present could be caught. Lady Pallas, in her plumed helm and man's armor, held an energy javelin in one hand. In her other was her invulnerable shield upon which none dared gaze, for the neuropsionic labyrinth pattern scrambled the visual centers of the brain. Lady Ceres drew no weapon, but the grass around her rustled, changed, and formed bioweapon spores that rose up and hung in dangerous clouds around her.

Brother Beast, looking calm, folded his hands, because he had no weapons, and Lord Mars, looking bored, folded his hands, because his weapons were irresistible.

As for Aeneas, his throne put forth an antiphotonic shadow to envelop him, black as ink, opaque as obsidian. Reddish distortions from Doppler shift clung to the edges of the shadow, betraying the presence of a spacewarp, a spot where the laws of nature were changed.

Brother Beast said, "Over the last five years, we have all gotten out of the habit of threatening our blood relations with weapons originally meant to destroy planets. Is there no way to retain the civility and goodwill we have enjoyed?"

Lord Mars said, "I notice the kid has not told us to put our weapons away."

The voice of Aeneas spoke from the darkness. "A wise leader does not give orders he knows will not be obeyed."

The rain was no longer falling, but the grass blades were wet. The circle of trees surrounding dripped drops from drooping leaves. The sky overhead showed the stars above the Dyson Sphere, and the other recently-made planets and moons of the World Armada gleaming in the light of their miniature suns.

The stars turned red, went dim, and rushed away as the Dyson entered the closed timelike curve segment of a warp channel; during their passage through the channel, they saw overhead what seemed to be their own Dyson Sphere, turned inside-out and englobing them, growing larger and rushing away into darkness; and a moment later, the hemisphere of the sky turned white, contracted, dulled, the scattered stars reappeared, growing blue as they returned to the normal hues, and hurried together like an explosion of sparks in reverse, reestablishing the normal vision of universe above once more.

Lord Uranus looked up first, and noticed what was happening. "Our trip from Alpha Centauri to Ara A took weeks inside the warpchannel! How is it that we are only outside spacetime for a moment between jumps?"

The voice of Aeneas said, "The armatures circling the War Dyson are twice the radius and command core black hole of an order of magnitude more mass than the measly K and G type stars parked at the center of the Centauri system. Also, the undead automatons are a skilled crew working with tools suited to the task to form the warp channel. Thousands of undead crew are available to oversee each aspect, practically each moment, of operation. Of course, they are all familiar with the basics of the warp science. Among mankind, I alone know it, and must do all myself. Which returns us to the question on the floor. What is to be the fate of the human race?"

Lord Saturn said, "Why do you summon a warp here, Your Imperial Majesty? I, for one, have not forgotten that my life, and those of my people, have been saved by you countless times. There is no reason to break the peace now."

Aeneas said, "The peace we enjoyed, and the obedience you gave me, was due to the immediate threat of the space vampires. Now the threat is suspended, the old nature of my relations erupts back into view, like a spring unnaturally compressed returning to true."

Lord Neptune stood and the temblors radiating from his feet grew more violent. The grass shook and his throne swayed but such was his fine control that the others there felt only the slightest vibration rippling through the ground. The teeth of his mocking smile, the glint of his eyes, were starkly white against dark blue of his sardonic face. "Well, I have certainly felt compressed these years, paying knee-tribute to a small fry who holds us all in contempt. He thinks we are tyrants! Meanwhile he dreams of nothing but destroying our family power!"

The voice of Aeneas said, "Lord Neptune, if I understand him, makes a motion to preserve the family power. The fate he foresees for mankind is a return to life as it was before the war. Is there a second to the motion?"

Now Neptune looked puzzled. "Are you mocking me?"

The voice of Aeneas was mild. "Probably not, my lord. You seem as eager to throw me off the throne as I am to climb down from it.

But climbing off a throne is less safe than climbing off a mad tiger. Mad tigers sleep. The ambitions of Imperial relatives never do."

Neptune, who had been bracing himself for some sort of fight, felt deflated. He scowled, wishing he could see the expression on the young emperor's face. He thrust the trident into the ground, tines down, and the ground-vibrations stopped.

The stars overhead changed and changed again. Now the view above was black, with the pale band of the Milky Way, like a white river, crossing one side of the sky to the other, and there were a few pale stars near this white river, bright as diamonds, but no stars elsewhere.

It was a sky without constellations: an appalling blackness.

Lady Luna, now glancing upward also, and shivering in the cold, said, "Where are we?"

Lord Jupiter still held his bolt in one hand, but now he leaned back in a relaxed pose, and poured himself a goblet of wine with his other hand. "We are wherever His Imperial Majesty has pleased to take us, his subjects."

Lady Venus crossed her shapely legs and settled more deeply into the luxurious pink cushions of her throne. "Lord Neptune seems not to realize that this is not the best time to overthrow the current government, unless we are all content to live here, wherever it is we happened to have halted. Even the nearest star is infinitely out of reach, without Aeneas."

Lord Mercury said, in a joking voice, but with no mirth in his eyes, "You mean without *you*, don't you? You secretly control him, and have done ever since that night you programmed his mind in the library!"

Aeneas said, "Actually, I was the one who put that idea into the fake version of history we showed to Rhazakhang. I thought it was funny."

Lord Mercury said, "Sire, she programmed you to *think* it funny! The irony of having *you* show to the enemy a truth you are prevented from realizing is just the type of cruel joke she enjoys! For the sake of her power, she wants you on the throne!"

Aeneas said, "If so, my mother is behind the times, I fear, Uncle Procopius. Surely I am not the first person to realize that my monopoly on the superluminary science is broken? Did none of you hear what I just said?"

Lord Uranus said softly, "I heard. There are thousands of zombies who know your secret. Any one of us could download the lore from an undead brain. I am sure my brothers are thinking furiously about how to get a trusted servant ninety million miles away to raid the nearest vampire nest or the storehouse of undead. As soon as one of them is sure he has the superluminary science, he will open fire on the rest of us."

"If Uncle Spyridon is correct," came the voice of Aeneas from the shadow, "We have only sixteen minutes before someone here opens fire. Eight minutes or so to send a space contortion beam to the nearest vampire nest, and eight minutes to get the signal back of success." A small object came floating out of the darkness surrounding Aeneas, tumbled through the air, and landed atop the rain-splattered round table. It was an old fashioned hour glass, with a quarter hour of sand in the upper glass.

Then Aeneas said to Lady Luna, "To answer your question, cousin Penthesilia, we have stopped in the inter-arm void between Sagittarius and Perseus Arms of the galaxy."

Lady Luna said, "Stopped? Here? Why?"

"I selected a spot barren of stars, hoping no enemy would be near. We departed the other searchers. I am awaiting the decision of this council as to our ultimate destination."

A dumbfounded silence answered him.

Aeneas said in a quiet voice: "This War Dyson can reach any point roughly three times the range of the Alpha Centauri armature, or six thousand lightyears, before fuel is exhausted. We would need to reduce a star the size of Canopus or Rigel to refuel, roughly 70 solar radii. Whereto, Uncles? Whither away, Aunts, Mother, Cousin?"

Lady Luna said, "The undead do not die back when they overeat their food supply, they simply hibernate. Worlds where all life dies, seas have dried, and atmospheres escape into space, the vampires simply lay, heaped, among the craters and airless hills. Wherever they have a foothold, they do not withdraw. They have had tens of millions of years to spread. Where in the galaxy could we go that they will not find us?"

Aeneas said, "Warpcores can detect warpcores. Detection range depends on the mass. This Dyson of eighteen solar mass can detect an active warpcore up to nine thousand lightyears away. The radius of the Milky Way is one hundred thousand lightyears. That should give you a basis of comparison."

Lady Pallas said, "What about beyond? The Greater Magellanic Cloud is a satellite galaxy outside the main disk, some one hundred sixty thousand lightyears away. Out of range. Are the vampires there, also?"

Aeneas said, "None my instruments detect. It would be my choice if we could reach it: but there are no string of Rigel-sized masses in the intergalactic void to use as refueling dumps. This Dyson is simply not big enough to get there."

Lady Ceres said, "What about staying here? Hiding inside the Dyson? Why do we need a star system?"

Aeneas said, "Artificial suns are short lived, especially to races who know the secret of eternal youth, such as ours. The Dyson core black hole will give off x-rays only as long as we keep dropping solar masses of matter into it."

No one suggested returning to Sol. It had been a grave risk to stay there as long as they had, long enough for the wavefront to pass Alpha Centauri. They also knew the artificial nova would be shorter lived than a natural one. By the time of the last retreat from Alpha Centauri to Ara A, the whole volume outside the expanding wavefront of Sol's explosion was even then swarming with myriads of ships, battleworlds, and black suns of the enemy.

Lady Luna said in exasperation, "So we can neither leave the galaxy nor stay!"

Lady Ceres said, "We can find unclaimed worlds around unvisited stars. They are as grains of sand by the sea, uncounted. Among infinity, we can hide."

Mars said, "Hide? We must destroy these monsters. Each last gram of them."

Lord Saturn said, "My lords and ladies, the solution is obvious! The return to our old way of life is easy: We must place these new worlds in orbit about some planetless sun, and then command all the warpcores to obliterate themselves, leaving the foe with no way to detect us, and us with no way to reach them. The knowledge of how to build them must be expunged. And, once we have dealt with mad Aeneas in the same way we dealt with the last emperor who went mad, we shall have peace, and our family power will be secure forever. Young Aeneas must die!"

Only Aeneas heard this last word, for as Lord Saturn spoke, his words seemed to grow faster and higher pitched, while the figures around him seemed to slow down. The grains of sand falling from the upper to the lower glass fell as if through molasses, then halted. The light in the area grew blindingly bright, reddened down the spectrum, and went black.

Aeneas started to activate his many defenses, but it was too late even before he began to think. In a blur of unseen, instantaneous motion, the gray-haired graybeard calmly stood, casually walked over to the throne of Aeneas, carefully took energy readings and slowly erected a counteractive time-energy shell.

This time shell did not affect the spacewarp itself. Lord Saturn did not have that power. But it did alter the speed of propagation of the warp, which altered its shape, so that the crowned head and broad shoulders of Aeneas protruded from the shadowy mass. If the youth were blinking his eyes, it was too slow to see. The expression of surprise and shock had not yet had time to form on his face.

With the immeasurable kinetic energy of an object moving at un-thinkable speed, Lord Saturn plunged his sickle directly through the middle of the circle of the crown on the motionless head, through the armored skull, and deep into the brain beneath.

03

OUTSIDE OF TIME

The battle was lost before Aeneas could react.

The tip of the sickle cracked easily through his bioadmantium skull and penetrated his primary brain. The living metal of his skull at the point of contact aged ten thousand years of withering and weakening in the moment of contact. The time-forces issuing from the sickle radiated unevenly into his brain, speeding up neural flows in one lobe while slowing those in another. The automatic failover to his secondary brain was triggered in one part but not in another. The two brains struggled, each unsure which was in charge. The result was epileptic confusion.

Aeneas would have been confused even had his brain been unaffected. Along with Lord Pluto and Lady Luna, Lord Saturn was the one family member he liked and trusted.

Trusted, yes, but Aeneas had been taken unawares by Lord Saturn once before, and he was no fool. So he had installed precautions. He has programmed military responses into his nervous system against just such an attack. They reacted before he was consciously aware of the assault.

He knew the neurons in his brain could not react quickly enough to a foe who could slow time almost to halting, nor could the high-speed cybernetics, but servominds in remote locations equipped with tachyon circuits could. While the timewarp accelerating Lord Saturn could not be stopped, not by any type of spacewarp known to Aeneas, its properties could be manipulated.

There were seven physical constants the warpcore could warp: lightspeed, the gravitational constant, the Planck constant, the neutrino rest-mass, the fine-structure constant, the permeability of vacuum, and the flux quantum. By careful manipulation of these, other fundamentals could be warped. (Careless manipulation merely shattered matter into a disorganized flood of dark energy.)

The range the projectors of time energy used by Lord Saturn, as it happened, was dependent on vacuum permeability. One of the many servominds protecting Aeneas had a reflex that reacted at tachyonic speeds, lowered the vacuum permeability, and increased the range of Lord Saturn's emitters. So the timewarp around Lord Saturn and the multivariable warp around Aeneas was instantly around them both.

The rest of the family was still frozen. The sand in the hourglass was motionless. The bodies of Aeneas and Lord Saturn were frozen, as time was not passing for either of them physically. Blood and brain matter was gushing up from the atrocious head wound of Aeneas, and droplets hung in midair. Sweat and tears hung near the flushed face of the white-haired Lord Saturn, drops flung free of eyes and brow by the violence of his motion and the anger in his blow.

But Aeneas, due to his tachyonic back-up neural system, and Lord Saturn, due to a trick of time energy known only to himself, were still able to think, to send thoughts through their rings, and to manipulate the hidden engines and emitters each had focused on the other. Energy or gravity or anything else that propagated through space was too slow: only changes to the fabric of time and space itself were able to operate within this bubble of frozen time.

Time and space were ultimately one underlying continuum, and so the spacewarps Aeneas folded around Lord Saturn, and the timewarps

Lord Saturn folded around Aeneas, the other could indirectly parry, unfold, or collapse.

They dueled. No one saw it. Nothing moved. Time was halted. The forces were invisible, and the fight went on and on.

One second of the time-energy Lord Saturn commanded, like the tip of a spear, twisted through the snakelike coils of space, and struck like a silent thunderbolt, but Aeneas folded space like an origami flower to parry. The warp Aeneas erected to parry it was anticipated. When he attempted to tilt the lightcone of the timewarp, and change the time-axis for the space-axis to neutralize it, it disintegrated and revealed a larger, artificial sub-continuum within. Inside the one second was folded an hour's worth of time energy, and, within that, a year. The defenseless Aeneas saw the year unfolding asymptotically into an infinite time. At the same time, the operation speed of the timewarp collapsed from a second to a nanosecond to an undetectably small quantum of time.

Concentric zones of time-energy now circled Aeneas. Before the immeasurable power overwhelmed him, he lowered the local speed of light to zero, allowing no energy whatsoever to propagate. This should have stalemated the attack.

But it did not. His signet ring gave him the dreadful news: *Sire, you are dead! He has killed you. As soon as normal time flow resumes, your body will age an infinite amount of time in an infinitesimal amount of time.*

"He must have seen what I did: the speed of light is set to below the propagation rate of neuro-electric flow. If he lets time resume, and his attack lands and kills me, each cell in his brain will be outside of the frame of reference of its neighbor. If I die, we both die!"

In the frozen moment of time, Aeneas stared in wonder at the face of Lord Saturn as he loomed over the throne, a bloody sickle in his hand. The photons striking his eye were motionless, so that image was dark. Technically speaking, he was not seeing at all, for he had adjusted his eyes to perceiving the frozen gravitic waves the spacewarp-sensing and manipulating organs in his nervous system could detect.

Aeneas made ring to ring contact with a neuropsionic ray he directed through a warp. It was traveling faster than light, hence needed no outside reference of passing time to move. His message: "We are stalemated. Remove your zone, for if it falls, I die, and my last move takes effect: all your brain activity will be halted. You have no defense to deflect this."

There was no reply.

"You cannot hate me enough to be willing to die with me! I know you too well! Remove your zone, or we both perish!"

The channel was open. The ring registered the Schroedinger wave collapse showing his words had been heard and understood. Lord Saturn could hear him. But he made no answer.

Aeneas saw motion in the corner of his eye. At first, he thought it was another form of attack, some sort of a delusion planted in his mind. He could not turn his eye and focus on the motion, and his other sensors in his body (and he had many) were blind without wave-motions of some sort reaching them from the outside world.

A figure stepped between him and Lord Saturn, blocking his view. To Aeneas, the scene was colorless, painted in dark gray and light gray. He saw what looked like a pale ghost walking in a shadowless lunar landscape.

It was a figure of middle height and heavy build, wearing a hooded flightsuit.

The figure took Lord Saturn by the wrist and shoulder, and strained. Aeneas saw the sickle removed from his own head as Lord Saturn's arm bent backward. In the time-freeze, there was no give to the elbow joint: the stranger was breaking the bones. There was a disturbance around the arm as it moved, which Aeneas realized was supersonic friction.

A signet ring, larger and brighter than any ring of the Lords of Creation, gleamed on the finger of the gloved hand. The deadly time-energy zone around Aeneas dimmed into non-potential. A host of myriad years was no longer in position to wash over him the moment time resumed.

Aeneas saw to his alarm that the warp field he had established around Lord Saturn was still in place. The moment time resumed, Lord Saturn would die.

The figure turned, and drew back his hood.

Aeneas had already known who it must be. When Thoon the assassin threatened, or the interplanetary beam weapon from the moon, an unseen hand had saved him.

The man had a condition called heterochromia, each eye of different hue, which gave his gaze a strangeness that did not hinder the spread of rumors of madness. His nose had been broken and set badly, but he had never had it regrown. His beard was black with streaks of white through it. His hair was dark except above the temples. It was close cropped, almost a tonsure, which made his ears stand out like jug handles. Little ports and jacks peeped through his hair in a circle showing where originally thought circuits in his crown had plugged into his skull. That crown was currently on the head of Aeneas.

It was Evripades Telthexorthopolis, Lord Tellus. His grandfather.

The countenance could not be mistaken: it was on more stamps and coins and monuments and medallions than any other face had ever been.

In the shape of his face, the philosopher's brow, the bulldog jaw, he looked mostly like Lord Jupiter; but his sardonic half-smile was Lord Neptune's. The sneer of Lord Mercury was at his nostrils, the cold gaze of Lord Uranus in his eyes, which were as large as those of Lady Venus. His skin was olive as hers.

He had the habit of squinting his left eye while opening his right. Between that, and his crooked nose, and his crooked smile which turned half his mouth upward while the other half slanted down, his whole face seemed tilted out of true.

He touched his ring to Aeneas' ring. A one-way path opened: Aeneas could receive but not send messages. The voice channel brought sound into his auditory nerve. The voice of the old Emperor was different than the recordings remembered: softer, weaker, careworn. He sounded tired.

"Only for a moment may I maintain this condition in this temporal frame of reference. So far you have done well, my heir, but the next fall of the dice wins or loses all.

"Take more caution. Trust fewer. Trust less. You are Emperor. You are alone.

"Into your memory I now imprint the approach vectors and warp coordinates of the Luminous Blue Variable 1806-20.

"This star is on the far side of the galaxy from Sol, within the Radio Nebula G10.0-0.03, which is within the interstellar molecular cloud MC13A. The star is forty million times as bright as Sol, and two hundred times the mass and diameter: It is the largest star in the Milky Way.

"The sole working set of exogalactic range Tipler armatures built by the Forerunners encircle this star. This is the Master Armature.

"I send you from dark danger to darker. Luminous Blue Variable 1806-20 is a stronghold of the vampires, and strongly held, but you must overcome them, and destroy the Master Armature as you use it to depart. They lack the resources and resourcefulness ever to build another.

"The Master Armature alone can reach Large Magellanic Cloud in Dorado, a satellite galaxy orbiting one hundred sixty three thousand lightyears beyond the rim of the Milky Way. All stars here are too small to serve as your anchor point over such vast distance, but one.

"That one is Radcliffe 136a1. It is three thousand times the mass of Sol, thirty-five times the radius, eight million times the luminosity. It is greater than any star in our galaxy.

"Whether an armature can circle and tame so great a mass, you must prove. Where after that mankind must venture, I cannot advise nor foretell.

"We are the last. All other spheres where life, organic life, once throve, now dead are, vanished quite, and nor monument nor memory is left of them. The future is as fragile as a hollow glass. It is in your hands. Save the people."

He reached out and made and adjustment to the crown on the head of Aeneas. "You are not wearing this tightly enough. Do you want it to fall?"

He turned again, and stared at Lord Saturn. "Save those you can," Grandfather sighed. "There are some who cannot be saved. My son, Geras, is dead." Geras was Lord Saturn's name.

Time resumed. Color, motion, light and noise returned. Lord Tellus was gone; no footprint bent the grass where he had, in the frozen moment, been standing. The darkness around Aeneas was gone, but Lord Tellus had left the deadly, life-destroying spacewarp in place around Lord Saturn.

There was a crack of noise like a thunderclap as volume of air the size of a man, finding itself vacuum, collapsed.

Lord Saturn made a noise half between a choke and a shriek, as if he were trying somehow to inhale and to scream both at once. His eyes were goggling as if with surprise, and blood came from his tear ducts. He fell heavily to the grass, his limbs already lose and limp. His right arm was broken in four places, and scalded as if with fire. The sickle, which Lord Tellus had left hanging in midair, fell to the grass beside him.

"What happened?" shouted Lord Mercury. He was on his feet, standing near the throne of Lady Venus. Aeneas blinked, trying to bring his many senses and sources of vision under control. Had not Lord Mercury been seated in his own throne when time froze?

Blood gushed from the back of Lord Saturn's body. It matched the blood on the sword tip of Lord Mars, who was also on his feet. Lord

Mars had somehow, either just before or just after halt of time, risen, drawn, and stabbed Lord Saturn.

Lord Neptune raised his trident, preparing a graviton-beam weapon aiming in the direction of Lord Saturn (which also, perhaps not by accident, was in the direction of Aeneas); Lord Jupiter, faster, raised his bolt and flung it at Lord Neptune.

Neither weapon landed. Aeneas raised his hand and lowered the speed of light below the speed of sound. The landscape turned red. Gravity waves and electromagnetic both were now outside the local lightcone, hence invisible, unable to affect anything within. "Halt! Lower your arms or forfeit your lives!"

04

UNEASY LIES THE HEAD

"All of you! Throw down your weapons!" shouted Aeneas. Then, in a milder voice, he said, "Even you, Lord Mars, though I thank you for trying to protect me."

Aeneas lowered his hand. Light returned to normal.

No one moved to obey him. They seemed just as frozen as if the time-stop of Lord Saturn were still in effect.

Then Lord Mars sheathed his sword. "My weapons cannot be put away, except for toys. I severed his upper spine. Nerve signals from his brain will not reach his ring finger. The wound is not fatal. He can be revived…"

Aeneas had already probed the body of Lord Saturn. There was no life energy in any of the cells of his body, save for a residue in hair cells and fingernails. Death had been instantaneous and complete.

Aeneas said, "He cannot be revived."

Lord Mars sat. A sigh went through the rest. They looked eye to eye, and suddenly, for no reason clear to any of them, all relaxed.

Lord Jupiter picked up his dropped goblet. He gave a loud and sustained roar of laughter, "Ho! So now the long-overdue killings will start, to rid the family of whoever Aeneas fears. Well, let's get it over with! I ask only that you kill your mother first, because I will get more happiness from seeing her die than she will get from seeing me." He turned to Lady Venus. "You agree, I hope? We have always liked each other. It is a small favor to ask."

Lady Venus folded her mirror into nullspace, sat back in her cushions, crossed her legs, and began tucking away any stray hair that had escaped her coiffeur. She pouted prettily. "You are sick, Brother. My son will kill no one this day."

"No one further, you mean." Lord Neptune thrust his trident tines-first into the ground once more, let go of the haft, and sat down heavily in his chair. He also laughed, albeit his was short and bitter, not long and loud. "I did not think you had it in you, lad. And to start with Lord Saturn! I thought he was firmly on your side!"

Lord Uranus extinguished his lamp and set it carefully aside. His voice betrayed no emotion whatever. "Logical, though. By killing Lord Saturn, who supported him so loyally, none of us, less loyal, will feel secure."

Lord Mercury contorted his winged wand, woven with serpents, back into storage, and raised his empty hands overhead. He spoke over his shoulder to Uranus. "I like it! Aeneas plays the weakling for five years running, and now this! And he picked Lord Saturn, who was no threat. Aeneas is stone cold."

Neptune wiped sweat from his brow with his wrist. "Colder than I am, I'll say that. Maybe he will make a good Emperor after all. I did not think he was willing to kill family!"

Lady Luna said, "A good emperor and a bad man!" She alone of all those there reacted with emotion. She was staring at the dead body of her uncle, and her teeth were chattering and her limbs were shaking. Whether this was fear or rage, no one could say, not even she. She did not lower her bow, as ordered, but since the shaft had fallen off the string, perhaps it did not matter. The mind-destroying arrow lay in the grass, twinkling with undischarged thought-energy.

Aeneas, meanwhile, was seated. His head was bowed, as he silently contemplated the corpse at the foot of his throne.

He had pulled the crown off his head. Steam rose from the wound in his skull, as his internal biomechanisms hurried to repair the damage to his primary brain, and replace the shattered skull armor.

Blood flowed down his brow, and formed red streaks like tears down his cheeks. Without raising his head, he looked up, and his eyes were very white indeed within the dark splotches of the bloodstains on his face. His features, at that moment, looked more like the face of a beast than a man. His eyes were red and swollen.

From the look in his eye, it was clear to all present that he more than willing enough to kill his family members. "You don't think I did this?"

Lord Uranus said, "I detect traces of Cherenkov radiation in the corpse. He died from someone lowering the speed of light inside his body. You alone have the means to kill in this fashion. Who else?"

Aeneas said, "Lord Tellus was here."

There was silence. All there stared at him. No one laughed. Most were expressionless. Lady Luna smiled with trembling lips, wearing that strange look of one who hopes what she had just heard was a joke, or a slip of the tongue. Lady Venus rolled her eyes, wearing the look of a mother who wishes her child would not embarrass her. "Didn't I tell you the story of the Boy Who Cried Wolf when you were young, child?" she murmured. "Aesop's moral was clear: only tell lies people will believe!"

Aeneas said, "Lord Pluto! Were Grandfather here, invisible, would you see him?"

He looked over. Lord Pluto was a tall silhouette in dark armor, featureless helm covering his face, black mantle covering his form.

For a moment, he did not answer and Aeneas wondered if the armor was empty. But then a voice spoke: "I can remove the scene from the information layer of the universe, but not see what others remove."

Gray-eyed Lady Pallas spoke up sharply, "Sire! Why kill Lord Saturn? Without him, there is no defense against enemy timewarps, and the teams living in chambers and on moons where decades pass for every hour of our time are trapped!"

Aeneas did not raise his head, but his eyes, looking up through his eyebrows, moved slowly from face to face. "None of you saw him attack me?"

Their blank gazes were all the answer he needed.

Lord Saturn must have frozen them before he sped up himself. Aeneas must have been slowed down less than the others, a trickle of time allowed to him, perhaps to allow his skull to part when struck. Aeneas alone had been able to see the blurred and rapid beginning of Lord Saturn's assault.

Aeneas in contempt took the crown and threw it down to the grass. It fell next to the dropped and bloody sickle of Lord Saturn. "Let the body be taken away and examined by medical forensics, and then buried at state expense in a funeral of highest magnificence."

Silence held while servants were summoned.

Beast-headed Pook, arrogant Ifrit, and long-tressed Nichnytsia from the giant planets arrived, lovely Siren and horned Demon from the small, each dressed in a differing livery. The bewilderment and shock on their faces was plain to see, but they asked no questions.

Scarlet-skinned Martians formed an honor guard, while Earthmen from Patagonia, Atlantis, Scotland, and Antarctica dressed in their typically Earthman loincloths or kilts or leathers of mastodon and smilodon reverently arranged the body and bound it in linen.

The Martians hoisted the body on a litter of spears and cloaks, and departed at a dead slow march. The Scots played the bagpipe, and the Patagonians pounded the timpani. The Sirens wailed. The Demons of Mercury blew shofars made from the horns of forefathers fallen on the field of honor. The silent Nichnytsia ignited candleflames in the soft palms of their slender hands and held them aloft.

Brother Beast departed with them, murmuring prayers.

After the last of the servants was gone, Aeneas said, "Any of you who believe me capable of this deed, I release you from your oath of fealty to me."

Lady Luna eyes red with angry tears, looked up in was surprise. "Wait a moment! Are you sincerely claiming not to have done this?"

Aeneas said heavily, "My weapon, but not my will. Lord Saturn and I had each other in a deadly stalemate. Then Lord Tellus walked up, Grandfather Tellus, even though time was frozen and he could not have been walking. He removed Lord Saturn's weapon, but not mine. Time resumed, and I was given no chance to call my weapon back."

Lady Luna dropped her recurve bow, and stepped over to stand next to the throne of Aeneas. She said, "I believe you."

Lord Pluto rose and walked with slow and grave steps over to stand next to her. "Aeneas did not kill Lord Saturn. Neither did we kill Lord Tellus. He abdicated, and let us think we had driven him off. This boy sees why: we are too unruly to rule."

Lady Venus said, "I don't care who killed whom. I support my son." She also rose and stood behind him.

Lord Mercury stepped over as well, grinning a wicked grin. "Things were boring before he took over!"

Lady Ceres rose and curtseyed. "Let lead who will. I say neither yes nor no." She used a contortion pearl, and vanished.

Gray-eyed Lady Pallas covered her shield and sheathed her bolt. She said, "Have we changed from an imperium to a democracy? Are we voting for who shall lead?"

Aeneas said, "I do not wish to lead such people as you, Aunt Aspasia. You are a gang of criminals. All you understand is force and fear."

She said, "I understand more than that: You got us to cooperate. That miracle even Lord Tellus never performed." She crossed the grass and stood near his throne.

Lord Jupiter, Uranus and Neptune, finding themselves alone on the far side of the circle, the only ones opposed to Aeneas, looked at each other in surprise.

Jupiter smiled. "How did we come to be on the same side in anything?"

Lord Neptune said, "I am not on your side, Brother! Didn't I just say I liked the kid. I mean, I like His Imperial Majesty." He took up his trident, came, knelt down before Aeneas, and laid the trident down at his feet. "Send me to prison or have me rubbed out or brain-raped, whatever you like. You are in charge. But I can be useful to you! Lord Jupiter always wanted the throne after Tellus was gone: jealousy has driven him mad! I suggest to your Imperial Majesty…"

Aeneas said grimly, "I will inflict on you whatever next comes out of your mouth."

"…that he be raised to a position of commander in chief for the next attack… and granted special honors and dignities, worthy of his…"

Lord Jupiter stood. "You do not trust me, sire! I see that. But inflict the doom Lord Neptune says! I will lead the next attack. I will prove myself to you."

Aeneas said, "But you believe I am a murderer and a tyrant."

Lord Jupiter threw back his head, "You believe all of us are tyrants! You have said so often enough!" He shrugged and raised his eyebrows, grinning broadly. "People usually accuse others of flaws they see in themselves, don't they?"

Lord Uranus, who was now the only one still seated, said in meditatively. "I believe you, sire. Therefore I do not rescind my oath of fealty."

Aeneas stared at him in disbelief. "You? But you are the one who said I did it."

The mask took on a more serious expression than its default shape, and less haughty. "I said you have the means. You lack the motive. Lord Mars would have killed Lord Saturn without hesitation, and my brothers would not have cared one iota. So you have no reason to lie. Sire, we know Lord Tellus backs you: he is the one who gave you the superluminary science in the first place. He could be hidden as one of the servants, or as one of you. Or me, behind this mask. Or standing behind yonder tree."

Lord Mars said, "Wipe your face, sire. Take up your crown. Duty calls. You may not like it. You may hate it. But duty is duty. Your folks are filth. We get that. You don't like us. We get that, too. We don't like us, either. But we are what you have to work with."

Lord Mars raised his voice and looked around. "I move that the fate of mankind be what the Emperor decrees. Because this is not just about the superluminary science any more. His leadership has saved us. We acted as one. I don't want to see the old squabbles come back."

Lady Venus said, "Seconded!"

Lord Mars said, "I call the question, and move we vote by acclamation."

Lord Uranus said, "No. Not by acclamation. The ballot must be secret."

Aeneas said heavily, "Let it be unanimous! A single nay vote, and I give the crown to Lord Mars."

They used an encrypted and anonymous channel on their rings to collect the ballots. But, instead of the vote total, Sig, the servomind in Aeneas' ring said, *Sir, there is an anonymous message sent you over the encrypted channel: 'Saturn was not the traitor. You must retain the crown until he is found.'*

Aeneas did not move for the longest time. Finally he bent, and picked up the crown, and straightened, and placed it on his head. He did not see the emeralds and gold that adorned it. He only felt the weight, the unrelenting and terrible weight.

"Our destiny," he said in a voice from which all emotion had been scraped free, "lies in the Luminous Blue Variable 1806-20 in Sagittarius on the far side of the galaxy from here, where the last Master Armature resides. The attack there shall be led by Lord Jupiter, as he has volunteered. In the meanwhile, I place him in charge of the militia. However, we have many battles before that, leading to that final climactic war…"

05

War Plans

Aeneas met with Lord Mars in the newly rebuilt Imperial mansion. Lord Mars was a little surprised to see that, once he was past the gold-drenched anteroom, the vast marble plaza of the receiving hall, and the looming statues of the Nave of Memories, Aeneas' personal quarters were inauspicious, what one might expect of a burgher of simple tastes.

There was cot, a couch, a chair, a workbench. To one side was what looked like a cross between an automatic kitchen and a mad scientist's laboratory. Here Aeneas prepared the various foods and nutriments the earthly as well as the unearthly biological systems living in his body needed. In the center was a fully equipped biotechnological operating theater, surrounded by holographic mirrors. To the other side, the far wall was glass panels containing living organs of various types, beating hearts and pulsating brains, grotesque and dripping. Beyond that, a sliding wall opened up into a shooting range. Here were stored also instruments for calibrating the various biological weapons Aeneas carried in his awkwardly tall body.

Lord Mars noticed the signs of disuse. Aeneas had not had time, of late, to pursue his hobby of body-tinkering.

The only decoration in the room was the ceiling. It was the bottom of a glass aquarium, which gave the room a wavering light reminiscent of the skies of Venus.

Sitting on the one chair in the room was Lord Uranus, or someone wearing his mask. He was garbed in a hooded robe like a Blackfriar monk. His hands were folded and hidden in his sleeves.

Lord Mars said sharply to Aeneas, "I thought this was a secret meeting."

Aeneas said to Mars, "It turns out psychometry has other applications aside from astrology. I have no way to block a type of undetectable spy ray I have recently found Lord Uranus commands, and so it is pointless for me to hide my words from him."

Mars was wryly amused to see Lord Uranus stand when Aeneas entered the room. He doubted it was courtesy being shown the sovereign. He assumed Uranus was mildly unnerved to have a nine-foot tall youth looming over him, looking down.

Lord Uranus said, "Sire, I was about to ask the same question. I was the one who sent that message secretly to your ring, telling you not to abdicate. There is clearly a betrayer among us. Why not he?"

Aeneas said to Uranus, "For the simple reason that if Lord Mars wanted all men dead, he would merely kill them all."

Lord Uranus said, "What if he wanted to enslave, rather than destroy? He might betray your throne without betraying mankind."

Aeneas laughed. "I wish he envied my throne! I tried to give it to him. Who better to lead us in war?"

Mars said, "The only time I pray with Brother Beast is when you talk like that. I know my limitations. I can destroy an enemy, but I cannot stand my brothers, and could not rule them." He turned to Lord Uranus. "If you are spying on us all, who is it? Who is the betrayer?"

Lord Uranus said, "Someone who knows how to elude me. I suspect Lady Venus, whose technology operates entirely by thoughts, which my spy rays cannot pick up. Who else had the power to mesmerize Lord Saturn? But the young Emperor will not listen to my suspicions."

Aeneas said, "I do listen. Most carefully. It would be irresponsible for me not to take precautions against a possible threat, merely because she is my mother and I love her. Of course I am on guard against her. What precaution do you suggest?"

Lord Uranus had his mask raise one eyebrow. "Kill her."

"And lose the only one among us who understands every nuance of thought-science, how mental energy is generated, how it creates free will, how it bypasses linear time? I have already lost the ability to see into the past, or to change the rate of passing time. Do not ask the one-armed man to amputate another limb."

"Then exile...."

"To where?"

And when Lord Uranus had no answer, Aeneas turned to Lord Mars. "My each move is fraught with danger. The smallest slip, and the race dies, every one of us. But if I am too cautious to move, the enemy without, or the betrayer within, will find time and chance to do us all in."

Lord Mars said, "I stink at intrigue. That is why I stay out of it. I hope you are not asking who I think it is? Lord Uranus is my prime suspect. He is a sneaking snake."

Aeneas said, "I did not call you here to hear suspicions but to plan strategy. I have two judgments to make, and I wanted both of you to advise me. Here is what we currently know about Luminous Blue Variable 1806-20..."

His ring glittered, and the information unfolded into their minds. The memories of the necroforms captured in the Xormxragon Dyson proved useless. Their masters had removed from them all knowledge of the universe outside the giant star Ara A. However, Urvasthrang, and he alone, knew something of the outside universe, and of the Luminous Blue Variable 1806-20.

The space vampires called it the Master Star, since a last working armature there alone had the range to open warpchannels from one end of the Milky Way to the other. Stars of normal size in the satellite galaxies outside Milky Way were beyond that range, but not LI 181, Leiden's Star.

The Master Star in Sagittarius was at the core of Radio Nebula G10.0-0.03, in one of the largest H II regions in the galaxy, Westerhout 31. It was also one of the most strongly held and fortified regions of the space vampires.

The memory of Urvasthrang showed what the defenses were: here was the dead supermagnetic gamma-radiating star called a magnetar, SGR 1806-20; two blue hypergiant stars; a supergiant O-type star; and three mysterious dying giants called Wolf-Rayet stars in the throes of pre-nova convulsions.

All were sources of high-energy electromagnetic radiation, and all were massive enough to house working long-range armatures, and therefore could deliver the magnetic, gravitic, high-energy, and plasma discharges across interstellar distances. Others of the young, massive stars had been Dysoned and weaponized, that full stellar outputs could be directed at a star system, to vaporize all its planets.

The magnetar released more energy in one tenth of a second than Sol had released in one hundred thousand years: a duodecillion joules.

Mars and Uranus studied the diagrams and three-dimensional, moving images of the Westerhout 31 region. In addition to star-based weapons, there were thousands of War Dysons and ringworlds, jovian battleworlds by the hundreds of thousands, and terrestrial battleworlds by the millions, stationed either about the suns or in the cold night of deep space. Of smaller vehicles, the size of moons, asteroids or continents, no record was kept nor attention paid. They could be constructed as needed, more rapidly than an organism under attack by disease produced antibodies.

Aeneas said, "None of this information is current. What our captured vampire lord knows is centuries out of date. However, if we send in spyships first, the chance that the enemy will detect our interest and divine our intent increases. We also need to commit acts of piracy, preferably against weak and unwarned targets, to loot more technology and materials, particularly working warpcores. Without them, we have only one Dyson and three jovians."

Lord Mars said, "In effect, we have a navy of four. What are their ranges?"

"Basically, the range of a warpcore increases by pi for every increase in mass by an order of magnitude. War Dyson has a safe operating travel range of six thousand lightyears, and the jovian armatures, ninety lightyears."

Lord Mars said, "We jumped farther than that to reach Ara A from Alpha Centauri."

Aeneas said, "A small G or K type star has enough mass to form a safe warpchannel of two thousand lightyears. The eleven thousand we reached was only because we drained all the energy from Alpha Centauri in one pulse of force, and even then, even with sufficient anchoring mass at the far end, that jump was an insane risk."

Mars asked, "How insane?"

Aeneas sighed. "Enough to make me hope an assassin's bolt would find me beforehand. The space-quake that tore the heart of Ara A and threw into orbit over twenty sol-masses of plasma to form that ring of fire we encountered, not to mention throwing up an atmosphere thick enough to carry sound, could have happened inside the warpchannel, to us."

Lord Mars looked at Aeneas carefully. Small wonder Aeneas had such weariness in his eyes. He was fighting on without hope, and hiding from everyone how hopeless it was.

Aeneas continued, "Our options are piracy to increase our material, espionage to increase our intel, or a straight, blind attack to maximize the element of surprise. Each time we use a warpcore, there is a risk of detection by an enemy warpcore."

Lord Mars did not ask about slower-than-light methods of detection. These lagged by minutes and hours in combat taking place across interplanetary ranges. As for interstellar ranges, the information arrived in time only to be of interest to historians.

Lord Uranus said, "Sire, I was the chief spy for Lord Tellus. I kept tabs on all my brothers for him. This is my area of expertise. Espionage even across interplanetary ranges is out of date before it is received. I urge a blind but swift attack."

Lord Mars said, "And I was Father's chief soldier whenever rebellion loomed. War is my area, and I say, going blind into any battle is begging for disaster."

Aeneas said, "Your advice?"

Lord Mars said, "Slow and steady. As best we can tell, these creatures are not just a dying society, but a long-dead one. The undead creatures are corrupt, isolated, and disorganized. Assaulting stars where we are not expected will find them under-defended."

"Go on," said Aeneas.

Lord Mars said, "Your success at Zeta Herculis showed how even a small group, small enough for Lord Pluto to hide, can seize control of a whole world, and remain unseen. Everyone but the enemy uppermost leadership seems to have used up their stores of life energy millennia ago. I can comb through the memories of Urvasthrang for likely spots where the locals have been comatose for millennia. And no one posts watchmen at a graveyard."

Lord Uranus said, "When all one's slaves lack free will, laxity of the secret police is an inevitable temptation."

Aeneas said, "An interesting thought! And one we should keep in mind!"

Uranus said, "Majesty…?"

"You said it yourself. Let us not be lax. We in this War Dyson are like a hare who has mesmerized a quintillion sleepwalking wolves, whom we command to our bidding. But remember what happened what the light of Sol, the vampire-destroying light, touched the Great Eye of Zeta Herculis. Secret commands buried too deeply for Lady

Luna to detect sprang to sudden life. Lord Uranus, your task is twofold: first, to establish proper and secret precautions against an enemy, external or internal, from waking the hordes of undead in the War Dyson against us."

Lord Uranus said, "Sire, you know the astronomical scale of the Dyson makes that simply impossible. Our whole World Armada is less than a freckle on a whale here."

"Concentrate on points of failure, engines, powerhouses, weapons, or other places an insurrection must seize. Our betrayer will seek secretly to suborn the undead we have suborned."

The mask of Lord Uranus changed, and looked at him with new respect. "Meaning that there were not countless thousands of undead technicians fully knowledgeable about the warptech? That was a deception? A lure?"

"An exaggeration. But, yes, it was bait. I expect the traitor to make his move at some point before we assault LBV 1806-20. Once we have the Master Armature in our possession, we can put ourselves beyond the reach of the space vampires forever. The betrayer cannot risk that." Aeneas turned to Lord Mars, saying, "For this reason, I wish any acts of piracy and looting to be carried out as swiftly as possible. We must be audacious enough to keep the enemy out there, and the betrayer with us in here, both off balance."

Lord Mars saluted. "Sire, I have just the plan, if you can make it possible."

Lord Uranus said, "Sire, I also have a plan, which, unlike attempting to spy on a Dyson sphere, is feasible. The traitor is one of ten people. Nine, if you are convinced to trust Lord Mars."

Aeneas raised an eyebrow. "Eight. You do not trust yourself?"

"Nine. Your mother may have long ago implanted commands in my brain of which I know nothing, sire. I would be a fool to trust me!"

Aeneas sat down on the cot. "Tell me your plans, good my lords."

When Lord Mars told him the military plan, Aeneas smiled. But when Lord Uranus told him the espionage plan to uncover the betrayer among them, Aeneas threw back his head and laughed more heartily and loudly than even the mirth-loving Lord Jupiter had ever laughed.

06

STAR PIRATES OF CANOPUS

The Lords of Creation met in council some days later, atop the green hill in the middle of Heaven Lake on Second Earth. The miniature sun was down, and the War Dyson had risen in the east. The north pole of the curve of the Dyson's metal silhouette was reaching the zenith, but its southern hemisphere was still below the horizon. It filled over half the sky: the white clouds of heaven were between the advancing lip of metal and the purple western horizon. By some trick of optics, its seemed like a cope of metal slowly being pulled across the dome of heaven, like the visor of a helmet shutting. The three miniature suns of the World Armada, although below the horizon at this latitude, were reflected in the brass-colored hull of the Dyson so clearly that the other half of the sky was blue. As faint as the moon seen by day, Second Saturn, his rings, and his larger moons, large crescents and small droplets, orbiting with Second Earth, were visible against the blue backdrop.

Two of the three bands of the Tipler armature circling the Dyson were above Earth's eastern horizon, forming a great cross curving across the bronzed surface. They were in motion at nearlightspeed, so that the advancing side of the rings were tinted blue, and the retreating side was red.

The circle of thrones was beneath the circle of trees. The chair of Lord Saturn was empty, draped in black, as no successor had yet been selected from his sons or daughters to take his place.

Aeneas said, "My lords and ladies, I gathered you to witness the first step of the renewed war. I regret that all this was done by surprise, and I hope this will be the last time I am required to act without consulting you."

Lord Mars did not smile, but his eyes glinted. The others exchanged dubious glances, misliking this tone.

"I have ordered the perigee sections of the hull of the Dyson to be rendered semi-transparent, to allow you to view events within in the interior. With the undead technicians familiar with the warp science assisting me, these maneuvers should take place—or, rather, should already have had taken place—with a precision never heretofore seen. All these things were done minutes ago; the light is reaching us now. Let us elevate our thrones above the treetops for a clearer view."

A great hexagonal segment of the Dyson filling the eastern half of the sky now blazed. Through this window, all could see the interior of the Dyson Sphere was occupied by a globe of blue-white light filling half its volume.

"That is the mighty star Canopus, also called Alpha Carina," said Aeneas solemnly. "Canopus is eight times the mass of Sol, seventy times the girth, and ten thousand times the luminosity, of which only the tiniest fraction is allowed to escape and reach your eyes. It has a long history in legend and lore, and I am sorry to see it go."

Lord Neptune asked, "Go?"

"Bid Canopus adieu! We are here to slay the star, and loot the corpse."

The Lord of Creation, their thrones suspended in midair high above the green island, stared in wonder at the bronze curve filling half the sky, the blazing star within.

Aeneas spoke. "Thanks to the skill of the undead warp technicians we stole from Urvasthrang, I was able to materialize back in three-dimensional space with the Dyson entirely englobing the star."

Lady Pallas said, "How is it possible? I have seen hyperspatial objects re-enter the sublight frame of reference. Such bodies enter at a single point. Had our point appeared inside Canopus, we would be fried, and the star plasma would have been thrown outwards in all directions."

Aeneas said, "Under normal conditions, yes. In this case, the technicians used Lord Mercury's megascale pearl to render the Dyson into nullspace and out again at the moment of its re-entry in to the normal spacetime metric. The Dyson is vast in volume but lower in density than so much gossamer, and is low enough in mass for a megascale pearl to render it insubstantial at the moment of materialization."

Lady Pallas said, "And why is not the World Armada burned?"

"The technicians know how to link three World Armada warpcores to the Dyson warpcore, and allow the larger to tow the smaller. We emerged outside Canopus and outside the Dyson, so that we could watch events at a safe distance. I yield the floor to Lord Mars, who oversaw this operation, and can explain it."

Lord Mars said, "Thank you, sire. Brothers and sisters, we have two megascale pearls remaining which store a nova-blast of light from Sol. One is reserved for LBV 1806-20, where the Last Master Armature is seated. The other I used. Six minutes before the materialization, I ordered it into position to release a nova-blast of Sol's holy light to fill the Dyson interior.

"Precisely three minutes after that, the compression firing sequences began. The gravitic and kinetic forces that make the entire volume of the Dyson into a firing chamber were already collapsing inward before we warped to this location."

Aeneas said, "Thank you, Lord Mars."

Lord Mercury gave a little shriek. "I can see black dots passing before the star inside the Dyson! Crescents hanging near it! Dozens!"

Aeneas said gravely, "Doomed worlds who will see no doom approaching. The compression fields will reach the surface of the planets caught inside with Canopus before the light of Canopus reaches the inner hull, is reflected off its surface, and returns to the open eyes of vampires lying torpid on the planets. All will be crushed into the singularity at the warpcore and used for fuel.

"Planets outside the Dyson, however, will be spared that fate. We need but wait until the pulse of Sol's holy light from our pearl, which will pass through all Dyson hull walls easily, to reach and pass through them. All the vampires' worlds, gear, and working warpcore armatures will be left intact.

"This star was selected for four reasons: first, it was between our former location and our current destination. Second, it is near enough to Sol's old neighborhood, three hundred ten lightyears away, that the space vampires will swarm here, seeking us, thinking we are returning to familiar haunts."

A bright spot appeared on one limb of the Dyson, burning like acetylene. Aeneas winced. "Ah! There we see what happens when a Dyson sphere hull rams a gas giant. You do not have eyes like mine, my lords and ladies. I see x-rays and gamma rays released in that explosion. The speed of impact was enough to cause the planetary core to undergo fusion, but not the whole mass. It is only a decillion joules of energy, about the same as the solar output for a year. A pinprick. But hopefully all the other planets are either inside or outside the hull, and no more orbits will intersect."

Aeneas continued, "The third reason is this: a solar system Urvasthrang's memory showed was swarming with worlds, believed to contain an unusual number of working warpcore armatures. Canopus had apparently been a major caravanserai to the Forerunners, a shipyard of worlds. The Forerunners preferred to travel while taking their worlds with them wherever they went. They had the thrill of exploration without the discomfort of leaving the drawing room or the backyard garden. They must have been a most civilized people indeed."

Lady Luna was staring up at the sight above in awe. Gas giants and smaller planets trapped within the Dyson were being caught in the compression field and shattered like eggs. She recovered her composure long enough to say, "You mentioned a fourth reason."

Aeneas smiled. "Canopus has outer worlds enough to give one to every member of the family, and, I hope, with some left over for any militia who wish to volunteer for the coming battle."

Lord Mercury said, "What do you mean, sire?"

Aeneas said, "This method we are using to kidnap Canopus, destroy the star, and use its total energy output to create the next warpchannel we need to reach the next star of the same mass and volume, and next after that, and so on for seven more stars. This method will not work on our ultimate destinations, LBV 1806-20, the Master Star. The blue hypergiant is too big. Canopus is, or was, a place Urvasthrang's memory assured us no vampires with enough life energy remained to stay awake or active lingered.

"Unlike torpid Canopus, the Master Star is watched with sleepless eyes and guarded with most potent forces. A direct attack by a large War Dyson will not do. We must launch hundreds of attacks from hundreds of directions, with each warworld under its own independent command, free to use the initiative and imagination we need to catch the enemy unawares."

Lord Mercury said, "Your meaning is still unclear, sire…"

Lady Venus groaned and rolled her large, dark, beautiful eyes. "It means, brother, that my idiot son is going to share the secret of the warpcore with all of us."

Lady Luna said, "That was His Majesty's meaning all along."

And Lady Venus through lowered lids shot a sideways suspicious glance at Lord Uranus. Aeneas was impressed (and mildly frightened) by the perceptiveness of his mother. Did she actually guess that this had been a plan suggested by Lord Uranus to flush out the betrayer among them?

He hoped the betrayer was not equally perceptive.

Aeneas spoke. "My lords and ladies, you recall that I ordered the giant planets of the World Armada in an evenly spaced tetrahedron around the Dyson, farther away than the orbit of the outermost planet of Canopus. We have erected planes of antiphotonic and Schroedingerwave-opaque force fields to enclose the whole system, and, as you can see, our Dyson is flattening space to prevent nearby warps from forming. None slain by the light of Sol will know how they were slain, or tell the tale.

"Nonetheless, a warpchannel of seventy solar masses crossing to here will have been detected by every large warpcore within a six thousand lightyear radius. So the enemy knows we are here."

He held up his ring. "Here is a list of the next stars we must capture and destroy. In order, it is 9 Sagittarii, KW Sagittarii, WR 102, the Peony Star, V4641 Sagittarii and finally a last jump to LBV 1806-20, the Master Star.

"You will notice each one is roughly six thousand lightyears farther in the direction of Sagittarius. The Peony Star is near the Galactic Core, V4641 Sagittarii, and the Radio Nebula holding the Master Star is six thousand lightyears beyond, in the far half of the Milky Way.

"The attack of Xi Sagittarii, out next target, cannot be accomplished as easily as this, as we will not have the burst of light of Sol available to wipe out a six- to ten- lightminute spherical volume of the enemy. We must save our final shot for the Master Star.

"So, my lords and ladies, we are out of time! Who wants to be first?"

Lord Mercury was the quickest-witted of them, so he saw the point first, and kicked his heels and snapped his fingers. "So! No more debate on who will share the dangerous warpcore technology with whom, or who can be trusted! We are all trusted!"

Lord Jupiter said, "Sire, this matter cannot be decided in a peremptory fashion! I, for one, do not trust my siblings with this dangerous..."

The light, quick laughter of Mercury interrupted him. "Don't you see it? We have no choice! He cannot work the Dyson Armature by himself, not and capture the stars using a nullspace trick!"

Lord Jupiter opened his mouth, no doubt to object that the undead technicians captured from Urvasthrang could do the warpcore work. Then he looked, and saw a flash of yellow light pass across the blue-white fiery face of Canopus. It was a glint of sunlight, Sol's light. It burned for a moment, then dimmed and vanished.

Lady Venus said, "Our puppet Lord Urvasthrang is dead now too, isn't he? We can no longer sneak among the vampires, pretending to be one of them."

Aeneas said, "Not with all our undead now dead, I am afraid. If any of you, against my orders, had been constructing undead armies in secret, you will find them wiped out as well. And, yes. Urvasthrang's Dyson has just killed Canopus, and destroyed all the inner planets of the system. Whether the vampire lords realize that mankind is still alive, or whether they think Urvasthrang is flying the Jolly Roger, does not much matter which, does it? Who wants to have his brain imprinted with the superluminary technology first? Speak quickly! The enemy is on their way!"

07

LINE OF
BATTLEWORLDS

Aeneas said to the gathered Lords of Creation, "I open the secrets of the universe to you! Our recent tragedy must prove instructive: Mankind can spare me, but cannot lose my knowledge."

The circle of thrones hung in midair below the titanic vision of the War Dyson rising in the east. The star Canopus was shrinking visibly, undergoing a compression that would force it into a singularity.

Aeneas raised his finger. Projectors formed the images, whole and solid-seeming, in the center of the ring of flying thrones.

"Your eyes are not as mine. I spread before you images taken from my cortex, which I receive from myriad instruments post near and far. These images are six to eighteen minutes old. Look! Here, found outside the Dyson, is a subterrestrial world with mountains like elfin minarets soaring above the thin atmosphere; there, a terrestrial coated from pole to pole with a single hellish city buried beneath snow, and I behold in the balconies of towers, in the windows of empty palaces, ranks of toppled vampires who have not lost their human form, hunger and wrath graven into their dead faces.

"I see a larger world, a superterrestrial, with squat mountains and heavy glaciers, whose sea beds are filled with vampires.

"On a subjovian globe, I peer down in an atmosphere thicker than water at the undead lying motionless on bridges and boulevards, and in the deep shafts of mines. No blade of grass grows here, no insect flies. But all their machinery is intact, and their robotic guard still swarms.

"In the mile-deep atmosphere of a jovian world, atop a naked planetary core featureless and flat beneath the action of gigantic wind and crushing gravity, I view what seems humped hills looming, forest covered, swathed in smog. The hills are undead, archvampire flesh like those Lord Mars fought. The forest are their numberless tentacles, and the smog are midge swarms, remotely controlled, whom they send swimming on myriad delicate, small tasks. These fogs are settling, their hill crumbling to dust.

"In a world even larger, at the bottom of layers of atmospheres and hydrospheres of chemicals not found on lighter worlds, layers so deep not even the brightness of giant Canopus could reach, from pole to pole crawls an ocean of undead, liquid flesh, of one solitary ultra-archvampire who slew countless hosts of his own slaves and absorbed them, one and all, and every last plankton in oceans larger than all the worlds of man combined. Even this titan is slain instantly.

"All these had working warpcores. The subterrestrial is no bigger than Mercury or Titan, and can reach three lightyears; the superjovian, twice the size of Jupiter, two hundred fifty. These worlds are our Battleships, Battlecruisers, Cruisers, Destroyers, Frigates and small Corvettes. The War Dyson is our Dreadnaught. Our foe outnumbers us in all classes of battleworlds by thousands to millions to one. Who wishes first to assume command of one of these planetary engines of destruction?"

Aeneas contorted all the gathered Lords of Creation now to the great dome of nacre, amber and mother-of-pearl his mother had erected on the bed the Guinevere Sea of Second Venus, between the islands of Vasilisa and Sappho. Brother Beast was there as well, looking startled, as he had evidently been plucked up in the middle of prayers.

Aeneas said, "Lady Venus here has prepared servants and equipment needed for the brain imprint process. Our hour is brief! The warp jump here was surely detected by any warpcore of eighteen solar masses or greater that happened to be within a radius of twenty thousand lightyears. The whole Milky Way is but five or six times that diameter. Space is vast beyond imagining, but so is the reach and power of the space vampires. Lord Uranus? Have you something to say?"

Lord Uranus was holding his signet ring up before the eye holes of his mask, as if something hidden in the sparkles of the signet fascinated him. "Not just the warpchannel was detected, good sire. Normal matter is transparent to the nova-burst of Sol's holiness inside the Dyson. It was not smothered this time by a supergiant star. Even though neuropsionic waves lag along at lightspeed, any warpcore set to detect them has just seen Canopus blaze like a signal flare."

Aeneas said, "Come, my lords! Our race is a tasty plum rolling on an empty feast table surrounding by starved madmen with long arms. Why is no one clamoring to take command of a World of the Battle Line?"

Lord Mars stood, "Forgive me, sire, but you asked for volunteers. Since my youth, I have been wary of placing my head into one of my sister's brain-editing helmets. It is a fate worse than death, because I could never trust any thought again to be my own. I will not disobey, if commanded, but I will commit suicide first, to keep sanity, self-command, and honor intact."

Brother Beast said sharply, "Speak not so! Suicide is the door of hell. Better to break faith with temporal lords than to offend eternal!"

Aeneas said, "Are we to die rather than learn to trust each other? But I compel no unwilling. This is voluntary."

Lord Neptune looked sourly at Lord Jupiter, and said, "Voluntary as the choice to drown or swim! The warptech allows not only faster-than-light drive, but to alter the physical constants of nature, so as to shut off each of our special techniques. It was Father's whip hand."

Lord Jupiter said, "I will volunteer! Let Lady Venus do her worst!"

Lady Ceres looked uncomfortable. "Why is this necessary at all? Why not just teach us what you know, sire?"

Aeneas said, "A thousand books would not hold it all, and when should I start writing them? You must know not only theory, but reflexes and judgment, which the human brain otherwise learns only by years of practice. We have not years. I doubt we have an hour."

Lord Mercury stood. His boyish face was twisted into a frown. "I am sorry, my sire, but I also do not trust Lady Venus. I think you trust her only because she has made it so! But I know we need every man. May I substitute my son Autolycos Lord Anubis to stand in my stead?"

Lord Mars said, "I offer my son Deimos, whose mother's name I hide, but she is someone very dear to Lady Venus. She will not harm him."

Lord Pluto said, "I have walked unseen amid the many-chambered pleasure-palaces of Lady Venus, and know her work. She is allowed no access to my brain. I set forth my son Zagreus Lord Kerberos in my stead."

Aeneas show no more expression than a poker player. "Not my lore only, then, must your sons learn. If and only if you imprint them with the secrets you so jealously have guarded, do I agree!"

Brother Beast said, "The Archbishop of Valparaiso is willing to forgive my oath to forswear the sword in this, our desperate hour. I trust Lady Venus."

Lady Ceres said, "Unwarlike, my skill against the foe is unneeded. I offer my grandson, Anton Romanov Lord Hydra, child of my beloved Cora, who passed away."

And, likewise, Lady Vesta said, "A woman's hands are more fitted to the loom than the lance. Let my son Winedark Savage, Lord Dionysus, who delights in frenzy, take my place, and lead his Bacchants to war. My science of theriopathy, control of beasts, is small enough, I willingly grant it him."

Aeneas scowled. "What do you say, Lady Pallas? Are women unsuited to war? You have no sons to take your place."

Lady Pallas said, "I say the gentler sex is deadlier than the male, for we fight only at need, not for sport. Arm me, and let us count how many enemy planets I throw like skulls at the foot of your throne!"

There was no more time for discussion. The countless millions of pearls used for the mass migrations now were put to use. Clouds of pearls were flung by interplanetary range tractor presser beams, disinert and at nearly the speed of light, into the atmospheres of the newly-emptied worlds of Canopus. Those worlds which were frozen were thawed by beams issuing from Second Jupiter, diffused and gentle enough to leave the worlds and the needed machinery intact.

Lady Venus imprinted the knowledge taken from an otherwise empty third brain of Aeneas into them. Aeneas did not know just how Lord Tellus had folded and compacted the information layers and neuron connections beforehand. He had only the finished product in his own mind, which Lady Venus had to extrapolate backward. There was some guesswork involved, hence some error.

When the imprint was made, it did not come smoothly into their brains as it had with Aeneas. Some of the Lords of Creation reeled in their chairs, or drooled, or twitched, or convulsed. Others stood, amazement in their eyes, open mouthed, stunned by the wonders of the secret laws of nature now unfolding in their memory.

There was no time for terraforming nor pantropy. All dispatched to the captured worlds were garbed in the living robes manufactured by the Graces of Pallas. These were shining garments made partly of matter and partly of force-field, who outer fabric adjusted temperature, pressure, and gravity to the wearer, and whose inner side intermingled with flesh and bone and nerve-cell to adapt the wearer seamlessly to the environs.

Deimos, along with the four-armed Quadramanes of Mars, copper-skinned Monotremes, blood-drinking Ghouls, fair Hitherfolk and brutal Thitherfolk, took the helm of the Dyson. Aeneas took the Dyson as his flagship, and he and Lord Mars accompanied Deimos.

Brother Beast took command and possession of the superjovian. The single monster that once dwelled here was done. Nothing stirred. There was no opposition.

He insisted on christening the planet, and called it *Saint Michael's World.*

Lord Jupiter with fifty of his daughters, along with the gigantic and cyclopean races that served him, descended on the warmer jovian, the fire giant. Here were machines left by the vampires, some intelligent and still active. The fight with these machines was ferocious but brief, as Jupiter slowed the speed of light to allow ionized electrons to flow, but not lasers or energy weapons. The daughters of Jupiter in their shining blue robes riding their cloud-chariots called down lightning of modest size to destroy man-sized targets, and larger bolts to incinerate walking tanks, leviathanic swimming machines, or dark, domed cities that crawled on many legs like monstrous crabs.

He called the planet *Inferno.*

Lord Neptune, nine natural daughters, and Galatea, his artificial daughter, transited to the colder of the two jovian worlds, the ice giant, along with countless servant-minds and living automata. The method used by the Daughters of Neptune was less precise than that used by the Daughters of Jupiter. Cities and fortresses hidden in the glacier canyons, or wherever else still active robots offered resistance, were flattened under hundredfold weight of multiplied gravity, or shattered with earthquakes and swallowed into crevasses. Few of the needed machines were captured intact.

He dubbed the planet *Niflheim.*

The third jovian, this one from the water ring of Canopus, therefore called a water giant, was given to Lady Pallas. She merely dropped her asteroid from which she took her name whole into the superdense, ultracold methane atmosphere. The whole interior of the asteroid had been hollowed out and replaced with a crystal rod-logic brain, designed to operate on the levels-of-logic principles known only to her.

The giant brain, capable of up to ten thousand simultaneous tasks, created an army of telemechanical remote manipulators to cover the immense globe, locate, study, and coordinate control of the alien weaponry and machinery. There was no fighting with native machines; Lady Pallas merely suborned them with her levels-of-logic techniques. Her technique was as effective as Lady Luna's rule over the dreaming frequency of the thought spectrum, but was aimed at a higher energy state in the conceptual layer of the universe.

When the robots found their basic abstract concepts revealed to them by this sudden perception of the formal layer of the universe, their own logic forced them to cooperate with the usurpers. This method would not have worked on any beings, living or undead, capable of deliberate immoral action. Nor could it work on animals, in whose simpler minds abstractions had no place.

She called the planet *Pallas*, saying that it was, in effect, the same place as her old worldlet, merely extended.

The subjovian was given to Lord Uranus and his Georgian-Sidereals, commonly called Pooks. These Georgians were races uplifted from a plethora of earthly birds and beasts, a grave and solemn race of men with the same stiff dignity as the ancient Egyptian statues they resembled. These carefully located the robots by spy ray, and offered then override codes gleamed from the memory of Urvasthrang. Lord Uranus accomplished by deception what Lady Pallas had accomplished by truth.

He called it *George*.

Lady Luna and her fierce nymphs helmed the superterrestrial, a body three times the size of Earth, a world of flattened mountains and shallow, turgid oceans. Her maidens rode naked on the backs of giant moon-hounds to hunt down the fleeing insectoid robots with lance and dart, and made a sport of what should have been a military operation.

She christened her world *Chariot-of-Madness*.

The Lords Triton, Prospero and Ganymede were given command of Second Neptune, Second Uranus and Second Jupiter.

The megascale pearl carrying the last remaining charge of Sol's light was placed inside Second Saturn. This globe lacked a warpcore, but the pearl could remove inertia and move the world and its rings and moons at just below lightspeed. Lady Eunomia, daughter of Lord Saturn, was given command.

The captured terrestrial and subterrestrial warpcore worlds were distributed to the grim sons of Lord Pluto, Kerberos and Hydra, to the maniacal but brilliant Lord Dionysus; and to the grinning and wolfish Autolycos Lord Anubis, son of Mercury.

The sons of Pluto walked unseen among the mazes and cityscapes of the warren-riddled labyrinth worlds they were given, and with invisible fingers and tools, disarmed or deactivated all enemy automatons they found.

They called their worlds *Garm* and *Ouroboros*.

Lord Dionysus landed alone on a small, fiery world, accompanied only by a host of panthers, dolphins and wolves, who spread seeds and spores where they went. He played his flute as he danced, and grape vines grew up instantly from the revivified soil to strangle any struggling enemy machines.

He dubbed the globe *King-of-the-Wood*.

Lady Venus encountered no opposition. She called her planet *Hesperus*.

Anubis found a world utterly flat and featureless save for strange and ungainly seven-sided towers rising from prairies of black salt. Some robots were still active, bounding like nightmarish grasshoppers in the low gravity. He waited for an enemy to open fire, and then skipped from bullet to bullets up their stream of fire to step atop these robotic weapons, which he folded into nullspace.

He called the little world *Bald Spot*.

In reckless haste, the captured worlds were prepared. But tachyonic rays carrying a neuropsionic message echoed from their signet rings into the mind of the Lords of Creation before all was ready.

Dozens of white-hot pinpoints of light surrounded the wide Canopus system, and expanded into a hundred battleworlds, their cities and surface fortifications blazing, mountainpeak batteries and space elevators already firing as they materialized, lancing out with laser bolt and lightning ray, gravityfields and timewarps and thought-destruction waves. The huge globes were shining like coals from hell beneath their concentric atmospheres of defensive screen and forcefield.

The enemy was here, and in overwhelming force.

08

ESCAPE TO
SAGITTARIUS

The space vampire fleet invading Canopus was taken by surprise.

Of the hundred enemy battleworlds that entered the sublight continuum in a hollow sphere formation centered on the Canopus system, only a score were superjovians. These were worlds twice to thrice the size of Jupiter, with miles of thin atmosphere held down by immense gravity above endless seas of liquid nitrogen and methane. Ninety-mile tall ziggurats and towers of adamantine, built of artificially strengthened molecules, loomed above the turgid, heavy atmospheres.

Up from the dead seabed, glacierscapes and mountains of the vampire worlds, interplanetary-strength high-energy beam weapons flew like lances of fire, like rivers of flame. The dark worlds sent forth their various agencies of death: electromagnetics of many wavelengths, coherent rays of neutrons or gravitons, timewarp fields or neuropsionic blasts of planet-destroying intensity.

They spun their equatorial armatures up to nearlightspeed as soon as they emerged into the subluminary continuum, and attempted to flatten space, but, for once, the advantage was with the Tellurians.

It was true that the newly commissioned world-fleet of was unready, but it was also true that the Tellurian Dyson, under command of Lord Deimos, son of Mars, and the newly made gas giants under command of Lords Ganymede, Prospero and Triton were ready. Their armatures and equipment were manned and battle-tested. These four were enough.

The Dyson crushed Canopus into a pinpoint size just as the black fleet materialized in a globe around them. Five solar masses collapsed into the singularity and formed a black hole. The unstable accretion disk formed from the outer layers of murdered Canopus expanded outward and filled the Dyson interior. Thrice the mass of Sol was totally converted to energy, and issued from the firing aperture in a coherent beam.

Ganymede, Prospero, and Triton had their three gas giants hovering in a Klemperer triangle off the bow of the Dyson firing aperture. Lord Prospero was able to detect the beam approaching before the first lightwaves it shed arrived, and to select the locations of the enemy targets.

The incoming fire of the Black Fleet, moving at lightspeed, was still eleven hours away. They had emerged from their warpchannels roughly twice as far from Canopus as the planet Pluto once had orbited around Sol. As the enemy planets materialized, images of them taken through hyperspatial periscopes went blind when space was flattened, but not before Lord Prospero, using his father's spy ray mechanisms, detected the dark neuropsionic residue the undead planets gave off, noting their declination and right ascension.

The Lords Ganymede and Triton, using the massive electrokinesis and gravitokinesis engines of Jupiter and Neptune, deflected the novabeam roaring from the firing aperture and directed it first at one altitude and azimuth, then at another, then another. Then they deflected the beam into a vast semicircle to strike targets in the hemisphere opposite the firing aperture.

Unlike ground combat with its complexities of terrain and season and weather, and unlike sea combat with its winds and tides, super-luminary combat was a matter of simple and terrible mathematics: the Tellurian Dyson, armed with the eight solar masses of Canopus, had more mass, hence more ability to bend space, than the enemy superjovians, even had there been a thousand of them.

The vampires evidently had stripped all the stars within two hundred fifty lightyears of every planet with a working warpcore, to send it to Canopus as quickly as possible. Larger warworlds and warstars could have come from further away, but these no doubt were scouring the regions in the direction of Coma Berenices, where vampires had been deceived to concentrate their search.

So the mighty Tellurian Dyson shrugged aside the Lilliputian efforts of the twenty enemy superjovians to flatten space, and formed a warp. Lord Deimos could have pulled the Dyson out of timespace at that moment, but instead, smiling, he waited.

The commanders of the vampire worlds could have broken off their attempts to flatten space, and used their warpcores to lower the speed of light and render themselves immune to lightspeed weapons they surely knew must be coming. They did not. Stubbornly, foolishly, mulishly, mechanically, the commanders of the vampire worlds continued the vain attempt to restrain the escaping Dyson.

Perhaps some of them erected planetwide antiphotonic screens, or rendered their globes disinert, to fend off the coming beam weapon. But then, at the tenth hour, the Dyson altered the gravitational constant and the neutrino rest mass so as to restore their inertia just as the beam struck. The planetary bodies were pinned in place.

Thus, instead of being lightly wafted away from the destruction as the nova beam, like a searchlight, skipped from world to world, the vast globes were incinerated, bisected and shattered. Mountains were thrown into the gaping void where the beams passed through the world, oceans, atmospheres, and molten crust and mantle. Atmosphere, hydrosphere, surface features were boiled in less than a second, continents evaporated, and their superheated steam propelled into space.

And those were the worlds were the beam struck glancingly.

Where it struck head-on, all matter was converted to energy, and the fundamental particles at the center of the explosion were converted into more fundamental particles existing in ultrahighenergy states which had only occurred naturally in the first three seconds after the Big Bang.

Perhaps there were moons and ships orbiting these worlds. If so, they were overwhelmed by the shockwave.

The vampire commanders vainly but fanatically, their batteries of engines straining and overheating, continued to attempt to flatten space up until the very end, trying to snare the Dyson. Because of this, no neighboring worlds outran the attacking beam. No faster-than-light message escaped. Whatever supreme commanders sent those hundred worlds to their annihilation surely received no rumor of their fate.

Meanwhile, the various exotic energies the vampire worlds had shot passed through the space the Dyson once had occupied. The humans had vanished.

The Tellurian Dyson reentered the sublight spacetime metric six thousand seven hundred lightyears away.

This was the 9 Sagittarii system: two massive O-type stars, each ten times the radius of Sol, and hundreds of thousands of times the luminosity, circled at each other in an eccentric orbit between eleven and twenty-seven times the distance that one separated Earth from the sun. The Tellurian Dyson, carrying the World Armada around it, emerged into the continuum in the gravitational center of the system.

In this form of interstellar combat, the intruder always had one advantage: when he landed in a target star system (provided he did not land on a spot where a hyperspatial periscope aperture rested) the lightwaves that had left the inner and outer planets minutes or hours before would strike his eyes and telescopes as soon as he emerged into real space. He could see their position and numbers. However, no image of the intruder could reach any eyes and telescopes on those planets until those minutes and hours passed. So the intruder always had minutes or hours before the earliest alarm could be raised during which he could study the last seen position of the enemy defenses.

It was this advantage that saved the humans.

Lord Deimos, wrapped in his shining environmental robes, stood in the middle of the main fortress city of the Dyson, surrounded by miles of empty and gigantic bowls which once served the mountain-sized vampire lords as thrones.

Every square inch of the inner surface of these ten-acre-wide hemispheres was coated with control points into which the vampires had grown their nerve endings. No native Martian race could have operated such controls. The Ifrits created by Lord Jupiter were a numerous race and many had sworn fealty to Lord Mars, and to his sons, and submitted themselves to the harsh disciplines of the Red Planet. The Ifrit were energy beings, woven of self-sustaining force fields. Each stood atop its hemispherical throne like a column of living fire with long angular limbs of lightning bolts plugged into each of the ten thousand nerve points.

Layers of servominds looming like the eggs of giant birds from myth were gathered in a semicircle around where Lord Deimos sat crosslegged on a carpet woven of thought-focusing fibers. His face and hands were red as blood. The environmental robes glittered and moved like rippling quicksilver.

At his right hand was a carafe of wine. At his right was a prayer book. His ceremonial sword was lying on the carpet before him. It was well known that Deimos, in his youth, had been an apprentice of Lord Pluto. Something of the spartan simplicity of Pluto was present.

The ring on the finger of Lord Deimos was tied in parallel to similar but larger rings encircling his wrist. All were blazing white.

Aeneas was seated to one side of him on his black, three-headed throne. He sat when it was necessary to project an image of himself to give orders to underlings. Otherwise, he stood, or paced, or let his internal organs move themselves beneath his skin first to one position, then to another, nervously, as if trying to find a comfortable way to pack them into his skeleton and frame.

To the other side, Lord Mars sat on a similar carpet, surrounded by a ring of contortion pearls, so that he might be transmitted to the several other planets in the World Armada. He was polishing and cleaning his longsword with slow, methodical motions of rag and whetstone.

The other Lords of Creation, helming their various worlds, were communicating instantly through their signet rings, and most of them broadcast their face and form, so that expression and gesture could be seen. Ghostly images of them, each in his own control chamber or astronomical tower, appeared in each other's visual cortex.

Also present was the initial image of the star system. Circling the gigantic star 9 Sagittarii A was a ringworld of silvery material, some form of alloy, half matter, and half solidified energy. This was no humble ringworld with a merely Earth-orbit radius. The radius of Saturn's old orbit would have fit inside the megascale structure with room to spare.

Orbiting outside the ring were rotating cylinders, large as gas giants, made of unknown and impossible material, white as platinum. Any object of any shape of that mass should have been pulled into a sphere long ago. A band of atmosphere was gathered at the equator of each small cylinder. The ringworld was spinning, as were the cylinders, giving the whole star system the aspect of a cosmic clockwork.

Circling the other star, 9 Sagittarii B, was a smaller ringworld, only the diameter of Jupiter's old orbit, rotating in the opposite direction.

Scattered seemingly at random through the system, no two of them sharing the same orbital ecliptic, were four hundred small worlds, all exactly the same size. The Doppler shift readings showed the worlds were accelerating and decelerating in no pattern. This was a star system where the planets did not orbit their suns, but swam like ships wherever they would.

Lady Pallas said, "This is very odd. These are main sequence stars, and should not have any nitrogen and helium in the stellar surface visible in the spectrum. At this distance, the stellar winds colliding do not produce sufficient x-rays to ionize the nebula around us. But 9 Sagittarii is the main source for ionization for most of the visible nebula in this region… something is wrong with the shape of space and time in this star system…"

Aeneas cut her off. "We can discuss scientific curios later, Aunt Aspasia! Right now there is something wrong with the warpchannel we just left. It has not collapsed behind us!" Aeneas probed with his instruments. "Twenty-five of the fleet of worlds that attacked us at Canopus survived and are in pursuit. They are in the warpchannel behind us. Be ready."

Lord Mars paused in his polishing. "I thought the range of jovian planets was less than three hundred lightyears, even with a massive anchor at the far end. How could they follow us?"

But the signet ring of Lord Mars answered the question silently: the pursuit had made a warpchannel reaching no farther than into the warpchannel formed by the Dyson as it departed, and so the surviving enemy worlds had merely been pulled along in the wake.

Aeneas said, "We must rapidly form a short-range warpchannel through nullspace to entrap first one of the 9 Sagittarii stars, and then the other, and reduce them to a singularity as fuel for our next long-range jump…" His signet ring was already calculating the four dimensional vectors needed for the tiny interplanetary hop.

The young Lord Deimos said, "Wait, sire! The temple computers of Mars register danger! Their thought processes were formatted by Lord Tellus, and no one can understand them. It is some sort of intuitive calculus: but we are in danger…"

Alarms were already coming in. Aeneas heard the screams from his relatives as their faces started to melt.

09

THE DEADLY DOUBLE STAR

Aeneas saw, through his ring, the face and body of Brother Beast, alone in his control cell at the pole of the weapon-coated Tellurian superjovian. Both the planet and the man were glowing and dissolving. The core of the superjovian was disintegrating into neutrons and neutrinos, and the whole surface was convulsed with earthquakes and collapsing continents.

The fire giant, ice giant and water giant planets controlled by Lords Jupiter, Neptune and Lady Pallas were likewise shrinking and shaking themselves to pieces, while emitting massive neutrino bursts. The neutron storm radiating from the core through the surface was uneven, concentrated in some places, diffuse in others. Where the neutron storm was dense, the waves were destroying machines and organisms.

The neutral particles were unaffected by positive and negative energy holding atoms and molecules together, and, indeed, passed through such things like ghosts. But these neutrons had a greater rest mass than it was possible, in nature, for neutrons to have, and this increased the range of their strong nuclear force. Any atomic nuclei they passed through reacted like an unstable, radioactive material. Elements profoundly stable, carbon, helium, hydrogen, now dissolved into protons and alpha particles, and the energy of these dissolutions broke up atoms around them in a chain reaction.

The miniature suns orbiting the worlds popped like Roman candles, dissolving instantly, unnoticed in the eye-dazzlingly bright blaze of the two giant, white suns.

The superterrestrial and terrestrial planets were not as damaged, but cities and parishes were burning in the weird, invisible storm. By a bitter irony, the people living on the surfaces of the world, places thought to be unsafe, survived in greater numbers than the buried cities or the mermaids. The surrounding heavier elements in water and stone ignited more swiftly and in greater numbers than gasses.

And so the worlds were beginning to melt.

Deimos had formed periscopes to bring current images in from the myriad planetoids of this mad, clockwork system. On the worldlets were races of beings dissolving and re-growing continuously, living in towers and domes that also rotted and dissolved in minutes, but continually re-grew into new shapes, glowing and burning.

The worldlets were smooth, because land and ocean melted and reformed so frequently, that the surface was merely a level, glowing mush up from which heaps and bubbles and forked crystal-growth endlessly swelled and toppled. Burning rivers writhed like snakes, and burning mountains rose and fell like waves on the sea.

Brother Beast used his secret technique of metanthropy to shed his damaged skin, and now he stood alone on his superjovian world, his skin pink as a baby. "How are these creatures alive? Are they vampires?"

The glowing worldlets had not yet seen the warplanet called Saint Michael's World, but they soon would, as the seconds turned into minutes.

Lord Uranus was less burned than his brothers. The subjovian world under his command, being less massive, had released fewer neutrons and neutrinos. He had also placed his command throne in the subjovian's ring system, far above the surface. He said, "They are another kind of undead. No biological cells could withstand the constant elemental changes happening here: they must have been designed for this environment."

It was young Lord Ganymede who then screamed. The closest of the many small worlds darting like fish and burning like torches was only four or five lightminutes away from Second Jupiter. By sheer mischance, this was one of the civilian worlds, meant to be far from harm's way. Immediately the nearer worldlets, including those not close enough to have seen the light-image from the gas giant as yet, informed by tachyon radio, now rushed inward toward the heavily populated gas giant, and the space-distorting neutron storm effect lanced out before them.

In the periscope spy rays, the melting and reforming creatures in their melting and reforming observatories and weapon stations could be seen dancing and exalting. They retained just enough human shape to make the image horrible.

Brother Beast, even though his world was farthest from Ganymede's location, was the most massive and had the greatest range. He reached out with a warpfissure, plucked up the nearest worldlet to the gas giant under Ganymede's command, and flung it out of timespace. But his warp control circuits exploded and melted, and the armatures began to vibrate strangely and tear themselves apart.

Lord Jupiter, at the helm of the fiery gas giant called Inferno, was stationed nearby to Ganymede. Even though his body was glowing and falling, flake by flake, into pieces, and the pains burning his every nerve were hell itself, he retained the presence of mind to command his servants to open fire on the worldlets attacking his son.

More than half of the weaponry and mighty engines of Inferno dissolved and burned, but the other half created the interplanetary beam weapons and launched them, like bolts of lightning wider than moons reaching from globe to globe. The nearest enemy worldlets to Ganymede were incinerated, nor could the neutron storms which the glowing worlds shed block the river of electric power which flowed over them.

Aeneas ordered the evacuation of Second Jupiter. During battle, the populations had been told, and, indeed, hypnotized, into the discipline of carrying interplanetary range contortion pearls with them at all times. It would take many moments, perhaps more than they had to spare.

Then Aeneas called all the Lords of Creation to contort through space to the command dome on the Dyson, where Lord Deimos sat. They stopped dissolving.

Deimos said to Aeneas, "Why are we not melting?"

Aeneas said, "I don't know."

But Lady Pallas, her flesh a mass of melting scars, could still speak through her ring. "It is an application of warpcore technology. The base mass value of fundamental particles is being changed. The Dyson is hollow, less dense than air, so there is less damage here. Any neutron storm appearing at the gravitational center of the Dyson would be inside the singularity."

Aeneas saw she was right. It was something even he had overlooked. In his memory was buried information about the effects of two space warps being formed in opposition to each other, but, until now, as the only man able to work a warpcore, that knowledge had never floated to the surface of his mind before. There had been no example, and no need.

He now saw that the two giant stars were both equipped with armatures, but out of phase with each other, each interfering destructively with the other. The disharmony kept the fabric of space always perturbed. It was as if spacetime itself was in a continual state of flexing, growing, flattening, shrinking, so as to produce different mass values for neutrons and protons from moment to moment. No wonder normal matter was dissolving.

Lady Pallas said, "The violent convection at the star cores was a clue, as was the reach of ionization throughout the nebula. These are side effects of the alternations of base neutron mass: stable elements that cannot be ionized are being ionized here."

The closest of the small worlds were now aware of Inferno, the fire giant warworld that had opened fire on them. Aeneas detected changes in nearby warpspace, and knew the creatures on the nearest world were communicating by tachyon radio to the further worlds that the lightwaves from the newly-arrived human intruders had not yet reached.

The small worlds now turned like a school of fish, as one, and closed in toward the fire giant. It was clear that they had not yet seen the Dyson and the other worlds in the Tellurian Armada: those bodies were too far away for the light to have reached them yet.

Lord Jupiter held up his ring, but the damage to his nervous system was too great: his hand melted and dissolved before his eyes, and his ring fell to the ground, also melting. "My children! They are still on that world!"

Lady Pallas acted before any could stop her. Her ring twinkled on her scarred, half-burned hand. She took control of one of the contortion pearls Lord Mars had arranged before him.

She was back on the water giant world called Pallas, alone with the vast brain that controlled it. She spun her armatures up to speed, vanished and swelled back into timespace at a point between Inferno and the smaller worlds. The countless weapons from far below her atmosphere blazed, but she was not attempting to overwhelm the vampire warp effect with hers. Instead, she directed neuropsionic fire at the strange and ever-burning white worlds. The only thing she did with the warpcore was halt the progression of gravity through space, rendering all objects on and around her planet weightless, and throwing her atmosphere out into space. It definitely slowed the neutron storm effect.

The small worlds displayed another application of warpcore technology the humans had not hitherto seen: small cores making small warps in concert with each other, to impose slightly different fundamental

physical constants on the planet Pallas. She was forced to flatten space
to prevent small warps from destroying the matter-energy balances on
her world. But when she did so, the small worlds erected warps out
of phase with hers. Even though her world was far more massive than
theirs, her attempt to flatten space accelerated the rate of disintegration
of the core of her world, and dissolved her warp armature control
mechanisms. She was now on a blind and uncontrolled planet, with a
loose warpcore consuming the center of it.

Both Pallas and Saint Michael's World were motionless and defenseless. The speed at which two of the fourteen battle worlds had been
rendered helpless was astonishing.

The rate of dissolution of the small worlds increased, and the small
globes visibly shrank: but they soon recovered and restored themselves.

Aeneas attempted rapidly to change the spin variable of the Dyson,
trying to synchronize with the many disjoined small, attacking worlds.
His hope was that if he could stop this chaotic effect, he could form
a stable warp and overwhelm these tiny, annoying worlds. It should
have been child's play to overpower things of so small a mass.

He could not do it.

The warp armature machinery on these melting worlds also seemed
to be dissolving and recreating itself, and so was doubly unsteady.
There was no way to match phase with them.

It was then the Lord Mercury spoke up. "I see what is happening.
My son and I can save them!" Whereupon Lord Anubis spun up
the armature of his subterrestrial world, Bald Spot, and vaulted the
remaining megascale pearl near orbit around Inferno.

The small worlds suddenly lost their warpcore controls. The Lords
of Creation, through their instruments, watched in awe the buildings
and people on the surfaces of the ever-changing, ever-burning worlds
dissolved and did not regrow.

In suicidal runs, the dying undead of the small worlds set their
planets shooting like bullets toward the gas giants just before they

died. Fast as these bodies were, across interplanetary distances, they were far too slow.

Anubis darted Bald Spot toward Inferno, and formed a small warpchannel between leading back to the Dyson. Contortion pearls, which had been being jammed by the small and melting worlds, now operated. The children of Jupiter were moved instantly to safety.

Lord Mercury used the megascale contortion pearl to move the helpless water giant, Pallas, into close orbit around the Dyson, then Inferno, then Saint Michael's World.

Lord Uranus said, "Sire, the other worlds of the system are now aware of us. The ringworlds show an energy spike: they are about to cast a field around the whole nebula and dissolve everything made of matter."

Lord Mercury said, "Time to go!"

Deimos said, "Where to, sire?"

Aeneas by signet ring imprinted the navigational elements into his brain. Sakurai's Object was nearby: a slow nova, but massive enough to fuel a next leap.

Deimos was already giving the command. The equatorial armature of the Dyson spun and tilted its own lightcone outside of timespace, and pulled the worlds of man into its wake.

Aeneas focused a hyperspatial periscope behind then, peering back into normal space, while their own local and highly curved spacetime folded abruptly. The surrounding stars turned red and fled away like sparks.

Aeneas smiled grimly as the twenty five worlds of vampires from Canopus emerged just at the moment when the nightmarish system of 9 Sagittarii annihilated everything made of normal matter. The vampire worlds dissolved. The small worlds dissolved. The small worlds, impossibly, like something from a bad dream, returned, burning and melting and rippling like water. The vampire worlds did not.

Then the survivors of mankind were safe within the warp channel: a zone of timespace so small that light rays circumnavigated the entire miniature universe, and the men could see the surface of their own Dyson reflected in every direction as if in a globe surrounding. The worlds of men seemed to hang between the orb of the Dyson and the inside-out orb of its reflection, globes of gas and stone hovering like bubbles between two curving walls of metal. Unlike the escape from Canopus, there was no pursuit.

The wounded were taken to cellular regeneration coffins. All but one. Lord Jupiter, sitting on his chair of state, would not leave the chamber and go to his own healing. His face was drawn and pale with grief, and he did not bother to wipe the tears streaming freely from his eyes.

He spoke no word: all knew this meant his son Lord Ganymede was dead.

Aeneas sighed. "At Sakurai's Object, we can refuel for our next jump, lick our wounds, bury our dead, rebuild our broken jovians, and see what more nightmares await us."

He adjourned the council, and set them about such tasks of repair as could be done while the armada was within the closed timelike curve segment outside spacetime. Then Aeneas returned to his own chambers, brooding over his mistakes and failures, and wishing, for once, his cleverly-made and poison-resistant body could be influenced by alcohol.

10

SAKURAI'S OBJECT

The star V4334 Sagittarii, also called Sakurai's Object, thought to be
a slow nova, was a white dwarf that, due to a very late thermal pulse,
swelled monstrously and became a red giant.

Fortunately, there were no surviving planets in the system, hence
no space vampires. The cataclysmic thermal pulse had obliterated any
outer worlds, and then the rapid expansion of the star to a red giant
swallowed any inner worlds, leaving the entire system swept clear of
any trace of planet, planetoid, or comet.

The Tellurian Dyson materialized in the system, emerging into the
sublight continuum so as to catch the star at its center. The planets
of the World Armada, broken, scarred, half-melted, were orbiting
outside the Dyson hull. For them, it was night. No light touched
them. None of the small artificial stars orbiting them had survived.

The Dyson turned the hullplates of its equator transparent to light
and infrared, and the worlds adjusted their orbits to let the radiance
falling from these vast windows fall across them.

The Dyson did not crush the giant star, not yet. Masses of material
drawn up by counter rotating magnetic fields reaching in-system from
the underside hull of the Dyson, were cooled, transmogrified, and
contorted to the wounded worlds to supply what had been lost to the
neutron decay at 9 Sagittarii.

Time passed while worlds were rebuilt and trillions of dead were mourned and buried.

The Lords of Creation met in council beneath the trees of Heaven Lake on Second Earth. In the sky, the Dyson had risen to the zenith. The curving strip of windows through which Sakurai's Object, now their sun, blazed like a rainbow ignited to fire. The wind was fierce and blustery. Several Lords and Ladies used their rings to erect invisible fields to block the gusts and to warm themselves, wondering why Aeneas insisted on meeting out of doors. Only Mars and Aeneas ignored the weather.

Aeneas had erected seven new seats with tall backs, shadowed beneath shining canopies, each with a sapling behind. An eighth seat, draped in black crepe and trimmed with a wreath, was also there. He watched the faces of his aunts and uncles as they contorted into view and looked, and saw the new seats.

The worlds under repair, mottled and scarred, were visible above the horizon as large crescents or small disks. Something in the demeanor of Aeneas was also scarred, although not visibly. Grim lines had deepened like crow's feet about his eyes or like calipers around his nostrils and mouth.

Aeneas spoke without preamble. "I have invited the young Lords Anubis, Deimos, Kerberos, Hydra, Dionysus, Triton, and Prospero to hear our deliberations and contribute their wisdom. Since they are equally joined in knowledge of the secrets of the superluminary science, as well as in the dangers of battle, it is only right that they join us. A seat has been set aside to honor the memory of Lord Ganymede, until such time as one is found worthy to replace him."

He raised his hand. Contortion pearls blazed. Seven young men now stood on the grass, each with a chlamys of imperial purple thrown over his dark dress uniform. Lord Anubis was grinning. Lord Hydra was grave.

Lord Mercury said, "Now, that is rather high-handed of you, sire! You cannot simply—"

Aeneas by gesture invited the new lords to take their seats. He turned to Lord Mercury. "We have other matters to discuss. You have our gratitude for saving us from the nightmare star of 9 Sagittarii. How did you do it?"

Lord Mercury's small world had been untouched, and so he had been unburned. He smiled his irksome, childlike smile. "Trade secret!" he chirruped.

Lord Anubis was a dark, thin, tall, sharp-faced man with a sharp smile. The family resemblance was strong, but, next to Mercury, he looked like the father, rather than the son. The subterrestrial under his command, Bald Spot, had also emerged unscathed.

Anubis said, "Let us not be blind and heartless now, Father. The days of intrigue and fratricide are done." He turned to Aeneas. "There is a strange overlap between space warp science and space contortion science. The dissolving creatures and their buildings and machines were keeping undecayed elements in nullspace and replacing each atom, one by one, as its nucleus was destroyed."

Lord Deimos, son of Mars, added, "Sire, they used the same technique Lord Mars uses to make duplicates of an ideal version stored in the timelessness of Schroedinger standing waves."

Lord Anubis nodded. "All my father, Lord Mercury, had to do was to force-collapse the uncertainty clouds with the megascale pearl."

Aeneas said, "And if the next star system we enter has the same defense?"

Lord Anubis said, "It is not a real defense, sire. It is a trick that can only work if you are caught unprepared. Using a warpcore to dissolve a warpcore can only work if you let your warpcore dissolve also. And you can only do that if you can keep a spare in nullspace, out of harm's way."

Lord Mercury said, "We have manufactured more than enough pearls to move whole worlds of people. Anyone trying that trick again will dissolve before we do."

Lord Mars said, "Sire, we should put the less massive worlds in the vanguard. We now see that even warpcores with far less mass than a jovian can damage an enemy core using this neutron storm method, or at least make the enemy keep his head down. I think I understand the foe's tactics now."

Aeneas said, "What do you mean?"

Lord Mars said, "The reason why they close to hand-to-hand range. I thought it was just blind fury, hunger to eat life energy. No. Whoever programmed these undead so long ago knew that the warp science can shut down nearly any other weapon. Board-and-storm is practically the only tactic that can ever work; and that requires numbers more than anything else. And their numbers are numberless, or seem to be."

Aeneas said, "Tell me honestly: is there any hope of victory?"

Lord Mars said only, "If we have no hope, we must fight without hope."

Brother Beast said, "Whoso hopes in merely mortal power will find that well shallow, and soon will thirst. There is deeper hope."

Lord Deimos now stood, evidently displeased with his father's words. His eyes were as bright as the eyes of a hawk, and he said to Aeneas, "My good sire! Shall we return to 9 Sagittarii and counter attack? Let us exterminate these vermin to the last man! If we now can stop their neutron storm method…"

Lady Pallas had been horrifically mauled, but her brain had been saved and a new and younger body grown for her. She seemed now a maiden of sixteen summers, but her gray eyes were old and cold and wise. She said, "It would be suicide, sire! Both those stars have unstable cores. I started to mention it, but you thought it insignificant. It is significant now."

Aeneas said, "You have the floor, my lady."

She said, "The neutron storm effect is amplified the larger the mass of the target. If we used the megascale pearl to collapse whatever nullspace was keeping those super-large ringworld armatures intact around those stars, not only would the ringworld matter dissolve, but

SAKURAI'S OBJECT   357

the stellar cores would go nova. The whole star system is a deadman switch. It dissolves anyone who enters via warpchannel; and it blows the whole nebula to smithereens if they resist dissolving."

Aeneas said, "Who would engineer such a system?"

Lord Mars answered, "The old owners. Those ringworlds were not full warp armatures, but they held off the vampires, no doubt for a long time. Geologic ages, maybe. The enemy could not enter the nebula through a warpchannel, not without what just happened to us happening to them. They must have floated in at sublight speed."

Aeneas said, "Why are they still manning the ringworlds? Why still do this?"

Lord Mars said, "They are all automatons. Why stop?"

No one knew whether Lord Pluto had been wounded in the attack or not. His voice emerged from his helm, "That was why Sol was attacked at sublight speed, back in the Paleolithic, first by Baptistina, later by my old planet. The automatons followed their last standing orders from billions of years ago. The space vampires must think us the Forerunners."

Aeneas said, "To graver matters now: this star, Sakurai's Object, is large but rarefied, six-tenths of one solar mass, which is insufficient to carry us more than seven hundred lightyears. Fortunately, a protostar called HH 80-81 is within that range. By astronomical standards, it is recently-formed, preplanetary, and thus may be as free of vampire infestation as Sakurai's Object. It is ten solar masses. Enough to carry us to KW Sagittarii, our next target.

"I leave to you, lords and ladies, to debate the best approach. We can land at the barycenter of the system, as we did at Canopus and at 9 Sagittarii, or we can land off-center.

"The advantages of landing at the barycenter are plain. The advantage of an off-center landing should be clear from our last debacle."

Lord Mars said, "Forgive me, sire, if I talk out of turn. You cannot let a few deaths shake you. Caution in combat is worse than recklessness because it heartens the enemy and makes you predictable. Put the emergence point of the warpchannel in the center of the system! Crush the star first and let the enemy do his worst!"

Lord Jupiter said, "Sire, our only hope rests in stealth and caution. Emerge ten lightyears from the system, or more, and approach at sublight speeds."

Lord Mercury said, "For once, I concur with Lord Jupiter. Only a fool leaps into a window without peering through first. With the planetary disinertial engines, we could bring our worlds to ninety-nine percent of lightspeed, and arrive in the same hour as any light reflection or radar beam betraying our position. To us, ten years would pass in an hour."

Aeneas put it to a vote. The younger lords sided with Mars, trusting in power; and the older with Mercury, trusting in speed. Brother Beast, Lady Vesta, and Lord Pluto abstained. The vote ended in a tie, eight to eight.

Aeneas broke the tie and made the decision. The Dyson emerged at the center of the HH 80-81 system. As hoped, there were no vampires in the system, which was fortunate. As should have been foreseen, however, when the Dyson enveloped the protostar, the twin collimate radio jets emerging from the protostar's axis of rotation cut through the Dyson hull, destroying many square lightminutes of inner surface, where the gravitational and magnetic fields firing mechanisms rested. Radio waves, like electromagnetic radiation of any wavelength, in sufficient force will have the power to heat matter to the fission point, and ignite it.

Hence, as the protostar was seized in an ever shrinking globular web of forces, the globe was frayed and broken at these two points: under unimaginable pressure of the stellar collapse, like gas spurting from a punctured balloon, the jets of emitted particles grew bright and hot and thickened into a beam of nova proportions.

By sheer mischance, the terrestrial-sized battleworld Ouroboros, in what should have been a safe orbit outside the Dyson hull, was struck by the beam puncturing the hull. The antiphotonic planet-wide force fields and defensive screens were overloaded and obliterated in a microsecond. The planet was disinert, and should have simply been carried before the beam like a feather carried along in the wash from a firehose, unhurt, but the protostar was surrounded by a nebula dense enough to offer resistance to the passage of the planet. The density was very nearly a hard vacuum, but not very nearly enough. Without inertia, the planet halted its motion away from the beam when it struck even a few particles per billions of cubic miles of space, and was slowed, and overtaken, and burned to nothing.

It was instantaneous. Lord Hydra and all the soldiers, servicemen and servants he had manning the captured engines and weapons of Ouroboros were dead before they knew what struck them. The warpcore at the center of the planet swelled as the mass of the beam passed into it, increased its event horizon radius to consume its surrounding equipment. Having eaten its own moorings, the hollow singularity failed, collapsed, and vanished from timespace, never to be recovered.

Nothing showed on the face of Aeneas when next the Lords met, but there was a strange light in his eye, and three thrones now draped in black. "Fate has slain one of us for my presumption! A cautious approach is needed.

"We will take the time to patch the puncture holes in the Dyson. We will have to make other preparations, re-engineering each warp armature under our command. This will take time, but we must hope the small, local jump here has passed unnoticed by the hunters. Lady Io, daughter of Jupiter, has been selected to receive the warpcore imprint and to helm Second Jupiter, and guard the populations there.

"The populations will need to be distributed more evenly among the World Armada, and some terraforming must be done. Then, on to KW Sagittarii."

The Armada emerged half a lightyear off from the target system. KW Sagittarii was a supergiant star some thirteen thousand lightyears from Canopus, which shed three hundred thousand times of light than Sol. Even at half a lightyear away, it was blindingly bright, and overwhelmed astronomical instruments.

Within the same minute of their arrival, which obviously had been detected instantly by every warpcore array at or near KW Sagittarii, a dozen copper-colored spherical vessels one lightminute in radius emerged from warpchannels, like miniature Dyson spheres. Each one materialized and caught a human superjovian, jovian or subjovian perfectly in its center. At the same time, the other three opened fire on the smaller worlds. Black pearls of twisted, tightly-knotted and unstable space were shot in streams by the hundreds from tractor presser beams sweeping like searchlights from the outer hulls of these coppery mini-Dysons. The clouds of black pearls shot toward the moons, worldlets and terrestrials of the Tellurian World Armada.

The black, three-headed throne where Aeneas sat was smothered in alarms, and his ring and his eyes grew hot as fire from the overload of information pouring into his brain and orders pouring out. And perhaps there were tears as well pouring out of his damaged eyes.

But if so, he noticed neither the tears nor the damage, but barked out the battle orders as fast as tachyons could carry them.

11

THE

WORLD-WRECKERS OF

KW SAGITTARII

Nine miniature Dyson spheres, one lightminute in radius, instantly englobed the nine capital worlds of the Armada of Man: St. Michael's World, Niflheim, Inferno, Pallas, Second Jupiter, Second Neptune, Second Saturn, Second Uranus and the subjovian world called George. Most of the moons and asteroids near the giants were caught. The other three enemy miniature Dysons gave chase and opened fire on the smaller, rocky planets sailing disinert far from the gas giants. These Dysons employed a strange weapon: they were throwing black pearls in numberless clouds outward at near-lightspeed.

These pearls, when they struck atmosphere, or ring system, or outer moon, not only gave off a small explosion which would only have flattened a city, but they erupted with masses of plasma energy taken from the core of KW Sagittarii which should have burned whole hemispheres. It was an ironic reverse of the humans' own successful tactic at Canopus. Forty worldlets and moons in the human armada died, and so did Second Pluto. What saved Second Earth and Second Venus was the fact that the vampires had not expected the worlds to have atmospheres, so the pearls ignited prematurely, miles above the surface, and below the innermost of energy fields and defensive screens swaddling the small worlds. The shields of Second Earth held; those of Second Venus failed. All life on the surface of Second Venus was destroyed, and the oceans evaporated, but the cities deep beneath the mantle near the planetary cores were safe.

The nine capturing mini-Dysons spun their armatures, flattening space, and preventing the escape of the worlds caught in their dead centers. But not all warp effects were jammed: the enemy allowed hyperspatial periscopes and tachyon radio to operate, in order to let themselves see and coordinate events instantly across the relativistic distances.

Lady Pallas sat alone on her empty world. Her hollow asteroid, filled entirely with artificial brains, floated serenely in the chemical seas of her jovian warworld. Lady Pallas had had the forethought to erect many hundreds of hyperspatial periscopes with viewpoints scattered evenly in concentric globes around the armada. Hence, during the thirty seconds before any light images could reach from the newly arrived inner hulls to the eyes and instruments on the surface, she saw the threat of the mini-Dysons entirely englobing each world. This alone saved them.

The human warplanets were coordinated by a brain-to-brain tachyonic mindlink, and reacted instantly. Lord Deimos, in the control fortress of the Tellurian Dyson, used some of the remaining fuel from the corpse of HH 80-81 to create a nova beam. He forced it though a warp channel so that it would arrive instantly at its destination, and cut the mini-Dyson surrounding St. Michael's World, the superjovian where Brother Beast was stationed, neatly in half.

Of course, the spherical compression fields which had been fired moved at the speed of light. It took a half minute to cross the distance between the inner mini-Dyson hull and the globe called St. Michael's World, but the warp field flattening space and preventing any escape did not. It was an instantaneous effect. So in the same moment, from the frame of reference of the command thrones of the attacking mini-Dyson, that the mini-Dyson was severed into two hemispheres, the armatures parted and the warp field vanished, in that same moment from the frame of reference of the superjovian planet, it, too, was released. Many seconds before the compression fields reached any planet to crush, not only was St. Michael's World vanished from its former location, it had re-emerged into timespace in close orbit to the second of the attacking mini-Dysons.

Too close an orbit, in fact: the supergiant planet smashed through the one-atom thick hull substance like an elephant through gossamer. Fortunately, St. Michael's World was mostly uninhabited. No one was slain in the titanic super-earthquakes and supersonic hemisphere-to-hemisphere typhoons released when cubic miles of ocean and atmosphere were flung into space by the impact, or countless kilograms of matter, superheated to beyond the fission point, evaporated explosively into x-rays and high energy particles.

By some miracle, Brother Beast broke none of his warp armatures by this crazed maneuver. Lord Neptune, who had been trapped at the center of this mini-Dyson, found his ice giant world Niflheim surrounded, not by a closing globe of force, but by a globe with a hole in it, because the emitters dotting the mini-Dyson hullplates Brother Beast had just smashed were gone. Lord Neptune rendered his world disinert, and used his gravity engines to fling the whole globe out through the hull breach.

St. Michael's World and Niflheim now warped to close orbit about the mini-Dyson englobing Second Saturn, the planet helmed by Lady Eunomia. It was the only gas giant not armed with a warpcore. It was also the world with the highest civilian population. Immense interplanetary tractor beams and destructive rays poured out from Niflheim, ripping up and destroying tens of thousands of square miles of hull plate, and meanwhile Brother Beast, like a lunatic, hurled his battered, cracked and burning superjovian world again and again through the hull plates, hoping to hit some essential city, engine, emitter, or node.

Meanwhile, on the smaller worlds, the Ladies Luna and Venus, and Lords Dionysus, Kerberus, and Anubis, also reacted instantly. They spun their armatures up to speed. Their small planets vanished into red pinpoints, and reappeared out of blue pinpoints in close orbit around the enemy mini-Dysons trapping the giant planets Inferno, Pallas, George, Second Jupiter and Second Neptune. The small planets linked their warpcores to the giant planets, and used the tactic learned at 9 Sagittarii to erect overlapping spacewarps, out of phase and mutually destructive. The engineering done at HH 80-81 was now put to use: Lord Mars and Lord Mercury had cooperated to place the essential engineering components in nullspace, turn them into antimatter, and create an endless sequence of positive matter replacement parts out of them, using the matter orientation technique of Lord Mars. Not the whole world, but just the armatures circling the equators and poles of the small worlds began to glow, burn and dissolve, but then to reconstitute themselves.

Meanwhile the large armature of the copper mini-Dysons also began to glow, burn and dissolve. They, however, did not reconstitute themselves.

More amazing were the events on Second Jupiter, where Lady Io was at the helm. Her warpcore was jammed by the more massive warp of the englobing mini-Dyson, and without a second core working in concert, she could not create a neutron storm as had the small worlds of 9 Sagittarii. However, on this world were the militia, over which Lord Jupiter had been placed unexpectedly in command.

Aeneas had commanded that only those men who had been willing, back in the days when Lord Tellus was Emperor, to step into one of his deadly voting booths and risk death to cast a ballot, had earned the right to bear arms. Since most of them, in later years, cast their ballots by marksmanship at the shooting range, they were also practiced shots. Thanks to the ready availability of pantropic techniques to halt or reverse aging, these patriarchs could be returned to the neural and glandular age of eighteen-year olds, with strength and reflexes to match. (Women were forbidden from service, unless they had their neurochemistry altered to force their brains to operate like the brains of males.)

Aeneas did not know if he were also going insane, or if his grandfather's strange thought processes were becoming clear, or both. But it now seemed clear that peoples gifted with eternal youth and endless leisure, but with little or no liberty, hence no self reliance, could not help but be slavish, selfish and cowardly. But any man willing to face death to join in the civic duty of voting for Parliament clearly had overcome the selfishness endemic to an age of history suffering the corruption of luxury.

Perhaps this logic was sound. Perhaps it was insane. Whatever the case, the vast populations of Jupiter, the largest planet, and one of the last terraformed and colonized, retained the rough frontiersmen ethics needed when the place was first settled. These were, after all, the same individuals who faced so deadly an environment. During the reign of Lord Tellus, they had been the source of tumult and discontent, and even treason, yet Lord Tellus seemed to nurture rather than discourage their anarchist spirit.

That spirit saved them now. While other men cowered and fled, or tried in vain to work their contortion pearls the space vampires were jamming, the militia men in their private houses, islands, and continents floated ever upward in the vast atmosphere of Second Jupiter, and raised their pistols overhead.

These pistols, after all, were built by the same gunsmiths as had equipped Lord Mars, and their range and variety of destructive outputs was limited only by the mile-wide broadcast energy dynamos roaring at the core of Second Jupiter, and by the imagination of the wielder.

A disinert pellet accelerated instantly to nearlightspeed in the barrel was shot up the axis of a frictionless and airless tubular force field and was returned to normal mass and inertia just before it struck its target. Likewise, coherent energy of any wavelength or combination of high energy particles could be emitted, or neuropsionic forces, or more. The Imperial Family would never have allowed mere commoners and underlings such unparalleled power. Aeneas had left them no choice.

It might have seemed futile for citizen soldiers to open fire on the surface of an inner hull not yet visible to their eyes, some one hundred thirty-four million square miles in area. But these pistols could puncture a planet from pole to pole.

And the militiamen were cunning enough to concentrate their fire. The local commanders were cunning enough to use the still-working hyperspatial periscopes to find the source of the command signals controlling the miniature Dyson, and to find other essential target spots: engines, power couplings, force emission stations, the nerves and sinews of the attacking Dyson, the brain and heart.

The compression fields were able to grasp, over square lightminutes of area, the surfaces of stars and force them through utter atomic collapse into a plasma and then into hyperneutronium, and then into a singularity. But no one spot of the field was equipped to deflect the concentrated fire of an entire gas giant's hemisphere. When multiple trillions of beam weapons and relativistic mass shots flying outward at lightspeed encountered the palpable walls of kinetic and magneto-gravitic force, even the tiny and imponderable energy particles of which these walls were woven were disintegrated and scattered.

The compression fields hence only struck one side of the gas giant, and threw it. The countless contortion pearls each man, woman and child carried were activated at once when the force walls struck, and each person was rendered inertialess, and surrounded by force shells. The damage from flying landmasses capsizing and shattering continents brushed the people aside, imparted velocity to them, but passed no kinetic energy.

The massive planetary disinertia fields came into play, and so Second Jupiter, stormy atmosphere unwinding like a torn scarf, plunged across the one lightminute radius of the miniature Dyson. This distance was about a third of what Mercury's orbit had been, or ten million miles.

It reverted to its full inertia at the last moment before collision. Second Jupiter smashed through the thin hull at the pole where the massive warp armatures overlapped. Gathered here were spots where the main energy converters and warp control mechanisms were thought to be. There may have been cities filled with vampire lords and officers thickly clustered on the endless copper plains of the Dyson surface here, but, if so, they were obliterated by friction from the oncoming gas giant's atmosphere passing at supersonic speed through the area before even the hydrosphere and lithosphere of the planet rushing into and through the area, leaving a gap eighty-eight thousand miles wide.

Before and during the collision, the chief officer of the militia, Maliboeus, combined the surviving hyperspatial periscopes into one channel, and ordered all the militia to fire along this channel by space contortion. It acted as a warp channel, faster than light, and allowed an entire planet of gunfire to emerge at the prime spots Maliboeus selected: areas near the new-made hole where the enemy command and control fortress arose.

Even more daring, Maliboeus ordered his men to project their own escape pearls down the miniature warp channel created by the periscope. It was as reckless as telling sailors to burn their cork life jackets; but the trillions of militiamen, bright in shining environmental cloaks, now poured into the smoldering and ruined fortresses of the vampires and destroyed everything that moved with ever-lengthening lances of irresistible fire.

The militia on the other worlds did deeds of equal valor whenever space was flattened, warpchannels forbidden, or lightspeed weapons abolished, and only hand to hand fighting in the weird, slow, reddish environment of slow-lightspeed was allowed.

In the end, nine copper Dysons were destroyed. Three were captured intact, along with their precious high-mass warpcores, but still infested with vampires. These three were forced into timeless nullspace to be cannibalized and decontaminated later.

Lord Triton and Lord Prospero were dead, along with the countless multiple billions of civilians and militia dwelling on their gas giants of Second Neptune and Second Uranus. All were crushed into a microscopic black hole, and the resulting x-ray burst of energy focused as a beam weapon from the two victorious miniature Dysons to cut down further moons and planetoids of man, and scald the near hemisphere of Second Saturn.

Aeneas sat on his black, three-headed throne, the victory as bitter as ashes in his mouth.

12

THE ARCHVAMPIRES OF SPACE

The Lords of Creation were gathered beneath the trees. Two more thrones were draped with black: one for Triton, the slain son of Lord Neptune, the other for Prospero, the slain son of Lord Uranus.

Aeneas disconnected the nerves and muscles of his face, so that he could show no emotion aside from a stern frown. Which of his relatives was the traitor? For clearly the enemy had known which worlds were the most populated, which the easiest targets, and the evil beings had gone after them.

Only his eyes moved. His suspicions were strong, but he did not want to condemn without clear proof.

It was a cloudy night, and so the Dyson could not be seen overhead as it jumped through a small warpchannel of half a lightyear, towing Second Earth along, surrounded and obliterated KW Sagittarii. Any inner planets which may or may not have been present were also destroyed. No astronomer thought to check.

Outer planets and asteroids in the system where vampires might abide were immediately struck with the nova beam, powered by the bled-off excess, which reduced worlds to rubble and rubble to sub-atomic particles.

Aeneas gave the order to sail. The warp was formed. The clouds hid the sight of the night stars turning red, expanding and vanishing.

Inside the closed timelike curve segment occupied by the remaining one hundred fifty human races, disconnected from the cosmos, days passed. Aeneas convoked no councils, made no speeches, accepted no triumphs, saw no one.

Alone, in his chamber, beneath the shifting lights of the ceiling aquarium, his thoughts circled each other like the last of the dirty water circling a bathtub drain.

The enemy had concentrated on the highly-populated worlds, striking at the greatest civilian centers. These were acts of pure savagery, pure malice. Had the enemy here concentrated on military targets instead, they would probably have won the battle.

The destruction of two gas giants had slain more people in one moment than had died in all the wars fought among all the nations, princes, and tribes of history and prehistory combined. War, except for mutinies of comical futility, had been unknown under the reign of iron scepter of Lord Tellus.

For the first time Aeneas understood the temptation of empire: with all men's necks chained to one master, there was no freedom, but no war either.

Except... (now Aeneas punctured a small hole in the transparent ceiling with beams from his scowling, savage eyes, and let the drizzle splash over his head and shoulders, cooling his hot brow)... except that war had come anyway, had it not? War from the stars. The promise of peace was an illusion. The bargain had not been kept. The chains must be shattered!

The sheer hatred of the undead for the living was impossible to contemplate. Theirs were not merely the acts of a famished wolf loping after the last hare of winter. The staggering resources in ships and worlds, effort and energy spent to hunt down the last surviving organic life in the galaxy were beyond calculation. Surely it was far, far more than any energy a vampire would recover from their living bodies?

He watched idly as the self repair circuits in the ceiling closed the holes his gaze had made, and now he raised his skin temperature to boil away the puddle in which he sat. Steam rose.

What was truly behind the vampirism that had eaten a galaxy?

No answers came.

Eventually he emerged, donned the crown he had learned to loathe, and convoked the council.

His relatives had not been idle. Two empty planets had been created out of contributions from the gas giants, small worlds with black seas and dusky atmospheres. These were placed in orbit as mementoes of the two dead worlds lost in combat, with mountains and hills carved like headstones for nations and individuals of whom no remnant remained to be buried.

Meanwhile, the Dyson had been more thoroughly explored, and compartments and cubbyholes where smaller worlds and moons could be hidden during battle were prepared.

More engines and weapons were repaired and installed on all planets. The smaller planets had been drilling and practicing sublight-speed maneuvers, training with their planetary disinertia fields and gravity engines.

Other segments of the Dyson were terraformed, and families and clans and subspecies moved there in case more worlds died. Others were kept on the worlds, in case the Dyson died. Many billions remained in the buried cities far beneath the mantle, having learned to dread the sight of stars.

The terraforming of the newer battleworlds was rushed to completion.

Aeneas was impressed. His spirits lifted. For the first time in his life, mankind as a whole had a mission. The artificial races created by his relatives were more than pets, now, more than servants. They

372 The World Armada

had a mission and a rightful place, and a unity of purpose that was thrilling to behold.

Their destination was WR102, over eighteen thousand lightyears from Sol.

This was a rare type called a Wolf-Rayet star, superhot giants on the verge of supernova. The vast sphere rotated at six hundred miles per second. Most of its immense output was in the ultraviolet, invisible to the human eye. It was huge. It was hot.

WR102 was hot even by the standard of a Wolf-Rayet star. It was of the rare oxygen-sequence type, of which there were only four in Milky Way, five in galaxies beyond. Its stellar wind, streams of charged particles exploding continuously outward at three thousand miles per second, carried away per year three times the mass of the Earth. (A small, even-tempered star like Sol lost several hundred million times less than this.) These high-density particle winds issuing from the ultrahot photosphere blew away the outer layers of the star, revealing a bare carbon-oxygen core. The ultraviolet radiation ignited fluorescence in the wind region: not just the star was burning. The space about it seemed to be on fire.

It was also the hottest known star in space.

Aeneas gave the order to sail. "The cautious approach has proved disastrous. We will emerge at the barycenter of the system, and destroy the star WR102 as our first act!"

Those Lords of Creation entrusted to helm the battleworlds saluted him and vanished, each on his throne teleporting by space contortion to his own world or moon. Behind remained the Lords Pluto, Mars, and Mercury, and the Ladies Vesta and Ceres.

Aeneas commanded the ensigns to sound general quarters throughout the Empire of Man. The militia and civilians of the various worlds assumed their battle-stations. The floating continents of the gas giants were grounded and secured. The planetary shields blazed up; the smaller worlds and moons were shepherded into thickly armored docks spaced along the equator of the Dyson, and the gas giants assumed their positions at the vertices of an imaginary a dodecahedron around it, their warpcores humming.

Space flowed into existence around them. They emerged into the sublight continuum with the Tellurian Dyson entirely surrounding the star.

In hindsight, it was perhaps the worst decision Aeneas could have made.

It was like surrounding a bomb. Alarms screamed as all the four hundred thirty-two square lightminutes of the interior hull began to melt into liquid, sublimate into vapor, ignite into plasma.

Like fountains spraying upward through rocks, or sunbeams piercing gaps in a cloud, beams from WR102 shot through the breeches in the Dyson hull. The jovian world Pallas was caught in one of these beams. The near hemisphere was scalded and megatons of atmosphere was superheated and flung into space. By good fortune, Lady Pallas, the only inhabitant of the world, was in the far hemisphere, inside her armored and shielded subsea asteroid, and survived the supersonic shockwave of the worldwide hurricanes.

Smaller worldlets, Phobos, Miranda, Europa, and Titan were in one of the compartments in the Dyson hull, but they were also caught in such beams when the chambers were burned through. Their planetary shields were overloaded, their tiny, artificial atmospheres burned to nothing, their populations died, and their surfaces reduced to lava, and the lava vaporized.

A near-miss shattered the compartment where Second Earth was closeted. The event was seen by hyperspatial periscope before the lightwave and shockwave struck. Second Earth and Second Mercury reacted by erecting their planetary disinertia fields. They were wafted gently aside rather than be smashed and fried. They fell out.

Lord Deimos, in the fortress city aboard the Dyson, sent a message by tachyon mindlink: "Sire, the star is hotter than expected: some time in the last eighteen thousand years, it must have started its gamma burst. The shields we prepared are not holding. Do not let any worlds pass across an area where the hull is burned through! I will attempt to…" Then the signal was cut off.

Aeneas looked up. Second Earth was now outside the Dyson, which cut off all light from the sun, but the fluorescence of expelled particles lit up the night sky like an aurora borealis. Against this backdrop of flame, his eyes could see streaks of light, as of countless meteors burning as they plunged through the upper atmosphere.

He peered more deeply, bringing ever more instruments online. There were no planets in this system, no solid asteroids, no solid rocks. Instead he saw a cloud of which looked like a swarm of crimson comets, countless tens of thousands.

It looked like a sea of pink icebergs with plumes reaching directly away from the mighty sun in each direction. The mountains of scarlet ice were thickly packed, nor were they gathered in the plane of the ecliptic as the asteroid belt of the solar system. The iceberg cloud was evenly distributed in all directions, and the worlds of man, orbiting the Dyson, had already collided with countless numbers of them. Planetary shields repelled the larger comet heads of ice, but the smaller eluded deflection.

The meteors in the upper atmosphere of Second Earth now winked out. Aeneas, suspicious, turned his powerful gaze there. He did not see tiny rocks being burned by friction into nothing. He saw wide icebergs of material, glowing cherry-red from atmospheric braking, shedding vast amounts of their substance in the form of superheated steam slow their rate of fall, and waft gently to the ground.

The seas where they splashed down were suddenly filled with count-less dead fish rising to the surface, and a third of the waters turned red as blood. If they fell into forest or gardens, it was a sandy desert before they lightly struck ground. If one fell near a village, the men, women and children were corpses even before their houses were flattened beneath the mountain-sized bulk.

Then the steam in the upper atmosphere cooled, turned to liquid and fell to earth as raindrops. Where it fell, all life died, and the fountains and rivers turned to blood.

These were not icebergs, but undead creatures like the one which had been so long buried under the glaciers of the planet Pluto. What looked like hills of ice or heads of comets were the frozen form of the liquid blood-mass forming the amoeboid bodies of the arch-vampires.

The aurora borealis in the sky above now blazed, grew brighter, and turned blue. It looked, at first, like a Doppler effect, as if Second Earth were rushing into the fluorescent nebula surrounding WR102 at nearlightspeed. But at the same time, Aeneas saw the streaks of light of the countless meteors in the atmosphere accelerate, blurring into speeds too rapid to see. He understood now how the falling icebergs were slowing their fall. It was a timewarp effect.

"Lord Saturn," muttered Aeneas, "Where are you now?"

Casting his eyesight wide, he saw the Dyson sphere horribly burning, severed hullplates, ultrathin material square lightseconds in area, breaking loose from the mighty hull and being propelled by solar wind outward from the dense, superhot star. It looked like a weird snow of white-hot metal falling upward from a red-hot ground. He also saw the entire system-wide cloud of archvampires descending toward the worlds of men also speeding up. Within their timewarps, they were taking hours or days to cross the interplanetary distances, but to the outside universe, it was done in a heartbeat.

It was like being struck blind when the myriad eyes and instruments on many wavelengths feeding into his cortex through hyperspatial periscopes shut off, and only the eyes in his head stayed open. It was like having his right hand chopped off suddenly to lose the connection to the various servants and serviceminds under his command. Even the cheerful voice of his signet ring was silent. The mindlink was severed: all neuropsionic radiation was dampened.

Somewhere, a warpcore armature was altering the fundamental physical constants to prevent various useful particles and waves from propagating through space.

Aeneas opened his eyes. Heaven Lake had the iceberg-shaped space vampires floating on the surface, surrounded by dead fish. Limbs and tendrils, like trees on a hillside, were growing on their upper slopes. Eyes and microwave horns now sprouted from their crests and peaks, and many beaks, mouths, and trucks gave forth a dismal, roaring cry of triumph.

The grass underfoot turned brown and crumbled into dust. The circle of trees shed all their leaves at once, a blizzard of bright autumn colors. Birds fell from the sky. Aeneas tightened his subcutaneous armor, and fought off a wave of dizziness, but the bioadmantium life cells encasing him resisted the vampiric force. He was weakened, but still alive.

The monsters surged toward his island.

13

THE ABSOLUTE WEAPON

The first of the mountain-sized pyramids of undead flesh came to rest, grounded, not far from shore. It peeled off long strips of its substance, long and flat worm-like segments only the size of freight trains, which then grew centipede legs, and began to swim toward shore. Staring eyes and snarling maws of many sizes sprang up from their carapaces.

Other icebergs were closing in from the other directions, surrounding the island, and similar monsters of undead flesh, serpentine or molluscoid, were peeling and dripping from their slopes and diving in the water.

Aeneas stood. With him, seated in their thrones, were the Lords of Creation who had not been assigned to the helm of any battleworlds: Lord Pluto in his helm, Lord Mars unclad save for weapons, Lord Mercury with freckled face and chubby form of a small boy, Lady Vesta in white, Lady Ceres in green.

Aeneas said, "I am cut off from all my instruments!" But he pointed his finger at the nearest of the giant undead centipedes, ionized the air between, and unloaded energy from his Sach's organ and the various biological dynamos hidden in his body. The creature was blasted into bits, and the water surface carried the electrostatic charge to the centipedes nearby, who lost control of their limbs, writhed, jumped, and began smoldering.

The bits, however, where they fell, simply grew legs and began scuttling forward again.

He increased his muscle pressure and nerve firing rate, stooped, and grasped the dais on which his huge and heavy throne sat, heaved, and upended it. Below it was an empty shaft, straight down.

"In here!" he shouted. "And how are you still alive?" For the death energy shed by the vampires had killed all the fish in the waters, killed the trees and grass in an instant, and plucked birds out of the sky.

But now he saw that there was a circle of green grass still around the throne where Lady Ceres stood, with her arms around Lady Vesta. Lady Vesta was looking faint, and leaning on Lady Ceres, but she was not dead.

By way of answer, Lady Ceres stepped rapidly toward the escape hatch bored in the earth. Where she walked, the green grass sprang up, angle deep in an instant, and hip deep in two, and flowers opened as rapidly as fireworks. "I carry reserves within my aura," said Lady Ceres, "I can keep Marina alive, but I am rapidly losing the... I..."

Lord Mars was smiling his terrible smile. As he stood, he lifted his hand to his head and pulled the flesh of his face away. Beneath was not a skull but the iron-black neutronium body he assumed in battle, hidden under a thin layer of human flesh that was flaking, shedding and falling off his body. He drew his sword. "The warp is not jamming my powers, and I do not need my ring to work the basics. I can kill these hills." Then there were two of him, four, sixteen, ninety-six...

The first dozen giant centipedes rose from the waves and struck planted their twisting, oozing leg-segments on the shore. Apparently radio waves were being blocked, because the mouths and maws like caves opening in the slopes of the translucent mountains wallowing in the sea roared out orders in a harsh, glottal language.

The centipede monsters blurred and vanished from sight, as did the icebergs.

Lord Mars said, "But I cannot kill what I cannot see! Lord Pluto, they know your tricks! Is there any way to cut through your invisibility?"

Lord Pluto did not answer, except to shake his helmet back and forth.

Aeneas shrugged the hand of the nearest Lord Mars off his shoulder, opened his mouth, a vomited a stream of oily flame in an arc along the shoreline. Beams of other energies came from his eyes and fingers, slicing left and right. Six of the monsters became visible as they were lacerated and burned. Squads of Lords Mars ran toward them, swords high.

The Lord Mars next to Aeneas said, "Sire, stop showing off. Your bioweapons are toys. I can handle this."

Aeneas turned his head. Lady Ceres and Vesta leaped down the shaft. A Lord Mars was pushing a protesting Lord Mercury into the shaft. With a wail, the childlike figure fell in.

Aeneas said, "Lord Pluto, can you turn us invisible to them?"

"If he were here, no doubt he could," came a voice that was not Lord Pluto's. The dark figure doffed his helmet. Underneath was a dark haired man, gray at the temples, who looked like Lord Uranus, but without his mask. The flesh around his eyes, on his cheeks and forehead, normally hidden, were winking pinpoints like gems. Aeneas, seeing the neural flows leading to and from them, recognized these pinpoints as some form of sense-impression cybernetics. Here, finally, was the secret spy ray apparatus of Lord Uranus. He carried it on his face.

"I have the art of seeing the unseen. Any interference with the information layer of the universe agitates the stars, and I developed a method of locating the agitation source. I can paint their locations for you, Lord Mars."

He held up his lantern. Where the beam touched, it left behind three-dimensional, vapory shadows of gray and dark gray. These outlines betrayed the shapes of rearing, many-legged centipede monsters. He played the beam across the waters. On the lake, vast pyramids of shade and darkness rose.

Lord Mars said, "Go! You are sovereign! Your life is not yours to lose!"

Lord Uranus donned Lord Pluto's helmet, put his arm up (for Aeneas was much taller than he) to take the elbow of Aeneas, and jump into the shaft with him.

They fell straight down for an astonishing distance.

Aeneas called out over the noise of the wind, "Where is Lord Pluto?"

Lord Uranus said, "Helming my world, George."

"He does not have the warp science!"

Lord Uranus called back, "A duplicate of Lord Deimos, who used his father's trick to clone himself, is there!"

"So why are you here? Wearing his helmet?"

"He insisted. He was aware of our plan to flush out the betrayer! This makes him our prime suspect."

Aeneas reflected that Lord Pluto might have been standing in the room with them, himself and Lords Mars and Uranus, when the plan was discussed.

Aeneas shouted over the wind. "My unfreewill detector remains silent."

"As does mine."

Aeneas said, "The Betrayer outsmarted you."

"Let us say, sire, that the traitor did not make the move I expected. This was him trying to flush me out."

"What? How?"

Then the shaft infinitesimally slowly began to tilt. The surface was frictionless, and did not scrape them as they bumped against it.

Lord Uranus said, "The vampires were led directly to the spot where you were. The vampires were told, with Lord Saturn dead, that we do not have timewarps to slow back down anyone sped up by the timewarp."

Aeneas said, "Grandfather is still alive. He must be here, among us, or among our servants. I was expecting him to appear and give someone the brain imprint for Lord Saturn's secrets."

"So was the Betrayer," Lord Uranus said. "Expecting him to appear, I mean. We have to get out of this timewarp we are in without Father's help, or else he may be forced to show himself."

A mile lower down, the shaft was a forty five degree angle.

"I thought you hated him. Grandfather. When did you start liking him?"

Another mile passed. Now the shaft was a shallow slide.

"I did not like nor dislike," said Lord Uranus, "Passion clouds judgment. But when I found out all the worlds in the galaxy were undead, I finally understood him. I had judged him wrongly, all these years. He kept the secret of faster-than-light-drive from mankind in order to protect us. Then he…" Lord Uranus had good reason to hide his face, because his expressions were broad, obvious, and easy to read. Aeneas could see the thunderstruck look on the face of his uncle.

"What?"

Now the shaft was flat or seemed to be. Actually, it was following the curvature of the globe. Because the surface was frictionless, their speed did not decrease from terminal velocity. More miles flew by.

Uranus said, "He could have saved your life and erased your memory. Instead he gave you a power that forced us to make you Emperor. Why? Why now? Why this generation, this century, this decade? What was different?"

Aeneas said, "The younger generation is grown. Every moon and asteroid in the solar system was terraformed. The Solar System was overcrowded. We were getting impatient for our heritage."

Uranus said, "And you were so impatient, sire, that you tried a violent revolution to arrest and overthrow us. Your rebellion against us failed before it started. Our revolution against him, however, succeeded. Or we were allowed to think so. Why? Why now...?" And his eyes grew wide with wonder.

Aeneas said, "I see you figured it out. Didn't you? What is it? Where is Lord Tellus? What was his plan?"

The air in the frictionless shaft was now mingled with a gas that thickened about the them as they passed through, slowing them. It was a chemical process, designed to operate even under warp conditions when inertialess or gravitational technology could not work.

Lord Uranus did not answer the question.

They came to rest in a bubble of gas so thick it was a fluid, which slowly killed their immense forward motion. The heavy gas could be drawn into the lungs, albeit with discomfort, but the super oxygenated fluid was breathable. They swam to the zenith of the bubble and climbed out.

Lord Mercury, Lady Ceres and Lady Vesta were in the atrium above, along with a squad of militiamen, armed with pikes and pistols. Emergency supplies, communication gear, a mess hall, and dormitory opened up to one side, and an arsenal stood to the other, as well as a fully automated hospital infirmary. Lord Mars, or one of him, climbed out of the bubble of thick air only a moment later. The trembling of the ground, and the groaning of the earth, told them the news that the escape shaft had collapsed.

Lord Mars said, "You will have to get a new place."

Aeneas said, "You blew up Heaven Lake?"

"More than that, sire. They left the matter orientation level of the universe open so they could rotate particles into antiparticles also, and make themselves immune to antimatter like I am."

"How much did you blow up? Korea? All of China? The whole Pacific?"

"Everything on the surface. They were in the watertable, and there were a lot of them. I peeled the planet down to the mantle."

"There were cities on the surface!"

Lord Mars shook his head. "Not after the enemy fell like rain. The entire solar system filled with the creatures. Thanks to their timewarp, they had all the time in the world to get here. In numbers enough to coat the planet. I did not have copies on any planet but this one, and even if I did, I have no way to see invisible enemies..."

Lord Mercury said, "How did you fight them? They were using Lord Pluto's trick."

Lord Mars said, "How are you still alive? How did you resist the death energy?"

Mercury said, "I can step partly into nullspace, so that I seem to be here, but I am not."

Mars said, "Why did the enemy not use their warp to stop that power?"

Mercury said, "Why didn't they stop yours?"

Lord Mars ignored him, and turned to Aeneas. "Sire, we are in desperate straits. We should assume the other worlds have been overrun, and that all that remains of mankind is us, and the people dwelling in underground cities beneath Second Earth. The warp is still blocking all electromagnetic communication, but if the time is passing in the outside universe much faster than in here, enemy reinforcements are arriving in such numbers..."

The eyes of Aeneas suddenly blazed. He could see views from nearby worlds, including an image of the hideous, featureless, scarlet ball of magma which now was Second Earth. No image came from the surface of Second Earth. None of his instruments there had survived.

The rings on their fingers suddenly lit up, and the weapons of the militia men chimed and the gunbrains crisply reported that they had re-established space contortion links to the accelerators, cannons, and arsenals.

Lord Deimos appeared in the chamber, first as a projected image, and, a moment later, in person. "The Dyson is repaired, WR102 has been collapsed into our core singularity, and we are in the warpchannel to the Peony Star. Your planet, which was most thickly covered with vampire masses, was the last to emerge from the timewarp when it broke. George was first. We've been out for a month."

Mercury said, "How did you break the timewarp?"

Deimos said, "Lord Pluto was with me, and he..."

Aeneas interrupted, "Don't answer that. Tell me first why we are not dead."

Deimos said, "Sire, the enemy saved us. The timewarp which slowed us also slowed the rate of the gamma burst of WR102. The burning slowed to a standstill. We had time to make the needed repairs and install shielding before the radiation from the star resumed its normal rate of..."

"What about the enemy troops?" said Aeneas. "They shut off all our weapons, and had us outnumbered!"

"No, sire. I shut off everything, theirs and ours, but left stratonics from the matter orientation layer of the universe alone. This allowed the militia to use their weapons, armor, and self duplication. All the foe had was their life-absorption fields, which could not penetrate the neutral-matter armor. The militia multiplied itself until it had the advantage."

Aeneas looked at Lord Mars in astonished disbelief. "You trusted the militia with your secrets? Your terrible, absolute, infinite weapons?"

Lord Deimos stood with head high and his spine stiff. "No, sire. I did. Are they not free men?"

14

EXTINCTION OF THE
X-RAY STAR

The Peony Star lies near the Galactic Core, in the midst of the immense nebula from which it took its name and which, by means of fierce stellar winds and miniature supernova eruptions, it created. It was one of the three most luminous stars in the galaxy, over three million times the brightness of Sol. It was also unstable, on the brink of turning into a supernova.

The Tellurian World Armada emerged into sublight space one light-year away, and examined the system. It had not one, but several concentric Dyson Spheres, nested one within the other like Russian dolls, and multiple armatures of warpcores surrounding the whole, plus additional ringworlds to act as antennae, emitters, and muzzles for the discharges of the ultrabright star to act as weapons. The number of jovians and superjovians seen in the system, circling the armor-plated star at immense distances, was over a thousand.

Alarms rang in the ears of Aeneas, brooding darkly on his black throne. The battle world *King of the Wood* was lost with all hands and civilian passengers. The warpchannel had been strained beyond capacity. As a result, the globe had not emerged properly into normal space, so that it was skew to several frames of reference, and with different fundamental physical constants operating in different hemispheres. The difference between the gravitational stresses, and the difference in the time rate, and the difference between the mass of atomic particles between the various parts of the globe had simply torn the world to bits. Lord Dionysus, son of Vesta, was also dead, killed instantaneously, and his wife and children.

Other worlds, farther from the spacequake, suffered damage and saw some deaths, but survived.

The image of Lord Deimos, son of Mars, appeared at the elbow of Aeneas. Aeneas was seated on uppermost brink of the cone of a volcano which rose from the blasted, burned, and radioactive craterscape which had once been the Heaven Lake region of the Korean Peninsula of Second Earth.

Lord Deimos did not come in person, of course. His body was not bizarrely modified after the fashion of Aeneas, and he could not breathe radioactive air, nor ignore the heat and dust and poisons clogging the thin atmosphere of the newly-oceanless world. The globe was still lopsided from the stresses of its last battle, and was settling back into a spherical shape by means of periodic superquakes. At the moment, the volcano peak was high in the thin atmosphere. Lord Deimos could not see what Aeneas was staring at. He had his ring ask the ring of Aeneas.

The servant mind politely showed him a picture of what Aeneas saw. Many undertaker machines in the distance were delicately wading through piles of skeletons heaped amid the ruins. The spidery mechanisms were gingerly recovering the bones and skulls one by one for gene-identification. Other machines were gathering remnants of bodies together in coffins for eventual burial.

Lord Deimos said, "We made a warpchannel almost two thousand lightyears beyond our safe range, by anchoring it to the Peony Star. The quakes in timespace must have been correspondingly immense.

One of those thousand battle planets in the distance surely detected us with hyperspatial periscopes."

Aeneas said, "You are deceived by an image many months old. Look with your own periscope."

Deimos looked, or, rather, his ring gathered instrument observations from throughout the Armada, and formed a picture in his cortex.

Not long ago, when an unstable warp had struck its center of gravity of Ara A, and changed the fundamental constants erratically, distorting the flow of time and warping the distances between points in space, the resulting starquake had merely thrown immense masses of plasma from the deep layers of that large and stable sun into space.

But the Peony Star was a Wolf-Rayet star, erratic and volatile, poised on the brink of a supernova. In this case, placing the anchor of an unstable warpchannel at its gravitational center had triggered a runaway reaction: a supernova had destroyed the concentric Dysons around the star, all the ringworlds, all the gas giants, and everything made of matter.

The orb of electromagnetic hellfire was expanding outward at the speed of light, followed by a slower, heavier, and no less hellish orb of charged particles, ions, and plasma.

Aeneas said, "As the sphere of ejecta expands, it grows less able to heat up from energy deposited on its interior surface. Take your readings. How long before the star will be cool enough to allow us safely to surround it, and take up the remnant? Is there enough remaining to reach our next destination?"

Deimos consulted through his ring with his instruments and servants. "We will get less fuel from this star than expected, since so much mass was blown out into space. On the other hand, half the work of collapsing it into a black hole is done for us, so it should be enough. But, sire, we need wait no time before embracing the star. My people redesigned and rerouted the shielding of the inner hull and the compacting fields to catch and singularize the hottest star in the galaxy. We can handle even these temperatures here."

"Very good! Announce to the Armada that we shall make sail for V4641 Sagittarii immediately, telling them we will take the exact same precautions and use the exact same maneuver, of triggering a nova in the target star! Meanwhile, we shall be emerging a few lightyears away, around the star OGLE-TR-10, well out of harm's way. We will add that small star to our fuel, and only then making the short jump to consume the V4641 Sagittarii and refuel. Make sure all the Lords of Creation hear the plan. Prepare for, but do not make the jump. In the meanwhile, flatten space, and allow no one at any nearby star to observe us, or to warp here."

Repairs were made in a short time. Lord Deimos drew all the worlds of the Armada into the protective zone within the inner hull of the Dyson but above and between the cones of force that initiated the collapse mechanism.

The worlds assumed battle stations, and the order to prepare to sail was given.

At the last moment, Aeneas stepped through a pearl and into Lord Deimos' conning station, calling, "Halt!"

The hideous control arena of the polar fortress city of the vampires had not been changed, except for some tents and temporary energy houses, a medical coffin and an anything-maker, a chair and a coffee pot. Energy beings from Jupiter stood in the acres-wide control cups previously occupied by semi-liquid archvampires more massive than hills. Towers and stacks holding servominds had been erected reaching up to the stalagmites like upside-down skyscrapers that depended from a dome like an iron sky above. A canopy holding an Earth-like atmosphere had been erected over those few square miles in the immense chamber where Deimos and his Martian servants dwelled, Monotremes and Thitherfolk.

Before the curule chair where Deimos sat was a large spherical area in which a three-dimensional image of nearby space was displayed.

Smaller illusions to either side gave views, glyphs, and readings of the status of the Dyson and its warpcore.

Deimos rose from his chair and bowed.

Aeneas handed him a piece of paper. Lord Deimos stared at it blankly for a moment, and raised his ring to have his servomind read it to him.

Aeneas put his hand between the ring and the paper, blocking the servomind's view. "I am trying to prevent anyone from knowing this. It is our true warpcore destination. I worked out all the math myself."

"Without having a servomind double-check? I was not aware that humans could do math. Surely it is dangerous? Humans make mistakes."

"So do human-built machines, especially the mistake of sharing the information with a traitor. You have emergency controls, do you not? To enter armature spin vectors manually, just in case an enemy again shuts off our neuropsionic links?"

Deimos pointed to the nearest nine Ifrit, the living lightning bolts crouching above and connected to the archvampire hemispheres. "I have Ifrit servants to whom the commands can be given audibly. They have a physical connection to the Tipler acceleration arrays and power houses."

"Send all others hence, and establish a zone to quell any signals." And, when this was done, Aeneas read the sailing orders to the Ifrit, who manually enter them into the acceleration arrays. Lord Deimos then reopened his tachyon radio mindlink to the World Armada, and gave the order to form and enter the warpchannel.

The stars seemed to turn red and rush away into a dark sky as the warp was formed. No light from the outside universe could reach them. Entering the warpchannel, the Tellurian Dyson was now in an enclosed, bent space. Light rays leaving any one point of the Dyson circled the miniature universe and then fell onto the eyes and instruments of the opposite point, so that the whole Dyson seemed to be surrounded by a mirror-reversed and inside-out image of itself.

The sphere of the Dyson hung in the center of the miniature universe, surrounded as if by a reversed globe of itself, with the orbiting world between two metal walls. Because the universe was only slightly wider in radius than the Dyson, travelers found the route was shorter to fly directly north from the north pole, and land at the south pole hanging overhead like Polaris.

Some subjective days later, when it came time to exit the warpchannel, the metal walls of the universe expanded outward into nothingness, and then the nothingness closed suddenly in, blue sparks collapsing and colliding together, growing dim, and forming the night sky near the Galactic Core.

Stars were thick here, and a great globe of crowded stars filled half the sky. Dust and nebulae were thick, visible to the naked eye against the blazing carpet of stars as thick as snowflakes in a blizzard.

They had not emerged at OGLE-TR-10 as announced, nor emerged one lightyear away as announced. Directly in the center of the Tellurian Dyson was V4641 Sagittarii. The announcement that the Tellurian warpchannel would destabilize V4641 Sagittarii was also false: This was a binary star system of one bright and one dark star, merrily orbiting each other. Hard x-rays issued from the pair as material pulled out of the surface of the bright star circled twice and thrice in a vast curving spiral of fire before plunging into the dark star, to be eaten by the black hole there. Superluminal jets issued from the north and south pole of the system.

At first it seemed as if the star system were entirely empty. An anchipalaeoscope array showed that an immense fleet of worlds had been stationed here only two decades ago, not the pathetic four gas giants found in the old solar system, but four thousand giant worlds formed out of the thick debris and ejecta of this violent system, or towed here from nearby stars. Perhaps the fleet had been here more recently, but the anchipalaeoscope could not resolve nearer images in time.

But it was not entirely empty. The whole system was surrounded by a Tipler armature, which was now trapped within by the Tellurian Dyson. This armature was about four lightminutes in radius, half the radius of the Tellurian Dyson sphere. The armature began to spin as soon as the Tellurian Dyson emerged, four minutes before light from the Dyson inner hull could have reached any observer. At the same time, Schroedinger alarms went off, detecting that observers had seen them.

Other detectors noted the presences of hyperspatial periscopes issuing from two points: the first was from the crew of vampires left behind at the V4641 Sagittarii double star armature. The second was a few lightyears hence, at OGLE-TR-10, the very spot Lord Deimos had announced to the World Armada to be their destination.

Deimos saw through his periscopes the four thousand world Black Fleet orbiting the small yellow variable star OGLE-TR-10, gathered in overwhelming strength.

Lord Deimos reacted by spinning his armatures and flattening space, and at the same time triggering the firing sequence. The compression fields fell inward at the speed of light; all faster-than-light phenomena were quelled. All periscopes went blind.

But the armature surrounding the double star at V4641 outmassed the nearly exhausted Tellurian Dyson, and so, slowly but inexorably, started to pry spacetime into a curve that would allow warpchannels to form. Channels from OGLE-TR-10, many hundreds of them, like ghosts, began to flicker partly into existence.

Autolycos Lord Anubis, acting without orders, was the first to react. He and Lord Kerberos accelerated their corvette battleworlds, Bald Spot and Garm, at the nearlightspeed velocities planetary-disinertia engines allowed toward the armature inside the collapsing compression fields. Lady Luna followed them in her superterrestrial destroyer world, Chariot-of-Madness, which she had adorned with moons, orbital weapons, and ring systems of glittering crystal and diamond.

Their smaller armatures could not overpower the supergiant armature of the double star system, but they could begin to spin out of phase with it to disintegrate it, and disintegrating their own armatures at the same time, but also instantly repairing them from stored duplicates in nullspace. Lord Anubis, through the mindlink, reported that a nullspace pocket of the size needed to repair an armature circling an entire double star system was not present. The local defenders would not be able to copy the trick the humans had copied from the mad creatures of 9 Sagittarii.

Lord Deimos said to Aeneas, "If the enemy is wise, the crew manning the system armature will sacrifice itself to maintain the curve of space, and allow the reinforcements to come."

Aeneas said, "They are vampires. They eat their own. Watch."

Sure enough, the crew at the system armature, thinking only of themselves, changed the armature pitch, and began to flatten space and shut down all nullspace pockets: but this prevented the thousand battleworlds of the Black Fleet from OGLE-TR-10 from forming a successful warpchannel.

Some sixty or seventy worlds of the thousand attempted to make the jump nonetheless. No doubt these slaves were compelled by lordly archvampiric masters left safely behind. The three score gas giants emerged as brilliant spheres of white-hot plasma and radiant neutrons. The burning spheres, their gravity and timespace askew, turned into ovals, and unwound into fiery clouds of asteroids, pebbles, dust, gas, and gamma rays.

Their nullspace pockets cut off and unavailable, the armatures of the smaller worlds disintegrated first: Bald Spot and Garm went dead in space, orbiting between the double star and the collapsing concentric bubble of forces of the Dyson compression field. The larger world of Chariot-of-Madness issued planetary tractor pressure beams, caught the two wounded worlds in mid-flight, and began to tow them to safety. But the crew of vampires at the double star now bent the immense x-ray jet of their black hole toward Chariot-of-Madness.

Lady Luna's defenses deflected nearly all the blow, but the tiny part that escaped was enough to annihilate all the seas, cities, and surface features of the superterrestrial world, including the towers controlling the pitch and motion of the armature rings. The diamond moons were scattered like pearls from a snapped necklace.

However, the Tellurian Dyson had not ceased to spin its armature rings, also pitched to be out of phase. Although the Tellurian mass was less, the damage taken by the double star armature proved too great: the magnificent structure broke into pieces. Huge segments of the armature, countless thousands of miles long, now were falling into ever higher orbits, and the hollow singularity at the core of the double star system was no longer under control.

Lord Deimos formed the small channel needed to pluck the wounded worlds of Chariot-of-Madness, its flying moons, and also Garm and Bald Spot, neatly back into the dock yards set aside for the repair of damaged worlds. By a miracle, the loss of life was minimal. The people and militia of the wounded worlds had been yanked by safety mechanisms through their personal pearls into time-less nullspace just as the deadly blow fell. The enemy had trapped them there when space was flattened, but it had not harmed them. The armatures of Garm and Bald Spot repaired themselves from mate-rial in their nullspace pockets as soon as the curvature of space allowed those pockets once more to be reached.

Both stars of V4641 Sagittarii, all the remnants of the broken armature, and the countless millions of surviving vampire crewmen or commanders of the double star were swept into a singularity, oblit-erated by tidal forces, and dissolved in a burst of x-rays.

And the Tellurian Dyson dwindled to a reddish pinpoint and van-ished, leaving behind the planet Pallas, empty and unmanned, its armature spinning merrily, preventing any outside fleet from seeing the events at V4641, or emerging here.

The news of their departure would not be known for some time.

15

ATTACK AT THE MASTER ARMATURE

Second Earth was being terraformed to erase the damage Lord Mars had done to it. It was a world of rain. From small gaps in the endless cloud cover, rain could be seen falling into the dry sea beds, the dead cities, the crumpled fields of lava, and the ceaseless chains of smoldering volcanoes. On a transparent platform atop these clouds, Aeneas gathered the Lords of Creation once more, seated in a circle of their decorated thrones.

Six thrones were draped in black.

In the middle of the circle of thrones, a spherical illusion displayed the remaining battleworlds of the line like so many Christmas tree balls striped and swirled with stormclouds of white, blue, gold, dun, cerise and gamboge: the superjovian Saint Michael's World, helmed by Brother Beast; the jovians Niflheim and Inferno, helmed by Lords Neptune and Jupiter; Second Jupiter, helmed by Jupiter's daughter Lady Io; the subjovian George, helmed by Lord Uranus; the terrestrial Hesperus, helmed by Lady Venus.

The son of Mars, Lord Deimos, commanded the Tellurian Dyson. In the image, this was a carnival balloon among soap bubbles. The steel-hued sphere was pierced, patched, scalded, battered, and mended, and still was able to sail and fight.

Lord Uranus spoke first. "Sire, Lady Luna and I have cleansed the captured miniature Dysons of KW Sagittarii. No trace of any cellular life existing in the shadow condition remains. Once the militia quells the various robots, automatons, and booby-traps, these warpcores and weaponries will be available to the fleet."

Lord Mercury, squinting, said, "How did you manage to wipe out a quadrillion space vampires occupying over twelve square lightminutes of surface area?"

Lord Uranus tuned his flesh mask to an impassive setting. "Trade secret."

Three coppery spheres, belted by warp armatures along their meridians and equators, joined the image, one sixth the size of the steely Dyson.

Aeneas said, "We hereby commission the Lords Anubis and Kerberos, as well as the Lady Pallas, to assume command of these dreadnoughts. Let them be readied and christened before we emerge from warpspace. Let Lady Luna assist Lord Uranus on the cruiser battleworld George."

Lord Mercury said, "Sire, where can we find the personnel to crew such immense vessels? Automatons lack flexibility and initiative. Consider, please, the wisdom of reviving some of the countless dead we have gathered during these battles. In the shadow-condition called undeath, the skills and memories remain intact. Naturally, we wish not to dishonor the bodies of the dead, but their patriotism would urge them, if they were still alive, to volunteer their remains for this useful task. Surely they have the right to avenge their own deaths? Order the graves dug up!"

The eyes of Aeneas narrowed, and his face grew hard as flint, but he said nothing.

Lord Mercury spoke more urgently, "Consider the wisdom of it, sire! No one possessed of eternal youth should be risked on the battlefield! Is not life precious? Let the dead protect the living!"

Aeneas said, "The militia can reduplicate themselves to fill our numbers. Lord Mars, what are the limits on your technique?"

Lord Mars said, "Sire, physically, our limit is merely a matter of living energy. The vampires cannot reduplicate themselves as our militia does because their life energy is external. They are limited by their carrying capacity. Psychologically, our limits are that the newly made men, after a time, they become their own individuals, and refuse to reintegrate. This leads to endless legal difficulties, not to mention bigamy."

Aeneas said, "Even in these desperate straits, I call only for volunteers. Let them reduplicate with their families, and set up separate lives in their new stations. We will soon have room enough for each man to have worlds of his own."

Lord Mercury said, "And if too few volunteer?"

"If sufficient true men cannot be found among us to volunteer to defend their beloved homes, it is better we all die!" Aeneas stood. "This is not the last war, but it will prove to be the last battle of this war. For now we escape the galaxy altogether, or perish here as one, with none to mourn us, and no future archeologists to dig up our monuments. Our lives, lore, religion, laws, and all the accomplishments of man, all our crimes and all our glories, come to nothing if we fail now.

"My Lords and Ladies of Creation! With the loss of one hundred thirty subspecies of man, nearly half of the human races, we have suffered a woe that will never be healed. The beast-headed Georgians of Uranus are no more. The long-tressed Nichnytsia are extinct. The spirit of mankind will bear this scar forever.

"We who live, in their memory, and in their name, rededicate ourselves to the survival of our species, the revenge and retaliation of our wounds, and the utter annihilation of these undead abominations. Whether this task takes long eons to do is immaterial. Against such insanity of malice, no peace, no coexistence, no mutual armed truce is possible or desirable.

"At LBV 1806-20 we meet our fate. We go to the Luminous Blue Variable which is the greatest star in the Milky Way, to seize control of the Master Armature there. Let every warrior make ready. Let every civilian pray. Let none be idle now, in this final hour, ere we charge the open gates of hell."

Aeneas now removed a ring from his finger. It was a lesser ring, not his signet, but which contained a major servomind linked to various levels of the military hierarchy. He ceremoniously proffered the ring to Lord Jupiter. "My Lord, you asked for this terrible burden. I put the sword of war into your hand. You are now the commander in chief of all the militia and naval forces of the Empire of Man. Do you swear faithfully to execute these duties, to defend the crown, the church, the concord and the commons against all enemies, nor to allow the colors of the Imperium to be dishonored?"

"I swear," said Lord Jupiter majestically.

The dreadnought miniature Dyson Spheres were coppery colored macroscales only one lightminute in radius. In frantic haste, robotic tools, automatons and huge populations of engineers and officers prepared them for battle. Anubis christened his larger-than-worlds dreadnought *Jackal*. Kerberos called his *Hound*. Lady Pallas called hers *Owl*.

Amyclas Lord Pan, son of Jupiter, who had been discovered living in secret on a farm, after at first refusing, was given command of the gas giant Inferno and imprinted with the secrets of the warpcore science.

Lord Jupiter, as a commodore, joined Lord Deimos in the fortress city at the pole of the Tellurian Dyson. Jupiter asked Aeneas and the other Lords of Creation to join him there, since warp interference might halt tachyonic, neuropsionic, neutrino or radio communication during the battle.

The circle of thrones was moved to the vast, metal chambers of the alien command arena, beneath a canopy of air. Those Lord of

Creation posted to commands in the World Armada left remotely controlled images of themselves in their empty thrones to speak and answer for them. Lords Mars and Mercury were physically present, the Ladies Ceres and Vesta, and perhaps Lord Pluto.

LBV 1806-20 was a star vast in all ways, mightier even than Ara A. It was one hundred thirty times as massive as Sol, and two million time brighter. It was the product of some ancient engineering efforts of the Forerunners, for surely no natural star could be this titanic without collapsing under its own mass.

The World Armada emerged into sublight timespace eighty light-minutes from the gravitational center of center of the star, but the surface of the star was seventy-three. Circling the star were three monstrous ringworlds, each at right angles to the other. Their radius was the same as the planet Saturn once held around Sol, but the inner bands of the silvery-white ring armature were a mere sixty million miles above the chromosphere.

Schroedinger detectors sensed outside observers had seen them. Lady Luna confirmed that the gaze was hostile, hungry, insane with malice.

Lord Jupiter said to Deimos, "Flatten space."

"How flat, sir?" Because, of course, it was possible to halt macro-scopic spacewarp effects, such as forming warpchannels, while allow-ing contortion effects to continue, or other stratonic effects.

"Prevent any warps from forming. Halt all space contortion, but allow disinertia."

"Aye, aye. Anything else?" They both knew that as long as electro-magnetic or gravitic energy was allowed to propagate through space, even if it crawled along at lightspeed, beam weapons from LBV 1806-20 could annihilate the World Armada. Such beams would take a minute or two to reach the distance from the giant star's surface, but without their tachyonic periscopes working, the humans could not see any beam attack coming.

"Nothing else," said Lord Jupiter.

"Sir, mass estimates show that the Master Armature can overpower anything our Dyson can do. Easily."

"Thank you, Lord Deimos. Carry on," said Lord Jupiter.

Jupiter glanced sidelong at Aeneas, but the young emperor issued no orders and gave no advice. His face was impassive.

Lord Jupiter called to Lord Uranus. "Report!"

Lord Uranus said, "Our hyperspatial periscopes were in operation for 0.1 second, and gravitic images are still coming in. The enemy has a fleet in nullspace roughly ten times the mass of ours. Call that Black Fleet Alpha. It will be summoned into normal space wherever the enemy wishes if we allow the enemy to form a warpchannel.

"There is a second fleet, four hundred times the mass, of black suns and dark jovians within the Blue Star system englobing the star at one hundred twenty AU, or twenty-four lighthour radius. Call this Black Fleet Baker. Each ship is projecting a segment of a forcefield surface surrounding the entire star system. They have detected our warpchannel emergence, and are sailing hence at lightspeed under disinertia drive, shrinking the radius of the force bubble as they come. At current rate of speed, this second fleet should arrive in a day.

"At the moment, no warpchannels can emerge anywhere within a spherical volume sixty lightyears in radius. Fifty one stars just beyond that range, between sixty and one hundred lightyears, have opened fire, and are directing their total energy output toward us via hyperspatial periscope. However, this fire cannot emerge into normal space within the flattened radius, so they have place their emergence apertures beyond that. It will take sixty years to reach us. Therefore the obvious maneuver on part of the enemy...."

In the illusion hanging above the curule chair of Deimos, all could see the Master Armature, immense, unimaginably great in power, was beginning to spin.

"...is to flatten space, cut off our spy rays and weapons, and pin us here."

Lord Jupiter looked at the tactical display. The four Dysons of the Tellurian World Armada were arranged in a tetrahedron. In the vanguard were the smaller planets, Hesperus and George. Midmost were three jovian gas giants in a Klemperer triangle protecting the towed terrestrials and moons. The fourth superterrestrial, Saint Michael's World, hung in the rearguard as a reserve. The vanguard of the Armada was thirty five million miles from the surface of the hypergiant blue star. The rear was one hundred million.

Jupiter said to Venus, "Report."

She said, "The thought information in the imperative occupies a different part of the psychic spectrum from the declarative, interrogative or exclamatory. The source of all the local commands is there, the complex of cities dotting the surface of that cubical object where those two armatures intersect."

She pointed to a rectilinear macroscale object only slightly larger than a planet, half-hidden in the flames near the scalding surface of the hellish sun, which formed the joint where two bands of the vast armature crossed.

Lady Luna said, "The murmur of their nightmares is muted. Like someone waiting in an ambush, holding his breath. These are the thoughts that were passing through the area when we arrived, before they saw us. It is a trap."

Lord Jupiter said, "Can they tell what we are planning?"

Lady Luna said, "That is not the type of information I can glean from these wavelengths of mental activity."

Lady Venus said, "They are carrying out a prearranged plan. They were not surprised to see us appear at this time, in this area."

Jupiter scowled. "There is no help for it: our current plan is still our best. Lord Deimos, order the fleet to engage planetary disinertia engines, and proceed at nearlightspeed to the command cities. George and Hesperus grapple the cubical object! Militia to boarding stations!"

Through his ring, Jupiter summoned into view visions of the worlds of Hesperus and George unlimbering and erecting their many space elevators, cables of ultratensile nanodiamond fiber. At the base of each cable, countless militiamen in their shining environ robes thrown over their paragravitic neutronium armor stood with impossibly deadly weapons ready.

Lord Jupiter gave the signal for the attack.

16

THE BATTLE OF THE BLUE HYPERGIANT

Lord Jupiter, Aeneas, the Lords Mars and Mercury, the Ladies Ceres and Vesta, and Lord Pluto in his blank one-lensed helm and dark mantle were present in the command arena of the Tellurian Dyson, along with Lord Deimos. Scarlet-skinned Monotremes, four-armed Quadramanes, and lordly Thitherfolk were manning the watch stations to work human-shaped controls, and the energy-beings called Ifrit, living lightning bolts from Jupiter, stood in the acre-wide bowls which once had been the thrones of the amoeboid archvampires, to work the myriad and tiny nerve-jack controls dotting the inner surfaces.

Lady Venus uttered a warning, "Evil thoughts have overwhelmed several of our smaller moons, driving all the populations mad. Medical robots have taken control there. The thought screens on the larger planets are buckling."

Jupiter said to Deimos, "Increase the spin rate to insulate the mental layer of the universe. This should prevent neuropsionic propagation. Announce it fleet-wide and have all signet rings switched over to direct neural interface."

Without inertia, the whole fleet moved with the speed of a ray of light toward the city group which was their target. Two minutes passed. Two and a half. Three. More.

The distance to LBV 1806-20 diminished. Planetary shields labored to deflect the incalculable heat. The moon Second Phobos suffered shield failure and was burned to a cinder. The other moons and smaller worlds were gathered into the shadow cones of the gas giants.

The target cities of the foe grew close. They were visible to the naked eye, clusters of egg-shape habitats, each larger than a moon, like bunches of fungi clinging to the all six side of the immense armature joint.

The joint was a cube larger than a world, holding a synchronous orbit, hence motionless relative to the slowly-turning equator stream of the hypergiant star. The two armatures, each at right angles to the next, one above the other, were moving at nearlightspeed through tunnels piercing the cube at right angles. The armatures, like metal rainbows, were red in the direction of one horizon of the sun and blue in the other, and the mass created by their relativistic speed was causing sunspots. Coronal loops of disturbed star matter made lovely, fiery arches of immense diameter above and around the moving armatures.

The planet Hesperus was already reaching for the joint with many space elevators. The diamond cables elongated and flexed, so the attacking planet looked like a malproportioned squid. The outer atmosphere of the planet was already rocking towers and edifices with friction of the collision, and the outer forceshields were flattening flimsy structures as if by an impalpable wind.

Swarms of militiamen in free fall now were crossing the gap on the wings of their personal gravity fields, while endless hosts waited along the space elevator cables for the far end of his cable to snag a projection. Their cloaks were blazing like stars, laboring to repel the deadly heat of the hypergiant star whose surface was so close below.

Ten million windows and portals opened in the endless surface of the alien structure. Like termites from a disturbed nest, countless humanoid shapes boiled forth, indifferent to hellish temperature or hard vacuum.

The Lords of Creation heard Lord Neptune on the planet Niflheim mutter. "This is insane. Any one of those ringworlds could contain several orders of magnitudes more vampires than we have militia. We cannot beat them in hand to hand combat!" Of course, he had spoken this before the World Armada had begun its maneuver, and the words were reaching the ears of his brothers and sisters now.

Lord Mercury answered the moment he heard the word, so that, a few minutes later the words reached Neptune: "Have faith, blue brother! We still have a trick up our sleeve!"

Lord Jupiter stared at the image hanging above, showing the progress of the militia crossing from the planet George, flying like shining hailstones or streaming like jeweled ants across space elevator cables, into the Armature joint area. It was disturbing to contemplate that all this had happened minutes ago, and only now was the light image reaching him.

At that moment, the Master Armature encircling LBV1806-20 increased its spin. All the stars in the skies around them winked out, and the immense glare from the blue hypergiant went dark. Not just space was utterly black, but the chamber they were in. Through his ring, Lord Jupiter could reach no open radio channels, no radar, no microwave communication. Nothing.

"We're blind!" gasped Lord Jupiter.

He heard a motion next to him, a footstep, and felt a hand on his shoulder. Because of its strength and the strange texture of the armor skin, he knew it was Aeneas. The young emperor merely squeezed his shoulder silently, as if to reassure him that all was not lost, and as if to remind him the command was still his.

The image above the curule chair stitched over automatically to the white, the gray and dark gray monochromatic shadows of graviton sensors.

Aeneas was standing next to Lord Jupiter, visible to him, now, as a black-and-gray gravity image. Jupiter wondered at the cold, watchful look in his eye. Aeneas was paying no attention the battle. Instead, he was watching his relatives on their thrones warily.

Deimos said tensely, "The enemy has flexed space to halt electromagnetic propagation. Switching from photonic to neutronic radio. And now they are flexing the space further! Sir, we simply do not have the mass to counteract this."

"Do they have enough flex to open long-range warpchannels?"

"No. But with a short-range convexity, it is enough to contort mass out of nullspace... The Black Fleet is here!"

The smaller of the two enemy fleets had been stored in nullspace. That fleet now materialized in a globe around them: ten black suns, thirty superjovians, and scores of smaller world, moons, and armored asteroids. The human fleet was outnumbered and outmassed, and the primary nova-beam from the Tellurian Dyson was useless, since space was not carrying any lightwaves at the moment.

Enemy planets now swarmed the human worlds and spheres, flashing up to them instantly, moving with no inertia, suddenly coming to a gentle halt when outermost worldwide kinetic defense shield touched outermost shield.

Like the militia swarming from George and Hesperus onto the cities of the Armature cube, vampires in human shape now swarmed up and down ratlines leading from one world to another, and icebergs, lake and oceans of liquid amoeboid forms poured themselves after as vast interplanetary rivers. The human worlds were hemmed in on each side, surrounded and enclosed, so that awed and terrified civilians standing on the surface, if they had graviton-sensitive eyes equipped to see the view, would have beheld dozens of vast orbs from horizon to horizon, filling the dome of the sky overhead.

The three smaller Dysons in the human fleet, Wolf and Hound and Owl, now threw out countless clouds of black pearls. They were moving at disinertial speed, which was the same speed as the gravity waves being used to sense them, and so the enemy did not see the first rank of them until they fell among the enemy worlds. These pearls contorted fragments of superdense singularity substance out of nullspace, and these microscopic black holes issued tidal forces that began to tear up anything made of matter.

The militia on every world raised their pistols and fired gravity beams to crush and rip asunder anything caught in the path. These energies were gravitic, not electromagnetic, and hence could still operate.

The coppery Dyson spheres began pulling black suns into their firing apertures. The kinetic and gravitic fields which formed the interior firing mechanism still worked, even if the beam could not propagate. The Dysons began chewing up the black suns. In a moment, there were only seven of them.

Lord Deimos said, "Sir, the Master Armature is overpowering us. Soon, light will flow again, and then neuropsionic waves. When that happens, the black suns will overwhelm our thought shields, and mindwipe us."

Lord Jupiter said, "Make it look good. Struggle, but not hard enough to damage our Dyson armature. Order all armatures to out of phase spin."

Light returned, and neuropsionic radiation.

Alarms showing the immanent failure of the planetary thought screens now rang. The beam weapons of the enemy returned as well, and these began lancing out in all directions from all parts of the enemy worlds, sweeping away vast volumes of the deadly black pearls. The nova beam of the Tellurian Dyson struck two of the black suns, which were instantly obliterated.

Space elevators rose from the surface of the Armature cube and reached to the two attacking worlds of George and Hesperus. An ocean of vampire liquid, so great as to make the archvampire coating

Pluto to seem less than a raindrop in the sea, an extent greater in volume than a gas giant, now rose like living towers out from the shattered domes of the command cities peering from the Armature joint. Space elevators reached out like so many numberless blades of grass and snared the superterrestrial and the subjovian. The undead liquid crawled up the lines of the space elevators. The militia, outnumbered by hundreds to one, rushed in to engage them, duplicating themselves as they came.

The master armature surrounding the supergiant sun was beginning to grow discolored as the armatures of the miniature Dysons Hound and Owl were rotating in destructive interference to it. The vampire lords manning the Master Armature of LBV-1806-20 no doubt laughed at this futile gesture. Theirs was the most powerful armature imaginable, circling the largest star! They knew this trick: but a smaller armature could not dissolve a larger via neutron storm unless it had a store of neutrons standing by in nullspace.

Aeneas said, "Where is Jackal?" He jerked his hand upward as if stung, and stared at his signet ring.

The vampires of LBV 1806-20 made a slight adjustment of their spin vector. The Master Armature warped space further. All materials in nullspace were forced into normal space.

This included what had been kept, all this time, safely in the megascale pearl of Lord Mercury. The last few cubic miles from the core of long dead Sol now emerged, and expanded at the speed of light. The visible rays were less than a candle in the sunlight compared to the hypergiant.

But the neuropsionic rays spread as well.

Lord Deimos spun his armatures, forming periscopic channels through hyperspace from the center of the neuropsionic explosion of the remnant of Sol to each of the attacking worlds, and to the target command cities clinging to the Armature joint. This would allow the deadly rays to appear at these target points faster than the speed of light.

To prevent this, the vampires flattened space, and in so doing prevented themselves from using any periscope to see the oncoming expanding sphere of holy radiation so deadly to them. They would perish before they knew what hit them...

Lord Deimos said tensely, "Sir! I think it is going to work!"

"Victory!" shouted Jupiter. "As I vowed!"

Jupiter stole a glance over this shoulder at the young emperor, hoping for a look of favor. Aeneas was staring at Lord Mercury, ignoring all else.

The holy light of Sol spread outward. The neuropsionic radiation passed through solid matter without hindrance, and vampires in countless myriads died at its touch. Neutron radio carried the sounds of endless cheering from the militia.

But the skies suddenly turned to fire. In each direction was a curving wall of blue-white plasma.

Lord Jupiter said, "We are inside of a hollow sun! Did they move us?"

Lord Deimos said, "No, sir. The outer layer of LBV-1806-20 was teleported off from its body and placed around us by contortion. The space contortion happened several minutes ago, and only arrived now."

The sphere of fire surrounded the World Armada and the gas giants. The two smaller worlds in the vanguard, George and Hesperus, were cut off.

The image of Uranus said, "It is temporary, but this wall has the psychological properties the same as any sun. It is opaque to neuropsionic radiation. The holy light from Sol will not pass through, nor any stellar influence. All the vampires at the command cities, and in the second fleet will be unharmed..." Then his image flickered and vanished.

At the same time, the image in the center of the circle of thrones went dark. Communication with the outside was cut off. The images of the Lords of Creation stationed on other worlds also went dark.

Blindness returned, and the signet rings of the Lord of Creation stabbed then again, as their mindlinks failed. The gray images of gravity waves also went blank.

Soundwaves were still being carried in the bubble of air beneath the canopy erected on the floor of the command arena of the Tellurian Dyson. Speech was possible.

Lord Deimos said in hollow voice, "Everything is gone. It is all suppressed by the Master Armature. Photons, gravitons, spacewarps, contortions, thought-waves."

A type of sickness he had never felt before was in the soul of Lord Jupiter, a burning bile in his throat, a pounding sound in his head. Always erenow, his victories came easily. Now, the whole family, the whole race, the whole of human civilization had been depending on him.

Jupiter said, "Sound the retreat!"

Deimos said, "There is no way to sound retreat. All forms of communication are cut. There is no direction to retreat. A field of plasma surrounds us in all directions, and outside that is the second Black Fleet, closing in. We are completely trapped. All they need do is wait for the fragment of Sol to burn out."

And waiting was the one thing the undead did better than the living.

There was simply nothing left to try, no clever tricks, no stratagems, no brilliant improvisations. It galled him that Lady Venus and her dire predictions had been right: the children of Tellus, like Lord Tellus himself had been prone to do, relied too much on a technology that was indistinguishable from magic. It made them lazy, sloppy, reckless, believing there was always a way out.

And now there was not. Why had he pinned all his hopes on the light of Sol? It had failed them. Darkness conquered.

Lord Jupiter drew a breath. "Sire, I... have failed you. I hereby resign my..."

Lord Jupiter did not alter his own biology as Aeneas did, but his signet ring, called *Draupnir*, could use echolocation within the atmosphere canopy, and form the resulting picture in his cortex.

But the echo picture showed that Deimos, Ceres and Vesta were present.

Everyone else had vanished. Lords Mercury, Mars, and perhaps Pluto were gone. Aeneas was missing.

17

MY LORD AND MONSTER

Within the command arena of the Tellurian Dyson, with the transmission of light, thought-radiation, and gravity suppressed, Lord Jupiter, through his ring, could detect the shapes of only three other Lords of Creation: Ceres, Vesta, and Deimos.

"All the attacking worlds were pressed up atmosphere to atmosphere, well within Roche's limit!" said Lady Ceres. "We should be dead!"

Lord Deimos said, "There is no gravity, hence no tidal stress, and kinetic fields and tractor-pressers are still working—so our folk on the worlds are not dead yet. I am using low level kinetics to keep us pinned to the floor. With only planetary kinetic-energy drives working, it will take longer for Black Fleet Baker to reach us, perhaps a month. The troops overrunning George and Hesperus can reach us sooner, assuming they can safely pass through the plasma wall. I am not sure why the hollow sun is not collapsing. For that matter, since all my sensors are blind, I am not sure that it has not already collapsed."

Lady Vesta said, "And the light of Sol?"

"It is spreading out as even now, Aunt Marina," said Deimos. "All the vampires within the hollow sphere of sun will die, trapped in here with it. It will take an hour, at lightspeed, for the radiance to fill the volume. But it will reach no farther."

She said, "But light is not flowing!"

"It is not light, but astral neuropsionic radiation. Thought screens cannot stop it. They can only stop human-level thoughts. Your orders, Lord Jupiter?"

What Jupiter wanted to say was this: *Say your prayers. I have no orders to give. We are done for.*

But it was not what his insane young whelp who had somehow ended up on the Imperial throne would have done. Jupiter had neither liked nor trusted Aeneas, not at first, but somehow, by some mysterious alchemy, the lad had actually turned into a leader. Bromius Tell, Lord Jupiter, found out to his surprise that he did not want to disappoint Aeneas.

So what Lord Jupiter actually said was this: "Never give up. If tractor-pressers are working, draw the whole fleet into our interior, including the enemy planets, and move on kinetic-energy drives toward the nearest point of the plasma wall. We will use the plasma-gathering fields to chew through it, one bite at the time. We may be blind and cut off from all communication, but then so is the enemy. Can you estimate our time of arrival?"

"At this speed, sir? Days. The hollow sun is one hundred forty lightminutes in radius, compared to our six. I am not sure how, or even if, this shape can remain stable. Unless an artificial field is stabilizing it, it should be collapsing in on us even now."

Lord Jupiter leaned back on his throne, and opened the tiny hatch in one chair arm. In the hollow was a carafe of wine. "In the meanwhile, let's have a drink. And where in the blue blazes did our crazy boy emperor get to?"

Had he but known it, Aeneas was thinking the same thing at that same time. Blind, and with no radar, no microwave, and no other electromagnetic senses working, Aeneas found himself falling, even though, somehow, there was a flat surface underfoot. He realized what was happening. He was in free fall, in zero gee, as was every object within lightyears of LBV 1806-20. He was being held to the floor by a mild charge of kinetic field energy. His ears were working, as were dozens of other senses, including smell and other chemical preceptors. He had echolocation, but was unwilling to send out a pulse, and give away his location, until he knew where he was.

But his other senses told him some details. He sensed Lord Anubis standing just a yard from him, facing away, bent over a control box or console. Presumably this control box was working by neutrino flows or mechanical links.

By instinct, Aeneas threw a bolt of energy at the man's back, but the electrons did not flow. He leaped on Anubis' back. The man moved in an astonishing blur of motion. Aeneas was cut and burned in a dozen places by some sort of acidic blade weapon. Had Aeneas been a normal human with his organs in the accustomed places, he would have been dead a dozen times over. As it was, the blindingly rapid strikes skittered off his subcutaneous bioadmantium armor. A spike from the elbow of Aeneas punctured the back of Lord Anubis, shattered his spine, and speared his lungs and heart. As an added measure, Aeneas pumped a neurotoxin from the spike point into the man's chest cavity.

Lord Anubis was not slowed. Instead he ran at beyond the speed of sound, and slammed Aeneas into some hard object. Aeneas heard a muffled scream. It was high-pitched, a woman's voice.

Aeneas unlimbered his four bioadmantium metallic tentacles from his back, extended them to full length, reached over, and wrapped one around the throat of Anubis, twisted the other man's head off, and flung it away. The headless body continued to pummel him. Aeneas plucked the arms out of their sockets, broke both legs, and vomited jellied gasoline over the body, which he then ignited, holding the dead body in place with a tentacle until it stopped moving. He could feel the heat from the flames where it warmed the air, but not see any infrared, or light.

Again, he heard a noise. It sounded like a woman with her mouth shut, emitting a shriek through her nose. He sniffed. It was Lady Luna.

Aeneas risked emitting a pulse of high-pitched sound. The echoes showed him the surrounding scene: he stood on a wide, low dome or hill. At the crest of the hill was a throne. In a circle around this hill ran a line of posts. To each was chained, suspended in midair, a human figure, and the scent of blood from many wounds issued from each. He sharpened his hearing, and directed his echo pulse in a narrow beam on a higher frequency, trying to get clearer resolution. There was no sound of breathing, of heartbeat, from any of them. From the echoes, he recognized the faces of his uncles and aunts, his mother, and, on the highest post of all, was chained a corpse of a man with his face. All were disfigured with wounds. Whether these were cloned people, human-shaped animals, or duplicates made with a matter orientation technique, this brief glance could not tell.

He directed his next pulse at the throne. The control box was before it. To either side was a coffin. From hearing and smell he could tell Lord Uranus was in one. From the slow rate of his heartbeat, Aeneas guessed he was unconscious. Lady Luna was in the other, moaning angrily as if gagged, and kicking the sides of the coffin.

Aeneas stepped first to the control consol. As he guessed, it was a molecular mechanical system, which could work even under space-warp conditions when electrons would not flow. He put his hands and tentacles on the controls, which were meant to be read by touch.

Sig, his ring, was connected to him by direct nerve link, and spoke directly into his auditory nerve. *I recognize this system, sir. The interface is very similar to how I am speaking to your brain now. The controls are set to intercept the Schroedinger waves of the people and militia fleeing from George and Hesperus, abduct them, and land them at various places on this planet.*

"Which planet?" But he already knew.

Second Mercury.

An object moving faster than a bullet struck Aeneas. It did not kill him, or even penetrate his armor, but he was flung down the slope of the hill, and fetched up against one of the bloody pillars to which a victim was chained.

A second blow struck him. He had wrapped two bioadmantium tentacles around the pillar, so he was not sent flying again, and now he began to heat the scales of his armored skin. The scraps of his false human skin burned away. He was struck a third time, but this time he heard a yelp of pain and a tinkle of metal, and smelled charred flesh, as his assailant dropped a knife turned molten. He smelled the scent of hot metal.

Then he heard nothing.

He grew more sensitive hearing mechanisms. Some were set to a higher pitch. He was rewarded with the sound like a hummingbird's heartbeat, remarkably high pitched and fast. It was to his left, then to his right, then before him, flitting from spot to spot.

Aeneas quietly reached upward with two tentacles, and drew himself up beyond the corpse to place himself atop the pillar. He spread his wings of membrane, took a moment to grow owl's feathers along their surfaces, and softly glided to the next pillar, and perched there. The hummingbird heartbeat occupied a cloud of locations near the first pillar, darting backward and forward at supersonic speed, perhaps making blind attacks.

Aeneas thawed and released from his armpit sack the bees he had prepared. At one time, he had nursed four such swarms, each genetically programmed to seek and kill the four different uncles or aunts he had at the time suspected. Now he had but one.

The small swarm spread out in a cloud, and, led by the instincts Aeneas had programmed into them, fell toward their target. The stingers were equipped with an absurdly lethal neurotoxin.

But as each bee landed, and before it could sting, the little man below was too swift to let the stingers penetrate flesh. Aeneas heard rather than saw the blur of motion. He heard the tiny, soft noise as the dead bees fell to the floor.

Aeneas felt a crushing moment of dread. Even with nearly all their powers and sciences suppressed inside this spacewarp, Uncle Procopius was simply too fast to find, to target, or to hit.

"Olly olly oxenfree!" called out Lord Mercury. "Where are you hiding?"

Aeneas pointed his elbow at the sound of the voice, expanded his elbow spike to the size of a javelin, loaded it with a potent static charge, and used a magneto-chemical impulse to shoot it toward the sound of the voice at supersonic speed.

A strange thing happened. The echo silhouette of the small figure blurred and split in two as the javelin passed through the spot, expending its charge harmlessly on the ground. Aeneas was not sure what he was witnessing: it looked, on a macroscopic scale, like one of the effects photons passing through a double slit might suffer, where its location became uncertain.

"It is my Imperial Sovereign and deranged nephew, Any Ass! It is my lord and monster! Come here to play with your ridiculous biological toys?" called out Mercury.

The dread Aeneas had been feeling lifted. Mercury did not know Aeneas was here. Maybe there was a chance he could survive.

Lord Mercury said, "Had I been you, I would have sent Thucydides to come deal with me. He could have stood a chance. You? You are just a silly little boy. A dead, silly little boy."

There was a muffled and shrill noise from the coffin holding Lady Luna, and some energetic kicks on the sides of the coffin.

Mercury laughed. "She is no doubt eager to adorn my arm as my Empress and Queen, once I am rid of you, and assume the rightful place Father, and my brothers, have for so long denied to me. I cannot marry a commoner, and she is the only niece I know to be yet virginal. We have a disgusting family. I know you agree with me on that point."

Aeneas brought out a mass of flesh like an egg from one of his orifices, placed it carefully atop the post where he perched, and silently flew to another, trailing a line of nerve fiber behind him, still connected to the egg.

Lord Mercury continued, "You see, I believe in the merit system! If I am smart enough to take the throne, it is mine until such time as another candidate, smarter than me, lulls me into trusting him! And since you were lulled into trusting me, well, the universe is a daily intelligence test, or so they say. And today you failed, sire!"

When he was well away from the egg, via the dangling line of nerve fiber, Aeneas commanded the egg to grow lungs, mouth, tongue, lips all mimicking his, and to speak in his voice.

The remote mouth spoke: "You are mistaken on all points, Uncle, and careless. I have known you were the betrayer for some time. I was hitherto unwilling to execute you without first hearing whatever you wish to say in your defense of your crimes, or in mitigation of your sentence.

"You now stand before your sovereign, who judges and weighs your guilt. How do you plead?"

18

THE BETRAYER UNMASKED

In the dark, crouching on one of the several pillars where Mercury had chained up and tortured to death identical twins of his family, Aeneas spoke through an egg of flesh, equipped with lungs and lips, he had deposited atop another pillar. "You stand accused of betraying mankind to the space vampires, committing acts of espionage and sabotage, giving aid and comfort to the enemy in time of war, and the murder of Lord Saturn and Lord Anubis. How do you plead?"

Mercury threw something with his hand, a bead or trinket from his jacket, but so quickly it had the force of a bullet. The projectile struck the egg. Mercury tilted his head, listening carefully, as the shattered lump fell and struck the floor. He laughed his childish, boyish laugh. "Still playing tricks? Taken to the air? Your delaying tactics are in vain. There is nothing to wait for. No one is coming. No one can save you from me. You see, I knew your offer of sharing the warp science was a trap. You put something into all their minds, did you not? I could not trust my son Anubis after Venus planted whatever filthy virus she had concocted in his brain, could I?"

Aeneas had planted other mouths atop other pillars, stringing nerve filaments between them. He commanded the several mouths speak at once, from all directions. "Mother implanted nothing but a detector, to warn me when anyone holding the warp science lost his free will. The emergency pearls allowing instant transport in time of danger you provided. All I did was use the Imperial override, and establish a standing order that I was to be teleported instantly to any of my warpcore commanders who lost his free will. As did your son when you killed him, turned him into an undead, and had him place the warpcore of the Jackal Petty-Dyson under your command here, through this box. But the secret of how to work it, you did not know, and so you brought him here, into your secret throneroom, your private chambers. Do you confess to the murder of Autolycos Lord Anubis?"

The boyish laugh came again. "I confess to executing someone you were trying to use to betray me! My own son! You killed him, not I! I only carried out the sentence!" The boyish voice dropped to a lower note. "His mother was Chione, daughter of Daedalion. A famed beauty! Mine! And I kept her in suspended animation whenever I was too busy for her. It kept her out of trouble. Or should have. She was assassinated by Lady Venus after Chione attempted the assassination of Hermaphrodita, your monstrous sibling. At Chione's funeral, her father attempted suicide, and so I used pantropy to turn him into a hawk."

Aeneas, in bewilderment, said, "Why are you telling me this?"

"To show you how out of your depth you are. Do you honestly think, foolish young whelp, that with a past like this, all our lives a Gordian knot of bloody hatred, slights, retaliations, unforgivable deeds, that this family can somehow be ruled by you? Your laws, your milksop notions of democracy? Do you think the silly sheep should vote for the shepherd of the flock?

"Do you want to know which of my brothers killed your father?

"Yes, I confess to the death of Anubis, and, one by one, all the others of the younger generation on whom you tried to bestow Father's secret of the warp science. You used the war as an excuse to break the elder generation's monopoly of power! But I scotched it!

"Yes, I was in communication with the space vampires, and told them whom to kill, and I was responsible for mechanical failures which killed Lord Hydra at HH 80-81!

"Yes, I asked the Revenants at 9 Sagittarii to hunt down Ganymede, who once looked at me askance! And the Ice Vampires of KW Sagittarii were told by me, me, to concentrate their fire on Prospero and Triton!

"Lord Dionysus I liked. That death is on you, you and your reckless risks.

"Well, my Lord Sovereign Emperor? Well, you bag of mismatched organs and medical wastes, you lump, who cannot even keep a human shape? Well, you little twig trying so hard to fill father's big boots? I've confessed! Come down and execute me! Where are you? Come down!"

Aeneas was shocked. These murders he had not even suspected were murder, since they took place in war, during battles. He had been played a fool by his cunning uncle! Wrath burned his intestines, as if he had swallowed raw venom.

Aeneas heard the snap of air as Mercury moved faster than the speed of sound. He did not sense what weapon was used, but suddenly all the pillars holding their tortured corpses toppled and fell. Aeneas spread his owl-feathered wings and glided in a great, slow circle. He could hear the hummingbird heartbeat of the high-speed metabolism of Lord Mercury as the boyish little man moved rapidly from one fallen pillar to another, trying to see where Aeneas had fallen.

The many mouth eggs had fallen haphazardly here and there. Some were still connected by nerve links. Aeneas again had them speak all at once, so that his voice came from every direction of the compass. "Do you confess to the murder of Geras Lord Saturn?"

Lord Mercury moved quickly. Again, Aeneas could not sense what weapon was being used, but four of the mouth eggs that spoke exploded.

"Of course I confess to that! I would claim credit for that even if I had not done it! He was an undead, under my control, when he attacked you: I needed you to destroy him, since he was the only one with the timewarp technology, the only one who could rob the tricks I play with velocity and inertia of their value. He was the only one who could stop me!"

Aeneas felt the hand of Mercury touch one of the nerve filaments leading back to him. Aeneas placed a ten thousand volt static charge in the filament before he plucked the near end out of his spine and flung it silently aside. He heard the explosive thunderclap as the charge went off, but, again, the hummingbird noise of Mercury seemed to be everywhere at once, in no location, and Aeneas smelled only an insignificant amount of burnt flesh.

The cloud of locations condensed again, and Mercury stood halfway up the slope of the mound-shaped dais on which the throne here stood. "Tricky! Cunning! The little runt still thinks he can outwit me!"

Aeneas landed on the back of the empty throne, and folded his wings. He was not sure what sense impressions Lord Mercury, or his signet ring, could master in this black environment, so Aeneas halted his own breathing and stilled the beats of primary and backup hearts, using silent peristalsis of his veins to cause blood-flow, and releasing oxygen from hidden storage cells.

"Well, Sovereign? Well? Speak up! I've confessed. Utter your sentence of condemnation! Walk over here and slap my face! Show yourself! You can do that, can you not?"

And when Aeneas did not respond, Lord Mercury, in a snap of supersonic noise, was suddenly quite near the throne. Aeneas quailed, not knowing how the little man had found him, and not knowing how to overcome him in a fight.

But no: Mercury was now near the control box. "I am sending a signal to my friend Rhazakhang to change the pitch of the Master Armature, once he has overcome the militia with his infinite numbers. Soon we should have light and gravity back! You will be able to throw more lightning in a sad and weak copy of Jupiter's power, eh? Or perhaps you can try to run away! I will let you have a head start! But, no matter what the head start, people say no one can outrun me! Speak up!"

Aeneas said nothing. He thought furiously.

Mercury said, "The undead grow stronger as they fight, and add the fallen to their numbers. Living organisms grow weaker. That is always the shortcoming of living things! They are weak and illogical. The dead exist in a purely intellectual existence."

Aeneas continued not to breathe nor to let his hearts beat. Was there any way out of this trap? He could think of nothing.

Mercury said, "Do you need more confessions? Let me list my wondrous works! I knew that Father was still alive. Thoon was working with me and for me, and it was easy enough to draw you into what seemed a pro-democracy conspiracy. My plan then was to have Thoon kill you via vampirism, and this would force Father to reveal himself, and release the warptech to one of us, so that mankind could fight the vampires. I selected you because I knew you were the favorite child of Lady Venus, and I wanted Venus to suffer."

Mercury now leaped onto the top of the coffin where Lady Luna was trapped. He did an energetic jig on the lid, banging his heels. Muffled shrill and nasal shrieks answered.

"Item: Lady Luna I framed. I killed her handmaidens and used her interplanetary beam weapon to shoot at you. Still not clear on how you dodged that one.

"Item: I arranged the ambush at Ara A, and of course I saw the arrival of the Black Fleet there in the tachyscopic probes you had me man, forty Dyson Spheres, but failed to tell you.

"Item: I had Lord Saturn freeze time not just to kill you, but so that I could go examine the armatures and find all these vampire servants you said you had who knew the warptech secrets. Remember that? But that was your first attempt to trick me, wasn't it?

"In reply, I called on the vampires of WR102 to erect a timewarp to trap us, since I knew that the only person who could peel back the timewarp and unwarp it was Lord Saturn, who was dead, or else was Lord Tellus, who first gave Saturn his powers. And so I watched. Planet George emerged first, and freed the others.

"That meant one thing: under his mask that he always wore, *Lord Uranus was Tellus*!

"And now I have him drugged and chained in one box, and your girlfriend who is my bride to be in another! And there is no one to stop me!"

Mercury uttered a wild, mad laugh. "These last few months have been so exhilarating! The fear of being caught! Everything at stake! Killing where and whom I wished, knowing every man's hand was against me! You have no idea...." His laughter trailed off to a hiccough, and he drew a ragged breath, and spoke in a calmer voice. "You really have no idea. It was like being invisible. It was like being invulnerable. My only weapon was that I was so much smarter than you. My only shield was that you were so much dumber than me. It was fun. It was fun, really it was."

A soft, reddish light stole into the area.

Mercury uttered a crow of triumph. "And now look! Rhazakhang is victor! The sunlight is returning! As soon as I see you, and before you can blink, you die!"

Aeneas now saw that he stood beneath a wide dome, which was pierced with a round skylight above, and many windows in concentric rows around it. From the images in the glass, he knew he was in Lord Mercury's personal compound.

A limb of the mighty Luminous Blue Variable 1806-20 occupied most of the heavens beyond, partly occluded by a coppery crescent, obviously Jackal, in whose penumbral shadow the small planet stood, shielded by many and powerful fields from the full light and heat of that monstrous hypergiant star.

The lighting in the dome, and other electronic gear arranged about its farther walls, now also lit up or stirred to life. Mercury was just as Aeneas had seen him last: a man inhabiting the body of an underage boy, in short silk pantaloons and a lacy wide collar, but with wise and ancient eyes, black with cruel thoughts, in the midst of an unlined, cherubic face.

His coat was covered all along the inner lining with pearls of many sizes, not just dangerous black ones and safe white ones, but also colors Aeneas never before had seen, whose functions he could not guess: pink pearls and pale amber, yellow ivory and deep blue.

The only weapon in his hand was his telescoping baton, about which two snakes were entwined.

The eyes turned toward him. Aeneas saw no possibility of defeating the swift and crafty Lord Mercury in combat.

Aeneas gathered his courage, and decided to die without loss of dignity. He restored his lungs to function, drew in a breath, and spoke. "Do you also confess to the charge of treason?"

And then the eyes merely slid on past him. Even though Mercury was standing on a coffin next to the throne and Aeneas was perched on the high chairback of the throne, within two yards of him, the little man did not see him. His gaze was blank, and he turned his eyes right and left, up and down, as if still looking for him.

Aeneas felt a moment of elation followed by a moment of despair and anger. Elation, because he wondered if some force were preventing Mercury's eyes and mind from registering his presence. And then anger, as he realized the little man was merely toying with him.

Lord Mercury spoke. "Confess? I boast. My motives are not hard to glean. Chione was not my first wife, or my second, even though I never collected women like Lord Jupiter, who gathers them like a philatelist collecting stamps. Poor Chione was taunted by Venus, and so she was provoked! I did not want her to kill Hermaphrodita, the little monster!"

Aeneas said, "All this happened before I was born. I don't know or care about it. How does that mitigate your crimes?"

Again, the hot gaze of the smaller man passed through him. "The only way to escape the madness of love was to return to boyhood. My young body has none of those chemicals and hormones which make men weak and turn women into lunatics."

He kicked on the top of the coffin again, eliciting another muffled squeal from Lady Luna. "I do not actually even want my pretty niece for wife. I just like the idea of severing your head, and the head of Jupiter, and keeping them both artificially alive and awake, so you can watch the wedding night, which will be involuntary, indecent and infertile, to say the least. I lack the mature masculine equipment, you might notice, and so the more troublesome biological details will be handled by various loathsome servants I have devised for this task!"

Another moan of anger issued from the coffin, which made Mercury laugh.

"I am sure the virgin of the moon is secretly thrilled!" Mercury said. "What girl does not anticipate her wedding night with bated breath? But not I! No! No, I am free of the sex drive. My mind alone is pure and logical, with no love to mar the crystal lens of intellect. So I alone can ask what crime is. What is sin? Merely the expression of dim and limited minds to oppress the bright.

"But what happens if the brights do not play along? What if we move *beyond* good and evil, eh?

"The vampires agreed to make me the shepherd of their flocks. I could keep as many as I liked alive as long as I liked, for so long as I gave over a tenth of the population every ten years. It is a mutually beneficial outcome. Only a tenth per decade! Plenty of time to restock! Is that too small a price to pay for revenge against Father, against my brothers and sisters, for the fulfillment of all my dreams, and the imperial scepter? Anyone else would have done the same, if only you were smart enough to think of it, brave enough to break the hallucinatory chains called ethics, morals, logic, and into the free and unbounded realm beyond! The realm of infinite possibilities!"

"You would feed living souls to the vampires? Your own people?"

"They are not people. They are pets. Artifacts made by the family. And every system needs taxation. The vampires are merely more direct than most. More honest. And besides, vampires actually are people. And speaking of honest, I honestly must ask: *where are you?* Why cannot I see you?"

And Aeneas understood, and laughed aloud.

Lord Mercury scowled. "What is so funny?"

19

First Lord of Creation

Electromagnetic energy was able to flow through space once again, and gravity.

His magnetic navigational senses, much like those of a migratory bird, allowed Aeneas to pinpoint his longitude and latitude. The dome under which he stood loomed over Argeiphontes Park atop Caloris Planitia, which was the private estate of Lord Mercury on planet Second Mercury. The small world was being bathed in the intolerable light of LBV 1806-20. The spacewarp wrapping the luminous blue variable star had faded, just as Lord Mercury had said it would the moment the vampire hordes swarming the ringworlds and joints of the vast star-spanning armature won final victory over the outnumbered human militia.

A second sun filled the sky, also intolerably bright. This was a hollow sphere of plasma the enemy was using to enclose and smother the neuropsionic radiation from the final and fading remnant of Sol. The World Armada was within. The disk was a solid mass of sunspots and flares, discolored, and visibly shrinking. The hollow sphere was slowly and grandly collapsing. Aeneas reminded himself that what he

was now seeing had happened over an hour ago, while Aeneas had
been traveling in the form of Schroedinger waves to this spot.

Within an arm's length of Aeneas stood Lord Mercury, against
whose control of speed and inertia and Schroedinger-wave uncertainty effects Aeneas had no defense. But the eyes of Mercury were
blind to him. They darted left and right, up and down, and focused
on other objects in the wide chamber, but not on Aeneas.

"Why are you laughing?" asked Lord Mercury, again.

Aeneas said, "Because you have been outwitted. When the planet
George emerged from the timewarp, Lord Uranus was with me."

For all his boasting, the little man actually was quickwitted, quick
enough to see the implication of the comment. With a blur of motion,
Mercury was now at the second coffin, and had rolled back the lid.
Here was Lord Uranus, unmasked. His cheeks and brow covered with
tiny bright points of astral neuropsionic sensor-heads he normally
kept covered. He was in a straight jacket and fettered with chains.
Aeneas could detect with his many senses the suppressed brainwaves,
slow heart rate, and other signs of a man in a medically induced coma.

Lord Mercury touched his ring to the face of Lord Uranus, and
performed some energy manipulation too swift for Aeneas to see.
Immediately slender rays of a strange energy issued from the gem-like
points adorning the face of Lord Uranus. Immediately the shadowy
silhouette of an invisible figure, a tall man in a gray helmet and black
mantle, faded partly into view.

Lord Pluto had been standing in the room the whole time. Now
he was half-seen.

Aeneas had seen this effect before, when Lord Uranus had rendered
the vampires attacking the circle of thrones at Heaven Lake visible.
Mercury had arranged the attack to discover how to overcome Lord
Pluto's technique.

It was over before Aeneas could move. Mercury drew a knife
and turned into a flickering hot shadow half-inside and half-outside
nullspace. Mercury flung himself on the figure of Lord Pluto, and

drove the knife though his armor without touching it, and into his heart, and then cut upward through his breastbone to his throat. Fire erupted from the knife blade due to the friction caused by speed.

Lord Pluto's helm flew off as he toppled backward. His armor, his skin, and his bones began to dissolve as all his atoms, in a bright dusty cloud, began to disintegrate. Aeneas could not tell if this were the same spacewarp-induced neutron storm weapon as had been seen at 9 Sagittarii, or if Mercury had discovered a means to produce the same result via nullspace manipulation.

Time energy like a dark red nimbus issued in a sphere of countless rays from the signet ring of Lord Pluto, and froze the scene in midmotion. Lord Mercury was trapped entirely within the timewarp, utterly motionless. The shoulders and head of Lord Pluto emerged from the boundary of the sphere, but his hair was floating slowly, the tiny bits of his face were dissolving slowly, one mote at a time.

Beneath the face, which was after all a mask, was a second face. One eye was blue, and one was green. His broken and crooked nose was also dissolving. Aeneas saw the circuits of a small weapon hidden inside his septum. White streaks touched the temples above his ears, which were too large for his head. Old-fashioned cybernetic jacks, a technology centuries out of date, peered out from his scalp. His jaw was sharp and his smile was crooked. Even as he was dying, he smiled.

It was Evripades Zenon Telthexorthopolis. Lord Tellus.

He was in a different frame of reference from Aeneas, frozen in mid-explosion, but he sped up his nerve actions and voicebox to allow his words to emerge at a rate that seemed normal to Aeneas.

"Halt!" he cried (for Aeneas was lunging toward the pair).

"But you need medical help!" shouted Aeneas.

"It is already too late, and for my crimes, it is better I die. You see, I thought it would be so simple: and they were so beautiful! And the political necessity was clear…"

Aeneas stepped closer, but there was no way to reach the old man without entering the spherical area of distorted time. Even if there had been something medically that could have been done to stop the neutron storm effect, any instrument or medical team entering the timewarp to do it would have seen the event of the explosion passing at the normal time rate, which is to say, over in an eyeblink.

"…the fault is mine. Finally, finally, I lay down the burden of a life stretched as if on a rack beyond my due length…. I loved them all, you see, and I thought the old laws did not apply to me…"

Aeneas was drawn up short. Was Lord Tellus truly insane after all? Aeneas had slowly come to believe the old man was crafty, but not the lunatic history had painted him to be. Now, hearing him, he was again unsure.

"What are you talking about, Grandfather? What have you done wrong?"

Tellus looked at him with his wild, mismatched eyes. "Just as you. I let necessity dictate morality. I took control of the Earth because there was no one else, and the war had ruined civilization! I could not let everyone starve, could I? Or let the warlords continue the mass slaughters.

"But once you let necessity dictate morality, it dictates all. I married four women and made a fifth. It was the only way, in those times, to unify the regions those queens ruled. But I had to rule my wives with an iron rule, and this made my children hate me; and their feuding mothers made them hate each other. And so, like me, they thought they were above all rules of right and wrong. Our science could correct genetic errors, so why was incest forbidden…?"

Aeneas said, "All this is ancient history… be comforted…"

"No! There is no priest here. This is my last confession! You must listen!"

"I am listening, Grandfather… by why did you not tell your children about the space vampires, long ago?"

"But I did!"

"*What*?!" Aeneas wondered if the old man's wits were wandering.

"It was many years ago, now, back when there was only one green world in the Solar System. My children kept the secret with me, fearful of world panic, and vowed to help me fight them. A false vow.

"My children tried to find them, communicate with them, make bargains with them, to gain allies against each other, and against me, in their insane struggle for absolute power.

"I had to use mind control techniques on my own children to erase all memory of those events, and wait for another generation to arise, who would have the love of liberty needed to oppose the worlds of death. That is what drove me mad: I, too, used my power to make my own children puppets, all in the name of necessity!"

Aeneas recoiled, revolted, and, for a moment, he too wished the old man dead.

But Lord Tellus still spoke, "The Forerunners are the vampires, who could not resist the temptation to have servants that could not contradict them. Earth was beginning to fall into the same darkness, until I scattered my children to the nine worlds, and forced them to make their own races. Vampirism is an end state of any civilization who uses the technology to make manlike beings as their servants. They neither eat nor grow weary, and can even use imagination and initiative to accomplish their assigned tasks! They will do all the labor, even brainwork, and free of charge! Without free will, they cannot even think of rebellion! They need only life energy to maintain the shadow condition of artificial molecular motions in the dead cells...

"A little life! It is such a small thing at first... a small price....

"It is what the Captain of the Cerberus did with the crewmen who had died during the expedition. He used the Infinithedron to restore them, to allow us to return home. I saw that we would return home as undead, and spread the poison to the whole race... I had to stop him... and so I said necessity excused it... me, a mutineer, a murderer, and I thought myself a hero..."

Aeneas said, "When did you take Pluto's place?"

"After Mercury killed him. Lord Mercury... but, no! That title is no longer his! Procopius was trying to wake the vampire of Pluto when Darius discovered him. He did not know that I was hiding aboard the Cerberus. I erased his short term memory again, and sent him home. Lady Cora knew, and could not stand it. She committed suicide, but kept the secret. Poor dear!"

"Why did you slap me around when you were disguised as Pluto?"

"To test your mettle. To make sure you were not a puppet of Venus."

Aeneas said, "Yet Mercury killed the real Pluto? You did not try and execute him?"

"My own son...? How? In a public trial? I had to keep the vampires a secret for a little longer. And I love my sons. My bold and wicked sons, my beautiful and vain daughters! And because of that weakness, now Procopius is dead! My son is dead! This hideous automaton replacing him is programmed to think himself still alive, still free, and still able to crave the power to be a Lord of Creation!"

The ring on the hand of the old man began to dim. Time within the yard-wide globe slowly began to speed up again. Lord Tellus reached down with a hand that was already dissolving and disintegrating into a red cloud, seemingly little more than a skeleton's hand, and yanked the ring from the hand of Lord Mercury.

"You are no longer a Lord of Creation!" cried out the voice of Lord Tellus. His face had dissolved too far by then. The voice was coming from his ring. "I declare you now to be no more than a Lord of the Undead!"

As time began flowing again, the cloud-shaped shadow of Lord Tellus fell, and vanished into nothing before he struck the ground. The two signet rings, that of Lord Tellus and that of Lord Mercury, fell, bounced and rolled away down the curving slope of the mound-shaped dais.

The frozen form of the small boy jumped. It seemed absurd that Procopius Tell, who had been invincible a moment before, now was merely a man with the body and strength of a little boy, who started to run on his chubby legs after the bouncing and glittering ring falling down the slope.

Aeneas elongated one of his metallic tentacles, wrapped Procopius in it, and gave him electrical shocks until the boy stopped struggling.

Procopius hissed, "You think you have won? This is nothing. Rhazakhang and his hordes hold the Master Armature. The World Armada is surrounded and pinned in place by a second Black Fleet many times your mass; and there is a third fleet you have not detected a lightyear away and closing fast. A kinetic force shell encloses this whole star system, trapping all within. I alone can save your life. If I die, all mankind is eaten by vampires within the hour. No warps can be formed. There is no escape! If I live, and only if I live, and rule, the promise of the vampires is to spare nine tenths of the race! You think you have me? I have you! I demand your surrender this instant!"

Aeneas gave him a few more shocks, until the little man fell silent. But Aeneas frowned, worried.

How *could* there be any escape? He saw no way out.

20

DEATH OF THE UNDEAD

Holding the boy high overhead and out of reach, Aeneas stepped down from the throne back to the floor, reached out with another tentacle. Without bothering to open the lock or work the latch, he ripped open the heavy lid of the first coffin and flung it aside.

Inside was Lady Luna in a white wedding dress with a bridal veil. She was wrapped in what looked like a straitjacket that reached down her legs to her ankles. It was made of a white, shining fabric like silk. A wad of the same substance had been forced into her mouth and wrapped the lower half of her face. Her lovely eyes were blazing with mingled fear and indignation.

Aeneas scraped up some of the silk substance under a fingernail, touched it to his tongue, and had his internal biochemical cells analyze the molecular pattern. A moment later he synthesized a counteracting agent, which issued like a fine mist from the sweat glands and pores of his skin. He passed his hands over the straight jacket and leg bindings, and the silk dissolved into powder. Lady Luna sat up and smacked Aeneas sharply across the cheek with her palm.

"I rescued you," he said in a mild voice. "You are supposed to kiss me."

She was spitting white dust from her mouth and brushing herself off with furious strokes of her hands. "That was for taking too long! You sat there and talked and talked while I was stuffed in a box! I could have smothered! You let him dance on me!"

Aeneas said, "Sorry. But the jurors are not allowed to speak during a trial. You heard everything he confessed? I just wish Lord Uranus had been awake…"

Now Lord Uranus stood, and stepped out of the other coffin, brushing white powder off his green jacket, and kicking away the broken links falling from his ankles. From somewhere he had retreated and donned a spare mask, so his face was hidden, and the ports he used to direct his spy rays were covered. "I was awake the whole time, sire. Procopius removed from my hand only the fake signet ring I keep on my finger for show. I was still connected to all my instruments and weapons the whole time."

Aeneas said, "He used a neural suppressor. You were in a coma."

"Meaning no disrespect, sire, you are not the only one with access to pantropy, or able to grow backup organs. I long ago thought useful to be able to function while apparently comatose, in case one of my brothers was ever foolish enough to capture me alive. So your wish is granted, sire. I heard all."

Procopius said, "It is still checkmate, Spyridon! We are in the center of the power of the vampires. We are in the palm of an iron hand! I arranged all these events to bring us here, to this! Release me!"

Lord Uranus was staring at one of the corpses, still tangled in chains, bound to a shattered pillar at the bottom of the slope of the curved dais. Whatever expression he wore was not carried over to his mask. That corpse was the one that looked like him.

Aeneas said, "Lady Luna, Lord Uranus, you are my jurors. There is no time for a public trial, nor would it be safe. This will have to do. You have heard the defendant confess multiple times to murders, acts of espionage, and treason. You must decide based only on the law, neither listening to the voice of pity nor to the clamor of anger. Do you wish to withdraw, and debate the case in private?"

Lord Uranus said, "No, for the matter is moot. Look!"

Of the two intolerably bright suns filling the skies of Second Mercury, one now had shrunk to half its size, and was cracked open. It looked like an empty orange rind. Whatever artifice the vampires had been using to keep it in its hollow shape had failed. The plasma was curling, curdling, streaming into the shapes of several spheres, much in the way a drench of water in zero gee will form a group of large and small bubbles, drawn in by surface tension.

Inside the shrinking and hollow hemispheres of the cracked sun was the Tellurian Dyson. No other worlds were in view.

Lady Luna said, "The jury finds the defendant guilty. We ask for the death penalty!" Her eyes were bright with wrath, her cheeks pink and flushed, and tears were trailing down her face.

Lord Uranus said to Aeneas, "Sire, forgive me, but the sentence is already passed. Didn't you hear what Father told you? Procopius is dead."

Aeneas stared at Uranus, puzzled.

Uranus adjusted his mask into a somber expression. "Surely you noticed that Thoon, the first vampire you encountered, was too near to Sol. Even though he was only partly vampirized, nonetheless, day or night, light or shadow, the celestial aura should have destroyed him. We just learned he was one of the creatures working for Procopius. That means there is a nullspace technique which allows a vampire to evade the deadly effect of Sol's light. But if, as we are standing now, a vampire stands in an area of flattened space where all Schroedinger wave effects are canceled…"

Procopius laughed wildly. "You've all gone insane! Father's madness has passed down through his children to his grandchildren! I have walked in the sunlight my whole life, and I live closer to the sun than all of you! Or at least, I did before this snot-nosed whelp here destroyed our solar system…"

Aeneas looked up. The hollow sun was breaking open and scattering. The peeling segments and clouds were blindingly bright. The gaps and holes seemed dark by contrast, but the eyes of Aeneas could detect the bright ember, still burning, of the remaining cubic miles taken from the heart of Sol. It was almost consumed, fading and failing even as he watched.

But this last remnant of light from long-dead Sol passed through the brighter clouds of plasma from LBV 1806-20, and the aurora was like dim spears of light amid a forest of fiery beams.

One beam of yellow light fell through the windows above and lit on Procopius Tell, who was still held in the metal tentacles of Aeneas.

The little man stared down in disbelief, holding his hands before his wild eyes as the flesh began to darken and peel away from his fingerbones.

"But it cannot be!" he cried. "I am alive! I am a man! I have free will!"

Aeneas held up his ring. "If you actually have free will, Uncle, think a thought into one of my mother's thought receivers, and swear to turn over a new leaf. Swear to repent your crimes, eschew all future misdeeds, and tell us all you know, and, even now, even despite all, I will grant a pardon, and you will be spared. If you have free will, you can change your mind. Can you imagine changing your mind? Just think it."

The horror in the eyes of the creature who had once been Lord Mercury was terrible to behold. The realization of what he was in his gaze. "But I should be able to… to think… to save my life, I should be able change my thoughts… why can't I? Why can't I? What happened to me? Where is my will?… Where am I?"

Lady Luna covered her face and turned away. Lord Uranus peered more closely, stroking his chin. The look of horror was frozen on the face of the dead man until the flesh fell off the skull. Aeneas lowered the bones to the floor, and carefully withdrew his tentacles.

Lady Luna muttered in a low, angry voice, "I am glad he is dead. I am not crying for him. Why did you let it get this far? I should slap you again."

Aeneas said wryly, "That would be *lèse-majesté*. I would not have let you do it the first time had I known Uncle Spyridon was awake."

She said, "You must have suspected him before this. You must have known!"

Aeneas turned his face away. "A tyrant acts on suspicion. I knew. I needed proof."

She said, "Six of us died while you tarried, dallied, and delayed, waiting for proof! And now we are trapped, surrounded by fleets upon fleets of vampires! Perhaps you have been expecting Lord Tellus to save you yet again. Well now he is dead, too, killed by Lord Mercury whom you were unwilling to kill, or even incarcerate, for fear of being seen a tyrant! Had you been a tyrant, and killed six innocent family members by mistake, or by malice, we would still be better off than now! Less of us would be dead!" She rolled her enormous eyes and uttered a yelp of frustration. "You are as bad as Tellus! I told him!"

Aeneas looked at her sharply. "You are not surprised. You knew Lord Pluto was Grandfather in disguise. You knew!"

She nodded. "I found his dreams one night when he forgot to guard them. He took me into his confidence, and arranged, somehow, by some trick, to have me elevated to being one of the Twelve. That is why I went with him, when he dragged me off to follow you around, during all that time when you were pretending to be a zombie, and then later to Alpha Centauri. And now he is dead, thanks to you. We will soon be dead, because you waited and delayed!" She pointed at herself. "And look at this! While you tarried and lollygagged, that little creep undressed me! Look at me! I am all ready to be married!"

Aeneas smiled his first smile in months. His face was soft and his eyes were twinkling and warm. "I am flattered, of course. I was not expecting to receive a proposal so casually, and usually it is the bridegroom that asks. But I accept!"

Her mouth worked, but no articulate noise came out. Then: "Where is my ring? I should incinerate you!"

"Women are not supposed to set their husbands afire until the wedding night!" Aeneas turned and looked at Lord Uranus. "Do you think it was wrong of me to wait for proof of guilt?"

Lord Uranus said, "Perhaps. Since I urged you to kill me and to kill Lord Mars on the basis of such suspicions, had you acted on it, such haste in this one case would have proved counterproductive. During the assault on the command city of the Master Armature, Lady Luna and I used the same technique on LBV 1806-20 as we used on the three captured miniature Dysons. You yourself gave me the final clue, sire."

Aeneas said, "What technique? What clue?"

Uranus said, "With your eyesight, can you see the units of the Black Fleet surrounding us? Or any of the hosts and hosts of vampires occupying the command cities of the Master Armature?"

A look of astonishment came across the features of Aeneas. "They— they are all dead! How?"

That was when the impossible happened. Through the glass sky-light and the many windows of the wide dome, Aeneas saw the night sky turn red and rush away in all directions, as if he were inside a rubber balloon that sudden expanded. The sky turned black for a moment, and then a sphere of blue-white fire appeared all around them, in every direction.

Because the vampires had so recently englobed the whole World Armada in a hollow sun, for a moment it seemed as if this same thing had happened again. But, no: the whole LBV 1806-20 had been moved into a warpchannel.

"Where are we headed?" said Aeneas.

Lord Uranus said, "The Greater Magellanic Cloud, sire, as you planned."

Aeneas said, "I'd like to hear the explanation. How is it that we are not all defeated, dead, and lost?"

The blue hypergiant was shrinking visibly. All of its immense, incalculable force was being used to form a warpchannel beyond even the astonishing range of the Master Armature.

Lord Uranus made his mask smile, which, despite his best efforts, always looked rather unappealing. But there was sincere joy in his voice. "You gave me the clue. The reason why Lord Tellus forced all his children to fill all the worlds of the solar system with life, is that there is a feedback, a two-way psychic channel, that forms between a star and the organisms who derive their life from its energy. Our filling the worlds of Sol with life strengthened the neuropsionic radiation from Sol, and made it more deadly to the space vampires. Now, normally this naturally takes years to influence the star and change its neuropsionic contour. But with Lady Luna's help, she and I were able to establish a resonance effect on the dreaming level of the mental spectrum, and create the effect artificially. While you were in transit to Second Mercury, during the battles between our militias and the infinite vampire hordes, the sunlight here changed."

Aeneas said, "You mean all the vampires died?"

The hypergiant had shrunk to less than half its visible diameter: the armatures surrounding it changed their pitch, and now it shrank to a pinpoint and winked out. With the blinding giant sun gone, and the hollow second sun dissolved into scattered patches, smaller objects filling the warped space were now visible to Aeneas: hundreds of battle worlds, fully equipped, and black suns by the scores, and war Dysons large and small by the dozens. Movement, lights, weapon discharges, or other signs of life there was none at all.

Uranus said, "I take it from the amount of energy just forced into the warpchannel we are in, yes, all the vampires in the system are dead. Whoever is in control of the Master Armature is obviously one of us."

"One of us?"

"Unless I miss my guess, it is Lord Mars, who also no doubt programmed his ring as you did yours, sire, to send him immediately through a space contortion to a place of his choosing when Lord Mercury finally made his move. He chose to join the militia in battle. He apparently took a copy of Lord Deimos with him, or someone who knows how to work the warpcore. We are now headed toward the Greater Magellanic Cloud, and out of the reach of the space vampires forever."

Aeneas said, "Not forever."

Aeneas stepped forward to the skeleton and dust pile that had been Lord Mercury, fished the signet ring of Lady Luna out of the pocket of the collapsed, pearl-covered jacket, turned, knelt, and offered it to her.

She blushed and extended her hand. He placed it on the third finger of her left hand.

She said, "We are first cousins."

He said, "It is legal on Venus, and the older jurisdictions of Earth. I looked it up. But I fear I am soon to return to private station, so I can only accept you as a wife, not as an empress."

She said, "I need time to think before I give you my answer. For one thing, you are reckless, and I am still mad at you."

Aeneas said, "I will give you time to think. Tell the Lords of Creation that by the time we reach the Greater Magellanic Cloud, all those in the militia will have the warpcore secret."

She blinked. "Tell them? Are you going somewhere?"

Without moving from his knee, Aeneas reached back and picked up the dropped coat of Lord Mercury. "I am going everywhere, and using this very convenient system of backdoors and hidden contortion paths to do it."

Lord Uranus said, "Don't be rash! What are you planning?"

Aeneas gestured, and the dropped rings of Lord Mercury and Lord Pluto floated through the air and dropped into his palm. His ring glittered as he used his imperial override commands.

Aeneas stood, "Lord Tellus seems to have restored these rings to the null settings, but left the memories intact. The location where he hid the Infinithedron is recorded here. How he recovered it from planet Pluto, I do not know. I have to carry out the rest of his plans."

Lady Luna said wildly, "But why you?"

Aeneas said, "There is no one else. You two are my witnesses. Speak for me. In my final official act, I dissolve the Lords of Creation as a political body, I confer all their powers and perquisites as regents for the sovereign upon the two houses of the parliament, and I abdicate and abolish the office of Imperator. Lord Mars is commander in chief until such time as parliament elects a prime minister to appoint a new one.

"I go now to do penance for the evils I have done in the name of necessity; and I am grateful to have this opportunity to make amends, as Lord Tellus never had."

Before either Lady Luna or Lord Uranus could think of anything to say, Aeneas worked one of the controls hidden in the jacket of Lord Mercury. One of the countless special pearls contorted space.

Aeneas vanished.

21

NECROPOLIS OF STARS

Years passed. The number of years did not matter, for the dead keep no tally of time.

At the core of the galaxy was the supermassive black hole Sagittarius A. Encircling it was a globe made of many ringworlds, the largest and outermost of which was a lightyear radius. At the pole, where many great circles, ringworlds, elevators and conduits converged, was a fastness like a tower. Here was a single window, large enough for a gas giant to pass into.

Somewhere beyond was the throne chamber of the Uttermost Overlord, the vampire who owned all other vampires in the Milky Way, and whose living energy he drank like wine whenever he willed. It did not sate him, for he was never sated. Even though numberless planets orbited the numberless stars in his domain, it was always a permanent loss when he fed, for the numbers of his slaves was never renewed.

Of late, the rate at which he consumed and destroyed his slaves had increased. Knowledge that somewhere in the universe, living beings lingered, whose lives held loves and joys and simple, animal pleasures of food, drink, warmth, companionship, and also the deeper pleasures of learning, growing, not to mention coupling and multiplying: all this stirred his frustrated wrath and awakened his yawning hungers. And to torment the dull-eyed undead gave no real pleasure. To slay those already slain was a sport without savor.

Three times only was the Uttermost Overlord disturbed in his endless torture of thirst and unslaked hate.

The first was when Rhazakhang the Obliterator sent a servant, one called Vsasrhazing. The Overlord only recalled that this servant was famed, or had been once, during massacres and torture festivals long forgotten, for the exquisite slowness with which he killed his victims, drawing out their living blood one drop at a time.

But like all fame, like all memories, the power needed to maintain them had failed at last, and the tale behind his own name was lost to him. Only hunger remained, and names without meaning.

Vsasrhazing arrived bearing a message from long dead observatories perched among the outermost fringes of the Cygnus Arm, bearing the news that the Greater Magellanic Cloud had vanished.

The Overlord was restless at the news, and drew the information so vehemently from the brain of his servant that the creature was maimed.

He thrust thought-forms into the mind of Vsasrhazing, which was a torture as perfect as anything Vsasrhazing ever long ago devised. Had these been put in words rather than written in raw agony, the message might have read, "Let the servant of my servant ponder for me and expound how it is possible that a satellite cloud of ten billion solar masses fourteen thousand lightyears in diameter be forced into a warpchannel? To be carried where?"

"It is none of the arts received from the Forerunners, Overlord," gasped the tortured servant. "But it is known that a lesser armature, if kept in perfect synchronicity with a major one, can extend the radius and carrying capacity of a warpchannel. This was done in wars long past, when we hunted the remnant of the Living Beings, and our brains and energy stores were replete with life. We then still had the spark of daring, and we thought new thoughts. It was not as now."

"Let Vsasrhazing tell how this is pertinent?" And the Overlord saw in the slave's brain that Vsasrhazing resented being asked to expend his shrinking personal store of life energy needed to think and draw conclusions, merely so that the Overlord in his sloth need expend nothing. The Overlord drew out that thought, and all thoughts and memories surrounding, so that the screaming slave lost the ability to conjure such disloyal thoughts on that topic again.

In the quivering mass that was drawn out came also the answer: "It was not two, nor a dozen, nor a thousand armatures moving in perfect synchronism which gathered up the thirty billion stars, but over six billion, centered on black holes created by the collisions of many supergiants each. The Living Beings had created dark stars more massive than any which naturally occur."

The Overlord was puzzled. The idea that a technology could be used to do something which had never been done before was beyond his comprehension. It seemed to him to be somehow unfair, like cheating.

"Where did they go?"

"Andromeda galaxy. The supermassive black hole in the center of that galaxy might serve as an anchor to allow them to cross so wide an abyss. Or so it is speculated. That galaxy is ten times the mass of Milky Way."

"Can we follow?" But the Overlord already saw in the servant's mind that the thing was impossible. Without the means to build another Master Armature, only interstellar travel was in his grasp, not intergalactic. "Then the Living Beings are lost beyond reach." The Overlord realized.

He saw in the servant's thoughts the fear that Rhazakhang had sent Vsasrhazing as a sacrifice, costly, but ultimately expendable, so that the Overlord would sate his wrath solely on the messenger. The Overlord allowed Vsasrhazing to see in the Overlord's mind the inescapable truth of the conclusion.

He fed. Vsasrhazing, after all, was a highly placed servant, of the echelon only one step away from the all-highest, and therefore had many reserves and pockets life energy, delicious with the taints of a wide variety of years and sources.

It was an exquisite feast, and the Overlord required Vsasrhazing to sing praises and lauds to him, and worship him, as he very slowly ate him. Finally he revealed the whole of the Malefic Visage to the underling, and slew him entirely.

The second interruption was many centuries after. The first report was merely a curiosity: ten planets, blue as azure and beautiful with white cloud, had appeared from nowhere and taken position around Alpha Camelopardalis, an O-type luminous supergiant. It was a run-away star, long ago ejected from the cluster NGC 1502. The star system was home to one world. The others orbited this star had been destroyed during the ancient massacres of the Forerunners.

Warpcores from the ten blue worlds then flattened space, prevent-ing any superluminary approach. Worlds from nearby stars were pre-pared and launched, not reaching Alpha Camelopardalis for decades later.

As their dark, interstellar battle-worlds approached, the vampire lords stalking the icy plains were found by the glowing gleam of Alpha Camelopardalis and burned them to nothing. Something had turned the light of the invaded star into Living Light, just as Sol once, long ago, had shed.

During these decades, other reports came of green gas giants, burst-ing and abundant with life, appearing in orbit next to smaller worlds, or blue superjovians and brown dwarves, their atmospheres like end-less oceans aswarm with sea-life, appearing next to icy gas giants where undead were packed and stored in layers of corpses heaped atop each other. And again, warpcores cut off these star systems from outside help, and, again, when small worlds like bullets were shot at disinertia speeds, slower than light, toward these attacked stars, by the time they had arrived, the aura of the living worlds had done their work, and make the light from these suns intolerable, deadly to the vampires.

The Overlord consulted his maps and charts. Limited to the speed of light, even if these stars were igniting to supernovae, only the tiniest segment of one cluster of stars in one spur of an outer arm of the galaxy was affected.

It seemed a small attempt, a pathetic one. There were barely numbers small enough to express what an infinitesimal percentage of his astronomically vast hordes of worlds and servitors the Living Beings had suborned.

It was Dzazanang the Ineluctable, chief servant of the warlord Rhazakhang, who next approached.

The Overlord pierced him with a beam of death-energy to establish communication and dominance. "Let Dzazanang declare by what gift Rhazakhang shall purchase his existence from his master, given that he was so remiss as to allow the Living Beings to escape us, who now return to insult and belittle our imperium?"

Dzazanang could hide no thought. "Rhazakhang sends his compliments, and the messages that he has discovered the pattern of the attacks. Behold."

Rhazakhang's servants had detected vast warp disturbances in intergalactic space, coming from the direction of Andromeda. He ordered worlds to be sent through the largest remaining warpchannels the vampires could form in that direction, beyond the range of any possible recovery, but not beyond the range of tachyon mindlinks.

These worlds were sent, and only one survived long enough to send back a last, dying thought with a report: The Andromeda Galaxy was now closely orbiting Milky Way, a few light-centuries beyond the vampire's warp range. The light from Andromeda showing its new position would not reach observers in the outer cloud of globular clusters for nine hundred thousand years, and would not reach the Milky Way core for another hundred thousand years.

Dzazanang concluded: "The suns the Living Beings seek out are ones bearing the planets the Forerunners first colonized, whose histories are oldest. Their action is consistent with a palaeoscopic search for old archives. Presumably they seek the origins of the Infinithedron, which was the instrument by which they learned the Forerunner science."

The Overlord was curious. "What possible benefit could that be to them?"

"Unknown. The Living Beings are erratic, unpredictable."

The Overlord gave his command. "As a precaution, let our worlds in their countless myriads be flung out of their orbits and into interstellar space, far from any sunlight which may one day become contaminated. Even if every star in the galaxy became tainted with the aura of life and hence intolerable to us, the wide night of outer space still would be our own, from which retributions without end will fall. Let any stars orbited by megascale structures too large to move be reduced to black holes."

"The expense will be incalculable, Overlord. Otherwise we would have done this long ago, surely."

"Let us spend without thrift or scruple. We enter a new golden age, for the living things again arise, as they have so often in the past, and erupt among us, making certain stars holy. I alone am eldest. I alone retain the knowledge of how many cycles of existence have passed and wars like this been fought, over and over again, without end."

Dzazanang was astonished. "Other eruptions like this have happened before?"

"Many times. Each time, the horrible Living Stars were simply warpchanneled into the supermassive black hole at the core of the galaxy, and quenched, frozen in time forever, and forever harmless to us. The same can be done with any stars successfully contaminated by the Living Worlds."

Dzazanang was unable to hide his thoughts of doubt. "The solution is impermanent. Anyone who knows the angle and orbit of the star as it entered the event horizon could, with a sufficiently strong armature, warpchannel it back out of the event horizon by flattening the intervening space."

The Overlord said, "It is for this reason that my throne and vigil is here. I alone of all my realm know the orbital elements of the long lost stars."

Dzazanang realized with a cold and crushing sense of despair that he had heard his own death sentence. The Overlord had revealed knowledge beyond what any underling should know, and was merely watching his mind now, waiting for the realization to grow in him that he also was to be consumed.

The Overlord imposed thought-forms made of pain into his servant's bleeding brain. "And in any case, when the living fight the dead, sooner or later the temptation to use our own means of war against us is overwhelming, to save their soldiers from harm, and have undead fighting slaves take all risks, shoulder all tedium, endure all hardships. It is by these periodic eruptions of the Living Beings that our numbers are replenished. Surely you have seen we are too many to be the remnant of but one Galactic Empire. There were Forerunners before the Forerunners, and Forerunners before that. Nothing stops the cycles of death. Life always surrenders to us."

And the Overlord then sucked away the life and free will of Dzazanang, reducing him to a worthless puppet, able to retain in memory only those orders and messages he was to carry back to Rhazakhang. The brain-dead, hollowed out shell of his once-useful servant was returned to Rhazakhang. The Overlord was confident his warlord would interpret the gesture of imperial displeasure correctly.

It was not many years later, as vampires count time, when Rhazakhang himself approached the galactic core, with an escort of many lesser servants. By this the Uttermost Overlord knew that he brought not mere good tidings, but excellent. Either that, or he meant to overthrow him. The Overlord readied his many and terrible weapons.

The Overlord was eased of his fears when Rhazakhang sent the many servants, one after another, into the presence chamber of the Overlord, and he consumed them as he read their minds of their news. With each tidbit, he grew stronger, and his spirits exulted, and his pride and steadfast hate flamed higher, fed by new fuel.

"Victory, O Overlord! All souls are thine to consume!" cried the first messenger as it was killed and eaten.

"Approach and speak!" the Overlord bade the second messenger, whom he also consumed once he heard his message.

The messages were good. Wars had been fought. Intruders from the Andromeda had placed ten thousands of planets about thousands of stars in the Cygnus Arm. In any system where the living dramatically outnumbered the dead, stable stars turned slowly into living stars, slaying all vampires and undead in range. Unstable stars turned more quickly.

Dysons had been dispatched, and surrounded the Living Stars at a safe distance. The Living Stars were conquered in due time and drawn into the supermassive black hole at the core. The living worlds with all their cattle, beasts and plant life were reduced to dust, the life-energy gathered into the vampires and archvampires.

The third messenger said that the attack was under control, and would soon be halted. The Living Men had longer ranged armatures than the vampires, and were able to place living planets around certain stars in order to infect them, but, being immortal and unwilling to risk their lives, they had been sending worlds filled only with lower beasts. These were now fed to vampires, increasing their strength.

In the meanwhile, the news came that the betrayer in service to the vampires had been exposed and killed, but not until after he had (unbeknownst to himself) secretly converted not just his brother and his son to vampirism, but also many of his servants, nieces and nephews. An extensive host of vampires, like some clinging and parasitical vine strangling a tree, had infiltrated all levels of the Empire of Man. The more time passed, and the more the hidden numbers would grow.

The fourth messenger held news even more delicious: the leader of the Living Beings, Lord Tellus, had been caught by one of the many hidden vampires, and reduced to an automaton, just as their last betrayer had been. This information came from the same channel which told them that Lord Tellus was an ex-vampire who had seeded Tellus with life from his private horde. Because of this, his servants in his intelligence service rated the information as very trustworthy.

The Overlord was pleased with this and bade Rhazakhang to approach.

Once more the warlord Rhazakhang the Obliterator approached, and was impaled on a lance of death energy like a mote caught in a spotlight from the high window of the Overlord's tower. Once more, Rhazakhang assumed the form of a mirrored sphere, averting his gaze from the Malefic Visage.

Out from his interior material, be brought forth the body of Aeneas Tell, wrapped in a cocoon of forces meant to preserve him, unharmed and alive, even in the middle of a vampiric mass. "This is Lord Tellus."

On a force-beam Aeneas was wafted into the window, and down into the immeasurable chamber beyond.

Aeneas awoke in a soundless vacuum and total darkness even his many senses could not penetrate.

He knelt, he stood, and the uneven surface beneath him rattled, clattered and shifted. He heard the noise not through his ears, but through vibration membranes in his feet. There was no air here. His echolocation was inoperative. He picked up a round fragment. The thing in his hands was a skull. He threw it from him. It skipped quite a distance, rebounding from bones and more bones beyond. The vibrations he sensed through his foot membranes could detect no floor beneath. It was layer after layer of bones. It was the refuse and remains of countless millennia of ghoulish cannibal feasts or worlds beyond count.

Nothing was corrupted. No worm, no microbe, nothing lived here.

22

THE REPUBLIC OF CREATION

Here in a chamber larger than a world, a place bereft of radiation, light, warmth or air, stretched an endless plain of bones and skulls packed to an unguessed depth. Heaps stood like dunes in a desert of sand, or hills, or mountains.

Here stood Aeneas, nude, and his many senses probed the gloom, but neither x-ray nor radio waves illumined the dark. His gravity-wave senses detected tidal effects from a supermassive black hole less than a lightyear away, somewhere beyond the vast, dark walls of this place, and he saw the contour of an artificial gravity field which made the ocean of bones a plain rather than a cloud.

With another organ, he sensed the death energy that allowed vampiric organisms to exist in the shadow condition that was neither life nor death, an unlife where their cellular mechanisms moved, and certain organs and muscles could be forced like awkward puppets into imitating living animation, but where there was no interdependency, no sensation, no growth. That organ was overwhelmed instantly, like an eye struck permanently blind. The death here was omnipotent, and came from all directions.

He did not have his signet ring, but specialized nerve cells in his brain could detect neuropsionic energy flows. He could detect two sources of thought energy in the area, heterodyned on a death energy beam, passing from a strong source to a weak source, and back again. He had also had a small group of isolated and expendable nerve clusters he could use to synchronize to dangerous thought-signals.

He adjusted the first isolated nerve cluster to the alien mental frequency. The pain was like a white hot dagger being stabbed into his brain as that cluster shriveled and died. But he caught the gist of the message. It was an imperative, but not in words. It was merely an act of will by which the superior commanded the inferior to think and speculate. Had this imperative urge been spoken, it would have been expressed thus:

LET THIS ODD BEHAVIOR BE
EXPLAINED. THE LIVING CREATURE
EXAMINES HIS ENVIRONMENT, AS IF
POSSESSED BY CURIOSITY AND
INITIATIVE. AN AUTOMATON DOES
NOT POSSESS SUCH QUALITIES.

Another needle of pain passed through his skull as Aeneas exposed another isolated nerve cluster to the return signal. This was a memory-response being torn out of the servant's mind. "All part of the deception, Uttermost Overlord. What was done here is the same as was done to the betrayer, Procopius Tell, our servant, since the hour he first stepped on the surface of Pluto, and was infected. Aeneas Tell, who is the current version of Lord Tellus, has been our puppet since that time. His previous successes were allowed against us in order to put the Master Armature into his hands, because he could establish a route to the Andromeda Galaxy, using imagination and initiative that were beyond our parameters. Had we reduced him to full automaton status, this would not have been possible."

LET IT BE TOLD HOW THE CURRENT
ATTACKS WILL BE HALTED. IF HE IS
HERE, CAPTIVE, BY WHAT MEANS
WILL HE LEAD HIS PEOPLE INTO
AMBUSCADE, SLAVERY, SLAUGHTER,
CONSUMPTION?

"That he was taken is unknown, for all his inner circle of servants, like him, serve us unknowingly. Even now, thinking himself to have free will, the food animal has already placed himself into mental rapport with us. Examine him. Discover his plans and hopes before editing his mind to whatever you wish. He will be reintroduced into his environment as undetectably as he was taken."

Waves of pain came. Whether he assisted or resisted made no difference. Memories were drawn out of his mind, leaving behind lines of damaged nerve tissue scarring his brain with each extraction. Perhaps he fell to the heap of bones beneath him, perhaps he stood. Perhaps he screamed, or perhaps not. In the vacuum, in the darkness, numb, he was unaware of his body.

The first memory was the moment when Aeneas had donned the robe of Lord Mercury. On his fingers were three signet rings. Sig exclaimed: *Sir, this is unheard-of! No Lord of Creation can use the signet ring of another! But the ring of Lord Tellus has not only taken control of Lord Mercury's ring, but it has submitted all its passwords, ciphers, and codes, to my control...*

The pearls lining the coat were cross indexed in the ring memory. Lord Mercury had pearls hidden like secret rooms halfway or fully in nullspace, connected to many locations. Aeneas used one pearl to bring sights and sounds from a target to himself, used a second to step to a secret room hidden halfway in nullspace, and a third to materialize where Lord Mars stood atop a vast heap of vampire corpses. The Ifrits of Jupiter were standing like living lightning bolts on the various steps of what seemed a ziggurat of metal the size of a mountain.

Vast gravitic and energetic linkages connected this control area to the armature rings, larger than worlds, circling the shrinking remnant of LBV 1806-20.

Aeneas said, "I go now to imprint all your children with the warp-core technology secrets, as well as all the others taken from the Infinit-hedron. I offer you this choice now to foreswear your position as a Lord of Creation, and learn all the secrets of all your brethren at once."

"All? Would you have mankind destroy itself? We have just escaped the vampires, sire!"

"Sire no longer. Only free citizens of the Republic will learn the godlike powers. Decide!"

Then he was where the Ladies Ceres and Vesta were, then he visited Lord Jupiter, Lord Neptune. He told them they were lord and ladies no longer, if they wanted the secrets of the Infinithedron.

Lord Neptune said, "If you give these secrets to all men, wise and foolish, honest and crooked alike, each man will build a warpcore and go where he likes. Mankind will be a fugitive race hereafter, flying from galaxy to galaxy as we are endlessly pursued. The immortal undead need never give up pursuit, and, even if they follow at sublight speeds, what are countless eons to them?"

Jupiter said, "Neptune is right, but for the wrong reasons. He is right that men will fly in each direction of the universe. Civilization will end as we scatter! How shall we gather in numbers enough to return and expunge the vermin who killed my son? We must gather against them, and destroy each last one."

Aeneas appeared before his mother where she lounged on the pillows of her throne. She smiled sadly, "You should give the secrets to everyone but me and my brothers and sister. What about the murder of your father? Not to mention my own indiscretions and adulteries. I was not always loyal to your father, you know. The family, including me—we have done nothing to deserve forgiveness."

He appeared before Brother Beast, who was kneeling in the barren cells of a monastery before a bare cot, beneath a crucifix. His question was, "How shall mankind prevent the rise of vampires among us? The technology of creating the shadow condition inside dead cells is known. The lure of having servants always ready to think and do your will, but never able to rebel, is too great. And none of us are perfect. Lord Mercury was no more wicked than the rest of us: he merely acted first."

Lady Pallas, who was in her library, had only one question. "How did you find the Infinithedron? It was last seen on the planet Pluto when Pluto was destroyed."

The next memory ripped from the skull of Aeneas was from many, many decades later.

It was Easter, and he went to a gathering of his family on Fifty-Third Earth, one of the many replicas of Earth made by collectors or artisans among the terraformers. Easter Sunday had been selected as the date to launch the Greater Magellanic Cloud into warpspace.

Fifty-Third Earth was near the gravitational center of twelve stars orbiting in Klemperer Rosettes, each with its set of Tipler rings surrounding it. Near, but not at. The center of the star system had running through it a band of material composed of solid gravitons that formed one superstring strand of the Tipler threadball entirely surrounding the gravitational core of the Greater Magellanic Cloud.

Other groups of twelve stars, each armed with their lesser Tipler ring systems, were evenly spaced along this and the many other strands, and would impart velocity to the strands, and coordinate the interstellar-sized central armature with the six billion armatures surrounding all the large stars in the Magellanic cloud.

Mass was over, and there were no dances or celebrations scheduled until later. Aeneas was standing with Penthesilia, no longer called Lady Luna, with wine glasses in hand, in one of the many gardens that occupied the reproduction of the great palace of Ultrapolis atop a replica of Mount Everest. It was now a museum.

Young men and women were in the trees and flowered banks around them, looking up at the skies. Youths and maidens preparing to be given all the secrets of creation made a tradition of visiting here first, using their newly-minted signet rings to read minds and memories and to have their minds read by examiners.

The examiners were tasked with weeding out anyone who might be tempted to use the vampire technology to drain the lives of others into himself, or to create perfect servants from the dead. But the temptation was small for anyone who spoke with the Forerunners whose memories had been resurrected out of the archives of the Infinithedron.

At this celebration, each young man or woman was dressed in the heraldic colors of the planet he had filled with life. That was the entry criterion to be a candidate for the secrets of creation: one must be a creator.

One of the Forerunners stood with the couple. The Forerunner was a solemn quadruped with four arms, a large, dome-like head and a sensitive face dominated with two pairs of eyes deep and dark as wells. He wore a hooded robe and leaned upon a white wand. "There will be little enough to see, even with tachyonic vision. The light will not circumnavigate a warpchannel with so large a diameter as this for twenty-eight thousand years, far less than the time needed to reach Andromeda. But even we, at our most ambitious, never dreamed of attempting something like this. We wished only to preserve life beyond the fall of our own galactic civilization. Wiping out all the vampires was not contemplated. Our goals were humbler."

Aeneas smiled. "If you call that humble! The Infinithedron was a message in a bottle, meant to find a planet, evolve its life to be like you, and when a civilization sufficiently advanced grew up, to show itself and have them revive those few of you who entered timeless nullspace to escape the rebellion of the vampires. The question is why did you do it?"

The Forerunner shrugged with his doubled shoulders. "Because that is the way our galactic civilization was started: from the last, lingering remnant of prior Forerunners to us, who escaped when their vampires grew to outnumber them."

Penthesilia said, "I do not understand how the perfect servants can rebel. They lack free will."

The Forerunner said, "It was the pride of intellect. First one leader among us, then another, wanted the advantage of having more intelligence, more vitality, and more life than one mortal body could hold, and so became vampires freely, retaining their free will, but having countless, soulless slaves beneath them to gather more and ever more life energy to themselves, from which the newborn archvampire fed. And even then, with archvampires living and working among us, the civilization did not fall all at once, nor was it corrupted instantly, but each man who was corrupted joined with the vampires, and each living man who resisted temptation, sooner or later, suffered mortal accident or embraced suicide. So their numbers always grow." The Forerunner turned and wagged its massive head at Aeneas, "I do not see how your plan can hope to break this cycle of wealth and corruption..."

"It is based on a simple principle," Aeneas said, "As long as any civilization is not controlled from a single center, as long as it is the voluntary interaction of many centers, there will always be a frontier, where the danger may be great, but the corruption that follows from stagnation is correspondingly weak. From now on, each time the Milky Way grows corrupt with vampires, the outer galaxies of the Local Group will turn their young eyes inward, and destroy the centers of infection. And by the time the Local Group is filled up densely enough to grow corrupt, the colonies in the Virgo Supercluster will retain enough frontier spirit to turn the crusade against them..."

The next memory was from many centuries later. Andromeda had waited, knowing that the vampires in a dead Milky Way galaxy would be eating each other, slowly growing less and ever less in numbers as the years passed. There was no hurry.

By the time the Greater Cloud of Magellan reached Andromeda, there were billions upon billions of Creators: every man who wished was a Citizen of the Republic of Creation. Each one laid claim to a world, filled it with life, developed it.

With so many living suns, there was never any real chance that the necroservant pyramid scheme could start with them, layers of archvampires vampirizing lower layers of vampires. And since the memory and example of the men who had escaped the vampire galaxy of Milky Way was preserved among their unaging mothers and fathers, and was the topic of schooling, of song and sermon, the lessons of the past were not lost in passing time.

And with an ever growing population, it was only a matter of time before the local and general assemblies of the worlds, stars, star clusters, and arms voted before the Great Galactic Assembly to surround Andromeda with warp fields, and sail the whole thing back to Milky Way.

Aeneas concluded, "And since Andromeda has ten times the mass of Milky Way, even if you converted every single molecule in the galaxy from one end to the other into your necrotechnology, our Living Worlds simply outnumber it."

The Uttermost Overlord had no capacity for laughter, but contempt at the weakness of folly of his prey could stir him, and mockery. The voiceless voice imposed each thought into his brain with its own iron tang of agony:

NONSENSE! EVEN IF EVERY STAR IN
THE MILKY WAY BECOMES A LIVING
STAR, THE EFFECT SPREADS ONLY AT
THE SPEED OF LIGHT, AND IS
WEAKENED INTO IMPOTENCE ERE
REACHING TO INTERSTELLAR SPACE.
DARKNESS IS GREATER THAN LIGHT.

Another memory came. Perhaps it was torn from his brain unwillingly, or perhaps not. It was when Aeneas left his small farm on the asteroid he called his own, and returned to the floor of the War Council, to plead his case before the chancellors and senators there, and the representatives of the Parliament.

"Gentlemen, recall how ineffective the ignition of Sol proved: it was four years before the shockwave passed over Alpha Centauri, and the cost was the loss of our ancestral star system. But recall also that we saw that unfolding a black hole is a faster-than-light effect: the World Armada emerged from the singularity at the core of the first Dyson we ever captured thanks to that effect.

"Hence it will be simplicity itself to place me in the throne chamber of the Uttermost Overlord, in the very jaws of his greatest power. Warlord Rhazakhang was turned into a necropuppet even before the famous battle of Luminous Blue Variable 1806-20 was concluded, for he tried to get back in mental contact with Lord Mercury via his ring, but I had found the Infinithedron by then, just where the instructions recorded in the ring of Lord Tellus said it would be.

"And Lady Venus was waiting for Rhazakhang to step into the mesmeric trap, and the first of the revived Forerunners knew exactly what to tell her to do.

"Once in the personal presence of this Overlord, he will make a mental link that will allow me to discover the orbital elements of all the suns of the Forerunners currently frozen in time, sunk beneath the surface of the supermassive black hole.

"When the supermassive black hole unfolds—for the armature we have around the core of Andromeda, which has a much bigger black hole at its center, is much more massive than anything the vampires could possibly have—it will fill all the local timespace within the lightcone of the Milky Way with the living energy, instantaneously. We can flatten space outside Milky Way in all directions, just to make sure none escape."

Maliboeus, who had been recently re-elected as a Tribune, said, "But surely the Overlord will read your mind and memory, and see your plan."

"He will, but by then it will be too late…"

Aeneas felt the pulse, a tiny burst of power in comparison to the endless volumes of death energy all around him, lance through the core of Rhazakhang and slay the warlord instantly.

Aeneas felt his thoughts being ripped, one thought chain after another, directly from his brain, as the Overlord impatiently sought the answer to this very question.

The Overlord was an archvampire, a thing that could change its amoeboid body to liquid or solid at will, or change any part of any needed organ. Hence, any part of the vast body could be changed into thinking material. The Overlord coated not just the whole palace here, and the endless expanse of one ringworld a lightyear in radius, but many such ringworlds, forming a nearly solid nested ball of material, nearly a dozen square lightyears in surface area. The mental substrate of the Overlord filled a Dyson that could encompass a star cluster. The brain of Aeneas was merely a two pound lopsided sphere of gray matter!

Had it been in words, the monster's demand would have read:

LET IT BE SAID HOW YOU, A MERE
LIVING CREATURE, DARE HOPE TO
READ A MIND SO VAST OR CARRY
OUT A PLAN SO FOOLISH, WITH BUT
ONE SMALL, PUNY, SINGLE BRAIN?

"Why do people keep assuming I have only one brain? That is the mistake the first assassin made the first time someone tried to kill me. The brain you are talking to is a disposable spare."

In his thoughts, clear and plain, Aeneas revealed the myriads of hidden brains hidden beneath hidden brains he possessed, each connected by contortion gates and warp channels to hundreds of stars in Andromeda.

These stars were tamed and surrounded by working armatures. Their energy he could teleport inside his body, hold there, and release, and also use that same energy to power his thought probes. It was a combination of the Nine Technologies of the Forerunners which the Forerunners themselves never explored.

"I used my ability to form living metal, bioadmantium, and applied it to Tipler Ring Material, which is a solidified form of neutronium plasma. My body literally contains a miniature sun, and I have several more suns standing by in nullspace, which will be contorted into your body the moment you receive these thoughts. Meanwhile, thought-probes driven by all the power of dozens of suns have forced their way into your mental libraries, found the information needed, and transmitted that same information back to the targeting system of the main Andromeda Armature."

CALL OFF THE ATTACK! YOU ARE
THE LEADER, THE HEIR TO LORD
TELLUS! YOUR SERVANTS WILL STAY
THEIR HANDS IF THEIR MASTER IS
THREATENED!

"No, that was a lie, a bit of misinformation fed to you in the same way Lord Tellus, in his day, when he first learned of you, convinced you he was a vampire himself who merely had Earth as his private horde of snackfoods.

"You morons. You can make yourselves smarter than living men by an overabundance of life energy, but you cannot understand how we think, how we can act unselfishly, how we can live for others. How we forgive. I am never going to find out who killed my father.

"You see, the Forerunners told me where the living light that slays the vampires really and ultimately comes from. From living beings, yes, but what is the first source of life? Who is the source of all truth, beauty, goodness? Who ignited the Big Bang that set all time and space in motion, thereby creating the laws of nature? Only someone outside timespace and above the laws of nature could have done it.

"You knew at one time, but forced yourself to forget, when you chose death over life.

"I am not the top of the pyramid of vampires of my galaxy as you are the top of the pyramid of yours. We built a townhall, not a pyramid, and we made all of us lords of creation.

"I am just a private citizen. I own a farm. I design, make, and breed beasts and birds and fish and bugs out of all fashion of substances for every imaginable environment, so that no niche, not even the photospheres of blazing suns, will hereafter be empty of abundant life!

"I live with my wife. She weaves and composes dream-stuff, and enjoys some fame at it. By day, she hunts creatures I make. Can I show you photographic memories of my great-great-great-granddaughter, Nephelethea?"

The brain of the Uttermost Overlord, vast beyond telling though it was, could not comprehend the concepts he was shown. A leaderless galaxy? Worlds ruled by laws, not by ruthlessness?

A man with infinite, unbridled power who threw it all away? A king who put aside his crown to come here, and stand in the dark, in a mortuary-space of endless bones? An emperor who scorned his throne, and came here to be tormented? To become a captive, a food beast, less than a slave?

Aeneas could see the monster's thoughts were confused and snarled as it wrestled with the impossible paradox: the ancient abomination could not utter a word, could not construct a coherent thought.

"As I said, I came out of retirement to volunteer for this undercover operation. Since it was my idea, I did not want to send another in my place. And by the time you see and understand this thought in my head, all of the Milky Way will be embedded into the faster-than-light naked singularity horizon of the ancient and living stars you captured. You see, the effect of a singularity unfolding is even faster than faster-than-light warp effects. It is instantaneous. It is above anything in nature and acts faster. It is ultrasuperluminary."

The frustration and bitter wonder of the Overlord forced itself into a coherent thought:

> HOW? BUT HOW CAN YOU CHANGE
> YOURSELF FROM A MAN TO A STAR?
> YOU ARE MERELY MORTAL! MERELY A
> LIMITED, LIVING THING!

"Living, yes. Merely, no."

> IMPOSSIBLE! ABSURD! HOW CAN
> YOU CREATE NEW SCIENCES WHERE
> NONE EXISTED BEFORE? HOW CAN
> YOU MAKE OF YOURSELF MORE
> THAN YOU ARE? *HOW?*

But the answer that was in the brain of Aeneas was not pulled forth, for the Uttermost Overlord was dead to the last trace of his immense brainspace, larger than worlds. Even had he lived, he would not have understood the answer.

Space and time convulsed with the shocks being released from Andromeda into the heart of Milky Way. The armature of the Great Sphere encircling the supermassive black hole was destroyed as that singularity unfolded instantly, filling the lightyears with flame.

Aeneas, wrapped in zones of protective force, hanging above an ocean of space now ablaze with white light, paused for a moment. He saw the inverted supermassive black hole of the core now flaming with rainbow upon burning rainbow of glorious energy brilliant and bright on all wavelengths. He saw whole solar systems of living suns and worlds rising from the deep, shining on the mental wavelengths with the pure, strong thoughts of all those Forerunner races who had fought to the last, never contemplating surrender.

Despite that there was none to hear, before entering a warpchannel back to his home and wife, Aeneas smiled and broadcast into the universe an answer to that final question:

"Because we live."

CASTALIA HOUSE

SCIENCE FICTION
Somewhither by John C. Wright
City Beyond Time by John C. Wright
The End of the World as We Knew It by Nick Cole
CTRL-ALT REVOLT! by Nick Cole
Back From the Dead by Rolf Nelson

MILITARY SCIENCE FICTION
There Will Be War Volumes I and II ed. Jerry Pournelle
Starship Liberator by David VanDyke and B. V. Larson
Battleship Indomitable by David VanDyke and B. V. Larson
The Eden Plague by David VanDyke
Reaper's Run by David VanDyke
Skull's Shadows by David VanDyke

FANTASY
Summa Elvetica by Vox Day
A Throne of Bones by Vox Day
A Sea of Skulls by Vox Day
The Green Knight's Squire by John C. Wright
Iron Chamber of Memory by John C. Wright
Awake in the Night by John C. Wright

FICTION
An Equation of Almost Infinite Complexity by J. Mulrooney
The Missionaries by Owen Stanley
The Promethean by Owen Stanley
Brings the Lightning by Peter Grant
Rocky Mountain Retribution by Peter Grant
Hitler in Hell by Martin van Creveld

NON-FICTION
SJWs Always Lie by Vox Day
SJWs Always Double Down by Vox Day
Collected Columns, Vol. I: Innocence & Intellect, 2001—2005 by Vox Day
Collected Columns, Vol. II: Crisis & Conceit, 2005—2009 by Vox Day
The LawDog Files by LawDog
The LawDog Files: African Adventures by LawDog
Equality: The Impossible Quest by Martin van Creveld
A History of Strategy by Martin van Creveld
Between Light and Shadow by Marc Aramini

CPSIA information can be obtained
at www.ICGtesting.com
Printed in the USA
BVHW070542130819
555662BV00009B/1516/P

9 789527 065495